MERCURY
INK

SIMON
PULSE

MICHAEL VEY

BATTLE OF THE AMPERE

ALSO BY RICHARD PAUL EVANS

MICHAEL VEY
THE PRISONER OF CELL 25

MICHAEL VEY
RISE OF THE ELGEN

MICHAEL VEY
BATTLE OF THE AMPERE

RICHARD PAUL EVANS

MERCURY INK

SIMON PULSE

NEW YORK   LONDON   TORONTO   SYDNEY   NEW DELHI

This book is a work of fiction. Any references to historical events, real people, or real places are used fictitiously. Other names, characters, places, and events are products of the author's imagination, and any resemblance to actual events or places or persons, living or dead, is entirely coincidental.

SIMON PULSE / MERCURY INK

An imprint of Simon & Schuster Children's Publishing Division

1230 Avenue of the Americas, New York, NY 10020

This Simon Pulse/Mercury Ink hardcover edition September 2013

Text copyright © 2013 by Richard Paul Evans

Cover illustrations copyright © 2013 by Owen Richardson

For information about special discounts for bulk purchases, please contact

Simon & Schuster Special Sales at 1-866-506-1949 or business@simonandschuster.com.

The Simon & Schuster Speakers Bureau can bring authors to your live event. For more information or to book an event contact the Simon & Schuster Speakers Bureau at 1-866-248-3049 or visit our website at www.simonspeakers.com.

Interior designed by Mike Rosamilia

The text of this book was set in Berling LT std.

Manufactured in the United States of America

2 4 6 8 10 9 7 5 3 1

This book has been cataloged with the Library of Congress.

ISBN 978-1-4814-0630-7

ISBN 978-1-4424-7513-7 (eBook)

To Abigail
You have brought healing and joy into many hearts,
but especially mine.

MICHAEL VEY
BATTLE OF THE AMPERE

PROLOGUE

The ES *Ampere*

**100 kilometers west of Naples in the Tyrrhenian Sea.
Aboard the Elgen Superyacht *Ampere*.**

"Is it as bad as first reported?" Chairman Schema asked. His voice was even lower and more coarse than usual due to the bronchitis he was fighting. Living at sea was taking its toll.

"Worse, Mr. Chairman. The Peruvian Starxource plant has suffered a complete bowl meltdown. More than seventy percent of the country is without power. The Peruvian government has declared a national state of emergency and they're mobilizing engineers to restart their coal and diesel operations from before. It will be months before they have restored even half their country's power."

Chairman Schema coughed. "The press must be having a feast."

"That's an accurate assessment. All the major television networks have reported the story. It's made the front pages of the *Wall Street Journal*, the *New York Times*, *USA Today*, the *Beijing News*, the *International Herald*, and the *London Times*. Unfortunately, the media coverage is having an effect. The governments of Taiwan and Zimbabwe are holding emergency discussions about the possibility of phasing out our plants. And three countries have put Starxource plant production on hold. Brazil has completely cut off negotiations with us."

Schema dabbed his feverish forehead with a handkerchief. "This is disastrous. Were the rats contained?"

"The ER were contained only because they were completely exterminated—more than a million and a half rats were killed in the bowl's meltdown."

Schema erupted in another bout of coughing. "Have we determined the cause of the meltdown?"

"The plant was attacked by a terrorist group."

"A terrorist group? The Shining Path?"

"No, a group called the Electroclan."

"Michael Vey," Schema growled. "He's just a kid."

"Then he's a very powerful kid."

"He's one of our *own*!" Schema shouted. "This is like Frankenstein; the monster has turned on its creator. So that was Vey's plan—to destroy our plant and stop our global expansion?"

"No. According to our sources, Mr. Vey's mother was being held captive in the Peruvian compound. His only objective was to free her. Dr. Hatch apprehended him, but then Vey's fellow terrorists attacked the compound to free him. The power plant was collateral damage."

"You're telling me that we lost billions of dollars as a side effect of a boy looking for his mother?"

"Yes, sir."

"Was Mrs. Vey at the compound?"

"Yes, sir."

"Then Hatch never released Vey's mother as he was directed."

"It would appear not."

The chairman screamed out a long string of profanities, which ended in an equally lengthy fit of coughing. "This is Hatch's doing! The man's gone rogue. Has he done anything we told him to? Have the rest of the electric children been released?"

"We don't believe so."

"Where was Hatch when all this happened?"

"He was at the compound."

"And where is he now?"

"He is on his way here—as per your summons."

"When will he arrive?"

"In about three hours."

"Alert security. Tell them to prepare the brig. They'll soon be accommodating a new prisoner."

"Yes, sir."

"Does Hatch have any of the electric children with him?"

"We don't know, sir."

"Then find out!" Schema shouted. "Under no circumstances are you to allow those children aboard this boat. Do you understand?"

"Yes, sir. What do we do if they're with him?"

"Turn the helicopter away."

"If they won't go?"

"Then blow them out of the air."

"With the youth aboard?"

"Yes, with the youth aboard! Are you an idiot? Do you have any idea how powerful those children are? They could take over the ship. Under no circumstance do we allow those children on this ship."

"And kill Hatch as well?"

"Did you think we were going to let him live? He knows *every-thing*. Hatch will never leave this ship alive."

PART 1

1

A Bad Dream

I'm Michael Vey. Last night I had a really weird dream. I was back home in Idaho, sitting at the table with the cool kids in the cafeteria at Meridian High School. (For the record, I'm not one of the cool kids.) My girlfriend, Taylor (who is one of the cool kids), was sitting on my right side in her cheerleading outfit. My best friend, Ostin, was on my left, eating cheese pizza and garlic bread. The rest of the table was filled with a bunch of cheerleaders and basketball players. As usual, Ostin and I looked as out of place as chocolate doughnuts at a Weight Watchers meeting.

The school's basketball team was joking with me like they did at Maddie's party, calling me "Li'l Norris"—short for *little Chuck Norris*—and trying to outdo one another with their Li'l Norris jokes.

Drew, the basketball team's star point guard, said, "Li'l Norris is so tough, dark is afraid of *him*."

"Yeah?" said Spencer. "Li'l Norris is so tough that the road in front of Meridian High used to be called Li'l Norris Street, but it was changed because *no one crosses Li'l Norris and lives*."

Everyone laughed except Ostin, who looked confused. "I don't think it was ever really called Li'l Norris Street," he said.

"Shhh," I said. "It's a joke."

"Yeah?" said Drew. "Monsters check under their beds to make sure Li'l Norris isn't there."

"I got it; I got it," Spencer said. "Li'l Norris is so tough that he died ten years ago but Death is too afraid to tell him."

Everyone was laughing when a low, angry voice behind me said, "If Li'l Norris is so tough, why is he hiding in the jungle?"

I turned around to see Dr. Hatch standing behind me. I was paralyzed with fear. Suddenly everyone else vanished and it was just the two of us. Hatch leaned forward, close enough that I could feel his breath and see his eyes through the dark lenses of his sunglasses.

"I'm going to find you, Vey," he whispered. "And when I do, I'm going to hurt you."

That's when I woke up in the jungle.

2

Number Fifteen

It took me a moment to remember where I was. Some kind of Amazonian jungle insect-beast was crawling on my face, and as soon as I realized it, I sat up, wildly brushing it off. Someone started laughing. A young native girl was on her knees on the ground next to me. She was wearing a dress made of tree bark and was holding something that looked like one of the dream catchers my mother used to hang on her wall. I also noticed that my foot had been packed in dark dried mud, wrapped in leaves, and tied up with jute twine. Surprisingly, my ankle wasn't aching anymore. "Hey," I said to the girl.

She gazed at me with dark, intense eyes. "*Dzao an, hen keai.*"

"I have no idea what you're saying," I said. "I have no idea what any of you have been saying."

She smiled, then set down the dream catcher and ran out of my hut.

Now what? I thought. I lay there for a while, wondering what I should do. I still didn't know what the tribe had planned for me. It crossed my mind that I should try to escape. But where would I go? The jungle had to be at least as dangerous as this place, and I'd only get more lost—if that were possible.

Out of nervousness, I sat up and started making lightning balls and throwing them against the wall, which wasn't exactly smart. You know how they say that people in glass houses shouldn't throw stones? They could also say, people in thatch huts shouldn't throw lightning balls, because the wall will catch on fire. It did. I had to use my shirt to beat the flames out. I had just extinguished them and was sitting back on my mat, pulling my shirt on, when the chief walked into my hut flanked by two warrior tribesmen. There was still a lot of smoke in the room, and the chief looked at the burned spots on the wall, then back at me. As usual, the warriors just stared at me with angry expressions, like they wanted to skewer me with their spears, then eat me.

"Good afternoon, Michael Vey," the chief said.

"Uh, hi," I replied, not sure how I was supposed to talk to a tribal chief. My eye started twitching. I still didn't know how the guy knew my name. Just the fact that he spoke English freaked me out a little.

"How is your ankle?" he asked.

"It's not hurting like it was."

"Stand," he said.

I slowly stood. My ankle was still a little sore, but it was not nearly as painful as it had been the day before.

"It feels better," I said.

He nodded. "The jungle medicine is strong. By tonight it will be healed."

I didn't know what medicine they had used, or even when they had wrapped my ankle—I had slept through it all—but whatever they'd done was nothing short of miraculous. "Thank you," I said.

He stepped closer to me. "How did you dream?"

"I had weird dreams."

He looked concerned. "What did you dream?"

"I dreamt about this guy called Dr. Hatch. He said he would find me."

The chief frowned. "Then he will find you."

His saying that chilled me. Hatch had found me twice before, and both times I had barely escaped with my life. I couldn't imagine being lucky three times. "It was just a nightmare," I said.

The chief just looked at me gravely. *"Wo syiwang jeiyang,"* he said. Then he said in English, "We can hope."

"Do you know where my friends are?" I asked.

"The woman with the two boys is deep in the jungle. They are safe."

"What about the others? The ones like me."

"They are not safe. The Peruvian army is hunting them—as they are hunting you. You must leave the jungle soon."

"Why is the Peruvian army hunting us?"

"I do not know their ways." After a moment, he said, "Come. There is someone you must meet."

"Who?"

"You will see." The chief turned and walked out of my hut. The warriors stood next to me.

"Janchi lai!" one shouted.

I followed the guards outside. We walked maybe twenty yards to the edge of the clearing where there was a small hut set apart from the others. We stopped at its door.

The chief said to me, "When you go, there is someone you must take with you." He turned back toward the hut and raised his hands. *"Hung fa,"* he shouted. *"Gwo lai!"*

A moment later a young woman came out of the hut. She looked like she was my age—pretty with dark red hair and freckles. She looked at me curiously, then at the chief, as if awaiting an explanation.

"She is one of you," the chief said.

"She's American?" I asked.

The girl stepped toward me. "He means I'm electric. Like you. You must be Michael."

I looked at her quizzically. "How did you know that?"

"Because I know all the electric kids except for the last two the Elgen hadn't found. You're not a girl, so you must be Michael Vey." She reached out her hand. "I'm Tesla."

As my hand neared her, electricity began to spark between my fingers. I pulled back, afraid to shock her. "I'm sorry," I said. "I'm not trying to do that."

She just gazed into my eyes. "It's all right. You can't hurt me."

I still kept my hand to myself. "Are you sure?"

"I'm sure," she said.

"What's your power?"

"Have you met any of the others like us?"

"Yes."

"Have you met Nichelle?"

I stepped back from her. "Yes."

"Don't worry, I'm not like her. Actually, I'm the opposite of Nichelle."

"You mean you're not a psycho Goth freak?"

She grinned. "I meant my powers. I don't suck away electric powers. I enhance them. Here, shake my hand." She stuck out her hand again. "Go on."

I just looked at her.

"C'mon," she said. "You won't hurt me. Promise."

I hesitantly reached my hand out. The closer I got to her, the more intensely my electricity sparked. When we touched, my hand was glowing pure blue-white, almost like it was in the rat bowl.

"You have a lot of electricity," she said. "It . . . tickles."

"Tickles?"

"Yeah. I usually don't even feel it." She stepped back from me and my electricity lessened. "You're very electric. Far more than any of the other Glows."

"You were amplifying my electricity?"

"Yes. But I wasn't really trying. If I tried, I could make you produce ten times that. At least."

"That could be useful," I said.

"Dr. Hatch thought so."

My heart froze at the mention of him. "You're with Hatch?"

"Not anymore."

"Why are you here—in the jungle?"

"The Amacarra rescued me. I escaped from the Starxource compound by crawling out through a pipe that runs underground. . . ."

"The Weekend Express," I said.

She looked surprised. "You know about that?"

"It's the same way I got out."

"Then you know it just drops you out in the middle of the jungle with a lot of snakes and stuff. It was dangerous, being alone in the jungle. I'm not like you. I don't have any powers of my own. I probably would have been eaten by something if it wasn't for the Amacarra."

"Why were you here in Peru in the first place?"

"Hatch was using me to amplify the electricity the plant was producing. Do you know how the plant works?"

"The electric rats . . ."

She nodded. "I was able to increase the amount of electricity they produced by more than three times." She cocked her head. "So you also know about the rat bowl."

"I broke it."

"What?"

"Actually my friends broke it. I just helped."

She looked at me in amazement.

"What kind of name is Tesla?"

"Actually, it used to be Tessa. A few months after I was captured by the Elgen, Hatch added the *l*, in honor of Nikola Tesla, the great inventor and pioneer of electricity. He's the guy who invented the Tesla coil."

"Like in science," I said.

She nodded. "Hatch thought changing my name was pretty clever. Tesla is also the name of one of the Elgen boats."

"They have boats?"

"Practically a whole navy."

"Why?"

"It's where they live. If they lived in any real country, they'd probably be arrested. So they made their own country."

"You've seen their ships?"

"Only the *Ampere* and the *Volta*. The *Volta* is a science boat. It's where they do their most secret experiments. It's not as nice as the *Ampere*. The *Ampere* is where all the Elgen brass are."

"Brass?"

"You know, the bosses. Hatch's boss."

"I didn't know he had a boss."

Tesla grinned. "I don't think he does either. I'm pretty sure they don't like each other. Hatch calls them the board of jesters."

"You should change your name back. Tessa's a pretty name."

She thought about it for a moment. "I like that idea. It could be my declaration of independence." She nodded. "Call me Tessa."

"Tessa," I said. "So how long have you been here?"

"I've been in Peru for more than two years. I came three weeks before they turned on the Starxource plant. But I've been in the jungle about six months. I think. It's hard to keep track of time out here. It's not like the Amacarra have calendars."

"You've been here for six months and the Elgen still haven't found you?"

"They sent guards out looking for me." Tessa looked at the chief. "But the Amacarra know the jungle. They protect me."

"I am sorry we cannot protect you now," the chief interjected. I had forgotten that he was even standing there. "There are too many of them coming. The dark magic of the *Chullanchaqui* is too strong for us."

Tessa turned to me. "Do you know what's going on out there?"

"When we shut down their power plant, all the guards came after us. But now the Peruvian army is looking for us too. The chief said we'll have to leave their village soon."

Hearing this upset Tessa, and she began to tear up. "Then we'll leave," she said to the chief. "You've risked too much for me already."

The chief frowned. "It is with great sadness that you leave," he said. "You are Amacarra, Hung fa." He turned and walked away.

I let Tessa compose herself before I asked, "What's a *Chullancha-qui?*"

"The natives believe the *Chullanchaqui* is a demon who lives in the Amazon jungle. It appears as a friend and lures people off into the jungle where they are never heard from again. The chief thinks Hatch is the *Chullanchaqui.*"

"He's right," I said.

Tessa nodded, then said, "I have a lot of questions. Do you want to go into my hut and talk?"

"Sure," I said. I followed her inside. Her hut was nicer than the one I'd stayed in. The walls were decorated with bright red and green parrot feathers, and the ground was completely covered with a thick mat woven from leaves. We sat cross-legged across from each other, my back toward the door.

"Nice place," I said.

She grinned. "For a jungle hut." She looked at my mud cast. "What happened to your foot?"

"I hurt it while I was escaping from the Starxource plant. I woke up this morning with this mudpack on."

"Is it broken?"

"I don't know. I'm hoping it's just sprained."

"The medicine they put on it will help," she said. "Your face keeps twitching. Are you feeling okay?"

"I have Tourette's syndrome," I said. "It makes me blink and gulp—stuff like that. Especially when I'm under stress."

"Tourette's," she said. "I've heard of that. Is it contagious?"

"No. It's genetic," I said. "You won't catch it."

She nodded. "Before I came to Peru, there were two of you that the Elgen couldn't find—you and a girl. Did they ever find her?"

"Taylor," I said.

"Then you know her?"

I nodded. "I know her."

She looked at me for a moment, then said, "You like her."

"Why do you say that?"

"I can tell by the way you said her name."

I didn't realize I was that obvious. "She's my girlfriend."

"Where is she?"

"She's out in the jungle with the rest of the Electroclan."

"What's an Electroclan?"

"That's what we call ourselves. They're my friends. Some of them used to be with Hatch. You might know them. Ian, Abigail, and McKenna. Zeus."

Her eyes narrowed. "Zeus? You're with Zeus?"

"You know Zeus?"

"I know them all," she said. "I knew Zeus the best, since Ian, Abigail, and McKenna were locked up for insubordination. I'm glad Dr. Hatch finally let them out."

"He didn't. We rescued them."

"And Zeus?"

"He came with us."

"That surprises me," she said. "But he always was a wild card."

"He still is."

"So how did you meet up with them?" she asked.

"It started when Hatch kidnapped my mother and Taylor. I went after them."

"Have you ever met Dr. Hatch? I mean, face-to-face?"

I nodded. "The last time I saw him he tried to feed me to his rats."

She grimaced. "Hatch made me watch someone be fed to the rats. That's what he does to the guards who disobey him. How did you escape?"

"I absorbed the rats' electricity. It made me too electric for them to touch."

"You can absorb electricity?"

"That's how I stopped Nichelle."

She looked surprised. "You stopped Nichelle?"

"Yes."

"No one's ever stopped Nichelle." Suddenly, Tessa looked up. *"Ni yau shemma?"*

I turned. The young woman who'd been in my hut when I woke up was standing in the doorway looking at us.

"Hung fa. Ta bi laile. Tade jyau hai hwaide. Wo syu bang ta."

"Hau, hau," Tessa said. She looked at me. "I guess you have to go."

"Where?"

"She said your foot is still hurt. She needs to work on it some more."

I lifted myself up. "Yeah, it's still a little sore. It was nice meeting you."

"Same here," she said. "Though kind of surreal."

"What do you mean?"

"You're kind of a legend. Like Bigfoot or the Loch Ness Monster."

I looked at her quizzically.

"It's just that everyone at the academy has talked about you for years. But I never thought I'd ever really meet you. Especially not in the middle of the Amazon jungle."

"I never thought I'd be in the Amazon jungle," I replied.

3

A Rushed Departure

I followed the young woman back to my hut. When I got there, there were two stone bowls on the ground next to my bed. One had a thick, green substance in it. The other one also held liquid, but it was dark and watery with purple flowers floating in it. There was also a pile of fresh leaves next to the bowls.

"*Dzwo,*" she said, pointing to the mat.

I guessed she was telling me to sit, so I sat down. She knelt down, untied the jute twine, and peeled back the leaves around my ankle.

"*Fang sya,*" she said.

"What?"

She pushed back on my chest.

"You want me to lie down?" I asked. I partially lay back. "Like this?"

She laughed and pushed me again. "*Fang sya.*"

I lay back. She set the leaves aside, then began peeling the hard clay from my foot. When it was all off, she washed my foot with warm, sweet-smelling liquid, then began rubbing some kind of salve on it. She kneaded my foot for nearly an hour. The massage felt really good, and the concoction she was rubbing into my ankle made my skin tingle. I started to sit up to look, but she gently put her hand on my chest to stop me. *"Ching bu."*

"Sorry," I said. "Just looking." I lay back and closed my eyes. After my ankle was fully coated she wrapped it in fragrant leaves, then gently tied it with the same cord as before. Then she came around and began running her fingers through my hair. "This is, like, better than a day spa," I said, even though I'd never actually been to one and she couldn't understand me anyway.

She didn't speak any more but continued to massage my scalp and gently tug on my hair. I had no idea what this had to do with healing my foot, but it felt really good.

After a few minutes she began to sing.

Hen ke aide,
bu syi huan wo,
tai ke shi,
yin wo ai ni.

Hen ke aide,
Wai gwo haidz
Ho ni li wo,
hwei ni syang wo,

Wo syi wang, hwei
yin, wo ain ni,
jye nyu haidz
hwei syang ni.

She sang the words over and over. I had no idea what she was singing, but it was pretty and soothing, and she seemed sad singing it. At one point she got particularly emotional. I partially opened one eye and saw that she was crying. She was still singing when I fell asleep.

I had another dream. I was alone in the jungle when a tiny Peruvian man with a wooden leg came to me. "We must hurry to someplace safe," he said. "*He* is coming."

"Who's coming?" I asked.

"*El Chullanchaqui.*"

"Who is that?"

"No time to explain," he said, running off into the jungle. In spite of his size and wooden leg, he moved quickly as I ran after him, deeper and deeper into the trees. The farther into the jungle we went, the darker it got, until it was nearly dark as night. Finally we stopped in a place that was too thick to hike through. The branches of the trees around me were snakes, snapping at me.

I looked at the man fearfully. "I thought you said you were taking me someplace safe."

"There is no safe place anymore."

"Who is *El Chullanchaqui?*"

He looked at me and smiled. "Me." Then he disappeared.

I woke, gasping. It was dark around me, and the hut was slightly illuminated by the glow of my skin. The girl was gone. I took a deep breath and rubbed my forehead. *I've got to stop dreaming*, I thought.

It was about a half hour later that the young woman returned. I could see her silhouette in the entranceway. She wore flowers in her black hair and dozens of red and purple beads, which shone against her bare shoulders and neck. She looked pretty.

"*Hen keaidi, ni laile.*" She reached her hand out to me.

I took a step toward her and realized that my foot felt completely better. I touched it, then looked at her and smiled. "Thank you."

"*Bu yung, sye.*" She took my hand and led me out to the center of the village, where there was a large fire blazing. The natives looked at us as we arrived, their faces lit by the flickering flames. They were sitting around the fire on mats woven from palm leaves. There were many more women than men, and I guessed that the warriors were out patrolling the jungle.

I sat down on a mat next to the young woman, who looked very happy, her face blanketed with a contented smile.

"It's a pretty night," I said.

She didn't speak.

"I can't believe that you fixed my foot. Doctors in America can't fix a foot that fast."

She looked over at me, her eyes gazing deeply into mine.

"Hey, glow boy. She doesn't speak English."

I turned around to see Tessa walking up to us. At her approach the young woman frowned, then quietly stood and walked away. In the shadow outside of the fire, I could see Tessa's faint glow, which was comforting to me. My own glow increased as she got nearer. She sat down next to me.

"What's going on here?" I asked.

"It's a funeral dinner. That's why the women are wearing those red and purple beads."

"A funeral dinner? Who died?"

Tessa gave me a funny smile. "We did."

I stared at her. "They're going to kill us?"

She laughed. "No, glowworm. When someone leaves that they won't see again, they consider them dead."

"That's . . . creepy."

"It's their custom. I mean, it's not like Americans don't have weird customs—like, carving faces into pumpkins and putting candles in them. Or hanging lights on Christmas trees. How weird is that?"

"I never thought about it that way."

"That's because it's what you're raised with. Same with them. Unfortunately, their customs won't be around much longer."

"Why is that?"

"The Amacarra are going extinct," she said. "There used to be thousands of them. Now this is all that's left. There are more old people than young. Soon they will be down to less than a dozen people."

"Why are they going extinct?"

"Same reason the American Indians did," she said. "Disease. The shrinking forest. The modern world."

The young woman returned and handed me a stone bowl filled with a yellow substance, mashed like potatoes.

"Wo gei ni chr, ke aide."

I didn't know what she said but thanked her. She left us again.

Tessa asked, "Do you like Meihwa?"

I looked down at my bowl. "I don't know. I've never tried it."

Tessa burst out laughing. "No, Meihwa is the girl who's been taking care of you."

I looked up at her. "Oh, sorry. She seems nice. She mostly just looks at me and laughs."

Tessa grinned. "Of course. She's only twelve. And she thinks you're cute."

"How do you know that?"

"Because she calls you *henkeai*."

I looked at her blankly. "Yeah, I've heard that. What does it mean?"

"It means she thinks you're cute."

I wasn't sure what to say to that. "She's cute too."

Tessa smiled. "If we were sticking around, the chief would probably marry her to you."

"She's only twelve."

"The Amacarra marry young."

"Then it's a good thing I'm not sticking around," I said.

"Good thing," Tessa repeated.

I changed the subject. "So what's in the bowl?"

"Mashed bananas," she said.

"Bananas," I said. "Then it's good for our electricity."

"Yes. But I don't think the Amacarra know that. It's just what they eat."

I picked out a piece of something white and fibrous from the fruit. "This isn't banana."

She took the piece from me and put it in her mouth. "It's piranha."

"Piranha?"

"Yeah."

"What does it taste like?"

She looked at me with a wry smile. "Chicken, of course. Just be glad it's not the *yasyegump*."

"What's that?"

"Squashed termite larvae."

"They eat that?"

"Sometimes," Tessa said. "It takes some getting used to."

"I don't think I'd ever get used to it."

"You'd be surprised at what you can get used to," Tessa said.

"Do they eat much piranha?"

"Yes. Maybe because it's so easy to catch. The river is full of them."

"What do they use for bait?"

"The Amacarra use spears to fish, so there's no bait. But I've seen the Peruvian jungle men fish, and they use just about anything. I once saw a man cut a callous from his foot, put it on a hook, and fish with it."

My dinner was looking less appetizing by the second. "We're eating foot-fungus-fed piranha."

"I told you, the Amacarra use spears. Go on, don't be a chicken. It's good. Besides, *eating* piranha is a lot better than the other way around."

Just then an older woman with gray hair walked up to us. I could tell that Tessa liked her by the way her face lit up when she saw her. The woman held out a bowl of food to Tessa. Tessa took the bowl then said, "*Sye sye, muchin.*"

The woman smiled. "*Buyung kechi,*" she said. She touched Tessa on the cheek, then walked away.

"How did you learn the language?"

"I only know a little. If you hang out long enough, you start picking up things. Like this is how they eat." She held up her hand with three fingers together. "You hold your fingers like this and scoop it up." She lifted a lump of the stuff to her mouth and ate it.

I imitated her, dipping my fingers into the pasty goo, then put it into my mouth. Honestly, it wasn't that bad. I would never think of eating fruit and fish together, but, in a jungle sort of way, it worked.

We ate a moment in silence, then I asked Tessa, "So what are you going to do after we get back to America?"

"I don't know. I guess I'll just try to live a normal life. Whatever that is."

"You could, like, work for an electric company. Or with scientists."

She raised an eyebrow. "I could if I wanted the Elgen to find me."

"Sorry, bad idea," I said. "Do you think Hatch will ever stop looking for you?"

She frowned. "No. Hatch never gives up. And he never forgets. It's something he's proud of." She slowly exhaled. "What about you? What are you going to do?"

"I'll go home with my mom. Finish high school."

"That sounds nice," she said. "Home." She looked at me then asked, "Do you think Hatch will leave you alone?"

"No." After a moment I asked, "How did Hatch get you?"

"I was nine. They kidnapped me from my room."

"That's horrible."

She looked down. "It was pretty traumatic. But the Elgen psychologists, they"—she paused—"help you forget."

"So you don't remember your family?"

Her expression fell. "I remember some. I had a little brother. And my mother was just about to have another baby. He'd almost be six by now."

"You could find them."

"No. I can't go back," she said.

"Why not?"

"It's not my world anymore."

"It could be."

Her expression grew more sorrowful. "No. I've seen too much." She slowly shook her head. "I've done too much. I don't belong anymore. They wouldn't want me."

"Of course they would. I bet they think about you all the time."

Her eyes looked pained. "No, it just wouldn't work anymore."

"Why are you saying that?"

Her eyes flashed. "Because it's true. When the Elgen take you, they do things to you. They change you. You're not the same person you were. They convince you that your family doesn't really want you anymore. They make you angry at them. They get you to denounce them."

Hearing this made me heartsick. "Did you denounce your family?"

She didn't answer, but I could guess the answer from the pain in her eyes.

"You know that Hatch and the Elgen are liars, right?"

"Logically, I do. But this stuff is programmed into you as a kid. It takes root and grows into who you are. Pretty soon, you can't pull it out anymore because it's all that's left of you. Even if you know it's not true, it's all you know." Her voice fell. "It still feels true. And deep down inside, you're afraid that they're right. . . ."

"They're not right," I said. "The Elgen can twist the truth all they want, but they can't change it. A million lies can't make a single truth."

"But they can bury it so deep you'll never find it," she said. She took a deep breath. "Can we talk about something else?"

"I'm sorry," I said.

Just then an Amacarra tribesman ran into camp. He was speaking excitedly and his hands flew wildly around him, as if he were swatting at a swarm of bees. Everyone around us stilled and the chief's expression grew solemn. Then he stood and walked over to us. "The army is near. It is time for you to go to the river. *Ma shang.*"

"Now?" I asked Tessa.

"*Ma shang* means 'immediately,'" Tessa said, setting her bowl down on the ground.

The chief shouted something and a woman ran away from the fire, then returned carrying two woven blankets. "You must wear these," he said. "To hide your glow."

We put them around us, like cloaks, so that only our faces showed. A half dozen warriors surrounded us.

"Come," the chief said. "We must hurry."

I looked across the fire. Meihwa was looking at me. A tear, glistening from the light of the fire, ran down her cheek. I waved at her, but she just turned away.

The expedition was composed of Tessa and me, the chief, six warriors, and the old woman who had served Tessa food.

The Amacarra village wasn't far from the river, less than a half hour by foot, and we hurried through the jungle as fast as we could run, over fallen trees and around quicksand, with hardly a wasted step. Everyone moved quickly, even the elderly woman, who I had trouble keeping up with. Every now and then the chief would turn back and say to me, "*Kwai, kwai ba!*" Which I took to mean, "Run faster!"

We moved without speaking, and a few times we heard the echo of gunfire in the distance, which only increased our pace. I wondered if the army had reached the Amacarra village and if they would harm the villagers.

At the river we walked down a small incline to a dugout canoe. Two caimans were on the shore next to the canoe but turned and splashed into the water at our approach, their thick tails making final flicks at us before disappearing in the dark brown water. Two of the warriors got into the canoe, while the others began cutting large fronds from the trees that overhung the bank, piling them next to the canoe.

"Get in," the chief said to us.

Tessa turned to the old woman. There were tears in both their eyes. "*Muchin,*" Tessa said and they embraced. The tension around us was thick and in spite of their emotion, they held each other for only a moment before they separated. The woman took off one of her necklaces, a long string of bright red seeds, and put it over Tessa's neck. I now understood that the old woman had come with us only to say good-bye.

"*Kwai ba!*" the chief shouted. "*Mei o shr jyan!*"

The pair embraced once more, then Tessa turned and climbed into the boat. She turned back one more time to look at the woman. "I will never forget you, Mama," she said.

The old woman touched her hand to her heart.

I climbed into the boat after Tessa.

"Michael Vey," the chief said. "Look at me."

"Yes, sir."

"I have dreamed a dream. Over the water, a choice will come to you. You must choose between the lives of a few you love or the lives of many you do not know."

"I don't want that choice," I said.

"No one would wish that choice. But fate does not bend for us— we must bend to it. Now go! *Chyu ba!*"

The tribesmen motioned for Tessa and me to lie down next to each other, then they pulled our blankets up over us and covered us with the broad green leaves they had collected.

The floor of the canoe was rough and pungent and looked as if it had been pounded out with rocks. Beneath the blankets our glows were bright enough to easily see each other. The boat was narrow, so our bodies were pressed tightly together. My glow was brighter wherever her body touched mine. I was anxious, and my electricity arced loudly between us.

"Can you stop doing that?" Tessa whispered.

"I'll try."

With some effort, I made the arcing stop, though an occasional buildup would jump between us, especially from our heads, which were touching.

"It's so cramped," she said. She pulled the necklace she'd just received up around her throat, then slid forward until my head was against her chest. "Is this better?"

"That's better," I said. I could hear her heart pounding rapidly. Lying against her like this made me think of Taylor. I remembered how she'd held me that night by the pool outside of Mitchell's house. I wished she were with me now. Actually, I wished we were back at Mitchell's house.

The tribesmen pushed the boat away from the shore, and I could hear the rhythmic slap of their paddles against the water as we slipped out over the cold, dark river.

"Who was that woman?" I asked Tessa.

"That's Aigei," she said. "But I call her *muchin*, for mother. She's been like a mother to me since I was found."

Considering that she had been separated from her real mother at such a young age, I wondered what that meant to her.

"That's a pretty necklace she gave you," I said.

"It's made from *huayruro* seeds. It's supposed to bring good luck."

"We could use it," I said. I had no idea where we were going or how long we would be in the boat, but I gathered it might be a while. After a little while Tessa fell asleep, but I couldn't sleep. At least not at first. I was too worried—not just about us, but about my mother and my friends. I lay awake for what seemed like a long time before sleep overtook me.

4

A Surprise Reunion

I awoke to one of the tribes-
men shaking me. I rubbed my eyes and looked up. It was dawn, and
Tessa was already sitting up, her hair matted to the side of her head.
She pulled her hair back from her face. "I think we're here."

I lifted myself up and peered over the side of the boat. We were
docked, but all I could see was more jungle. "Where's here?"

"I don't know," Tessa said. "Somewhere downriver."

"With your old friend Jaime," a voice said.

I spun around. Standing behind us on the shore was Jaime, the
Peruvian man who had brought us into the jungle.

"Jaime!"

"Mr. Michael," he said, stepping forward. "Let me help you out."

"Help her first," I said, looking at Tessa.

Jaime offered her his hand, but she grabbed the side of the canoe
and climbed out by herself. I got out too.

When I was on the bank he said, "Congratulations, amigo."

I looked at him quizzically. "What for?"

"For still being alive," he said. "And for making some serious trouble. *Mucho caos*."

I'm pretty sure that that was the first time in my life that someone had congratulated me for causing trouble. "More than we planned on," I said.

Tessa looked at Jaime suspiciously. "How do you know this guy?"

"He's the one who brought us into the jungle."

"How did you meet him?"

"I'll tell you later," I said. "But we can trust him. He's a friend."

She still looked unsure. "You're from Idaho. How do you have a Peruvian friend?" She looked directly at Jaime. "Are you an Elgen?"

"*Ufff! Que locura!*" Jaime said. He looked her directly in the eyes. "Do not insult me. I would rather cut out my own heart and feed it to the piranhas than to be called one of those demons."

"That's pretty graphic," she said.

"We have not the time to chitchat," Jaime said. "We must hurry. You have angered the Elgen wasps, and they are looking for someone to sting."

"Where are we going?" I asked.

"Into the jungle," he said. He turned to the tribesmen. "*Feichang, sye sye.*"

They slightly bowed. "*Bukechi,*" they replied. They immediately paddled away from the shore until they were in the middle of the river and headed upstream.

"Those guys are strong," I said. "They didn't even rest."

Jaime turned back to me. "They have not time to rest," Jaime said. "Neither do we. Come. *Vámonos!*"

We followed him through a path in the trees that quickly disappeared, overgrown with foliage and snarled tree roots that rose like snakes through the jungle's dark soil. Even though it was morning, beneath the canopy it was dark enough that Tessa and I could see our glows.

We had hiked more than an hour into the jungle when the foliage in front of us suddenly lightened into a small clearing, exposing an elaborate campsite built next to a stream.

"We are home," Jaime said.

"It's not my home," Tessa said, looking around.

I surveyed the camp with wonder. "How did you get all this stuff back here?"

"With much work," Jaime said. "This is our base to monitor the Elgen."

The camp consisted of two large nylon tents, a cooking spit, a generator next to at least a dozen plastic gas cans, and a metal communications tower that rose as high as the trees but no higher. About fifteen yards from the camp Jaime suddenly stopped, holding his hands out. "*Alto.*"

In spite of my B+ in Mrs. Waller's eighth-grade Spanish, I didn't recognize Jaime's command to stop, and Tessa and I just kept walking.

"I'm starving," Tessa said. "I hope he's got something to eat."

Jaime lunged at me, grabbing me by the arm. "*Párate!* Stop! Do not walk any farther."

I hadn't seen him coming for me and instinctively pulsed. Jaime screamed as he fell to the ground. I looked down at him. He was holding his arm and moaning. "*Ay caramba, caramba, caramba!*"

"I didn't mean to do that," I said. "It's just habit."

"You are worse than the *anguila*," Jaime said, still grimacing with pain. "You must not walk any farther." From the ground Jaime pointed toward a twitching pile of fur lying near the second tent. "See? It is a trap."

"Who would set a trap out here?" I asked.

"I did. It is a safety."

"A safety?" Tessa replied. "I think you're using that word wrong."

Jaime rose to his knees. He picked up a fallen branch on the ground and threw it into the clearing ten feet in front of us. There was an immediate eruption of gunfire and bullets that tore through the wood, shredding it into slivers.

"Whoa," I said.

"That totally could have been us," Tessa said. "Swiss cheese."

"That is my safety to make sure no one enters my camp when I am gone. Before we go in I must deactivate the sensor."

"I'm for that," Tessa said.

Jaime took a small, black cylindrical object out of his pocket. It was about the shape and size of a lipstick tube, with a single red button on top. He pushed it. "It is safe now."

Looking at the quivering animal near the edge of the clearing, I wasn't about to step into the firing zone. "Are you sure it's off?"

"Yes. Look." He lifted another piece of wood and threw it into the clearing. This time nothing happened. "It is turned off." He pointed toward the gun. "There is no light on the turret." He climbed back to his feet and stepped forward, still rubbing his shocked arm. "We are safe. I will go first."

He walked into the clearing, with Tessa and me close behind.

"That was pretty cool," I said. "How does it work?"

"It is simple, amigo. There are two guns." He led me to one of the machines. The turret was run by electric motors mounted onto steel pipes that Jaime had wrapped up in leaves. The contraption looked simple enough, and my first thought was that Ostin could probably build one of these from spare parts he had in his bedroom. The thought of that made me miss him.

"It is a robotic sentry that runs off a program from my laptop. I bought it from an American company that makes them for paintball guns."

I touched the gun's barrel. It was still warm. "They make these for paintball guns?"

"Yes. I just made some adjustments." He pointed to the other side of the clearing. "The other one is over there behind that tree. They are very fast. Each one can move so quickly it can follow up to four targets at the same time."

"How does it know when to shoot?" Tessa asked.

"The guns are activated by movement. They shoot anything that moves past its camera." He turned back to me. "I put these here to keep my equipment safe from Elgen when I am not here. If they

were to get our communication codes, it would endanger everything."

"It seems . . . extreme," Tessa said.

"Our cause is extreme," Jaime said seriously. "The sentry is very
effective, but so far all it has shot are monkeys. That is good."

"Not for the monkeys," Tessa said.

"Monkeys and whatever that thing is," I said, looking at the animal, which had finally stopped twitching.

"What is that thing?" Tessa asked.

Jaime pointed to the pile of fur. "That, senorita, is dinner—the
osohormiguero."

"Lovely," she replied.

I walked up to examine the beast. It had thick, spiky fur and a
long body about four feet in length, not including its tail, which was
curled up around its belly. I still couldn't tell what it was, and I had
to push it over with my foot to see its head. It had small dark eyes
and an elongated snout. "It's an anteater," I said.

"*Was*," Tessa said. "I think its ant-eating days are over."

"Yes, you call it an anteater," Jaime said. "It is most tasty."

"I've had it before," Tessa said. "It was okay." She looked at Jaime.
"Do you have anything to drink?"

"The water barrel is there," Jaime said, pointing to a five-gallon
white plastic bucket. "You must lift the lid. The cup is hanging next
to it. Be sure to look for spiders. They like the water."

"I'll keep that in mind," she said. She unhooked the tin-handled
cup hanging next to the bucket, then lifted the bucket's lid. For a
moment she just stared. "There's something dead in here," she said
dryly. "Actually, there's like a million dead things in here, but there's
one really big dead thing."

Jaime walked over and looked in. He took another cup and lifted
out an eight-inch insect. "It is only a walking stick. Not poisonous."

"I feel so much better now," Tessa said. She skimmed the top of
the bucket, dumping the contents of her cup on the ground three
times before scooping up a cup of water clear enough to drink. She
drank down two cups, then filled it up again and brought it over to

me. There were small things floating around in it, mostly mosquitoes and fleas, but I drank it anyway.

"Thanks," I said.

"It's funny how we adapt, isn't it? In the academy days I would complain if my water didn't have a slice of lime in it. But after being in the jungle this long, hardly anything bothers me anymore. I once ate a roasted armadillo. The Amacarra roll them up and cook them in their own shells."

"What I wouldn't give for a cheeseburger about now," I said.

"Sorry," Jaime said. "No cheeseburgers. But I do have food." He disappeared into the first tent and returned carrying two boxes, which he handed to us. "I was only making a joke about the anteater," he said. "We cannot make a fire to roast it. The Elgen soldiers could follow the smoke. But trust me, it is very delicious."

"I'll take your word for it," I said.

We opened the boxes. Inside was a ham sandwich sealed in cellophane, a package of crackers with soft cheese, quinoa cake, a Sublime chocolate bar, a piece of fruit I'd never seen before, a bottle of Inca Kola, and a yogurt drink.

"Real food," Tessa said. "*Muchas, muchas gracias*. It's been so long."

"Yes, thanks," I said. "I'm starving."

"Come inside the tent to eat," he said. "We will talk." Jaime lifted the mosquito netting around the second tent. We ducked under the netting and went inside. The interior was a square, about twelve feet by twelve feet, cluttered with crates and barrels. There was a small collapsible plastic table against one side of the tent with a ham radio and a digital clock. Stacked up next to the table were long crates with the word PELIGRO stenciled on them.

Jaime grabbed himself a box of food, and all three of us sat down on the tent's vinyl tarp floor.

"I like this Inca Kola," I said. "It tastes like bubble gum."

"You have this in America?" Jaime asked.

"No," I said. "At least not in Idaho."

"Shame," he said.

I lifted the fruit.

"What is this?"

"Granadilla," Jaime said. "Try it."

I peeled it open. Inside, the fruit was gray and looked like mucus.

"It looks like snot, " Tessa said.

Jaime laughed. "Yes, Americans call it 'snot fruit!' Try it!"

I looked at it for a moment, then took a bite. It actually was quite good. Tessa just looked disgusted.

"I just threw up in my mouth," she said.

I ate the rest of the fruit, then took hers as well.

"There's something I'm wondering," Tessa said. "How did the Amacarra know to find you here?"

"A few days ago, when I saw smoke coming from the compound, I asked the chief to keep an eye out for Michael and the others."

"So that's how he knew my name," I said.

"Yes. I told him about you." Jaime looked at Tessa. "But I am surprised that he did not tell me about you."

"They were looking out for me," Tessa said.

Jaime shook his head. "Our affairs are not the Amacarra's affairs. But the Elgen have been bad to them."

"Do you know where my mother and friends are?" I asked.

"Your mother and Tanner made it to the rendezvous site. They are now safe with our people."

Hearing this filled me with a powerful sense of relief. "And what about the rest of the Electroclan?"

Jaime's expression turned. "They have been captured."

My relief vanished. "The Elgen got them?"

"No. The Peruvian army."

I shook my head. "I don't understand why they're hunting us."

"It was my country's electricity you stopped."

"Do you know where they're being held?"

"They are at a jail in Puerto Maldonado. But we are sure they will take them back to Lima to be tried."

"Tried? For what?"

"For terrorism."

"Terrorism! We're not terrorists! The Elgen are the terrorists. We were helping your country!"

"They did not ask for your help. The way they see it, you put my country out of power. Shops and businesses shut down. Hospitals are on backup generators. People will go hungry. The power outage cost my country millions and millions of dollars. Only *we* know that what you did was good."

"That's not fair."

"No. But that is how it is in the world—the wise are hung and the fools are glorified, at least while they are living."

I raked my fingers back through my hair. "What will happen if they try them in your courts?"

"They will probably find them guilty of terrorism."

"What will they do to them? They're just teenagers."

Jaime's voice came slowly. "If they are found guilty, their age will not matter."

"What will they do to them?" I asked again.

Jaime hesitated. "They will probably be executed."

My blood ran cold. "They can't do that."

"My country abolished the death penalty in 1979, but not for treason and terrorism."

"We can't let that happen. *I'm* not going to let that happen. How many soldiers are there?"

"More than you can fight," Jaime said. "Maybe as many as four thousand soldiers. Even if our organization risked everything and came out in the open to help you, we could not rescue your friends."

"An army couldn't," I said. "But a mouse can get in where a lion can't."

He looked at me. "That is true."

"I could sneak in and rescue them like we did in Pasadena. Are they still in Puerto Maldonado?"

"You will never get close. There are many patrols, and they have built fences. I am certain that they will be moving your friends soon."

"They'll fly them to Lima?"

"No, they will not fly," Jaime said. "They must have been warned about Tanner, because they did not bring any aircraft into the area. And Tanner destroyed all the Elgen helicopters."

"But you said that Tanner's gone."

"The Elgen and the army do not know that."

"Then they'll have to drive them to Lima," Tessa said.

"There is only one road to Lima," Jaime said. "It is a mountain road and very narrow at spots. That is your best chance of stopping them. It could be like Thermopylae."

"The what?" Tessa asked.

"Thermopylae is an ancient place in Greece where three hundred Spartans held off tens of thousands of Persians. It is a narrow place that a large army can't march through. If only a few people can get through the door at a time, it doesn't matter how many people there are."

"If we stop the trucks in front, the rest will be trapped behind them," I said.

"Then what?" Tessa asked.

"In the confusion, I'll sneak in and free my friends."

"They will be guarded," Jaime said.

"I can take care of that," I said.

"But you will still be surrounded by the entire army," Jaime said.

"If we had everyone's powers . . . ," I said.

Jaime looked skeptical. "Those powers did not stop them from being captured."

"But if they were enhanced." I turned to Tessa. "Could you enhance everyone's power at the same time?"

"I enhanced a half million rats' power at the same time," she said.

"If we had even ten times the power, Taylor could reboot all the soldiers at the same time, and we could just walk out of there. Zeus could fire real lightning and destroy any weapon. McKenna could go supernova and melt everything in sight."

Jaime looked at me. "It is still a big risk. We need to talk to the voice and see what he says."

"You can contact the voice?" I asked.

He looked around cautiously, then nodded. "Yes."

"What's 'the voice'?" Tessa asked.

Jaime looked at me, then Tessa. "We cannot speak of the voice around her."

Tessa turned red. "You don't trust me? I followed you into the middle of the jungle, and you don't trust *me*?"

"Tessa, it's okay," I said. "He's not trying to insult you. He's just got to be sure."

"Then *get* sure," she said to Jaime.

Suddenly, Jaime froze. "Do you hear that?"

We stopped talking to listen. "No," I said. I looked at Tessa.

"I don't hear anything," Tessa said, still sounding annoyed. "In fact, it's kind of quiet."

"Yes," Jaime said. "Exactly." He stood. "Just a minute." He parted the door and walked out of the tent.

As soon as the tent's flap shut, Tessa asked, "What's this voice?"

I looked at the door to make sure Jaime was really gone, then back at her. I lowered my voice. "After we escaped from Pasadena we went back to Idaho. The Elgen followed us. We were hiding from them at a tanning salon when a woman came in and handed me a cell phone. There was a man on the other end. He knew who we were and where we'd been. He knew all about the Elgen. That's how we got down here. He flew us down."

"Who is he?"

"I don't know. All I know is that he hates Hatch as much as I do."

"Why is he so secret?"

"Because secrecy is his most important weapon. You can't fight an enemy you don't know exists."

She nodded. "That makes sense." She looked around the place. "What if this voice tells you not to go after your friends?"

"I'll go anyway."

"They mean that much to you?"

"They're my friends," I said. "You don't abandon your friends."

For a moment she was quiet. Then she said, "It wasn't like that at the academy. We got along because it was a rule. But everyone was in competition with one another." She looked at me seriously. "Friends or not, I don't think it's a good idea going up against the army. You'll only get caught."

"I have to," I said. "And I really need your help."

She looked down. "I don't know," she said. "I have to think about it. If Hatch captures me, he'll punish me for running away."

I looked into her eyes. "Tessa, I can't do it without you."

She took a deep breath. "I just don't know. I have to think about it."

I sighed. "Think about it. Because either way, I'm going."

The silence between us grew uncomfortable and I began gulping. After another minute I said, "Jaime's been gone a long time for just checking around."

"Maybe he had to use the bathroom," Tessa said.

I stood. "I'm going to go see what he's doing."

I walked out of the tent. At first I didn't see anything. I took a few steps before I saw Jaime lying motionless on the ground.

"Jaime?" I started walking toward him. "Tessa!" I shouted.

Tessa came to the flap of the tent and looked out. "What is it?"

"Jaime's on the ground."

"Did he have a heart attack?"

Someone shouted, "Put your hands on your head and walk out of the tent! Now!"

I looked up as a squad of uniformed Elgen guards emerged from the jungle. Their guns were pointed at us.

"Now!" the guard shouted again. "Both of you. Or we'll open fire."

"I'm not going back," Tessa said, her voice pitched with terror. She ducked into the tent.

I put my hands on my head. "Don't shoot."

"Don't try anything, Vey," one of the guards said. "Or we will. And tell the girl to get back out here before we shoot up the tent."

I turned back. "Tessa, come out!" I shouted. "They'll shoot."

"Tessa?" the short guard to my left repeated. "Was that really Tessa, aka Tesla?"

I didn't answer.

"Jackpot, boys," the guard said. "It's two-for-one day at the Happy

Mart. Vey *and* Tessa. Hatch is going to be happier than a monkey on a banana boat."

Tessa slowly walked back out. She was shaking.

"Beautiful little Tessa," the guard said, grinding his teeth. "Remember me? Carvelle?" He walked up to her. "I always had a thing for redheads. And then you had to go and run off." His expression turned dark. "Hatch was so upset when you went missing that he fed your bodyguard to the rats." His eyes narrowed. "He was my cousin."

Tessa swallowed. She looked pale, like she might faint.

"Did someone radio base?" a guard asked.

"There's no coverage," the captain replied. "We'll radio it in back at the river."

"Look at that tower," another guard said. "They've been communicating with someone."

"Let's find out who," the captain said. "Search the tents."

Four of the guards disappeared into the tents.

I was twitching a lot and electricity was sparking around me wildly. Under duress it always did, but with Tessa standing next to me it was crazy. It was even sparking between my legs, climbing from my ankles to thighs like a Jacob's ladder.

"Stop sparking!" the main guard shouted.

"I can't help it," I said.

"Then I'll help you," another voice said. Two of those yellow-and-red-striped darts struck me in the side.

I collapsed to the ground, groaning as I fell. But I was still sparking. The darts started smoking, then blew. My energy immediately returned.

"It's Tessa," Carvelle said. "She's making him more electric. She's got that way with men."

Three darts hit Tessa. Then another three darts hit me. Tessa fell to the ground about two yards from me. My electricity stopped.

Tessa was almost breathless with pain. My own pain was agonizing, but she seemed less able to handle it.

"Let's move it," the captain shouted. "Pedro, Pair, and Sanchez, secure the radio. Find out who they've been broadcasting to. I want all codes, logs, and frequencies. Then we're going to pack that thing out of here."

"Yes, sir."

"Johnny and Ryan, you have Vey. Cuff and RESAT him. And be careful, he's slippery. Carvelle, since you and Tessa are such good friends, she's all yours. RESAT her, too."

"My pleasure," Carvelle said, pulling the white RESAT box out of his pack. "I'm going to keep it turned up a bit high just to be sure you're not enjoying this, sweetheart. Every time you scream out with pain I want you to think about my cousin in the bowl."

Tessa began to cry.

The men connected the RESAT to my leg, then they rolled me onto my stomach and pinned my arms behind my back and banded them together.

"Should we band his legs?" one of the guards asked.

"Only if you want to carry him out of here," another replied.

"That would be negatory." He laughed. He smacked me in the head. "Sorry, boy. No free rides on this train."

Out of my peripheral vision I could see them cuffing Tessa's hands as well. She was still crying but not struggling. She looked as if she was having difficulty breathing. The RESAT was set way too high for her.

When we were both secure they dragged Tessa, on her back, to the center of the camp and lay her next to me; then the men left us to join the others searching the tents, leaving just two guards to watch over us. That's all they needed. With the RESATs we could barely even breathe, let alone escape.

With some effort I looked over at Jaime. He was so still I wondered if he was dead. But I hadn't heard any gunshots and he'd been cuffed, which wouldn't make sense if he were dead. Then I saw the dart sticking out of his hip. It was not like one of the RESAT darts—it was more like a needle. They had tranquilized him. Of course they had. The Elgen only killed when their foe had no value. Jaime had value. They would torture him for information. They would break him and learn about the voice. They would know everything. Our cause would be lost.

Then I noticed something else. Something on the ground next to him. The small black remote to the robotic guns had fallen out of his pocket.

"Tessa," I whispered.

Only her eyes moved toward me. Her cheeks were stained with tears mixed with dirt.

I struggled to take a deep breath. "No matter what happens, don't move a muscle. Not a muscle. Understand?"

I gestured with my eyes to the remote.

She followed my gaze to the device, then looked back at me. She looked scared but blinked in understanding.

On my stomach, I inched my way toward Jaime. If I could get close enough, I could roll over onto the remote and activate it with my fingers. Moving was slow and painful, and I had to rest after each exertion, hoping that the guards didn't notice me and that the other guards didn't finish their search before I got to Jaime. I was about two feet from the remote when the rest of the guards emerged from the tents, their arms loaded with papers and equipment.

"We've found a treasure trove, gentlemen," the captain said, his arms laden with boxes.

Then one of the guards glanced over at me. "What's he doing?"

"He's going for that thing," another said, pointing to the remote.

"What is that?" the captain asked. "Someone get that."

With everything I had, I rolled onto my back over the remote.

"Get him!" the captain shouted.

Slightly arching my back, I got the remote in my hands and moved it around in my fingers. As the first guard reached me, I pressed the button. The entire campsite exploded with machine-gun fire.

"Ambush!" a guard shouted, before falling to the ground riddled with bullets. The sound of bullets whistled past me, one so close that it caught a flap of my shirt, ripping the side of it open.

The guards shouted in panic, making their situation worse as they went for their weapons to combat their unseen assaulters. The firing probably lasted less than twenty seconds, but felt much, much longer. I closed my eyes until the firing stopped, the stench of smoke falling low to the ground. I fought coughing. I dared not even move my head enough to look around to see if anyone was left. I was afraid to look at Jaime and Tessa.

When it had been quiet for nearly thirty seconds, I pushed the remote button again, then slowly raised my head enough to see the turret. The red light above the gun was off. I breathed out in relief, then fell back again, my body racked with pain. The Elgen guards were lying all around me, but no one was moving.

I looked back at Tessa. She was shaking.

"It's off," I croaked.

She tried to speak but couldn't. She was drenched with sweat and her blouse looked as if she had showered in it. The RESAT was set way too high. I worried that if I couldn't get it turned off soon that it might stop her heart. But I could barely move myself and I doubted that I could cut myself loose, even if I could wriggle myself to the nearest guard and unlatch his knife.

That left Jaime. I had to get the dart out of him. I rolled over again, then pushed myself up over him. I felt around until I found the dart, clasped it with my fingers, then rolled off, collapsing on the other side of him. I had the dart. Now he just needed to wake up.

5

Into the Darkness

It was nearly a half hour before Jaime stirred. About five minutes before Jaime woke, Tessa began convulsing, and then her eyes rolled back into her head and she passed out. I struggled back to her and even tried to kick the RESAT, but I was too weak.

Jaime groaned, then his eyes opened.

"Jaime," I said.

He looked at me.

"Help."

He sat up and looked around at the fallen guards. "What happened?"

"Turn this off," I gasped.

He walked on his knees over to me. His hands were still bound behind his back.

"I can unfasten it," Jaime said.

"No. If they're unfastened without being turned off, they power up to full. It could kill me."

"How do you turn it off?"

"The guard right there put it on me. He should have the control."

Jaime crawled over to him and felt through his pockets. "I think I found it."

"Push it," I said.

My RESAT powered down. I took a deep breath, then pulsed as hard as I could, melting my wristbands. Then I crawled over to Carvelle and turned off Tessa's RESAT. She immediately gasped for air, as if she'd just come up from under water. I detached the machine and threw it into the jungle, then put my head against her chest. To my relief her heart was beating.

"Cut me loose," Jaime said.

I stood up and walked over to him. Careful not to touch him, I grabbed his bands and melted through them.

"*Gracias*," he said. He stretched out his arms, then rubbed his wrists. "*Muchas gracias.*"

I went back to Tessa. Her eyes were still closed. I gently rubbed her face, wiping the mud off her cheeks. Her eyelids fluttered, then opened. She looked into my eyes, still too weak to speak.

"Are you okay?" I asked.

She took another few breaths, then said softly, "Yeah."

"Let me take care of your bands." I grabbed her bands and pulsed. With the enhancement of Tessa's returning power the band didn't melt, it vaporized. She brought her hands to her face and began sobbing. I put my arms around her and she fell against me, her face buried against my chest. When she had settled a little, I asked, "Are you okay?"

"I thought I was going to die," she said.

"What happened?" Jaime asked. "How are the Elgen guards all dead?"

I turned back to him. "Your remote fell out of your pocket. I pushed it."

Jaime looked at me with admiration. "You are very clever," he said. "Very, very clever." He looked at the radio and papers scattered around the campsite and his expression turned grave. "Were we compromised?"

"I don't know. I heard them say that they didn't have radio coverage here."

"*Madre de Dios*," he said. "*Esquivar una bala*. We were lucky. We need to get out of here. The Elgen usually travel like *lobos*. And their radios have tracking devices. We need to leave before these guards are found missing."

"Where do we go?"

"We need to radio the voice," Jaime said. "But we cannot carry the tower. We will have to find a mountain."

"Where?"

"West of here. It is also in the direction of the mountain pass the army will take to Lima."

"How long will it take us to get there?"

"To the mountain it is several days without packs. But we have much to carry. The radio and decoder are very heavy. I will need a gun and ammunition. And we will need food." He sighed. "It took me a month to carry all this in. We must leave in minutes. We must burn everything we do not take."

"But won't they see the smoke?" Tessa said.

"Yes, but it is too much for us to carry," Jaime said. "We must take that chance and be gone before they arrive."

"I'll start the fire," I said.

"No, we must be ready to go before we start a fire. In case they are near."

"What do we need to do?" Tessa asked, forcing herself to her feet.

"Help me pack the supplies," he said to Tessa. "Michael, the Elgen have helped us. Please gather what they have dropped into a pile. Then we will soak it with gasoline."

"On it," I said.

Jaime and Tessa disappeared into the tent while I walked around the camp and picked up all the papers and books the Elgen had already brought out. I piled them in the center of the clearing, then dragged some logs over and made a fire pit.

As I was finishing, Jaime and Tessa came out carrying three large backpacks. Jaime took two of the guards' utility belts and fastened them around his waist. I took one of the backpacks from Jaime, and we carried the packs outside the clearing. I turned back toward the camp. "Are we ready to start the fire?"

"*Sí*," Jaime said.

Laying down my pack, I went back and emptied three five-gallon cans of gasoline over the pit. Then I created a lightning ball and threw it onto the pile. It burst into flames as tall as me. Black smoke began rising above the canopy.

"*Pronto*," Jaime said. "We have just revealed our location. We must go."

I started to put my pack back on when I had an idea. "Wait. The turret guns."

"What about them?" Jaime said.

"Can you put them on a delay?"

"A delay? Why?" Then a knowing smile lit his face. "Ah, *entiendo*." He went over and punched something in on the sentries' computer. As he returned he picked up the remote, pushed it, then tossed it into the bushes. "Thirty seconds should be enough."

"What did he do?" Tessa asked.

"He put the sentry on a delay. That way if an Elgen patrol walks into the camp, it will give them time so they'll all be within range."

"You are clever," Tessa said.

"Come, clever boy," Jaime said. "*Vámonos!*"

6

A Wet Day

Hiking through the thick of the jungle was difficult and exhausting, especially after all we had been through. The jungle was hot and wet, as were we, though most of the moisture that soaked our clothing was probably our own sweat.

About an hour after leaving our camp, we heard the firing of the sentry guns.

"Sounds like the Elgen found our camp," Tessa said.

"Or a monkey," I said.

"Poor monkeys," Tessa said.

We walked the rest of the day and continued hiking at night, our trail lit by Tessa's glow and mine. Jaime knew the jungle well and, with a compass and machete, kept us moving at an exhausting pace. It must have been at least two in the morning when Tessa suddenly stopped walking. "I've got to stop. I can't walk any more."

"Me too," I said. "I'm exhausted."

Jaime looked at us. "Okay. We can sleep for a few hours. But not too long."

Tessa shrugged off her pack and dropped it on the ground. "Better than nothing," she said.

I took off my pack too. My shoulders were chafed from where its straps dug into my skin. "Do we have anything to sleep on?"

"The tent and tarp are in her pack," Jaime said. "It is big enough for two." He took off his own pack, checked for insects, then sat down on the ground against a tree.

"What about you?" I said to him.

"I must stand guard," he said. "We cannot take chances."

I felt bad for him. I knew he was exhausted too. "Thank you," I said.

"It is my job," he replied.

Tessa opened her pack and brought out a small vinyl tent and a rolled-up tarp. There were no blankets, which, considering how warm the jungle was at night, weren't necessary.

With Jaime's help, we set up the tent, then Tessa and I climbed inside. I took off my shirt, then Tessa and I spread out the tarp and lay down. The ground was warm and spongy.

"I can't believe how loud the jungle is at night," I said.

"That's when most things hunt," Tessa said. "Or flee."

"Including us," I said. I breathed out heavily. "It's hard to believe it's just been one day. We've escaped the Peruvian army in an Amazonian tribe's canoe, hiked through the jungle, been captured by the Elgen, destroyed our camp, and fled into the jungle. That's like a thousand times more than what had happened to me my entire middle school years in Meridian, Idaho."

"I could use a little more dull," Tessa said. She looked at me. "Do you think we'll ever have normal lives?"

"If Hatch has his way, normal won't be what we think it is."

"What do you mean?"

"He wants to change the world."

"One person can't change the world," Tessa said.

"Of course they can," I said. "Every idea starts with just one person."

"You're right." She was quiet for a moment, then she said, "How do you think the Elgen found us?"

"Probably el-readers," I said.

"I forgot they had those," she said. "The guards once used them to find Torstyn when he was out hunting." She frowned. "That means they could still track us."

"That's probably why Jaime is pushing us so hard." I looked at her. "Don't worry about it. They got lucky last time. This is a big jungle, and they don't have helicopters anymore. We're just a needle in a very big green haystack."

"I hope you're right," she said. She closed her eyes. "Good night, Michael."

"Night, Tessa," I said.

"Thank you for saving my life today."

It was still dark when Jaime woke me.

"We must go," he said.

It took me a moment to remember where I was. The jungle was still impossibly noisy with the sounds of insects and wildlife. I sat up and yawned. "Did you sleep?" I asked.

"No. I will sleep tonight."

I gently shook Tessa, who fought opening her eyes. "What?" she said angrily.

"*Vámonos!*" Jaime said.

"What?"

"It's time to go," I said.

She opened her eyes. "We just went to sleep like two minutes ago."

"It has been three hours," Jaime said. "I am sorry, but we must keep going. We must stay ahead of the Elgen."

"Even Elgen sleep," she said, rolling back over. "Wake me when there's a sun."

Jaime looked at me helplessly.

I put my hand on her back and shook her. "C'mon, Tessa. We better do what he says."

Still nothing.

Frustrated, Jaime said, "You can sleep after you are dead."

I turned and looked at him.

"Is this not an American thing to say?" Jaime said.

"Not really." I shook her again. "C'mon, Tessa."

After a moment she breathed out heavily. "All right already." She sat up and rubbed her eyes, then looked around. "It's still night."

"No, it is very early morning," Jaime said.

"You're a glass half full kind of guy, aren't you?" Tessa said.

Jaime just looked at her. "What?"

"It could be worse," I said. "Jaime hasn't slept at all."

She frowned. "Sorry. I'm just grouchy when I don't get enough sleep."

We folded our tarp and tent, returned them to Tessa's pack, then started off again.

The route we cut ran parallel with the river. It would have been much easier and faster to walk along the bank, but we kept our distance from the water. It wasn't long before I discovered why. Shortly before the sun came up we stopped to rest on the crest of a hill. Jaime left us for a few minutes, then returned.

"Be very quiet," he said. He led me to where the hill started to slope toward the river. Peering out between the trees, I could make out about a quarter mile south of our vantage point, the Río de Madre de Dios below us, its pale brown water shimmering beneath the moon's glow. Jaime touched his ear, and then I heard it. Somewhere in the distance was the whine of an outboard motor. A moment later he pointed and whispered, "Look."

A motorboat filled with Elgen guards sped by. They held spotlights and guns, both of which they panned against the banks.

"They are patrolling the river," Jaime said. "It is the second Elgen boat I have seen."

"As long as they stay on the river, we're okay, right?"

He turned and looked at me. "We still must cross the river to get to the highway."

I looked back down at the wide river. "We have to swim across that?"

He nodded. *"Sí."*

"Aren't there, like, alligators and piranhas in there?"

"And snakes," Jaime said.

"At least we've got that to look forward to," I said.

When we got back to our camp, Tessa was sitting on a log eating some jerky.

"Vámonos!" I said.

"Oh please, not you too," she said. "It's bad enough hearing it from him." She shrugged on her pack, then stood. "Where'd you go?"

"Jaime wanted to show me the river. The Elgen are patrolling it."

"For a moment I thought maybe you guys had left me."

"Thought or *hoped?*" I asked.

"Why would I hope you would leave me?"

"So you could sleep."

"I'll sleep after I'm dead," she said.

We hiked all day, taking only a few short breaks to eat and drink. Jaime said little and even though he hadn't slept, kept us going at a brisk pace. Tessa was stronger than she looked, and, in spite of our difficulty getting her up, once she was walking she just kept on. By twilight I could see that Jaime was finally starting to lose it. As the sun set I grabbed his arm.

"You need to sleep," I said.

He looked almost confused with weariness. "We must keep on."

"We'll be okay," I said. "You can't keep walking like this forever."

He looked around a moment, then said, "Okay, Mr. Michael. We will camp here. I will take the first watch."

"No. You need to sleep. We all do."

He looked at me anxiously.

"Look, no one is going to find us. I couldn't find me here."

Finally he took a deep breath and said, "Okay. Okay."

We found a dark thicket of trees where we set up our tent and covered it with leaves and vines. By the time we were done you could have walked over it and not seen it. Then Jaime gathered dead leaves and threw them in a circle around the camp.

"What's that for?" I asked.

"If someone comes near, it will wake us."

"As tired as I am," I said, " I don't think dynamite would wake me."

"There's no way dynamite would wake me," Tessa said.

All three of us climbed into the tent, and Jaime pulled a cover of leaves down over the tent flap, sealing us in. It was a two-man tent (Tessa joked, "It's okay; there are only two men, right?"), and it was cramped with three, but it was also cozy and dry. Not surprisingly Jaime was asleep within minutes of lying down, which was unfortunate since he snored loudly. After one especially loud snort, Tessa laughed. "So much for the camouflage."

Even with Jaime's snoring, Tessa also fell asleep quickly. Her face was next to mine, and for a moment I just looked at her. It was strange how little I really knew about her yet how close I felt to her. Hard times will do that. As I looked into her beautiful face, I wondered about Taylor. I wondered if the soldiers were hurting her. The thought of it made me twitch. I pushed it out of my mind. There was nothing I could do about it now, and there would be plenty of time to worry about that later. And now, in our nylon cave, for the first time in a long while, I felt safe. I closed my eyes and fell asleep.

The sun was already up when I woke. From the look of it, it had been up for quite a while. I felt more rested than I had in days. Tessa was already awake and looking at me.

"Hey, handsome," she said. "You gonna sleep all day?"

"If I can," I said, rolling over.

"Sorry, not an option. You can sleep after you're dead."

I grinned as I sat up. "Where's Jaime?"

"He went to find water. He said to give this to you for breakfast if you ever woke." She handed me a box with a sweet roll and dried bananas and papaya. "You're gonna love that sweet roll. Jaime called it castana bread. I was tempted to eat yours and tell you that we were eating monkey brains for breakfast."

I raked my hair back from my face. "Yeah? What stopped you?"

"No idea," she said.

We folded up the tarp and had begun taking down the tent when Jaime returned.

"*Buen día, hermanos*," Jaime said. "I found water." He handed me a wet, cold canteen. I passed it on to Tessa, who drank thirstily.

"Oh, it's cold," she said.

"*Sí*. I found a spring."

She handed the canteen back to me. The water was not only cold, it was sweet and delicious. "Good water," I said.

"Good water in the Amazon if you can find it," Jaime said.

I screwed the lid back on the canteen. "What's on the schedule today?"

"We are close to a mountain," Jaime said. "This afternoon we will set up the radio."

The thought of this encouraged me. "And talk to the voice?"

"That is my hope," Jaime said.

"Then let's get going," I said. "*Vámonos!*"

"*Vámonos!*" Jaime repeated.

"I still hate that word," Tessa said.

We finished breaking down the tent, repacked our gear, then set off again. Even though the hike was mostly uphill, we all felt so much better having slept that it seemed easy. We reached the mountain's peak around three in the afternoon. From our new vantage point we could see above the forest canopy.

"This is the place we will set up our camp," Jaime said.

Tessa and I put up the tent while Jaime worked on reassembling the radio. When we had finished, Tessa went inside to rest and I went to see if Jaime needed any help. He looked up at me as I approached.

"Anything I can do?" I asked.

"*Sí*. I need you to climb a tree as high as you can with this," he said, holding out a coil of wire.

I took the wire. "What is it for?"

"It is the antenna for our radio. I would do it myself, but I weigh too much to reach the treetop."

"No problem," I said. I surveyed the trees around us until I decided on the one that looked most scalable, then I tied the end of the wire around a belt loop of my pants. "Wish me luck."

"Be careful," Jaime said. "The branches may be wet. Do not fall."

"Not planning on it," I said.

The tree's trunk was about four feet wide, and its bark was smooth and gray. I climbed up about fifty feet before the branches were too thin to support me.

"How's this?" I shouted down to Jaime, who was now standing with Tessa at the base of the tree looking up.

He put his finger over his lips, then gave me a thumbs-up. I tied the wire as high above me as I could, then I climbed back down the tree. It was much darker below as the sun was beginning to set.

"You're practically a monkey," Tessa said. "I'm impressed."

"I was always climbing the trees around my apartment," I said. I turned to Jaime. "Sorry I shouted. I just forgot."

"We must be careful," he said. "The Elgen are hunting. I do not think they are close, but I have been wrong before."

"Can we call the voice now?"

He glanced down at his wristwatch. "In a little while," he said. "Now we should eat."

We walked back to the tent. "What's for dinner?" I asked.

"Sandwiches," Tessa said.

"Again?" I said. "No pizza?"

She smiled as she handed out the sandwiches. "I almost forgot that pizza existed. How would that be right now—a thick, hot, cheesy slice of pizza?"

"Heavenly," I said. "With a chocolate shake."

"Now you're just torturing me," she said.

We ate for a moment in silence.

Then Jaime said, "We have pizza in Peru."

"Is it any good?" Tessa asked.

"I think so. But not so good as American pizza."

Just talking about it made my mouth water. I didn't think we could be farther from a real pizza. Suddenly my sandwich didn't taste as good.

"What do you like on your pizza?" I asked Jaime.

"Sausage and olives," he said.

"And you?" I asked Tessa.

"Veggies. I used to be a vegetarian," she said. "But that was before the jungle. What about you?"

"Pepperoni," I said.

"Did you know that in Italy, pepperoni is not what you think it is?" Tessa said. "It means 'little peppers.'"

"Like hot peppers?" Jaime asked.

She nodded. "Green peppers."

"Then what's pepperoni?" I asked.

"*Salame*," she said. "Americans in Italy always get that wrong."

"You've been to Italy?" I asked.

"Of course. I used to be part of Hatch's family," she said. "I've been everywhere."

"Oh," I said, nodding. "I keep forgetting that you used to be one of them."

She spun at me. "One of *them*? What did you mean by that?"

I was caught off guard by her reaction. "I didn't mean anything by it."

"Don't judge me," she said angrily. "I was nine years old when they took me. If they had found you at that age, you would have been one of *them* too."

"I wasn't judging you," I said.

"It sounded like it," she said.

"I'm sorry. I didn't mean to."

Jaime looked back and forth between us, then down at his watch. "It is time," he said. "We can radio now."

Tessa relaxed a bit. I was grateful for the interruption.

We finished eating, then Jaime pulled a small LED flashlight from his pocket and lit our path as we walked back to the radio. He sat down in front of it. "Michael, you sit here," he said, motioning to his left side. I sat down next to him. He handed me the radio's plug. "Take this. But do not pulse too strong. You could blow up the radio." He turned to Tessa. "Do not make him more electric."

"I'll try not to," she said. She stepped a few feet back from me and sat down.

Jaime handed me a headset. "Put this on."

Jaime and I both put on headsets, and then he nodded for me to begin. I lightly pulsed and the digital readouts on the radio lit up.

"Less electricity," he said.

I reduced my pulse. Jaime turned a few switches, then dialed in a code. The sound of static burst over my headset. Jaime lifted the microphone to his mouth.

"Lightning Rod, this is Southern Cross. Over."

There were three beeps, then a voice said, "Southern Cross, we read you. Please confirm."

"Diez, uno, uno, uno, nueve, seis, dos."

"Confirmed. One moment, please."

There was a pause, then the voice I recognized came over the radio. "Southern Cross, please give us an update."

"We are in the jungle, but safe."

"Have you any jewels?"

"A diamond and a tourmaline."

"Tourmaline? This is unexpected, but very good news."

"Yes, it was a surprise."

"Have you encountered any resistance?"

"We escaped an attack. We were forced to abandon our base."

"Was protocol followed?"

"Yes, sir. Everything was destroyed or carried with us."

"Good. We have learned that Hatch has been summoned back to the base. The chairman is very displeased with him. We believe he will be terminated."

"Madre de Dios!" Jaime exclaimed. "This is *mucha* reason for a fiesta."

I grabbed the microphone. "This is Michael. Do you have my mother?"

"Do not speak your name on air," the voice said sharply.

"Sorry," I said.

A moment later the voice said, "She is safe."

"Can I talk to her?"

"She's not here. But I can arrange for you to speak."

"Do you know anything about the rest of my friends?"

"Your friends have been captured by the Peruvian military. They are being held under tight security in Puerto Maldonado. We expect that they will be transported to Lima for trial."

Jaime looked at me and nodded in confirmation.

"We've got to rescue them," I said.

"We don't believe that a rescue attempt is advisable. At this time, our best option is diplomacy. We have connections in the consulate."

"You can get them released?"

The voice paused. "We'll do our best."

"Your best? What does that mean?"

"I'll be honest with you; it's a long shot. But it's certainly not as risky as attempting to defeat an entire brigade of the Peruvian army. That would be certain suicide."

"Suicide or not," I said, "I have to try to save them."

"We cannot agree to that," the voice said. "When we brought you and your friends here, we knew we were taking a big risk. But you did it—knocked out the Elgen's largest Starxource plant, rescued your mother, and escaped. You succeeded, but there are costs to all success. You have to accept that."

"I can't accept abandoning my friends. I'm going after them."

"We forbid it," he said. "Taking on . . ."

I didn't wait for him to finish. I took off the headset and handed it to Jaime. Jaime looked at me with an annoyed expression but continued listening. A moment later he said, "He is not listening. Yes, sir. Yes, sir. Over." Jaime switched off the radio.

"What did he say?" I asked.

"He said I should do my best to talk you out of it."

"Good luck with that," I said.

"But Michael—"

"I'm going to rescue them," I said angrily. "Are you with me or not?"

Jaime just looked at me. Tessa looked down, avoiding my eye contact.

My face began twitching, and I held my hand up to my cheek. After a moment I said, "Fine. Then I'm going without you. Both of you."

Jaime crossed his arms. "How will you go without me? You do not know the way."

"I know the road is across the river. I'll just keep walking until I find it."

"And if they catch you?"

I looked him in the eye. "I'll tell them everything I know about the voice."

Jaime flinched. "You would not."

"This is war; you're either my friend or my enemy. There is no middle ground. So which is it?"

"We are your friend. We want the same thing as you."

"I don't think so," I said.

Jaime sat thoughtfully for a moment, then breathed out slowly. "I will take you to the road, and I will wait for you. But if you fail, you must promise to not speak of us."

"Agreed," I said. I turned to Tessa. "Are you with me?"

She frowned. "I'm sorry. I can't."

"Can't or won't?"

She didn't answer. Angry, I walked back to the tent.

Tessa followed me. She grabbed my arm. "Michael, I'm sorry. It's just—this isn't my fight."

"How is this not your fight? This is your world too, and the Elgen are trying to take it. If we're not willing to stand up to them, who will?"

"The Elgen are big, and we're just . . . us. We can't stop them, we can't even slow them down. You're crazy if you think you can take on an entire army. You're not Superman."

"No. I'm just crazy. But they're my friends. And I have to try."

She just stood there, speechless and staring at me.

"I don't need you," I said, turning away. "I don't need either of you." I got down on my knees and crawled into the tent.

It was a while before Jaime and Tessa got in. None of us spoke. Long after Jaime started snoring, I just lay there in the dark. My stomach was tied up in knots.

The truth was, I did need Tessa. And Jaime. But most of all I needed my friends. I missed them more than I could say.

PART 2

7

The Surrender of the Magicians

Rumors spread quickly through the Peruvian military force that the eight teenagers they were hunting in the jungle were more than just young terrorists. They were part of an occult group called the Electroclan and workers of black magic—a rumor that gained credence when it was discovered that some of them actually glowed in the dark.

Peruvian culture holds deeply founded superstitions, and even after the teens had surrendered, many of the soldiers refused to go near them. Others, in spite of their strict orders to bring the terrorists back alive, pleaded with their commanders to shoot the teens and bring back their lifeless bodies.

The Elgen's Elite Global Guard, who were consulting with the Peruvian army, helped spread rumors of black magic among the lower and more ignorant ranks of Peruvian soldiers, hoping that if enough of them believed it, they might pressure their superiors into turning the Electroclan over to the Elgen—which was their objective to begin with.

The chief Elgen officer working with the Peruvian military was Captain Welch, a senior member of the Elite Global Guard and third in authority to Dr. Hatch himself. He had tried, unsuccessfully, to convince, bribe, then threaten the brigade's commander, General Panchez, into releasing the teens into Elgen custody. The general wouldn't budge. His orders came from the top. The Peruvian president himself had demanded that the Electroclan be brought in for trial. The terrorists' capture had already made international news, and the Peruvian citizens demanded justice. In actuality, justice wasn't the president's main concern—it was his approval rating. With the loss of their electricity, the country was in crisis and people wanted someone to answer for their suffering. Like all successful politicians, the president understood public opinion well enough to know that if someone's head didn't roll, his would. And the general understood that if the president's head rolled, his would roll along with it.

Even though Jack and Zeus still wanted to fight, with more than five hundred armed soldiers surrounding them, there was little they could do but surrender. Taylor was the one who had made the decision, waving a torn piece of her blouse over her head.

"We give up!" she shouted. "We surrender."

A heavily accented military officer with a megaphone shouted, "You stand up now with your handses on your head!"

"The dude can't talk," Jack said.

"They're Peruvian military," Ostin said. "They're not Elgen."

"That's good, right?" Abigail asked.

"It's not good," Ostin said. "We'll find out if it's better."

Taylor was the first to obey the order. "Don't shoot!" she shouted. She put her hands on her head and slowly stood, followed by the rest: Ostin, Jack, Zeus, Abigail, McKenna, Ian, and Wade. Once they were all standing, the soldiers quickly closed in around them.

"Now you kneel down," the commander said when he was near.

He was a stocky, bald man wearing a black beret and green camouflage.

"Make up your mind," Jack said. "Stand up or kneel down."

"Just kneel," Taylor said.

When the Electroclan were on their knees, two patrols of Peruvian soldiers approached them carrying guns and RESAT boxes. More than a hundred soldiers held their guns on them, while the advance team—who had never seen or used the RESATs before—fastened the machines on each youth, including Ostin, Wade, and Jack.

Then their hands were cuffed behind their backs and their legs were shackled with a twelve-inch chain dangling between the two ankle manacles. Potato sacks were put over their heads, which was disorienting for everyone except Ian, whose vision was only slightly impaired by his RESAT.

A long, nylon rope was tied around all of their waists, and they were led in a single-file line out of the jungle to the waiting army vehicles. Walking roped together and blindfolded through the thick jungle was difficult. The chains between their legs caught on rocks and tree trunks, and each of them fell more than once. Ostin fell the most, eight times, leaving dark bruises and cuts on his arms and legs.

Once they were out of the jungle, the rope connecting the teens was cut, then each of them was taken to a separate vehicle—still bound, hooded, and surrounded by soldiers.

Under heavy security, which included two tanks and more than eighty armed personnel carriers, the soldiers drove in a convoy six miles to the Puerto Maldonado jail.

The army had commandeered the Puerto Maldonado city jailhouse for the purpose of holding the terrorists. They had released twelve of the jail's fifty-seven occupants, then crowded the rest into two tiny cells so they could utilize the remaining eight cells for the new prisoners. Then they built three twelve-foot-high electric fences around the jail, which were patrolled by guard dogs and more than fifty soldiers.

The general had been warned by the Elgen that the teens had

already escaped from two high-security facilities, and Panchez was taking no chances. The young terrorists would not escape him.

Upon their arrival at the jail, the teens were fingerprinted and photographed, then each was taken to a different cell. Ostin was the first to be processed, and after he was locked in his cell, he sat down on the cool, concrete floor, swatting at mosquitoes, rubbing his bruises, and grumbling.

"I've never even been grounded before," he mumbled. "Now I'm in jail. And I'm only in the ninth grade."

Ostin had studied Peru in seventh-grade geography and, as usual, had learned everything he could about the subject—including the country's history, Incan lore, the country's invasion by Francisco Pizarro, the current political structure, national exports, and even its national anthem, *Himno Nacional del Perú*, which he still remembered. He also remembered that the country reserved the death penalty for acts of terrorism, which frightened him since the soldiers kept calling them "*terroristas.*"

"We didn't do anything to them," Ostin said, hitting the concrete wall with his fist—which he immediately regretted. "We attacked the stinking Elgen, not them. It's not the same thing. What have they got against us?"

The cell he was being held in was a hot and humid ten-by-ten-foot square, with rough concrete walls and floor, both of which had fungus growing on them. There were thick rusted bars on the window, which had been boarded over by the army. In the corner of the room, there was a bucket for a toilet, and a single naked lightbulb hung from the ceiling.

"There's got to be a way out of here. Think, think, think." He rubbed his temples, which always made him think better. "We've got to escape. What do I know about escape? John Dillinger escaped from jail twice. Houdini. David Hoodoo . . ."

Five years earlier, when Ostin was ten, on a summer vacation trip to his aunt's home in Las Vegas, his parents had taken him to a magic show where the magician, the Magnificent David Hoodoo, had escaped from a bank vault suspended thirty feet in the air. He had also made a fully grown African elephant disappear onstage. While the crowd applauded wildly at the illusion, it vexed Ostin that he couldn't figure out how either trick was done. He had resolved to figure them out but never got around to it. After he returned home, he was distracted by Shark Week and a new interest in robotics.

"That won't work. The thing was staged. This isn't." He pounded on his RESAT. As the teens were checked into the jail, the Peruvian soldiers had removed their hoods, handcuffs, and foot shackles but had left the RESATs connected.

"Idiots," Ostin said, looking at the box fastened to his chest. "They don't even know what the thing does. It doesn't work on normal people. It's not a Taser—it's the opposite of a Taser." He examined the box. "Wait a minute. . . . Does this thing work like a Taser?" He reached around and unfastened the box from his chest, which was no more difficult than removing a backpack. Red and green diodes began flashing wildly on the plastic-coated box, followed by a soft, high-pitched squeal. The RESAT was designed to activate if it was tampered with, but for a normal human, it was as pointless as trying to drown a fish. He used the metal clip of the RESAT's buckle to pry off its back, then set the plate aside and examined the circuitry.

"Yep, there's the capacitor. It's huge. I bet it holds a million volts. What's this . . . oh right, of course. Hmm, I bet if I . . ."

It took him less than half an hour to figure out how to rewire the machine. When he was done he held the wires two inches apart and electricity sparked between them.

"Mega-epic voltage," he said. "This will blow them out of their boots." He thought for a moment, then said, "No, it needs to do more than shock them." He carefully reexamined the circuitry. After another five minutes he smiled. "So that's how it does that. Clever. If I divert this right here . . . Now we're talking." He grinned. "Now I just need someone to test it on."

8

Interrogations

As soon as all the teens were secured, the army began interrogations. Taylor, who they guessed to be the leader of the group, was the first to be taken from her cell. As she walked, handcuffed, out of the room she wished Michael was with her, then felt bad for thinking such a thing. *No. Anyplace but here.*

She was escorted down the hallway by two Peruvian military police who she tried to reboot but was unable to with the RESAT sucking out most of her power—though she did get one of them to trip. At least she thought she did. He might have just been clumsy.

She was brought to the interrogation room—a small, rectangular cell with a two-way mirror on one wall. In the center of the room was a square, wooden table with two chairs facing each other. The chair closest to the door was already occupied, and as she entered she could see the back of a man's head, or at least the Elgen helmet he was wearing, the ones the Elgens always wore around her.

The soldiers walked Taylor to the empty chair, which faced the mirror. One of the soldiers pulled out the chair while the other unlocked Taylor's cuffs.

"Thank you," she said. She rubbed her wrists, which were already sore from the cuffs.

The seated man looked at her for a moment, then said softly, "Please have a seat."

Taylor glanced at the two soldiers flanking her, then slowly sat down. The two soldiers left the room. The man seated in front of her looked Peruvian, though he was taller than most of the soldiers she'd seen. He was young and, under different circumstances, she might have thought he was kind of hot. There was a pad of lined paper in front of him with a pen. The last time she'd sat down with an adult like this was during her faculty interview for varsity cheerleader.

For a moment the man just stared at her, as if sizing her up. Then, to her surprise, he smiled at her. "Welcome," he said. He put out his hand, but Taylor didn't take it. He held it out for a few seconds, then cocked his head and put his hand back in his lap.

"My name is Cesar," he said. "What is your name?"

He spoke almost without an accent, and Taylor thought he sounded too pleasant for what he was doing. Taylor just pursed her lips and stared at him. After a full minute of silence he said, "Your name?"

"You already know who I am," Taylor said. "If you didn't, you wouldn't be wearing that helmet."

"That is true," the man said. "I just want to hear you say it."

"I'm not a toy," she said. She turned her head away from him.

"I don't think you're a toy. I'm just trying to develop a . . . rapport."

Taylor didn't respond. The man looked at her for a moment, then said, "You're not going to talk to me?"

She didn't answer.

"Could you please tell me where you're from?" He shifted in his chair. When Taylor didn't answer he said, "From your accent I am guessing that you're from the United States; perhaps somewhere in the west."

"Why do you keep asking me things you already know?"

The man looked at her for a moment, then stood up and walked over to Taylor's side and crouched down next to her. He spoke softly, just above a whisper. "You know that you're being watched and recorded. I am not going to hurt you. But if you don't cooperate with me, then they'll just get someone else who will make you cooperate—someone with more . . . forceful methods. Perhaps one of the Elgen's people."

Taylor still didn't look at him. "So it's the good cop, bad cop routine," she said.

"Excuse me?"

"It's on every cop show in America. One of you plays the nice cop who acts like he cares about me, while the other plays the bad cop who wants to bust my chops, so I confide to the good cop."

He nodded. "I see. Good cop, bad cop. I'll have to remember that. But this is not an American TV show. The Elgen corporation is very influential, and they want you very badly. I'm not with them; I'm with the Servicio de Inteligencia Nacional. We are called SIN."

"You call yourself SIN? Is that supposed to make me trust you?"

"I suppose in English that it is an unfortunate acronym. But we are like your CIA. We collect information about groups that are a threat to our country."

She looked at him incredulously. "You think *we're* a threat to your country?"

"You and your colleagues *are* a threat to my country," he replied. "So you can talk to me, or you can talk to someone who is . . . not me."

Taylor just looked at him for a moment, then said, "What do you want to know?"

He walked back to his seat and picked up his pen. "We'll begin with your name. What is your name?"

"Taylor."

"Taylor what?"

"Taylor Swift."

He looked at her coolly. "Okay, Miss Swift. What state in the United States are you from?"

"Utah."

"Utah," he repeated. "Tall mountains. Who sent you here?"

"What do you mean?"

"Who sent you to Peru? Someone wanted the power plant destroyed; who was it? A rival corporation? A foreign military power?"

"It wasn't anyone. We didn't come down to destroy the power plant. We came down because the Elgen were keeping my friend's mother captive."

"What friend?"

Taylor looked down for a moment, then said, "Just a friend."

"Someone we have in captivity?"

She looked at him. "Yes."

"Which one?"

"Ostin," she said.

He wrote something on the pad.

"How did you get to Peru?"

"We flew."

"Are you sure?"

She nodded.

"Which airline?"

Taylor swallowed. "Uh, Delta."

"We have checked the records of every airline that flies into Peru, and there is no record of you and your friends ever arriving."

"We drove," Taylor said.

"You drove to Peru?"

Taylor nodded.

"Are you sure?"

She nodded again.

"How long did it take you to drive from . . . Utah?"

"A little over a week."

"Really?"

She swallowed. "Give or take a few days."

"Where are the cars you drove?"

"We sold them once we got down here."

He tapped his pad with his pen. "Are you sure?"

"Yes."

"To whom?"

"I don't know who they were. Just some guys we met. I think they were probably drug dealers because they paid in cash. They didn't want us to ask a lot of questions."

"And where are your passports?"

"They took them from us."

"The . . . drug dealers who bought your car?"

"Yes. I mean, no. The passport people."

"The passport people?"

"Why do you keep repeating everything I say?"

"I just want to be sure that I am understanding you. The passport people took your passport. You mean the passport agents at the border."

"If that's what you call them."

He nodded. "They don't usually keep them."

"They kept ours."

"Did you cross the Panama Canal by ferry, or did you just drive around it?"

Taylor squinted. "We drove around it." Then added, "It was faster."

He nodded. "I'm sure it was." He looked at her for a moment, then stood. "Okay, Taylor Swift. Thank you for your cooperation. One last question."

"Yes, sir."

"Do you plan on holding a concert while you're in Peru?"

Taylor blushed.

"But if you drove from the U.S. to Peru in one week, you should be a race-car driver instead of a famous singer, because it would take at least three weeks if you never stopped. But what is most impressive is that you drove around the Panama Canal. I've heard of people walking on water, but driving on water is even more miraculous."

He leaned forward. "I'm disappointed in you, Taylor Ridley from Meridian, Idaho. Aside from your first name, I don't believe you've told me a single truth since we began. I don't think you have any idea how much trouble you're in. You've cost this country millions and millions of dollars."

"Bill me," Taylor said.

The man grinned. "They just might, you know. The cost will be your life." He leaned forward. "You don't really understand how serious this is, do you? You and your friends have been branded terrorists. The punishment for terrorism in this country is execution."

Taylor's eyes began to well up. But still she didn't speak.

"All right, then," he said, turning toward the door. "We'll see how you do with the Elgen interrogators." He turned to go.

"Wait," Taylor said. "I'm sorry."

He stopped and looked back. "You're sorry?"

"Yes, sir."

"And what am I supposed to do with that?"

"I'll tell you the truth."

He looked at her for a moment, then said, "Will you?"

She exhaled slowly. "I'll tell you what I can. I promise."

"We'll see what good your promise is."

"What I told you about my friend's mother was true. That's why we came."

"Which friend?"

Taylor swallowed. "Someone you don't know. Look, you need to know something. You've got the wrong guys."

"You're telling me that you didn't blow up the power plant?"

"I'm telling you that the Elgen are the bad guys. They're not here to help your country. They're here to take it over. Once they control all your electricity, they will control your country. We did you a favor." Taylor looked into his eyes. "I'm telling you the truth. We didn't come to blow up an electricity plant. We're a bunch of teenagers. At home I'm a cheerleader. We only came to Peru because they kidnapped my boyfriend's mother."

"Who kidnapped your boyfriend's mother?"

"The Elgen."

He just looked at her. "And why would they do that?"

"Because they were trying to catch us."

"Then you shouldn't have come."

"I know. But it was his mother."

He nodded. "So, did you find her?"

"Yes."

He looked at her skeptically. "And where is your boyfriend's mother now?"

"She got away."

"With your boyfriend?"

"Yes."

"What is your boyfriend's name?"

She hesitated. Finally she said, "Michael."

"Michael what?"

"Michael Vey."

He stared at her for a moment. "I'm supposed to believe this?"

"Believe what you want to believe," Taylor said. "But why would a bunch of high school kids come to Peru to blow up an electricity plant?"

He crossed his arms. "That's what I'm trying to find out. But you haven't told me anything that makes sense."

"I've told you the truth. You can believe me now, or you can believe me after the Elgen take over your country."

"My country. Speaking of which, how did you get into the country?"

She hesitated.

"I need to know."

She paused a moment longer, then slowly breathed out. "There are people besides us who know how bad the Elgen are. They flew us down in their plane."

"What people?"

"I don't know anything about them."

"I'm sorry, that's not a good enough answer."

"I'm telling you the truth. They only talk to us by cell phone. I don't know who they are. The guy calls himself 'the voice.'"

The man rested his chin in his hand and looked at her.

"You have to believe me."

The man nodded. "I believe you."

Taylor frowned. "You have to help us. The Elgen are bad, bad people."

He paused a moment longer, then said, "Thank you. I'll pass that on to my superiors. That's all for now." He reached back and rapped his knuckles on the door. *"Terminamos ya."*

"What are you going to do with us?" Taylor asked.

"You'll be taken to Lima, where you will go on trial for terrorism."

Taylor wiped a tear from her cheek. "I told you, we weren't attacking your country. We were fighting the Elgen."

"What you did was a direct assault on our country."

"If they find us guilty, what will they do to us?"

"If you're lucky, they'll keep you in prison until you're a very old woman."

The thought of it sent chills through her. "That doesn't sound lucky," she said.

"It is compared to the alternative."

"The alternative?"

The man looked her in the eyes. "You'll never be an old woman." The man stood and opened the door. *"Traigame el siguente."*

Behind the two-way mirror an Elgen captain lifted his phone and said into it, "Four, two, Charley, Alpha, Vixen, Omega."

"Go ahead," someone returned.

"This is Captain Moyes. I need to speak immediately with Captain Welch."

"Just a moment, sir."

A minute later Captain Welch answered. "What is it, Moyes?"

"We've just finished the first interrogation."

"Which one?"

"Sixteen. Tara's twin."

"Anything interesting?"

"The most vital information we've gotten yet. The kids aren't alone."

"What do you mean, they're not alone?"

"Someone's helping them. They're part of a resistance."

"You're sure of this?"

"Absolutely."

"Well done. I'll alert Dr. Hatch."

9

A Clever Distraction

An hour after Ostin had been incarcerated, a single soldier walked into his cell. Ostin was lying on his back on the thin, flea-infested cot, staring at the cracked ceiling. The guard had no gun but held a wooden truncheon in one hand. "Stand up," he said.

"*Qué pasa?*" Ostin said, slowly rising.

"Stand up. *Hazlo!*"

"Okay," he said. "Don't get your panties in a bunch."

The guard looked at him without comprehension.

Ten minutes earlier, Ostin had reattached the RESAT to his chest, and when he was arm's length from the soldier, he tapped on the box. "Can you turn this thing down? It's too strong."

"No. Put your hands in front of you."

Concealing the RESAT wires in his hands, Ostin held his hands out. As the guard brought the cuffs near, Ostin touched the bare-ended wires to the guard's arms. There was a loud snap of electricity, and the man collapsed to the ground without a scream.

Ostin looked down at him. "I told you it was too strong." Ostin crouched down next to the man to make sure he was out. "So that's what it's like to be Michael." He carefully rolled the wires back, then quickly undressed the guard and put on his uniform. The guard was an inch shorter than Ostin, and the uniform fit well except for being a little snug in the waist.

When Ostin had finished changing, he handcuffed the guard's hands behind his back, stuffed the man's socks into his mouth, then wrapped a sheet around the man's head to keep him from spitting the socks out. He took the guard's key and bludgeon, peered out of his cell, and when he saw no one, walked out into the corridor.

The jail was small, a single corridor about sixty feet in length, with doors on each side. Ostin had no idea which cells his friends were being kept in, so he tried the key in the first door next to his, opened it, and quickly stepped inside. Zeus was lying on the bed, his face bent in a grimace. Sweat was beading on his forehead, stress from a RESAT that was set too high.

"*Oye!*" Ostin shouted.

Zeus sneered. "Eat my shorts, you ape."

"I'll pass," Ostin said, stepping closer.

Zeus looked over at him. "Ostin? How did you . . ."

Ostin took the wires from the RESAT and hooked them to Zeus's machine. "I'm going to unfasten this."

"No, don't," Zeus said. "It sets it off. It could kill me."

"Shouldn't," he said. He set his own RESAT on the bed next to Zeus. "I rewired this to counter yours. I'm ninety-nine point six percent sure that it will work."

Zeus looked at it a moment, then said, "Are you sure?"

"I just told you how sure I am." Ostin grasped the closest fastener on Zeus's RESAT, then unlatched it. The RESAT immediately lit up.

"It's powering up," Zeus said anxiously.

"I know," Ostin said. Suddenly the machine began to squeal.

"Ostin . . ."

"Does it feel different?"

"No."

"Then don't sweat it."

Zeus didn't feel it getting stronger. If anything, his pain was diminishing.

"I think it's working," Zeus said.

"For a minute," Ostin said. "We've got to get it off you. The capacitor can only hold so much electricity before it will blow."

"Now you tell me." Zeus frantically unfastened the rest of the clips, then pushed the box away from him. He fell back against the wall and took a deep breath, groaning in relief.

"You're welcome," Ostin said, grabbing Zeus's RESAT and prying off its back.

"Thank you," Zeus said. "I'm going to blast those guys to the next city."

"Bad idea," Ostin said. "We're still surrounded, and they've still got guns." He yanked a few wires off the RESAT, then snapped on the back of the RESAT and gave the box back to Zeus. "Here, put it back on."

"I'm not putting that on," he said, looking at the flashing lights.

"It doesn't work anymore," Ostin said. "It just looks like it does. If you walk out there without it on, they'll know something's up."

Zeus slid his arms through the straps, and Ostin clipped the fasteners back in place. He looked at Ostin. "What's next?"

"We need to find the others. Then we're going to capture a few soldiers, put on their uniforms, and walk the rest of us out of here. That's the only way we're going to get past all those guards."

"Do you know what's outside this place?"

"Other than like ten thousand soldiers? No. We need Ian. If there's a weakness, I'm sure he's already found it. Do you know what room he's in?"

"No. I had a hood over my head when they brought me in."

"Yeah, we all did." Ostin walked to the cell door. "All right, I'm going to open it. When no one's watching, I'm going to cross the hall and open the door across from us. Get ready to run."

Ostin opened the cell door a half inch and peered out. No one was in the hall. He turned back to Zeus. "It's clear. Come on."

Zeus walked up behind him. Ostin looked out again, then they both ran across the hall. Ostin shoved the key in the door, unlocked the cell, and pushed the door open.

"It's us . . . ," he said, as the door swung open. There were at least twenty dirty and angry-looking Peruvian convicts staring at him.

"Sorry, wrong room," Ostin said, stepping back.

"Atacquenlos!" a large, bearded man shouted.

"Vámonos!" another shouted, rushing toward Ostin.

Ostin froze in the doorway, paralyzed by fear. Zeus pushed Ostin aside and with both hands extended, blasted the approaching men. The electricity from his bolt splintered off, traveling through all of the men simultaneously, and all of them fell to the ground, one of them grasping his chest. Zeus grabbed Ostin and pulled him out of the room.

"Wrong curtain, man," he said, pulling the door shut. They went to the next door, which Ostin, though still shaken and fumbling with the key, managed to unlock. This time he opened the door more cautiously. At first neither of them saw anyone. Then Zeus pointed to the corner. "There she is."

Lying on her back on the concrete floor next to the far wall was McKenna. Her back was arched and her long black hair was splayed out around her. Zeus pushed Ostin inside the cell and shut the door behind them.

"McKenna," Ostin said. Then he realized that she was convulsing. "No!" He rushed to her side. Her entire body was seized and her eyes had rolled back in her head. "It's killing her!" Ostin shouted. "It's too high!"

"Shut it off," Zeus said.

Ostin fell to his knees on the ground next to her. He fastened the wires of his RESAT to hers and practically ripped the machine off of her. She immediately gasped, then fell still.

"McKenna!" Ostin shouted.

Zeus put his finger on her throat, then his ear to her heart. "It's not beating."

"CPR," Ostin said. He began pressing on her chest, then listened. Then repeated. "I can't get anything," he said.

Zeus pulled him off her. "Stand back."

He put his hand over McKenna's heart. "Hold on." He shocked her, and her entire body jumped. He put his head on her chest. Nothing. He leaned back and tried it again. "Come on, McKenna." Her body jumped even more. Then she groaned. He put his ear to her chest. This time he could hear her heart.

"It's beating."

Her eyes opened, then she began to cry.

Ostin knelt back next to her. "I'm so sorry," he said. "I'm so sorry." He wiped the tears off her cheeks. She looked up at him gratefully.

When she could speak she said, "Thank you."

"Anything for you," he said.

"We've got to hurry," Zeus said. "Before they find out we're gone."

"Can you stand?" Ostin asked.

"I think so," McKenna said. "Just help me up."

Ostin stood, and, taking her hands in his, helped her to her feet. After she was standing, her legs buckled a little and she fell into him. He wrapped his arms around her, holding her up until she could stand on her own. "Sorry," she said.

"It's okay," Ostin said. "Take your time."

Zeus looked at them impatiently. "Not a lot of time."

"We can go," McKenna said.

Zeus pulled open the cell door and looked out into the hallway. "It's clear. Give me the key." Ostin gave him the key and Zeus crossed the hallway to the next door and opened it. Inside was Ian, who in spite of the effect of his RESAT, was still able to see what was going on and was sitting up expecting him.

Zeus waved McKenna and Ostin over. Ostin took McKenna by the arm and helped her across the hallway into Ian's cell.

"I saw you do something to this," Ian said, touching the RESAT.

"I can disable it," Ostin said.

"Then do it," Ian said. "It's killing me."

Ostin attached the wires from his RESAT to Ian's, then began unfastening the buckles. Ian slipped the box off, groaning in relief. "Thanks, man. I owe you."

Ostin began dissecting the RESAT. "You're welcome."

"And for saving McKenna." Ian walked over to McKenna and put his arms around her. After years of being imprisoned together in the academy's dungeon, McKenna had become a sister to him, and he had yelled out for help as he watched her struggling with her RESAT. "How are you feeling?"

"I'm better now," she said, glancing at Ostin.

Ostin smiled, then continued working on Ian's RESAT. When he'd rewired it, he replaced the rear panel and handed it back to him. "Here you go. It's best to keep them on."

"I get it," Ian said, rebuckling the machine.

"Where's everyone else?" Zeus asked.

Ian said, "Jack, Abigail, and Wade are in the next three cells on this side. Taylor's in the last cell on the opposite side, but she's not there. They took her down to interrogate her."

"Not good," Zeus said.

"No, it might be good," Ostin said. "It's just the opportunity we need. We'll wait in her cell for the guards to bring her back, then jump them. But we still need to get the others. Ian, you need to tell us when to move."

"Jack's in the cell next to us, then Wade, but we should get Abi first. She's in a lot of pain."

"Then let's go," Zeus said.

Following Ian, they hurried down to Abigail's cell. Abigail didn't see them come in. She was lying on the ground facing the wall, writhing in pain. Zeus ran to her side. "We're here," he said.

She rolled over to look at him, her cheeks stained with tears. "It hurts."

"I know. We'll get it off. C'mon, Ostin. Hurry!"

Ostin fastened his machine to hers, and Zeus pulled her RESAT off. She rolled onto her stomach and sobbed, while Zeus gently rubbed her back. "It sucks, you know? You can take away everyone's pain but your own."

"Are you okay?" McKenna asked, crouching down next to her.

"I think these guys are meaner than the Elgen," Abigail said.

"I don't think so," Ostin said. "I just think they don't know how to use the RESATs."

"Where'd they even get them?" Zeus asked.

"I'm sure they're a gift from the Elgen," Ian said.

"You can bet on that," Ostin said. He stood. "We better keep moving."

Zeus cradled Abigail in his arms and lifted her. "Thank you," Abigail said, draping her arms around Zeus's neck.

"What's going on out there?" Ostin asked.

Ian said, "There's some activity in the front, but we're still clear. Let's get the other two."

Everyone but Ostin stayed in Abigail's cell until Ostin had freed Wade, then opened Jack's door, at which point the group gathered in Jack's cell.

"Jack!" Wade shouted when he saw him.

"Hey, man," Jack said. "It's good to see you." They guy-hugged.

Zeus walked in carrying Abigail. "What happened?" Jack asked.

"They had her RESAT set too high," Zeus said.

"I'm gonna bust some heads," Jack said.

"I'm with you," Zeus said.

"Time for phase two," Ostin said. "Ian, what's going on outside the jail?"

"Nothing good," Ian said. "There are thousands of soldiers. They've constructed three supertall barbwire fences around the jail, so even if we get out, we'd have to somehow get through the fences."

"Then they've built their camp outside the fences, so after the fence we'd have to walk through the middle of thousands of soldiers."

"Yeah, I'm sure they won't notice us," Zeus said sarcastically.

"They didn't notice us at the Starxource plant," Jack said. "We walked right through their cafeteria. If we split up . . ."

Abigail looked frightened at the prospect. "I think they would notice me. I don't look at all like a Peruvian soldier."

"You'll need one of their assault masks," Jack said. "And uniforms."

"What we need," Ostin said, "is a distraction. And I know where to find it." He suddenly smiled. "Oh, this is going to be good."

"What's that?" McKenna asked, taking Ostin's arm.

"We're sitting on a powder keg just waiting for a spark," Ostin said. "The army took all the prisoners who were already in here and shoved them all in one cell, like sardines. They're as tightly strung as a banjo."

"Two cells," Ian said. "There's one near the front, and the other is at the end of the corridor, next to Taylor's cell."

"Even better," Ostin said. "So here's the plan. I heard some of the soldiers talking on the transport here. They didn't know I spoke Spanish so they weren't being real discreet. The bottom line is, these guys want us alive. Someone high up has ordered it."

"Why?" Jack asked.

"I don't know. Maybe it's for public relations. Maybe it's just so they can properly hang us, but whatever the reason, they're protecting us. So here's my idea. We start a fire—"

"Wait, you want to start a fire while we're still locked in here?" Abigail asked.

"Yeah. They won't let us burn. Then, if we let out the other prisoners, and they see the smoke . . ."

"Prison riot," Jack said.

"And they'll have to come save us," McKenna said.

"Exactly. Except that the ones saving us . . . are us," Ostin said.

"You lost me," Wade said.

"Jack you, and I will be dressed up as soldiers. We'll be the ones rushing everyone else out of the jail to keep them safe."

"Only one problem," Wade said. "How do we start a fire? Rub sticks together?"

"You're kidding, right?" McKenna said.

Wade looked at her. "Oh. Right."

Jack shook his head. "Dude, you're so dumb."

Wade frowned.

"Where do we get two more soldier uniforms?" Abigail asked.

Ostin turned to Ian. "Are they still interrogating Taylor?"

"Yeah."

"Are there soldiers with her?"

"Two of them."

"Perfect. We hide in her cell. When they bring her back, Zeus zaps them and we take their uniforms."

"Then we better hurry to her cell," Ian said. "We don't know how long the questioning will last."

"Let's go," Jack said. He opened the door. "Ian, is it clear?"

Ian looked around. "Looks good."

"Stay close to the wall, people," Ostin said.

They hurried in single file down to Taylor's cell. Ostin opened the cell door, and they all went in.

"When the time comes," Ostin said, "everyone needs to stand against this wall. We don't know how far they'll actually come into the cell, and if they see one of us, we've got a problem. Zeus, as soon as the doors open, be prepared to drop them. When they're down, Jack and Wade will pull them into the cell and put on their uniforms. Ian, you've got to let us know their progress so we can be ready for them."

"I'm on it."

"Then how do we get out of here?" Jack asked.

"There's only one way out of this hallway," Ian said. "But there's a guard stationed next to the door."

"Taylor will have to do her mind thing on him," Ostin said. "Then where do we go?"

"We go left, then walk straight out through the front lobby."

"What's outside?"

"Soldiers. Lots and lots of soldiers."

"Any vehicles nearby?"

Ian looked around. "A truck, two cars, a motorcycle, and a transport van."

"Are there keys in any of them?"

He concentrated on it. "Not that I can see."

"I can hot-wire it," Jack said. "It will only take me a few minutes."

"Then what are we facing?" Ostin asked.

"There's a single gateway that goes through all three fences. The checkpoint has three guards with machine guns, two more inside the booth, and a tank on the outside."

"So we can't run it," Ostin said. "We'll just have to convince them that we're transporting the terrorists to safety."

McKenna touched Ostin's arm. "What do you want me to do? Besides light fires."

"Keep safe," Ostin said.

"I'll do my best," she said.

Just then Ian said, "They're coming."

"How many soldiers?" Ostin asked.

"Two. One on each side."

"Where's Taylor?"

"She's in front."

Ostin looked at Zeus. "Ready?"

Electricity sparked between his fingers. "Born ready," he said.

Jack and Wade pressed themselves up against the wall near the door.

"Ian, give us a countdown," Ostin said.

"Thirty feet," Ian said. "Twenty-five, twenty, fifteen . . ." His voice softened to a whisper. "Ten, five . . ." They could hear the sound of the key in the door. Jack glanced at Zeus, who nodded. The door opened and the two soldiers pushed Taylor in.

Taylor saw her friends before the soldiers did. She looked at them, dumbfounded, trying to figure out why they were in her cell. Then one of the soldiers looked at Zeus.

"Surprise!" Zeus shouted, blasting both of them and knocking one of them out the door.

"Too much!" Jack said. "Take this one, Wade!"

Wade jumped on the first soldier while Jack reached out into the hall, grabbed the other soldier by his feet, and dragged him back into the cell.

"Sorry, man," Zeus said. "Got the rush on."

"I feel you," Jack said. "I bet that felt good."

"Not for them," McKenna said.

Ostin pushed the door shut. "Ian, are we safe?"

"I don't think anyone saw us."

"Taylor, come here," Ostin said, leading her by the arm to the bed. Taylor still looked confused. "How'd everyone get in here?"

"I let them in," Ostin said. He attached his RESAT to hers. "Let's get this thing off."

"You can't take it off," Taylor said, pulling away from him. "It goes off if you mess with it."

"It's okay," McKenna said. "He solved it."

Taylor looked at McKenna. "Then why is yours still on?"

"It's to fool them," Ostin said. "I disabled it. But they don't know it. These dudes don't even know how they work."

"Then get it off me," Taylor said.

It took Ostin less than thirty seconds to release her RESAT. When it was off, she fell back on the bed. "Thank you."

"Now I need to rewire it."

Zeus and Abigail tied up the soldiers as Jack and Wade finished putting on their uniforms.

"What's the plan?" Taylor asked.

"We're going out the front door. We need you to do your mind trick thing with the guards there."

"Why would they let us out?"

"We're setting the place on fire and starting a riot. In all the confusion, we'll look like we're trying to get you out to safety."

"How do I look?" Jack asked Abigail.

"Like one of them," she said. "Except taller. And better looking."

Jack smiled.

"How about me?" Wade asked.

"You look like one of them," Abigail said.

"Guys, we've got a problem," Ian said. "There's a soldier headed to Zeus's room."

"Is anyone else with him?" Zeus asked.

"No, he's alone. I don't see anyone watching either."

Zeus walked to the door. "Then I'll take him out." He opened the door and stuck his head out. "Hey, amigo!"

The man turned toward him.

Zeus reached out his hand. "Got a present for you." He shot a single bolt nearly thirty feet, bouncing the man off the wall and to the ground. Zeus stepped back in. "He's down."

"Time to go," Ostin said, setting aside Taylor's RESAT.

"Wait, what about my RESAT?" Taylor asked.

"Here, take mine," Ostin said. "It can shock people."

She put her arms through its straps. "Thanks."

"What does it look like out there?" Ostin asked Ian.

"Surprisingly quiet. It's like everyone's having a siesta break."

"Which cell has the prisoners?"

He pointed to his left. "Right there, the cell next to us, left side of the hall."

"Zeus, you better come with us," Ostin said. "In case the convicts come at us like those others did."

"You got it."

"I'll be your prisoner too," McKenna said.

"I'll take Abi," Jack said.

Abigail nodded.

"And me," Taylor said.

"No problem," Jack said. "I can handle both of you."

"Not hardly," Taylor said.

"Looks like it's you and me, buddy," Ian said to Wade.

"All right," Ostin said. "Prisoners in front, guards in back. Put your hands behind your backs so you look handcuffed. No one leaves the room until Zeus and I have let the prisoners out." He turned to Zeus. "Ready?"

"Let's do this."

They walked out to the cell next to theirs, and Ostin unlocked the door. Zeus kicked it open. There were at least twenty prisoners crammed into the room. *"Estamos escapando!"* Ostin shouted. *"Salganse ahorita! Huyan!"*

The prisoners just stared at Ostin, confused at seeing an American in a Peruvian soldier uniform telling them to escape.

"Come on!" Ostin shouted. *"Motín!"*

They still just stood there.

"We haven't time for this," Zeus said. "Stay in your cage, you rats."

"No, start the fires," Ostin said. "That's the plan."

"Right," Zeus said. He blasted the mattress with both hands. It burst into flames. The convicts jumped back, then, looking at Zeus in horror, fled the room. Ostin, Zeus, and Taylor ran back to Taylor's cell. "Come on!" Zeus shouted.

"McKenna," Ostin said. "Light the mattresses on fire!"

"Love to." Her hand burst into flames, and she lit the mattress. Then she and Zeus went to each of the cells, lighting the mattresses until smoke poured out of the cells and filled the hallway. An alarm went off.

Ostin opened the cell door for the other prisoners, who didn't need any persuading to get out, though they stayed away from Zeus.

"Everyone take their positions!" Ostin shouted. "Taylor, we need them to let us out now."

They walked to the door at the end of the corridor. *"Abran la puerta!"* Ostin shouted.

Taylor concentrated. Immediately the door opened. Soldiers rushed into the building with guns and fire extinguishers.

"Ian, which way?" Ostin shouted.

"Follow me."

When they got to the outside door, one of the soldiers pointed a gun at them. *"Alto!"*

The man suddenly collapsed to the ground.

A soldier standing behind the fallen man said, "Amigos, this way!"

"Who are you?" Ostin asked.

"Apúrate!" the man said, grabbing Ostin's arm. "We haven't much time."

"Are you with Jaime?" Taylor asked.

The man looked confused. "Jaime?"

"The voice," Taylor said.

He hesitated a moment, then said, "The voice. *Sí.*"

Another alarm went off, and outside the fences the soldiers were emerging from their tents. "Please. Hurry."

They followed the man over to an idling prisoner transport van. He opened the back doors. "Everyone in, hurry."

Suddenly there was a huge explosion about a hundred yards west of the camp. Men started shouting and two sirens went off.

"Get in!" the man shouted.

When everyone was inside, the man shut the doors behind them, then ran around to the passenger's side and climbed in. He shouted to the driver, *"Vámonos!"*

The van pulled forward, needling through the growing crowd of soldiers who had come to fight the fire. They drove up to the first check station, where they were stopped by a guard with a machine gun. He spoke to the driver. *"A dónde vas?"*

"Estamos sacandoles del encendio. Orden del general."

The soldier looked at the teens in the van. *"No puedo dejarte ir."*

The man in the passenger seat fired something, and the soldier dropped to the ground. Then the man pushed a button on a hand remote, and there was another explosion—this one closer to the jail—taking out a hundred-foot section of the fence.

"Vamos!" he shouted to the driver.

"Distraction," Ostin said. "Clever."

The van drove quickly in the opposite direction of hundreds of soldiers who were running toward the jail. Within just a few minutes they had passed out of the military compound.

"We did it," the man said through a speaker box. "We got away."

Everyone in back clapped, except Ostin, who looked conflicted. Jack punched him in the shoulder. "Lighten up, dude. You and that awesome brain of yours broke us out of there."

Wade also punched Ostin in the shoulder. "Yeah, you're the brain man."

Ostin still didn't look happy. "I didn't get us out of there; those guys did." He turned to Taylor and frowned. "Why didn't he know Jaime?"

Taylor shrugged. "Maybe they don't use their real names."

Ostin frowned. "Something doesn't feel right. Can you read their minds?"

Taylor looked over at the driver, who was divided from the back by a thick, bulletproof Plexiglas sheet braced with a metal caging. "I don't know. I'll try." She put her hand against the metal siding of the van.

Ostin knocked on the plastic partition between them. The man turned back. "Yes?"

"Where are we going?"

"Someplace safe, amigos," he said. "Someplace very safe." He turned back toward the front.

Taylor looked at Ostin with wide eyes. "We've got to get out of here," she whispered.

"Why?" Ostin asked.

"They're taking us to the Elgen."

10

Out of the Frying Pan

The mood in back of the van changed from relief to terror.

"What do we do?" Abigail asked.

"Try the back door," Jack said.

"There's no handle," Taylor said. "You can only open the door from the outside."

"Can you shock them?" Ostin asked Zeus.

"Not through that plastic screen."

"What if I melted through it first?" McKenna said.

"If you shock them, they'll crash," Taylor said.

"I'd rather take my chance with a car crash than with Hatch," Zeus said. "At least with the crash I've got a chance of surviving."

Taylor looked back at the men, then knocked on the plastic behind the first man. "Where are you really taking us?"

"I told you. Somewhere safe."

"Where is safe?"

"You know all you need to know," he replied.

"Who are you really?" Ostin asked again.

At first neither of them answered. Then the driver laughed. "Soldiers of fortune."

"No," said the other. "Underpaid soldiers."

"Not anymore," the driver said. "Soon we will be sunning on the beaches in Argentina."

"You're Elgen scum!" Jack shouted.

"No." The man in the passenger seat turned back. "We are not with the Elgen company. But they pay better than the Peruvian army."

"You know they'll kill us," Taylor said.

"What they do is not our concern," the driver said. "And the Peruvian government will execute you anyway. Your chances are better with the Elgen company."

"You've never met Hatch," Zeus said.

"Met what?" the man replied.

"Manuel," the driver said, his voice suddenly pitched. *"Mire!"*

In the middle of the road ahead of them was an army tank. Its cannon was pointed directly at them.

"That's not good," Ostin said.

"Who is that?" Taylor asked.

"Looks like the Peruvian army isn't as dumb as those two think they are."

"Que hago?" the driver asked.

"No sé! Vire!"

"Pueden reducirnos a cenizas!"

"No van a matar los chicos."

"What are they saying?" Taylor asked.

"They're trying to figure out what to do about the tank," Ostin said.

Suddenly machine-gun fire exploded around them, blowing out the van's tires.

"Everyone down!" Taylor shouted.

The teens fell to the floor. There was a loud screech as the tires shredded off and the truck's metal rims hit the payment.

"*Mi Madre de Dios!*" shouted the driver.

"*Firme!*"

The transport veered off the road and everyone bounced around in the back. Bullets tore through the front and side windows of the cab, ripping apart the front of the van. A stray bullet hit Jack in the arm. "Ah!"

"They got Jack!" Wade shouted. "They got Jack!"

"Calm down!" Jack shouted. "It's just a flesh wound!"

The van tipped up on two wheels, then slid down a small dirt slope where it crashed into a grove of small trees, tumbling everyone in back. When the motion stopped, everyone was quiet.

"Everyone okay?" Jack asked.

"I'm okay," Abigail said.

"Me too," McKenna said. "I just hit my head."

"I'm okay too," Taylor said. She had a small gash on her forehead and blood was running down the side of her face.

"You're bleeding," Ostin said.

"I noticed," she said, wiping the blood from around her eye.

Ostin moved closer to her. "It doesn't look too deep."

Zeus said to Jack, "You okay, buddy?"

"Yeah. Stings a little."

"I can help," Abigail said. She took Jack's arm and the pain went away.

"Thanks," Jack said.

"Anytime," she replied.

As they lay there, dozens of Peruvian soldiers surrounded the vehicle. Soldiers pulled open the front door of the van, then dragged the bodies of the traitorous soldiers out of the cab.

"*Están muertos.*"

A soldier looked into the window at the youth, then stepped back. "Everyone come out of the truck," a voice said.

"We're locked in!" Ostin shouted. "We can't get out."

"*Apúrense!*" a voice shouted. "*Scales antes que reventa el combi!*"

The soldiers swarmed the back of the van. "We will open the door," one shouted. "If you run, we shoot."

"Should I blast them?" Zeus asked.

"No. There's too many of them," Taylor said.

"And they've got us outgunned," Ostin added.

"Maybe they're going to shoot us for trying to escape," Wade said.

"They have a tank," Ostin said. "If they wanted us dead, they would have just blown us up. Besides, they probably just think we were kidnapped by those dudes."

The back doors of the van swung open, revealing dozens of guns pointing at them, including two mounted machine guns and a flamethrower.

"Can you say *overkill*?" Ostin said sardonically.

"Come out," one of them shouted in English. "One at a time."

Ostin breathed out slowly. "Failed again," he said.

"Michael," Taylor said, holding her head. "Where are you?"

PART 3

11

An Electrical Storm

In the Tyrrhenian Sea. The ES *Ampere.*

"**A**re we in agreement?" Chairman Schema asked. Two hours earlier he had called the board together for an emergency meeting. An ominous, dark atmosphere permeated the boardroom.

Board member Eleven broke the silence. "I'm not comfortable playing judge and jury," he said. "We're voting to execute someone."

"Perhaps you'd be more comfortable spending the rest of your life in prison," Two replied.

"If they don't hang you first," Ten said.

"No," Schema said, shaking his head. "There is no other option. Hatch must never leave this ship alive." His gray eyes slowly panned the table. "We must be unanimous as a board. This is no time for dissension."

"Then I'll abstain from voting," Eleven said.

"I will too," Seven said.

"As will I," Six said.

Schema looked at the three of them with disgust. "I didn't realize the board had cowards on it." Everyone turned away from the three except Schema, who stared at them coldly. "So be it," he finally said. "Let the record show that board members Eleven, Six, and Seven are irrelevant."

"I make a motion that we vote," Two said.

"I second the motion," said Ten.

"Is there any more discussion?" Schema asked. When there was no response, he said, "All in favor of the motion, say aye."

The room was a chorus of ayes.

"Any opposed?" He looked at Eleven, Six, and Seven, who remained silent. "The motion carries."

Schema's secretary walked into the room. She leaned over and whispered in the chairman's ear. Schema nodded. "Have we confirmed who's on board?"

"Yes, sir," she replied. "Just the pilot and Dr. Hatch."

"Alert security to their arrival," Schema said. "Land them." As she turned he looked over the board. "We've reached our decision just in time. I've just been informed that Dr. Hatch's transport is landing on the ship."

The Elgen helicopter dropped quickly beneath a low-hanging canopy of black-gray clouds, hovering a moment before settling onto the ship's pitching helipad. Hatch almost threw up. White-knuckle landings on a rocking deck were just another on a long list of reasons for Hatch to dislike their corporate sea base.

"We've landed," the pilot said.

Hatch nodded. "So we have."

The pilot shut off the engine, and as the rotors slowed, two armed guards, one tall and lanky, the other short and muscular, approached the helicopter. Dr. Hatch opened the helicopter door and stepped out, looking at the guards with a wry smile. "Now why would you be holding guns?"

"Sir, please step away from the craft," the tall guard said.

"I asked you a question," Hatch said sternly.

"Please step away from the craft," the guard repeated.

Hatch looked back and forth between them, then said, "As you wish."

The muscular guard walked around Hatch and looked inside the helicopter.

"Visual inspection clear, sir," he barked to the other guard.

"Were you expecting someone?" Hatch asked.

"We need to check you for weapons, sir," the first guard said. "Please put your hands above your head."

Hatch shook his head with annoyance. "Is this really necessary?"

"Yes, sir."

Hatch complied with the command and the muscular guard patted him down, then stood back at attention. "He's clean."

"Does Chairman Schema know you're treating me this way?"

"These are the chairman's orders, sir," the guard replied.

Hatch nodded. "How unfortunate."

"Follow me, please," the tall guard said. Hatch followed the guard, while the other guard walked behind him, his gun drawn.

Schema's secretary buzzed the chairman as Hatch and the guards entered the waiting room. "They're here, sir." She nodded to the tall guard, who opened the boardroom door. Hatch stepped past him and into the room. He noticed two more guards inside the room. The board was silent on his entrance.

"I see there have been some changes since my last visit," Hatch said, sitting down "Thank you for sending the welcoming committee."

Chairman Schema, who was seated at the far side of the table, just glared at him, his anger barely contained beneath a veneer of forced civility, like the clattering lid on a boiling pot.

Hatch coolly returned his gaze. "You wish to say something?"

"Dr. Hatch, you were given specific instructions and deadlines to dismantle the biogenesis program. Instead, you flagrantly disobeyed our orders, leading to the destruction of our largest facility, leaving seventy percent of an entire country out of power, and doing irreparable damage to our reputation."

Hatch showed no emotion. "We were attacked by terrorists. How is this my fault?"

"You were attacked because you failed to obey our order to release the Vey woman!" Schema shouted. "Your refusal to do so resulted in the attack."

"That's not wholly accurate. The group attacked us for their own political agenda."

"Political agenda." Three laughed. "They're teenagers. Their only *political agenda* is free Internet."

Hatch looked at Three, his eyes dark and fierce. "As I said, they have a political agenda."

Schema continued, "The damage done by your impudence has set us back years, if not outright destroyed our chance for short-term success."

"Don't be stupid," Hatch replied. "Do you really believe that any country will walk away from free electricity? Our plant being shut down was not our fault—but the poor handling of the situation is completely *yours*. We were attacked by a sophisticated and powerful group of anarchists and terrorists. When they attacked our plant, world sympathy should have been with us, not against us. But instead of invoking public sympathy, you apologized. What was going through your mind? What you did was tantamount to Roosevelt apologizing to the world after Pearl Harbor. Your stupidity turned public sentiment against us." Hatch looked around the table at the board members. "Really, this is our leader? Our chairman? This is the man we trust with our future?" He turned and faced Schema. "You have done enough damage!"

Schema pounded the table with his fist. "Enough!"

"Indeed it is," Hatch said, glaring at him. "You are no longer fit to run this organization."

Schema jumped up from his chair. "How dare you!"

Hatch also jumped up, simultaneously slamming his fist down on the table. "How dare you! You have led this group from one disastrous decision to the next. Your shortsightedness is exceeded only by your stupidity."

Schema was red in the face, his veins bulging from his temples. "Guards, take him to the brig."

"I'm not done," Hatch said, pointing at Schema. "It's time the Elgen became who we were meant to become. It's time for a change, but not the one you brought me here for." Hatch's eyes panned the room as his voice softened. "Yes, I know why you brought me here. You can't fire me. I know too much. I hold each of your lives in my hands. You didn't bring me here to fire me—you brought me here to silence me."

No one spoke.

"Don't worry. It's not going to happen. If anyone will be silenced, it will be our illustrious chair."

"Guards, take him out of here!" Schema shouted. "Now."

The two guards walked up behind Hatch.

"Sir, put your hands behind your back," one of them said.

"So it begins," Hatch said. He looked around the room with a confident, dark smile. "Does anyone here, besides me, of course, object to the chairman's scheme to put me down?" He looked back and forth between the group. "Answer carefully, your decision will hold consequences."

"Even in complete failure you're defiant," Two said.

Hatch looked at her. "You've always shared the chairman's animosity for me. It makes me wonder what else you share."

The woman blanched. "How dare you!"

"How dare I? You have no idea how much I'm willing to dare."

"You're a fool," Two said. "We are fortunate to be rid of you."

"Don't be too sure," Hatch said. "The day is not over yet."

Two chuckled. "Are you so obtuse or arrogant as to think that this board will change their minds?"

"The day will reveal who is truly obtuse," Hatch said. "And no, I don't believe that you will change your mind, but the less *obtuse* board members will. And my *arrogance* is not unfounded. Mark my word, friends: Those who don't support me will live to regret their decision. Sooner than you imagine."

Seven stood up. "Mr. Chairman, is this treatment of Dr. Hatch really necessary?"

"I agree," Six added. "Dr. Hatch has provided much to our organization. There wouldn't even be a Starxource initiative if it wasn't
for him."

Schema looked around the room. "Anyone else disagree with my
actions?" he asked softly. "Would you like to resurrect the discussion
on Dr. Hatch's reprimand?"

Eleven also raised her hand.

"Seven, Six, and Eleven," Schema said, looking at the three in
disdain. "You are relieved of your board membership and are under
house arrest until we decide your fate. Captain, see that there is a
guard stationed at each of their rooms."

"Yes, sir," the guard barked back.

Schema looked around at the rest of the table. "Is there anyone
else who wishes to join them?"

No one spoke.

"Take these fools away," Schema said.

As Hatch and his two guards boarded the elevators near the center of
the boat, Hatch said to his escorts, "I'll give you one more chance to
prove your loyalty to me." He paused for emphasis. "Not for my sake,
but yours."

"Shut up!" the first guard shouted. "You're insane."

Hatch smiled. "So be it."

The elevator doors opened onto the bottom level of the ship, and
Hatch was marched down a long corridor to the brig. The *Ampere*'s
brig consisted of four cells, six foot by six foot, with padded walls and
electric locks. Being on the ship's bottom level, the brig was situated
less than seventy feet from the engine room, so the cells and the outside corridor were always noisy, reverberating with the sound of the
yacht's massive diesel engines.

The second guard opened the first cell door and stood to its side.
"Welcome to your new home. Get comfortable. You're going to be
here a long, long time."

"I don't think so," Hatch said. He turned to the first guard, who
was still clutching Hatch's arm. "Are you going to take my cuffs off?"

The guard shoved him into the small cell. "Maybe tomorrow," he said. "But probably not."

"You don't have tomorrow," Hatch said.

"He's a nutcase," the second guard said. He slammed the door, which locked with a loud buzz and electric click. Both guards turned to go.

"One more thing . . . ," Hatch said after them.

Both guards turned back.

"Let me tell you something that many have learned the hard way." He leaned toward the bars and his voice fell to a low, guttural growl. "I never ever, ever forget."

"Like an elephant," the first guard said, laughing.

"Come on," the second guard said. "Just leave the nutjob in his cage."

Suddenly the corridor lights flickered. Then the lights at the end of the hall went dark.

"Gentlemen," Hatch said. "I believe there's an electrical storm coming."

Both guards drew their weapons, the first a submachine gun, the second a Colt sidearm. Suddenly the second guard dropped his handgun and began screaming. His face was red and he was violently shaking his hands in the air. "My hands! They're burning!"

Then the first guard also threw his gun to the floor and fell to his knees, pulling off his boots. "My feet!"

The two guns suddenly lifted into the air and flew to the end of the hall. Torstyn, Quentin, and Kylee emerged from the darkness, walking toward the brig. They casually walked past the two guards, who were on the ground writhing and screaming with pain. Kylee pulled the electric keys from the second guard's pocket without even bending over and unlocked the door.

"What took you so long?" Hatch asked.

12

The Takeover

"Get up," Quentin shouted at the guards, "before Torstyn explodes your brains! Then strip to your underwear and get into the cell."

The second guard stood. With blistered hands he quickly tore off his clothes. "Whatever you say, sir."

The first guard pulled off his boots, then just lay there. He looked like he was in shock.

Quentin looked down at him. "You have a problem with my order?"

"No, sir. I can't . . ." He grimaced. "My feet . . ."

Quentin looked at the man's feet. They were bright crimson and severely blistered.

"Then crawl in," Torstyn said. "Or should I just melt you here?"

"No, sir," the guard said. He hurriedly pulled down his slacks, screaming as they brushed against his feet. Then he crawled into the cell, whimpering.

"Both of you on your knees with your hands on the back wall," Hatch said. "And don't waste my time."

When both guards were against the wall, Hatch shut the cell door behind them.

"Just a few minutes ago you both were laughing," Hatch said. "What happened? Did you lose your sense of humor?"

Neither guard answered.

"I asked you a question."

"No, sir!" they shouted in unison.

Hatch turned to the second guard. "What did you call me? A nutjob?"

"I'm sorry, sir," the second guard said.

Hatch turned from the cell. "Not as sorry as you will be. Come on," he said to his youths. "Let's go pay a visit to the board."

The four of them walked down the hallway, back toward the elevator.

Hatch picked up the guard's pistol, put it in his right pocket, then pulled the satellite phone from his left pocket.

He pushed a button and just seconds later a voice answered. "Engage," Hatch said, then he stowed the phone back in his pocket. He turned to Quentin. "Where are Bryan and Tara?"

"They're covering the main floor," Quentin said. "I'll let them know we're on our way."

"No, have them meet us here," Hatch said.

"Yes, sir," Quentin said. He pulled out his cell phone and dialed a number. "Tara, it's Q. Come down to the first floor. Use the forward elevator." He returned his phone to his pocket and turned back to Hatch. "They'll be right here."

Less than a minute later the elevator stopped on the floor. Tara and Bryan stepped out.

"What's going on up there?" Hatch asked.

"Everything's calm. I think the board members are still meeting."

"Does anyone know you're on board?"

"Two window washers spotted us," Tara said.

"And?" Hatch asked.

"They jumped overboard." Bryan laughed. "Tara made them think the boat was filled with cobras." He turned to Quentin. "One of them did the most awesome belly flop. It was epic."

Hatch didn't look amused. "Did anyone see them go over?"

"We don't think so," Tara said. "We didn't see anyone else. And we could barely hear them screaming."

"All right, listen up. The three board members loyal to me are under house arrest on the second floor. We're going to free them, then pay the board a visit. There are currently fourteen guards on board. Four of them—Woodbury, Spafford, Harlan, and Mull—are loyal to me and are awaiting my orders. We've locked two in the brig, and the other eight will need to be neutralized. A helicopter with twenty of our best soldiers is on its way from the *Faraday*. It will touch down in exactly twenty-eight minutes. Quentin, I need you and Tara to make sure they encounter no resistance on landing, understood?"

"Yes, sir," Quentin said.

Tara nodded. "Yes, sir."

"Kylee, Bryan, and Torstyn are with me. We'll take out the three guards on the suite level, then meet up with our four guards on deck." He turned to Tara. "Did you see any guards on the bridge?"

"Two."

Hatch looked Tara in the eyes. "Dispose of them."

"Yes, sir."

"Quentin, take out all communications. I don't want an SOS going out to any other ships in the fleet. Not all of them are loyal to me yet."

"Yes, sir. I'll take out the bridge before we get there."

"Don't take out any of the controls or radar. We still need to float this tub."

"Yes, sir."

"Also, take out the video console. I don't want them seeing us on the second floor. I'll give you five minutes. Call me after it's down."

"Yes, sir."

"Go."

Tara and Quentin stepped into the elevator. It was less than five minutes later that Hatch's phone rang.

"We have the bridge, sir. The consoles are down."

"Good. Stay there until I arrive." He turned back to Torstyn and Bryan. "Let's end this."

13

Mutiny

Inside the boardroom, Schema looked somberly over the group.

"Then it's unanimous," he said. "Once we reach open sea, Dr. Hatch will be exterminated." He burst out in a fit of coughing, then breathed out slowly. "It will be a relief to be free of him."

Two Elgen guards, Spafford and Mull, stood watch outside the boardroom door with their guns drawn.

There was a loud beep on Spafford's communicator. He turned to Mull. "It's time."

Mull nodded. He glanced once more down the hallway and then, together, they opened the boardroom doors and walked in, closing the doors behind them.

"Gentlemen," Schema said. "You'll have to leave. This meeting is still closed."

The guards leveled their guns at the board members. "You are all under arrest. Put your hands on top of your heads. Now!"

"What are you doing?" Schema asked.

Two secretly pushed a button under the table.

"I said, now!" Spafford repeated.

"I suggest *you* drop your weapons," Two said to the guards. "I've alerted the guards."

"Shut up!" Mull shouted. "And get on your knees and prepare to meet the admiral of the Elgen fleet."

"The admiral?" Two said.

"Admiral Hatch," Spafford said.

"Have you gone raving mad?" Schema said.

Then the door opened and Hatch walked into the room. He was flanked by Quentin and Torstyn and followed by the three disposed board members.

"Guards, subdue him!" Schema shouted, pointing at Hatch.

Hatch just shook his head. "Clueless as always," he said. "They don't take orders from you." He turned to Spafford and Mull. "Well done, men."

"Your little coup won't work," Two said. "I've alerted the guards. It's just a matter of time before you're back in the brig."

Hatch looked at her for a moment, then said softly, "You've alerted what guards?"

Just then the boardroom door burst open and a dozen guards in black uniforms ran into the room. They were led by a squad captain dressed in purple.

"*Those* guards," Two said. She turned to the captain. "Thank goodness you're here. Dr. Hatch has gone rogue. Arrest him."

The captain just looked at her, his eyes narrowing in contempt.

"I gave you an order!" she shouted.

"These aren't ours," Schema said to Two in a low voice.

"You're correct, Schema," Hatch said, looking more amused than angry. "Which, honestly, I find refreshing, as it's so rare that you're right about anything these days. But, I suppose, even a broken clock is right twice a day."

"What are you up to, Hatch?" Schema said.

"I'm relieving you of your command," Hatch replied. He turned to the captain. "Secure them."

"Yes, sir." The captain turned back toward the board table and shouted, "Everyone stand with their hands behind their backs. Now!"

None of the board obeyed, but looked to Schema for direction. Schema stared at Hatch defiantly.

"You were given an order," Hatch said.

No one moved.

"No?" Hatch said. "Okay, then. Captain Welch, shoot one of them."

"Yes, sir," the guard said. "Which one?"

"It's your choice."

He turned his gun on Three.

"Wait!" Schema said, holding up his hand. "You don't have to do that. We'll do what you say."

"Indeed you will," Hatch said. He turned to the captain. "Next time someone hesitates to follow an order, *shoot them*."

"Yes, sir."

Hatch looked at the board. "Leadership is such a burden. You know how it is, Schema. If you threaten to cut off someone's finger for breaking a rule, you're going to have to cut off a few fingers before everyone figures out that you mean what you say. So which one of you is going to be our demonstration? It's your decision. Here's your first opportunity to show us. Everyone stand up."

Everyone quickly stood.

"Now sit down."

They sat down.

"Stand up!"

They stood up.

"Now . . . stand down."

Half of the board sat down, the other half wavered, confused, crouched somewhere in the middle. Everyone looked at Hatch nervously.

"What do you want us to do?" Four said.

Hatch grinned. "I'm just toying with you," he said. "Sit down."

Everyone sat.

"What's your point, Hatch?" Schema said.

Hatch's grin turned to a scowl. "My point is I've listened to you fools for too long. From now until the end of your miserable lives, you will do precisely what I say. Everyone stand."

They all stood.

"Secure them," Hatch said to the captain.

"You heard him," the captain barked. "Everyone put your hands behind your backs. Do it now!"

Everyone obeyed. Two of the soldiers walked around the room zip tying the board members' hands together. Suddenly, Ten spun around, attempting to grab the soldier's gun. One of the guards fired an electrode from across the room, dropping Ten to the ground.

"Secure him," the captain ordered.

Two soldiers grabbed Ten, tied his arms behind his back, tied his feet together, then dragged him away from the table, laying him at Hatch's feet.

"What are your orders, sir?" the captain asked.

Hatch crouched down next to Ten. "Were my orders too complex for you?"

"You're not going to get away with this," Ten said.

"Of course I will," Hatch said. "Throw him out."

Schema said, "You don't need to do that, Hatch. He's sorry. Aren't you, Ten?"

"I'm most certain of that," Hatch said. He turned to the captain. "Open a window for me." He pointed to the middle panel of the external glass wall. "That will do."

The captain pointed his submachine gun at the tempered glass and pulled the trigger, ripping out a large section. The smell of gunpowder filled the room.

"There's your exit," Hatch said to Ten. "I hope you're a good swimmer."

Ten was trembling. "I'm sorry. I'll do whatever you want."

"Will you?" Hatch asked.

"Yes, sir."

"Good. I want you to drown."

Two soldiers dragged Ten over to the hole in the glass, then turned back to Hatch. Hatch nodded. The guards lifted the man and threw him out. The sound of his screaming could be heard until a distant splash ended it.

"Good-bye, Ten," Hatch said. He turned to the captain. "Think he can swim with his hands tied behind his back?"

The captain shook his head. "No, Admiral."

"I don't think so either," Hatch said. He looked over the rest of the board members. "As I was telling you, you always have to cut off a few fingers before they get the point. Anyone else care to test my resolve?"

The board members just stared at him fearfully.

"Maybe you do learn. Take over, Captain."

"You will comply with our every word," the captain said. "All of you come to this side of the room and kneel."

Everyone except for Schema hurried to the starboard side of the room, next to the glass. The captain walked up to Schema and pulled him out of his chair, forcing him to kneel, then kicked him in the stomach. Schema gasped, then fell to his side, coughing fiercely.

Hatch turned back to the three displaced board members, Six, Seven, and Eleven. "Take your rightful places," he said.

The three expelled board members hurried back to the table. Hatch looked at the other board members. "Funny how things change. Just an hour ago you pitied these three. Now you would give anything to be one of them, wouldn't you? I told you there would be consequences." He turned and looked at Schema, then slowly walked up to him. "Living in Peru, I couldn't help but learn a little about the Incan culture. They were far more advanced than most people real- ize. They created architectural feats that stump our modern archi- tects. They created massive pyramids that we cannot duplicate. They performed successful brain surgery.

"True, they had their brutal side and practiced human sacrifice, but here, too, they showed their keen intellect and understanding of the nature of politics. Whenever an Incan king conquered another kingdom, the fallen king was sacrificed in front of his subjects so there would be no mistaking who was in charge."

Schema turned pale. Hatch crouched down in front of him. "You didn't really think I was foolish enough to come back here unprepared?" Hatch rose and faced the kneeling board members. "Just another example of your chairman's remarkable shortsightedness." He turned back to Schema. "You are relieved of your chairmanship. Be grateful I haven't relieved you of your life."

"You'll pay for this, Hatch. This is mutiny."

"*Admiral* Hatch," Hatch said calmly. "Of course it's mutiny. And pay? Where exactly would I send the check? To whom? If you're implying that this scenario might somehow end differently than me in charge and you in prison, you can disabuse yourself of that notion. There is no cavalry. Everyone answers to me. That's the inherent problem with delegation, Schema. Somewhere along the line the power gets . . . short-circuited." Hatch turned to the captain. "Captain, lock them all in the same cell in the brig. Cell One."

"Yes, Admiral." He spun around. "All of you on your feet. Now!"

The members of the board all struggled to their feet.

"What are you going to do to us?" Two asked.

"You will be given a trial. But don't worry. I will be just as merciful as you planned on being to me." He turned around. "Captain of the guard, I want *former* chairman Schema hung upside down by his feet. I want the last of his loyal subjects to know that he's been conquered."

"Yes, sir."

Schema turned white. "Don't do this. You need me."

"I need you like I need a kidney stone," Hatch replied. "Take him out."

Two soldiers lifted Schema to his feet and carried him out. Six other guards walked the rest of the board members out.

As they exited Quentin started to laugh, followed by the rest of the teens. Hatch smiled. "That was more amusing than I thought it would be. I'm almost sorry it's over."

14

C10 Information

After the board members had been removed, Hatch walked to the head of the conference room table. He pulled out Schema's former seat, pausing before sitting. "You have no idea how long I've waited for this. Please allow me the pleasure of savoring this moment." Hatch took a deep breath, then slowly sat in the chair. A dark smile crossed his face. "It's about time."

Seven began clapping, and she was quickly joined by the others still in the room.

"Thank you," Hatch said. "You may sit. Quentin and Torstyn, let me have you up here next to me. Quentin at my right, Torstyn at my left."

Everyone sat, the former board members in their assigned seats, the teens taking the empty seats closest to Hatch.

Hatch stood and walked up to the cabinet against the port wall and opened it, exposing a whiteboard. "The information I am about to share is C10."

The teens' expressions turned more somber.

"Is that understood?"

"Yes, Admiral," the teens replied.

"Call me sentimental, but you, my electric eagles, may still call me 'sir.'"

"Yes, sir."

The board members looked at one another. Eleven raised his hand.

"Yes?" Hatch said.

"I'm sorry to interrupt, Admiral. But what is C10?"

"Explain C10, Quentin."

"Yes, sir. C10 is the highest level of Elgen confidentiality. It means that what we are about to be told may not be repeated outside of Admiral Hatch's presence, even with one another. The penalty for divulging C10 information is death by torture."

"Is that clear enough?" Hatch asked.

"Yes," Eleven said. "Thank you."

"Let me see the Elgen salute," Hatch said.

The youth raised their left hands to their temples. The other board members watched, then imitated.

"Very well. What I'm about to share with you is called Operation Luau." Hatch wrote the words on the whiteboard: OPERATION LUAU.

He turned back around and tossed the pen on the table. "We need a land base. We need a place to carry out our experiments and build larger EMP weapons—a base far away from prying eyes, and invisible to the CIA, KGB, MI5, Mossad, or even any local government. A place with political autonomy. I have found just the place in the South Pacific, midway between Hawaii and Australia, near the islands of Samoa and Fiji—the Polynesian island nation of Tuvalu."

"Tuvalu?" Bryan said.

"If you've never heard of Tuvalu, don't worry, neither has anyone else—which is precisely why it is of interest to us. It is the world's fourth smallest country, behind Vatican City, Nauru, and Monaco, and consists of three reef islands and six atolls.

"Unfortunately for them, the islanders declared independence from Britain in the 1970s. This was highly unwise, as they are little more than an island of hula dancers and fish spearers. They have no military, spend no money on defense, and have no means of defending themselves outside of a puny, impotent police force. Their navy consists of a single Pacific-class patrol boat provided by the Australian government for maritime surveillance and fishery patrol. Even the *Tesla* could blow it out of the water.

"Tuvalu is facing an energy crisis. Rising ocean levels have damaged two of their diesel-motor power plants. Unfortunately for them, their third stopped working two months ago."

"Fate has been kind," Six said.

Hatch looked at her. "Fate is an excuse for people who are too stupid or too weak to make their own future," he said. "We sabotaged the plant. Then three weeks later we engaged our Starxource plant, operating on Funafuti atoll, in Vaiaku, the capital of the island nation. We are now in complete control of the country's energy.

"In preparation of our arrival, we have, as we did in Peru, built a rehabilitation camp for the reeducation of the natives.

"This is my plan: We will gather the Elgen fleet at the Peruvian Port of Callao, where we will load up with supplies and evacuate our troops from our Peruvian Starxource plant, leaving behind a squad of soldiers to guard what's left of the plant. From there it will take us two weeks to reach Tuvalu."

"How will we reach the island without them knowing?" Quentin asked.

Hatch put both hands on the table and leaned forward. "Oh, they know we're coming. But we won't encounter resistance. In fact, they plan to greet us with flowered leis and luaus. This is a diplomatic visit to celebrate the opening of our Starxource plant.

"We have invited the Tuvalu prime minister, governor general, and entire parliament to a celebratory feast. I am assured by our local Elgen administration that they are most eager to demonstrate to us their gratitude.

"As we feast, the *Faraday* will move into place outside the capital city. Our troops will disembark, while the *Watt* patrols the surrounding oceans. Any vessel trying to enter or leave the islands will be sunk.

"When our troops are in position, power will be shut off throughout the island so there will be no communication on the island or to those outside of it. Only our facility will be powered. The government will be put under arrest and imprisoned while our troops move in and capture the whole of their puny police force. They will be locked in their own jail with the men they have arrested, which should make for some entertaining moments.

"One of our advance groups will seize the country's sole radio station, from which I will, the next morning, address the people and introduce them to their new state of affairs. Every citizen will be required to register with our internal police board. Those who resist will be locked into our prison and sent through our reeducation process.

"In the meantime, the *Ohm* and the *Volta*, with a contingent of two hundred guards, will dock on the island of Nanumanga, which will be cleared out of all inhabitants. This is where we will build our new laboratories and weapons-production facilities." Hatch looked around the room. "Are there any questions?"

No one spoke.

"All right then. Quentin and Torstyn with me. The rest of you may retire for the evening. It's been a long day. Get some rest. We have much to do over the next five weeks."

While the rest of the youth and board retired to their rooms, Hatch, accompanied by two guards, led Quentin and Torstyn to the chairman's suite. The guards opened the door, and once inside, Hatch picked up the room phone. "Send housekeeping to the admiral's suite immediately." Pause. "Yes, the chairman's suite. Thank you."

He set down the phone, then lifted a crystal decanter of Scotch, poured three glasses, then brought them over to the table on a silver platter. He offered the glasses to the teens, and they each took one. Quentin started to raise it to his lips, but Hatch stopped him.

"Just a moment, Quentin. Have I taught you nothing? Never

imbibe before you know what you are about to imbibe. This pretentious little draught is the Balvenie Fifty, a rare fifty-year-old specimen of one of the finest single-malt Scotches ever distilled. A single bottle retails at more than thirty thousand dollars. So what I poured you there is a three-thousand-dollar taste. Therefore, it behooves us, out of decency and respect for the beverage, that we should thank former Chairman Schema for his fine taste in Scotch." Hatch lifted his glass. "To Schema. A buffoon who knew his drink."

They all raised their shots. Hatch closed his eyes as he drank, then set the glass down. "Worth every penny."

Quentin choked a little on the drink, which made Torstyn smile.

Hatch looked at the teens. "I invited you here to mark this occasion," he said. "A day which will live in infamy. Today marks the beginning of a new world order. The world is changing, my friends. The autonomy of nations is already slipping from their citizens' grasps and they don't even know it.

"It is self-evident that the supranational sovereignty of an intellectual elite is preferable to the archaic and outdated design of democracy. The belief that the average human, steeped in superstition and religious conditioning, has the ability to make rational decisions for society's governance is beyond ridiculous, it is unabashed stupidity.

"Today we have taken the conclusive step toward world government. I don't mean in the pantomime, impotent sense of a league of nations, rather an elite overclass prepared to rescue the dumb masses from themselves.

"You, my two apprentices, will someday take this gauntlet from me. You shall rule the world and the world will be better for it. So let us mark this momentous occasion with a toast." Hatch again filled their glasses. "To the Elgen elite."

"To the Elgen elite," they echoed.

All three downed their drinks.

15

The Dragon and Its Beast

Just minutes after the toast, there was a knock on the door. "Housekeeping."

"Come in," Hatch said.

The door slowly opened and a portly, middle-aged Italian woman in a white-and-turquoise housekeeping smock looked in timidly. "Chairman Schema?"

"Mr. Schema doesn't live here anymore," Hatch said. "I'm your new boss. Is it just you?"

"Yes, sir."

"What is your name?"

"My name is Patrizia."

"Okay, Patrizia, you'd better call for help. This room reeks of Schema. I want you to disinfect it—I want it scrubbed from top to bottom. I want you to change my linens, rugs, and towels—in short I want you to sterilize or replace every piece of fabric, including the drapes. You may begin by removing Mr. Schema's personal belongings from the closets and drawers."

The maid looked confused. "Where shall I take the chairman's things?"

"He is no longer the chairman and you are not to refer to him by that title anymore. Do you understand?"

She swallowed. "Yes, sir."

"I don't care what you do with his personal artifacts." He rubbed his chin, then said, "No, actually, I do. Throw them overboard. I don't like clutter, and he won't be needing them anymore."

She looked around at the beautiful art. "Everything, sir?"

"Everything. Now call your colleagues and get to work. I want you done and out of my room in two hours. A minute longer and you'll spend the night with the former chairman in the brig. Do you understand?"

"Yes, sir."

"Very well. Get to it." Hatch turned back. He took another drink. "Quentin, I want you to make sure everyone's accommodations are acceptable."

"Yes, sir."

"Go to it. When you're done, report to me on the forward deck."

He stood. "Yes, sir."

"Go along with him, Torstyn."

"Yes, sir."

The maid had already called the rest of the housekeeping crew and was working frantically, piling the linens in the center of the room. Hatch smiled to see her so motivated. He grabbed the bottle of Scotch and walked to the door. He turned back to the frantic woman. "One hour, fifty-eight minutes, Patrizia. I've set a timer. I will be back then. Hopefully, you won't be escorted out by one of my guards."

"Yes, sir," she said, too frantic even to look at him.

Hatch walked out of the room.

Hatch took the elevator to the bridge level and walked out onto the deck, the pungent smell of sea spray filling his nostrils. He sat down near the bow, kicking his feet up on the chair next to him. He lifted the Scotch and took a swig, then set the bottle down next to the chair. He had been there for about thirty minutes when Quentin walked out to him. "Everyone is happy with their room, sir."

"Where is Torstyn?"

"He's in his room."

"Very well," Hatch said. He was still looking out over the water. "Q?"

"Yes, sir."

"Have you ever read the Bible?"

Quentin's brow furrowed. "No, sir. It wasn't allowed at the academy."

"That's a shame." He turned to Quentin. "It's fabulous fiction, really. Hogwash, of course, rubbish and drivel. But, every now and then, the writers got it right. Did you know that it prophesizes of us?"

"I didn't know that, sir."

"Two millennium ago they wrote of our day." Hatch looked back out over the water. "And I saw a beast rising up out of the sea, having seven heads and ten horns, and on his heads a blasphemous name. Now the beast, which I saw, was like a leopard, his feet were like the feet of a bear, and his mouth like the mouth of a lion.

"The dragon gave the beast his power, his throne, and great authority. And all the world marveled and followed the beast.

"So they worshiped the dragon who gave authority to the beast; and they worshiped the beast, saying, 'Who is like the beast? Who is able to make war with him?' And authority was given him over every tribe, tongue, and nation.

"And all who dwell on the earth will worship him. . . ." He took another drink from the bottle, then turned back toward Quentin. "The seven heads and ten horns, the number seventeen, represents the seventeen electric children. And the dragon gave them their power, as I have given you yours. Just as I will give you thrones and great authority. And the people of this world shall fear you and they shall worship me." He smiled. "By the time they know who we are, it will be too late." He laughed. "I'm rather prosaic tonight, wouldn't you say?"

"Yes, sir," Quentin said.

"Or maybe I'm just drunk."

Quentin looked down. "About the seventeen. What of the others?"

"The other Glows? They'll come around," he said. "Eventually. Even Michael Vey. If I have learned one thing from life, it is that you can't fight destiny."

Quentin bit down on his cheek. "Yes, sir. Do you need anything else, sir?"

"To be left alone," Hatch said.

"Yes, sir. Requesting permission to retire to my room."

"Get out of here," Hatch said.

Quentin turned and went back inside. Hatch looked out over the setting sun. He held up his thumb, covering the halved red-orange orb. Then he lifted the bottle again. "To the dragon," he said. "And his fearsome young beasts."

It was after dark when Hatch carried what was left of the Scotch down to the brig. The engines were being serviced, so the bottom-level corridor was quiet for a change. The guards outside the cells saluted and stood at attention at Hatch's approach. "Admiral, sir."

"At ease, sailors," Hatch said. He handed out his bottle. "Have a drink."

"We're on duty, sir," they both said.

"Right answer," he said. "Here," he said to the closest guard, "hold my bottle."

At Hatch's appearance the crowded board members all stood, their hands still tied behind their backs—everyone except for Schema, who had been tied upside down by his feet to the outer bars, his back toward Hatch. He had been hanging for more than three hours and was unconscious. There was a pool of vomit on the floor beneath him.

Two pressed against the bars. "Cut him down, Hatch," she said. "I demand it."

Hatch looked at her incredulously. "Did I hear you right? You *demand* it?" His eyes narrowed on her. "Is that really what you said?"

Two swallowed, her look of indignation quickly evaporating.

Hatch smiled. "You, Numero Dos, are in no position to *demand* anything." He moved his face next to the bars. "And the next time you make such an imperious statement, you will join Ten bobbing for kelp in the Tyrrhenian Sea. Do you understand me?"

She began trembling. "Yes."

"Yes, what?"

"Yes, sir . . ."

"Yes, *Admiral*," Hatch corrected. He looked at the rest of the prisoners, who were cowed against the back wall of the cell. "If any of you get that wrong again, you will regret it for the rest of your greatly diminished life. From this moment on you will only address me as Admiral Hatch."

He started to turn.

"Admiral," Two said.

Hatch turned back. She knelt down and bowed her head until it touched the floor of the cell. "Please, Admiral. Please release the former chairman. He won't live much longer like this."

Hatch looked at her with intrigue. "So I wasn't wrong. You do care about him."

She looked up. Tears were streaming down her cheeks. "Yes, Admiral."

"You have feelings for him?"

She swallowed. "Yes, Admiral."

"Do you love him?"

She hesitated, caught up by her emotion. "Yes, Admiral."

Hatch started to laugh. "Oh my." After a moment he said, "How much?"

"What?"

"How *much* do you love him?"

She looked at Hatch fearfully, certain that his question was a trap. "With all my heart."

"With all your heart." Hatch laughed. "I've seen your heart, lady, and there's not much there."

She didn't answer, but bowed her head.

Hatch exhaled. "Okay, you say you love him, I'll have him cut down." He flourished his hand. "For *love's* sake."

She looked up in surprise. "Thank you, Admiral. Thank you."

"As long as you agree to take his place."

Her expression turned from relief to horror.

"For *love's* sake," Hatch said. His eyes narrowed. "Or doesn't your *love* go that far?"

She hesitated a moment, then said, "Yes, Admiral. It does. Thank you for your kindness."

Hatch looked at her for a moment, then shrugged. "Hmm. Surprising." He turned to the guard. "Make it so."

"Yes, sir."

Hatch shook his head as he reclaimed his bottle. Then he said, "All you need is love." He turned and walked back down the corridor, humming.

PART 4

16

Against the Current

Jaime, Tessa, and I continued our hike west through heavy jungle for two more days. At times the silence between us seemed as stifling as the jungle's humidity. Jaime was angry. He was breaking orders and was leading me only because I had threatened to expose the voice if he didn't. Tessa still hadn't changed her mind about helping me rescue my friends, though I was pretty certain she felt guilty about it.

Late afternoon of the second day, Jaime led us up the steep slope of another hill, then abruptly stopped and dropped his pack on the ground. "This is where we will camp for the night."

"It's not even dark yet," I said.

"Come with me," he said. I followed him to a break in the trees. "There," he said, pointing to a mountain on the opposite side of the river. "That is our destination. It is close. We can make it by tomorrow."

"If it's close, then we should keep going," I said. "The army could move them at any time. They could be traveling right now."

"No," Jaime said, shaking his head. "If they are traveling right now, then it is already too late. We do not want to cross the river at night. There are things in the river that feed most at night. And we cannot make a fire to warm or dry ourselves after we swim. It is best that we wait until the morning. Once we reach the hill, I will make radio contact again. I will ask our people to tell us about the movements of the army."

I looked back out over the river. "All right," I finally said. I had to give him credit. In spite of his disagreement with my plans, he had been more helpful than he had to be. I think that secretly, despite his orders, he wanted me to rescue my friends. "Thank you."

He looked at me with worried eyes. "Tell me that after you do not die."

Food was running low. All we had left from Jaime's camp was some beef jerky, dried banana chips, and hard rolls with packages of soft cheese. While Tessa and I set up the tent, Jaime left us to look for food. He returned about an hour later with a lumpy backpack.

He laid the pack down and fruit spilled out. Tessa held up an egg-size fruit with dark purple scales.

"What's this?" she asked.

"It is the *aguaje*," Jaime said. "It is delicious and very good for you."

She peeled back the fruit's skin and took a bite. "It tastes like a carrot."

"It is very popular," Jaime said. "Women who live near the rain forest eat it very often. They say it makes them more beautiful."

"I feel more beautiful already," Tessa said sarcastically.

Jaime handed me a different fruit. It was yellow and shaped like a bell pepper. "This is the *cocona*. It is also called the Amazon tomato. It is not sweet, but good to eat."

I took a bite. Its taste fell somewhere between a lime and a tomato. I ate until I'd finished the fruit, then wiped the juice dripping down my chin.

"Thank you," I said. "Was this hard to find?"

"Not so hard, but you must know what to look for. There are many fruits in the jungle, but much of it is poisonous."

We finished eating, then set up our camp. It was the earliest that we had gone to bed since we'd started our journey.

I woke early the next morning. Tessa was still asleep, her soft breath rhythmically filling the tent. Jaime was gone again. I sat up, then crawled toward the tent opening. It was dawn and a new sun had begun its climb over the jungle canopy, painting a baby-blue sky with creamsicle-orange clouds.

Jaime had nearly finished packing up the camp except for our tent. He looked over at me.

"Good morning," I said.

"*Buenos dias*," he replied. "Have some fruit."

"Thank you," I said. "You've already packed up."

"*Sí*. We should get an early start."

"How long have you been up?"

"Maybe two hours. I went down to the river to watch for Elgen patrols. One boat went by an hour ago."

I held up a piece of brown fruit. "This is new," I said, examining the avocado-size fruit.

"The *piton*," Jaime said. "I found it this morning."

"It looks like a mango."

"It is a wild mango."

"I love mangoes," I said. "The greatest fruit ever invented."

Tessa crawled out of the tent. "What's the greatest fruit ever invented?"

I held up the fruit. "The mango."

"I love mangoes," she said. "Especially in smoothies with sweet-ened condensed milk."

"That's not going to happen," I said.

"Eat it all," Jaime said. "We cannot carry much across the river."

"We're crossing the river today?" Tessa asked.

"*Sí, senorita.*"

"Good. That means we're getting close."

We finished eating, then Tessa and I packed up our tent and we all hiked down to the river.

Before coming out into the open of the riverbank, Jaime looked for several minutes through his binoculars, then set them down. "It is time to cross the river."

"Where's the boat?" Tessa asked.

"There is no boat," Jaime said.

"Then how do we cross?"

"We swim."

She looked at him in disbelief. "You're kidding, right?"

"No. I am not kidding."

"I don't swim. I almost drowned in a hot tub once."

I turned to Jaime. "We've got a problem."

"There is no other way across the river."

"You can't swim?" I asked.

"I don't swim *well*," she replied. "And this isn't a swimming pool. It's a big, scary, muddy river with things in it that eat people. Why can't we just take a bridge?"

"There is not a bridge for a hundred kilometers," Jaime said.

"Then let's get a boat. I mean, how are you going to take the radio across?"

"I have a waterproof bag. I will carry it across."

"You should put *me* in a waterproof bag and carry me across," she said.

"What if we found a log and floated across?" I said.

"We do not have time," Jaime said.

"I don't think we have a choice," I said. "Tessa, will that work?"

"There's still all those creatures in there. What if they're attracted by our glow?"

"The jungle people swim in the river all the time," Jaime said. "It is safer than crossing a street in Los Angeles."

"Not real comforting," Tessa said.

I looked Tessa in the eyes. "Come on, we'll be okay. I'll be right beside you."

She looked exasperated. "All right. Just make sure it's a really big log."

"We'll do our best."

Jaime and I went into the jungle and after ten minutes of looking, found a log about seven feet long. In spite of its size, it was very light—like balsa wood.

"This will work," Jaime said. "This is the kapok tree. Natives make boats out of it."

We carried the log to the river's bank. Then Jaime secured the radio in his waterproof bag, leaving as much air in the bag as possible before sealing it shut. Then we fastened all our packs to the log and pushed it partway into the river.

"Remember," Jaime said, "the current is strong. You must swim hard with the log."

He waded into the dark water, holding the radio in front of him. "*Vámonos!*" he shouted, and then he plunged into the water on top of the bag and began kicking fiercely as the water's current grabbed hold of him.

"Let's go," I said to Tessa.

Tessa glanced at me fearfully but still walked forward toward the log.

"I'll get in front," I said.

"No," she said. "Get behind me. In case I let go."

"Don't let go," I said.

"Like I'm going to on purpose!" she said. "It's a log. There's no handles!"

I moved behind her. "Here, just hold on to the pack's straps; it will be easier than holding the log."

"Okay, okay." She stepped into the water. "It's gross and dirty."

"So are we," I said. "C'mon, let's get it over with." We heaved the log into the river. The log submerged with us in tow, then quickly popped up again. Tessa clung tightly to the straps. She was terrified.

"I hate water!" she shouted, dripping and sputtering.

"You and Zeus," I said.

"Don't put us in the same sentence," she replied.

The current pulled us about twenty feet out into the river, then swept us forward.

"We've got to swim hard to get across!" I shouted.

"How do I swim and hold on?"

"Just kick!"

We both kicked as hard as we could but made little headway against the powerful current. Jaime was twenty yards downstream from us but was already approaching the opposite bank. We were having more difficulty, as the log put us at the mercy of the river.

"Más rápido!" Jaime shouted to us. "Swim more fast!"

We both kept kicking as hard as we could. We were quickly becoming waterlogged as the river repeatedly washed up over us and our log.

"Keep going," I said. "We're almost halfway there."

I realized that by the time we reached the opposite shore we were going to be separated from Jaime by several hundred yards. Although he was only ten feet from the opposite bank, Jaime was still swimming, trying to keep up with us.

Suddenly Tessa screamed. "What's that?"

"What?"

"In front of us."

I looked forward. There was another log ahead of us. Except it wasn't moving downstream.

"It's just a log," I said. "It must be stuck on something."

"I don't think it's a log."

I looked again. It wasn't a log. It was a massive caiman. "Oh, crap."

"Michael . . ."

"Climb up on the log!" I shouted.

We both tried, but the log just rolled back with us, dunking us underneath the water.

After our third attempt, Tessa shouted, "I can't!" She turned back. "It's coming!"

"Jaime!" I shouted. "Caiman! Caiman!"

He was far enough away that he looked at us without

comprehension. "Get your gun!" I pointed toward the approaching caiman. Jaime began swimming toward the bank.

"Michael!" Tessa screamed. She closed her eyes as the caiman opened its mouth just five feet in front of her.

"Enhance me!" I shouted. "Give me everything." I pulsed the hardest I ever had. So hard, in fact, that the water around me actually sizzled. The reptile shook violently, then turned sideways and sank. Suddenly, all around us, fish began popping up on the river's surface. They were everywhere, dozens of them.

"I'm going to faint," Tessa said.

"Don't do that," I said. "Just keep kicking."

It was another ten minutes before we were close to the opposite bank. Jaime had abandoned the radio and ran down the side of the riverbank to help us. He waded into the river up to his shoulders and grabbed the front of the log and pulled us in to shore. Tessa and I stumbled up to dry ground, then fell to our knees, exhausted. After she'd caught her breath, Tessa screamed at Jaime, "Don't you ever make me do that again!"

"*Senorita* . . ."

"Don't you '*senorita*' me!" she shouted. "I almost got eaten by a crocodile."

"Caiman," I said.

"Sorry," he said.

"Yeah, I bet you are," she said.

Jaime looked at me sheepishly.

Tessa took off her shoes and poured the water out of them, then put them back on and stood up. "*Vámonos*," she said.

I looked at Jaime and shrugged.

We were wet and uncomfortable, and the hike from the river to the top of the mountain took us six more hours. The one good thing was that by the time we reached our destination our clothes were mostly dry—at least as dry as one can hope for when hiking through a tropical rain forest.

From the mountain peak I could see the highway stretching east and west for at least five miles in both directions before it disappeared into the jungle. I could see why Jaime chose this point to attack. The roadway was steep and rugged, and the jungle seemed to spill over the asphalt as if attempting to reclaim the road.

Jaime looked out toward the east with his binoculars, then handed them to me. "That is the direction they will come from."

I lifted the binoculars and looked out over the fading ribbon of asphalt. "Are you sure this is the only way they can get to Lima?"

"*Sí.* This is the road they came on. I saw them. The road will go through Cuzco, then west to Lima."

"Is it possible that they've already passed?" I asked.

"No. Look closely. There is fruit and dead animals on the road that are not flat. That many trucks would not miss anything."

I looked out again and could see that he was right. There was some pretty bloated-looking roadkill. I handed him back his binoculars. "Thank you."

"We will make camp, then radio the voice and see what he knows."

We set up our camp a little off the peak on a mild downhill slope where the canopy was thicker. As we had no idea how many days we would be waiting, we took the time to carefully conceal our camp—gathering banana leaves and palm fronds to cover our tent. Jaime created a trip line of vines that would warn us if someone was near.

The sun was fading in the west when we finally stopped to eat dinner. Jaime handed us some reddish-orange pods he had cut open with his knife. The inside of the fruit was white, like boiled lobster, with a dark bean in the center.

"I've never seen this," Tessa said.

"It's cacao," Jaime said. "Chocolate."

"Finally something decent," Tessa said.

"It will not taste like a chocolate bar," Jaime said. He pulled out some of the beans. "You suck the flesh off of the cacao bean. Then you chew the bean."

Tessa and I followed his lead. The fruit surrounding the bean was actually quite good, but the bean itself was bitter with only a vague semblance of chocolate flavor.

"This isn't chocolate," Tessa said, clearly disappointed.

"It is what chocolate is made from," Jaime said.

"Could have fooled me," she said, spitting out the seed.

"You can have this," I said, giving her the last *piton*.

We finished eating, then we gathered around the radio that Jaime had concealed behind our tent. We were high enough up that I didn't need to climb any trees to mount an antenna. I didn't need to power the radio either. Apparently I had sufficiently recharged the batteries during our previous transmission.

Jaime flipped a switch and the lights of the radio came on. He handed me a headphone. The crisp crackle of static drowned out the jungle's symphony.

"I want to listen," Tessa said.

"I only have two headphones," Jaime said.

"I'll share," I said. I flipped the two earpieces around and Tessa sat next to me, both of us holding a speaker to one of our ears. Jaime dialed a number, then said, "Lightning Rod, this is Southern Cross. Over."

Nothing came back. Jaime signaled again. "Lightning Rod, this is . . ." He was interrupted by three beeps, and then a female voice said, "Southern Cross, we read you. Please confirm."

"Diez, uno, uno, uno, nueve, seis, dos."

"Please repeat the last two numbers."

"No," he said.

"Confirmed," the woman said. "One moment, please."

There was a pause, then the voice said, "Southern Cross. Are you still in possession of the jewels."

"Yes."

"We are pleased to hear that. At least not everything has gone wrong."

"What do you mean?" Jaime asked.

"Things have taken a turn for the worse. Hatch has gained control of the Elgen. He has imprisoned the chairman and commandeered the Elgen fleet."

"*Qué piña!* It could not be worse."

"Our source has learned that Hatch plans to secure a land base so the Elgen can train soldiers and ultimately build weapons of mass destruction."

"Weapons of mass destruction?" I said. "You mean nuclear weapons?"

"No," the voice answered. "The Elgen are developing high-potency EMPs."

"I know about EMPs," Tessa said. "Quentin is an EMP. He can shut down machines and stuff."

"That is right," the voice said. "A powerful enough EMP device could create an electromagnetic pulse that could conceivably shut down all electrical devices for many thousands of miles."

"Then EMPs don't kill people," I said.

"They will most definitely kill people," the voice replied. "It's estimated that up to ten percent of the population would die immediately. If you destroy all electrical devices, you shut down hospitals and all health devices. Anyone on life support would die."

"But hospitals have backup generators," Tessa said.

"An EMP doesn't just stop the source of power, it permanently destroys all electronic circuitry. Lights won't work. Cars won't run. Communication will be shut down, including all cell phones and radios. Gas stations won't be able to pump gas; grocery stores will lose refrigeration; food will rot and people will starve. All business will be brought to a standstill. There will be riots in the streets and looting. It is believed that an EMP may, in the long run, produce as many casualties as a nuclear weapon."

"How long would it take to get power again?" I asked.

"The problem is, the machinery required to repair or rebuild the infrastructure is also powered by electricity. It might not be possible for a country to rebuild itself."

"That's incredibly stupid," Tessa said.

"It's shortsighted," the voice replied. "But electricity has always been the Achilles' heel of the modern world."

"How will that benefit the Elgen?" I asked.

"The Elgen will offer aid by helping to rebuild the country's electrical grid to run off their Starxource plants, ultimately putting them in complete control of the world's power and economy."

"Where is this land Hatch plans to conquer?" Jaime asked.

"Hatch's target is a small country in the South Pacific called Tuvalu. The Elgen have already been there for more than a year and have already constructed a Starxource plant as large as the Peruvian facility that will serve as their administrative building and reeducation center."

"Doesn't the country have an army to defend itself?" I asked.

"No. Tuvalu is the size of a small American city. All they have is a police force, and there are more than a hundred Elgen guards to every police officer. The Elgen are also much better armed and trained. The Tuvaluans are a simple people. The Elgen will either slaughter them or turn them into their work force."

"You mean they'll make them slaves," I said.

"Very likely," the voice said.

"*Qué lío!*" Jaime said. "They are pure evil."

"The location of Tuvalu is strategic. It will give the Elgen unrestricted access to Hawaii, Australia, Taiwan, China, India, the Philippines, and Japan."

"This is most horrible news," Jaime said, rubbing his forehead. "What can be done to stop them?"

"We have leaked information to the leaders of Tuvalu, but it's falling on deaf ears. The Elgen have just solved the country's power shortage and are being heralded as heroes. But we have one other chance to stop them. Prior to their attack, the Elgen fleet is sailing to the port of Callao, west of Lima, to pick up the remainder of their force still quartered in Puerto Maldonado. There are thousands of guards stranded after the attack of the Starxource plant.

"They will also be refueling and stocking up on supplies. We estimate that it will take them four or five days to complete their preparations. But once they have left the port, there will be no stopping them. We must strike before they leave."

"What are your orders?" Jaime asked.

"Sink the *Ampere* while it's in port."

"What's the *Ampere*?" I asked.

"It's the Elgen's superyacht," Tessa said. "I've been on it. It's very cool. It has a helipad, sushi bar—it even has a disco."

"The *Ampere* is the Elgen command base," the voice said. "It's where Hatch operates from."

"How are we supposed to sink a ship?" I asked.

"You and your friends destroyed their largest and most secure Starxource plant. We're confident that you can sink a ship."

"Yeah, well, I don't have my friends with me," I said. "And the last time we spoke, you told me not to go after them."

"We were only protecting you," the voice said. "We believed that the chance of your success against their army was less than the chance of our success. But that's before Hatch took over. Now we are certain that we have no chance of diplomacy. The Elgen will be pressuring the Peruvian government for blood. You need to rescue your friends. Jaime, do all in your power to assist Michael in this cause. Call in assistance if you have to."

"Yes, sir. Do you know where the others are?"

"They are still being held in Puerto Maldonado. They nearly escaped but were recaptured outside the compound. Our sources tell us that the army is preparing right now to move them to Lima. So if you expect to breech their compound, you'll have to move fast."

"We have a different plan," Jaime said. "There is a narrow highway they will have to pass through on the way to Lima. We believe it is a place where we could stop them. We just need to know when they are moving."

"Very well. We'll alert you when the army is moving."

"And then what?" I asked.

"After you have rescued your friends, we will instruct you on everything we know about the Elgen fleet and the *Ampere*. Is there anything else you need right now?"

"I want to speak with my mother."

"I'll arrange for you to talk. I will give you a time during our next communication."

"Wait, I have a question," Tessa said, leaning forward toward the microphone. "Do you know anything about the Amacarra? Are they okay?"

There was a long pause. "The Amacarra tribe no longer exists."

Tessa turned white. "W-what do you mean?"

"The army massacred the tribe for harboring terrorists."

Tessa's eyes welled up with tears. "No!"

"I'm sorry. The army has been ruthless."

I put my hand on Tessa's back.

Tessa grabbed her beads, and tears began falling down her face. "My mama . . ."

There was a long pause, then the voice said, "I'm sorry, but we must sign out. There is one more thing you must know. We have been compromised."

Now Jaime turned white. "How?"

"The army learned of our existence while interrogating the others. They passed it on to the Elgen. They don't know who or where we are, but they now know that we exist. We have called a few of our agents in the field to come in."

"This cannot be true," Jaime said, putting his hand over his eyes.

"I wish it weren't. We will contact you when the army starts to move. Over."

The radio went dead. I took the headphone and gave it back to Jaime. The dread was palpable. It was as if a bomb had just gone off in our midst.

Jaime was the first to speak. "They know of us . . . ," he said, slowly shaking his head.

I looked at Tessa. She was sobbing.

"I'm sorry," I said, returning my hand to her back.

"They were so innocent," she said. She covered her eyes with her hand.

I didn't know what to say. I just kept rubbing her back. After a few minutes her sobbing slowed, turning to a soft whimper. Then she stopped completely. She held her hands at her temples, her fingers digging into her hair. Then she looked up at me. Her eyes were red and swollen. "They're going to pay for this. We're going to make them pay."

17

Rock Slide

After all the bad news we'd just received, the next few days passed in misery. We were low on food, and edible fruit was not very plentiful where we were camped. Now that we were close to the road, Jaime didn't dare go out foraging. "Too risky," he said. He told us that the army would likely send out an advance patrol before they moved.

The second day it rained hard and for most of the day we just sat in our tent, with nothing to do but sleep to escape the malaise. Jaime acted calm, but I could tell that he was going crazy inside. Tessa was not as stoic. She broke down crying at least a dozen times. The Amacarra tribe was the closest thing to family she had.

Early in the morning of the third day the rain finally stopped, and Jaime led us down the rugged terrain of the south side of the mountain near the highway. We needed to scout the pass to make our plans.

The road was covered on both sides by thick forest, which would be advantageous to us. The biggest question we faced was how to stop an army. Actually, we didn't need to stop all of the trucks, just the ones in front, creating a traffic jam.

The problem was, anything obvious might look like an attack and surprise was vital. If four thousand soldiers dug in for battle, we were through.

For nearly an hour we crouched down in the jungle, looking out over the highway, away from the road, in case an army patrol drove by.

"How many trucks do you think there will be?" I asked Jaime.

"Many," he said.

"Like how many?" I asked. "Twenty? Thirty?"

"Maybe two hundred. Or more."

"Two hundred? How will we know what truck they're being kept in?"

Jaime shook his head. "It will not be a simple thing."

"I can find them," Tessa said.

I turned to her. "How?"

"I can sense electricity. That's how I knew you were electric when I met you. It's the same way Nichelle sensed powers."

"Nichelle could sense powers?"

"If she didn't, she wouldn't be able to feed off your electricity. Hatch once had us walk through the academy blindfolded to find the electric kids. Nichelle and I are really not that different."

"Believe me, you're different."

"Personality-wise," she said. "Nichelle's all Goth and all that. But the scientists at the academy said we were similar in physiology. Nichelle was better at finding electricity than I was, but I can still do it. I just need to get closer than she did."

"How close?"

"Maybe thirty feet."

I looked at the lush jungle encroaching on the road. "That will work. We stop the convoy, then we'll move along behind the trees until you feel something."

"Then what?" Tessa asked.

"I shock the guards, we open the trucks, and we free my friends."

"How do we stop the trucks?"

"The question is, how do we do it without causing suspicion."

"Look," Jaime said. "That sign." He pointed to a yellow, diamond-shaped precaution sign that showed stones showering down on a road.

"Falling rocks," I said.

"We could roll large rocks into the road," Jaime said. "They would think it was a rock slide and not suspect us." He pointed to a rocky crag jutting out from the jungle. "There are rocks up there."

We followed Jaime back up the mountain. The terrace Jaime had seen from the road was littered with boulders from an earlier slide. Using a tree branch as a lever, we helped Jaime position a dozen or more large stones on the edge of the precipice.

"When they come, we will push the mountain down in front of them," Jaime said.

"Or on them," Tessa said.

"Just as long as we stop them," I said. The terrace was also high enough that we could see the highway for several miles in either direction. "This is a good lookout."

"*Sí*," Jaime said, sitting down on one of the rocks.

I pointed down to where we had first descended. "Tessa and I will wait there on the opposite side of the highway. After you stop them, we'll work our way down from behind the trees until we find them."

"Then how do we get away?" Tessa asked.

I looked back over the highway. "If they're chasing us, we'll have to head down the mountain. It's thicker jungle on that side. We'll have a better chance of hiding and ambushing them."

Jaime nodded with approval. "If we are separated, we will meet in Cuzco," he said. "There is a small hostel near the Plaza de Armas, the town square. It is owned by a friend of mine and will be safe."

"What's the name of the place?" I asked.

"Hostel El Triumfo," he said.

"El Triumfo," I repeated, committing the name to memory.

Jaime grinned. "Yes. The triumph. If we make it, then it will be well named."

I didn't like his "if."

By noon we had hiked back to our camp. We had a lunch of what Jaime had scavenged on the way back, mostly berries and some weird pod fruit that tasted like boiled Styrofoam. We also had snails, which Jaime had pulled from their shells and eaten raw. Tessa and I both tried one. I gagged and she spit hers out. We decided to stick with the fruit.

As the day waned, Tessa went back inside herself, silently fondling the red bead necklace her mother had given her when they'd said good-bye. I understood her anger. It's how I felt when Hatch took my mother. But I wondered if what had happened to her Amacarra mother had rekindled deeper feelings about the loss of her real family. I wouldn't have been surprised.

Around eight o'clock Tessa and I were just lying in the tent when we heard Jaime talking.

"What's he doing?" I asked.

Tessa sat up. "It sounds like someone's out there."

We crawled out of the tent. Jaime was standing near the radio. In front of him were two Peruvian men. Between them were three large packs and a duffel bag. As we approached, they turned to look at us.

"Who are these guys?" I asked Jaime.

"These are my amigos," Jaime said.

One of them started to put out his hand to me, then stopped.

"*Me electrocutará?*" he asked.

"*Espero que no.*" Jaime turned to me. "He's afraid you might shock him."

"I don't shock friends." I looked the man over, then said, "I'm assuming you're a friend."

He put out his hand and said with a heavy accent, "I am Xavier."

"And this is Pablo," Jaime said, pointing to the other man.

"I'm Michael. This is Tessa."

"*Hermosa,*" Xavier said, looking at Tessa. "Beautiful girl."

Tessa didn't smile. She looked at Jaime. "What's going on? Why are they here?"

"We need more help. Sit down," he said, pointing to the ground. We all sat. Jaime said to Pablo, "*Necesito su mapa.*"

The man retrieved a map from his backpack and unfolded it on the ground before us. Jaime pulled a small penlight from his pocket and shined it on the map. The words on the map were in Spanish, but I guessed it was a map of where we were.

"Our camp is here," Jaime said, touching his finger to the paper. He slid it down toward the single red line denoting the highway. "This is where we put the rocks. And this is where we will stop the army. You will be here." He pointed to a space across from the highway. "Your friends will be somewhere along this road. As you look for them, we will be watching you with binoculars. After you have found them all, you will go south through the jungle. To keep the army from following you, we will make a distraction over here." He touched a place about a quarter mile from where Tessa and I planned to start.

"What kind of distraction?" I asked.

"My friends have brought three gun sentries like the ones I had at the camp. We will make them fire on the army. They will think they are being attacked from down there," he said, touching the map. "While we will go back over the mountain and escape on the river, you will go south through the jungle as fast as you can go. In a few days we will find you and bring you to Cuzco."

"How will you find us in the jungle?" I asked.

"With this." He reached into the same backpack and brought out a small black iPod.

"An iPod?" Tessa said.

"It is like the one we gave you before," he said to me. "This too has a GPS signal. It will tell us where you are. I will also give you a small radio. But I will not try to contact you right away. The army will be searching these mountains and listening for transmissions."

"What if you're caught?" Tessa said. "Then what will we do?"

"I have friends in Puerto Maldonado that will help you. They know the signal of your device."

I looked at Jaime's friends. They were looking at us intently even though I doubted they understood a word of what Jaime was saying in English.

"You sure you can trust these guys?" I asked.

"With our lives," Jaime said. "They are proven. One more thing." He walked over and picked up a backpack, then walked back to us. "They have brought us food." Jaime dropped the pack between us.

"Oh, thank you, thank you, thank you," Tessa said.

"*Muchas gracias*," I said to the men.

"*Para servirle*," the older of the men said.

"Eat much," Jaime said. "You will need your strength."

I reached into the pack and brought out two Inca Kolas, a round of cheese, hard-boiled eggs, mini loafs of bread, some shish kebabs wrapped in foil, and some dip in plastic containers. We hadn't had protein in days, so after drinking some of our colas we unwrapped the kebabs. The meat was dark and cold but tasty.

"This is good," I said, stripping the meat off the skewer. "What is it?"

"*Anticuchos de corazón*," Jaime answered.

"Anti-what?"

"Cow heart."

Tessa grimaced. "We're eating heart?"

"It's meat," I said. "What's in here?" I lifted one of the plastic containers.

"*Causa*," Jaime said. "It is famous in Peru. It has potatoes and avocados and tuna fish."

"Jungle casserole," I said. "Are you going to eat with us?"

"We have food here. C*uy*."

"What's *cuy*?" I asked.

"Roasted guinea pig."

"Knock yourself out," Tessa said.

Tessa and I both ate until we were full. I had two eggs, half the container of *causa*, which I ate with my bread, two kebabs, and a banana, all of which I downed with a warm but delicious Inca Kola.

After we were full, we wrapped up everything we hadn't eaten and thanked the men again. They were sitting in their own circle eating and talking quietly in Spanish.

"We're going to sleep," I said. "*Buenas noches.*"

"Good night," Jaime said.

Tessa and I went back to the tent.

"That was good," she said. "I wonder how long before the food runs out and we're living off snails."

"I'm afraid we'll be eating snails very soon," I said. "Let's just hope we have my friends with us when we do."

18

On the Move

"Mr. Michael, Mr. Michael."

I opened my eyes to see Jaime leaning over me. It was still dark. "What?" I asked groggily.

"The voice has signaled us."

I sat up. "The voice?"

He nodded. "Come."

I looked over at Tessa, who was still asleep, then climbed out of the tent and followed Jaime to the radio. Our camp was lit by nothing but the moon, and Jaime had even covered the radio dials with leaves. I didn't see them at first, but in the shadows the other two Peruvian men were dressed and ready to go, standing next to their packs.

"How do they signal you?" I asked.

Jaime showed me a small blinking device that looked like a simple pager. "With this." He turned on the radio and a voice imme-diately came over the speaker.

"Southern Cross," a female voice said. "Do you read me? Southern Cross, do you . . ."

Jaime lifted the microphone close to his mouth and said in a soft voice, "This is Southern Cross."

"Please confirm," the voice said.

"*Diez, uno, uno, uno, nueve, seis, dos.*"

"Confirmed. Please receive this message. The army is on the move east on the PE-30C highway. I repeat: The army is on the move east on the PE-30C highway. Do you copy?"

"I copy," Jaime said.

"Transmission complete," the woman said. "Good luck." The radio went dead.

He looked at me. "It is time to go."

"I'll wake Tessa," I said. I went back to the tent. "Tessa." She didn't move so I lightly shook her.

She woke with a start. "What?"

"It's time," I said. "They're coming."

"Who's coming?"

"The army."

Tessa pushed her hair back from her eyes, then sat up. "Let's go."

She pulled on her shoes then followed me out. Jaime and the other men were standing near the outside of the tent waiting for us. "*Vámonos,*" he said.

We followed Jaime down the mountain, moving quickly through the dark jungle. Jaime's friends were fascinated by Tessa's and my glow, and Jaime reminded us to pull our sleeves down as far as possible.

It took us nearly forty minutes to reach the stony outcrop—twice as long as it had taken in daylight. Except for a few black stratus clouds, the sky was clear and the stars shone like punctured holes in a black curtain. The tension around us was as thick as the darkness. Or maybe it was just fear. Something told me it might be the last night of my life. I shivered at the thought.

From the edge of the outcrop we saw them. The lights of the army's caravan stretched on for miles, a long, dark snake, slithering steadily toward us, two abreast. It was the first time I fully realized how improbable our task was. I reminded myself that my friends were somewhere in that snake's belly and we were their only chance of escape.

"Look at all those trucks," Tessa said softly. "There's got to be a hundred of them."

"At least," I said. I took a deep breath of the crisp night air. "How long until they reach us?"

"Maybe twenty minutes," Jaime said.

"Then we better go."

He slipped the pack from his shoulder and propped it up against a stone. As he dug through it, he asked, "Do you have your GPS?"

I took the iPod out of my pocket and showed him.

"Good. And here is your radio. The frequency is 1717. Can you remember that?"

"Seventeen, seventeen. The number of electric children," I said. "Twice."

"*Sí*." His voice fell. "If you are captured, you must pulse and destroy the radio before it is found. Understand?"

I nodded. "Yes."

"When you have found all your friends, raise your hand to signal us. We will activate the sentries."

"Okay," I said.

"I will see you in Cuzco where?"

"Hostel Triumph near the town square."

"*Sí*. El Triumfo," he said. He looked into my eyes. "Good luck, Mr. Michael. Rescue your friends."

We embraced. I looked once more out toward our enemy, then nodded to Tessa, and we started down the slope, carefully making our way in the dark toward the highway. As quiet as we tried to be, our hike down was heralded by the screeching of birds and curious monkeys in the trees above us.

At street level we could no longer see the stony outcrop or the lights of the advancing caravan. We could only guess how close the trucks were. I got down on my knees and put my ear to the asphalt road like I had seen Native Americans do in old Westerns, listening for buffalo. I could hear the deep, low rumble of the distant convoy.

We crossed the highway about twenty yards down from the spot the rock slide would take place and disappeared into the darkness of the jungle, waiting behind the waist-high roots of a lupuna tree. Neither of us spoke and the only sound was the chattering of monkeys and the millions of insects around us that sounded like the buzzing of electricity.

"Do you think they'll be in the first truck?" Tessa asked.

"No. They'll probably want some kind of a buffer."

"Do you think they'll all be in the same truck?"

I shook my head. "We'll find out soon enough."

The minutes dragged on, raising my anxiety until my heart pounded like an African drum. I felt like a man with a noose around his neck, waiting for the floor to fall out from beneath him. When the caravan arrived, we could not only hear the rumbling of the trucks and the screeching of animals at its approach, but we could feel the convoy vibrating the jungle with a million pounds of metal.

Neither of us breathed when the first of the trucks' lights hit us. Then the first vehicles passed, a small jeep with a mounted machine gun followed by a tank. Behind it were five personnel transports painted in camouflage green. They drove past us without incident.

"Where's the rock slide?" Tessa whispered.

"Come on, Jaime," I said. "Roll the rocks."

Then I saw the problem. Jaime had miscalculated the density of the jungle. The rocks were crashing against trees, not even making it to the road. Only a few of the smaller rocks actually reached the asphalt, and they were small enough that they didn't even slow the trucks.

"It's not working," Tessa said, her voice pitched.

My chest constricted in panic as I watched the convoy pass.

"It has to work," I said. "This is our only chance." I turned to her. "Have any of my friends passed?"

"I'm not sure. The trucks are going pretty fast."

"We've got to stop them somehow."

"Try short-circuiting them," she said.

I focused on the nearest truck and pulsed. Nothing happened. "My pulse isn't strong enough."

"It was powerful," Tessa said. "I felt it. Can you magnetize them?"

"They're too heavy. It would only pull me to them." I thought for a moment. "But maybe if I didn't try to pull them toward me . . ." I looked at Tessa. "Enhance me."

She took my hand. "Okay, go."

I reached out, exerting as much magnetism as I could, focusing not on the vehicles but on the space between two of them. Suddenly two trucks veered into each other. There was a loud crash as they hit and locked bumpers, then one of the trucks, which was slightly ahead of the other, rolled over on its side, blocking the road. The crash set off a chain reaction as the vehicles behind them—their visibility limited by darkness—rammed into the vehicles in front of them. When the convoy had come to a halt, we could hear doors slamming and the shouts of soldiers furiously yelling at each other in Spanish.

"That should hold them for a while," Tessa said.

"Let's find my friends," I said. "Do you feel anything?"

"Not yet."

We moved quickly beneath the shadow of the trees, about twenty-five feet from the edge of the road. Suddenly, Tessa stopped and pointed at an idling green transport near our side of the road. "There," she said. "Someone's in that truck."

"Are you sure?"

She nodded. "Yeah. It's Zeus."

"You can tell who it is?"

"I can smell him."

"He doesn't smell *that* strong."

"Not him, his power. Everyone's power *smells* different."

I wondered what I smelled like. "Let's get him," I said.

The trucks were all jammed up next to one another, making it difficult to find a safe route. We crept to the edge of the jungle's shadow. Even though we were hidden by the dark, we knew that the soldiers might have night-vision goggles so we stayed low, moving cautiously. As we neared the truck Zeus was in, the driver's door opened and the driver got out. He walked around to the truck's rear and lit a cigarette. He was only about thirty feet in front of us.

"I can hit him from here," I said. While he was slightly turned, I made a lightning ball and threw it at him. I missed, and the blue-green sphere popped against the truck behind him. The soldier threw his cigarette down, then turned around to see what had made the noise.

"You missed," Tessa said.

"Yeah, I know." I quickly formed another one and threw it. This one caught him square in the back, dropping him to the ground. "Let's go."

We moved in until we were next to the man, hidden from the rest of the convoy by the truck.

"There's someone else in the truck's cab," Tessa said.

"I'll take care of it." I made another ball and lobbed it into the truck's cab. There was a flash of blue light, then the sound of a head hitting the dashboard. "Got him."

We got down on our hands and knees and crawled underneath the truck, coming up at its rear. The dented grill of the truck behind it was only six feet back. It looked as if it had rear-ended the truck in front of it then backed off. There were soldiers in the truck's cab.

"There are men in there," I said. "They'll see if we open the back door. I'll have to take them out."

"What's the door like?" Tessa asked.

I looked up from beneath the bumper. There were two doors. A thick chain with a padlock was wrapped between the door handles.

"It's locked with a chain."

"How do we get that off?" Tessa asked.

"I'll check the driver for keys."

As I started to crawl back, there was a massive blast of electricity, blowing the doors off their hinges and into the windshield of the truck behind us. For a moment we both froze, unsure of what had just happened.

"Zeus found his power," Tessa said.

"So much for stealth," I said.

Tessa and I crawled back under the center of the truck as soldiers began running toward us. Zeus jumped down off the truck's bed, his legs almost within reach of us. Electricity was sparking between his fingers and legs. He tore the smoking RESAT off his chest and flung it to the ground, then began blasting everything and everyone around him. "Eat lightning!" he shouted.

"Zeus!" I whispered loudly.

Zeus stopped and looked around. "Who said that?"

"Down here. It's me, Michael."

"Michael?" He crouched down. "Where did you come from?"

"Get down here. Fast."

He got on his knees and crawled under the truck. He stopped when he saw Tessa. "That explains why I was suddenly so powerful."

"I've always made you a better man than you are," Tessa said. "No hello, sweetheart?"

"I was a little busy," he said.

"It's good to see you too," she said coldly.

"I take it you two know each other," I said.

Tessa's eyes narrowed. "I thought I did."

Zeus said, "It wasn't all my fault. . . ."

"Great, you have history," I said. "You can settle this when no one's trying to kill us."

Tessa pointed a finger at Zeus. "Later," she said. "We'll talk later."

"Can't wait," Zeus mumbled beneath his breath.

"Can you sense anyone else?" I asked Tessa.

"There's someone over in that truck," Tessa said. "I don't recognize the smell."

"Do you know who it is?" I asked Zeus.

"No. We were all blindfolded."

"Let's get them," I said.

The truck was in the far row closest to the mountain, two vehicles back from where we were. It was dark, as Zeus had blown the lights out of the trucks around us. As we crept toward it, we could hear the shouting of soldiers, but the only soldiers we could see were either unconscious or electrocuted. "Keep your eyes open," I said.

From under the truck I saw a pair of boots. I made a lightning ball and threw it at the soldier. It exploded against his shin, dropping him to the ground. Then Zeus and I slunk around the back, while Tessa stayed sheltered next to its back wheel.

"Can you blow off its lock?" I asked Zeus.

"Yes, give me a hand," he said to Tessa, reaching his hand out to her.

"I'll do it from here," she said.

Zeus slid around the side of the truck, checked for soldiers, then pointed at the door and fired. Amplified by Tessa, the heat of his electricity actually melted the metal latch around the lock. "It's open," he whispered.

I ran around and pulled back one of the doors. McKenna was standing inside. Her skin was red and smoke was rising off of her. She had already melted through her cuffs, and her RESAT was on the ground and smoking as well.

"McKenna!"

"Michael?"

"Get down here, fast."

She ran to the end of the truck and jumped down. "It's so good to see you," she said. "What's happening? I'm suddenly superpowerful. My RESAT just exploded."

"It's me," Tessa said.

McKenna looked at her quizzically. "Tesla?"

"Long story," she said. "And it's Tessa now."

"Come on. We've got to rescue the others," I said. "Who's next?"

Suddenly there was a burst of gunfire. Bullets hit next to me on the truck.

"That was close," Zeus said.

"Looks like they've got night-vision goggles," I said.

"I have an idea," McKenna said. "Everyone close your eyes on the count of three. One, two, three."

We covered our eyes. McKenna stood up and flashed so brightly that even with my eyes covered I could see the light. She had literally turned the night to day.

When I opened my eyes she was crouched back down next to me. "That was crazy," I said. "They could all see you."

"They could see us anyway with their night-vision goggles," she said. "I just took care of that."

"I bet they're all blind now," Zeus said.

"Let's get out of here," I said. "Who's next?"

"I can't sense anyone," Tessa said.

I knew that there was a weakness in my plan. Tessa wouldn't be able to detect Ostin, Jack, or Wade. We needed to find Ian.

"They must be farther back. Let's keep going."

The four of us crept single file down between the trucks. Suddenly Tessa pointed. "There," she said.

Zeus and I crept low to the cab of the truck. The driver's-side window was open and I could hear Peruvian folk music playing from inside the cab. I produced a lightning ball about the size of a cantaloupe, then lobbed it into the cab's open window. It exploded louder than any I had made before. We ran around to the rear, and Zeus blew off the back door. Then McKenna and I climbed in while Zeus and Tessa stood watch. Ian was inside waiting for us. "Tesla sure makes me see a long way," he said.

"It's Tessa," she and McKenna said simultaneously.

McKenna melted off his bands. "I'm glad we found you," I said. "We need your help finding everyone else."

"We've got other problems," he said. "The soldiers are gathering on both sides. There's thousands of them behind us, about a hundred yards that way," he said, pointing toward the back of the convoy. "They're getting ready to move in."

"Are we surrounded?"

"Just on the road."

The sky was beginning to lighten a little as dawn was coming. "They're probably waiting for daylight. Where are the rest of our guys?"

"You passed Ostin," he said. "He's back there. The last I saw of the others, they were behind us."

"All the way back?"

"No. Maybe ten, fifteen trucks back."

We ran two trucks back and freed Ostin, who was overjoyed to see us all.

"What's the plan?" he asked.

"Simple," Tessa said. "Find everyone, run away."

"Who are you?" Ostin said, looking at her.

"Tessa," she said.

"Like Tesla," he said.

"Almost," she said.

"What do you do?"

"I make people more electric."

"Cool," he said.

"Wade's there," Ian said. "Seven trucks back. Just behind the jeep with the machine gun. But there are soldiers everywhere. Some are walking around."

"We better get off the road," I said.

We returned to the shadow of the jungle, passing all the trucks between us and Wade. When we reached Wade's truck, Ian stopped us. "There are soldiers in his truck and the truck next to him."

"I'll clear the way," Zeus said. "Turn it on, Tessa." He reached out and blasted both trucks with such force that it actually rocked them.

"Looks like we're good," Ian said. "For a minute."

We ran to the truck and opened the back door. Wade was still bound to the wall and unable to move. Ian hadn't mentioned that he wasn't alone.

"Stop!" a soldier shouted, pointing his gun at me. I pulsed, knocking the man back against the wall.

I ran in and grabbed Wade's bands and melted through them. He looked at me in disbelief. "Michael. Where did you come from?"

"Idaho," I said. "Let's get out of here."

"Did you find Jack?"

"Not yet," I said. "We've just got him and Taylor to rescue, then we're out of here."

We climbed down from the truck bed.

"Sorry, man," Ian said. "I don't know how I missed that guy in there."

"It's okay," I said. "I didn't. Where are Taylor and Jack?"

"I can't see them."

"What do you mean? You can't see that far?"

"No, with Tessa around I can see past the last truck. They're just not in any of them. They're gone."

"What do you mean, they're gone?" Wade said. "You've got to find Jack."

"I'm telling you, he's not here. Neither of them are."

"But you said you saw them earlier," I said.

"They were with us when we left."

I looked at Ostin, hoping he had an idea. He just shrugged. "Maybe they escaped."

I turned back to Ian. "So far all the transport trucks had big chains on back. Look for chains."

"All right." He was quiet a moment, then said, "I see one. It's the truck Taylor was in, it's open. But she's not there."

"How can you tell it's the one Taylor was in?" I asked.

"There's still electric residue." He kept looking. "I can see another truck open. There are leg manacles." He turned to me. "Jack escaped."

"Or someone let them go," Ostin said. "Are they together?"

"I don't know."

"Can you track Taylor like you did back at the academy?"

"I might be able to follow her residue. We've got to get close to the truck she was in."

"How far down?" I asked.

"About fifteen more trucks. But there are soldiers all along here."

"Back to the jungle," I said.

Fortunately, the farther back we went, the more the soldiers seemed unaware that their prisoners had escaped. They were just talking or sleeping, waiting for the road jam to clear. When we got to Taylor's truck, there was a RESAT lying on the ground with cut bands.

"This is where she was," Ian said.

"Her RESAT was cut off."

"It had to be turned off first," I said. "Or it would kill her."

"Who would cut it off?" Zeus asked.

"Probably the same guy who took them out," Ostin said, pointing at two soldiers lying facedown on the ground.

"Where did she go?" I asked Ian.

Ian looked around for a moment, then pointed south toward the trees. "Two sets of footprints. They ran off into the jungle."

"Jack and Taylor?"

"I don't know. But I can't see Jack anywhere else."

"Let's go," I said. When everyone else had disappeared into the jungle, I stopped at the side of the road and raised both hands.

"What are you doing?" Ostin asked. "They'll see you!"

Suddenly the sound of machine guns erupted from the hillside.

"They're firing at us!" Zeus shouted.

"No," I said. "They're ours. Let's get out of here."

All around us the soldiers began jumping out of their trucks, pulling out their weapons. As Jaime had planned, they were facing the opposite direction as us as we plunged unseen into the dark jungle.

19

Bounty Hunter

Taylor woke, groggy and dis-
oriented. She was moving, she could tell that, but not by her own
power. Someone was carrying her over his shoulder, fireman-style.
Her stomach hurt where the man's shoulder dug into it. The man
carrying her was muscular and lean, but panting heavily. *Who is it?*
She focused on his thoughts.

*I've got to rest. If I could get close enough to get his gun. Too bad he's
got that helmet. If Taylor could just reboot him . . .*

Taylor recognized Jack's thoughts.

I don't know how much longer I can go without water.

A few minutes later Jack said out loud, "C'mon, dude. I've got to
rest. We've been walking for hours."

"And we've yonks to go, mate," the voice said with an Australian
accent. "Keep walkin'."

Put down that gun, and we'll see how tough you are.

162

First chance I get I'm bucking wild on you.

Taylor felt guilty letting Jack carry her, but she was too weak to walk on her own. Her joints felt like rubber. *What did they do to me?*

Ten minutes later, Jack carried her over a stream. He slipped on a rock and caught himself before he fell, but not without twisting his ankle. She could feel his pain in his thoughts. When they reached the other side, he stumbled and, protecting Taylor, fell to his knees, then side, letting Taylor fall on top of him.

"Get up!" the man shouted.

"What are you going to do, shoot me?"

"I might."

"Do it. Then you can carry her yourself."

"Up with you!" the man shouted.

"I need rest. And I need water."

There was a short pause, then the man said, "All right, ya bludger. Just five minutes. You can drink from the stream."

Jack forced himself to his feet.

"Don't try anythin' stupid or I'll shoot ya both."

"I'm not running," Jack said as he stumbled over to the stream. He knelt down on the bank and splashed water in his face, then cupped his hands and drank from it.

"I'm sure it's got all sorts of nasties," the man said, drinking from his own canteen.

Jack took another drink. Then he walked back over and fell down next to Taylor. He noticed her eyes fluttering. She forced them open and looked into his eyes. "Jack?" she said weakly.

"Shhh," he said, shaking his head.

"Where are we?"

He put his finger over his mouth and tilted his head toward the man. For the first time Taylor saw who Jack had been thinking about. The Australian was tall, dressed in the black-and-red uniform of an Elgen district leader. He was holding a pistol. He also wore the attack helmet the Elgen donned whenever they came after her, which explained why she couldn't reboot him. He suddenly looked at her.

"So yer awake, are ya?"

"Who are you?" Taylor asked.

"An opportunist," the man said. "You're a very valuable catch, sheila. There's a bounty on yer head. Two and a half million soles. That's almost a million dollars American. And my pack mule here," he said, pointing his pistol at Jack, "has a fifty-thousand-dollar bounty."

The man walked closer, but kept his distance. "Now that you're awake, let me tell you how this works. If you try to escape, I shoot yer friend here. If he tries to escape, I shoot you. And don't pretend you don't care. I was in Pasadena at the academy when yer group shut it down. I know about you Electroclan. You look out for each other."

"Where's everyone else?" Taylor asked.

"No idea," he said. "Probably still with the army, 'less someone rescued them. I 'spect that's what the whole bloody jam up was about."

"Why are we with you?"

"The Peruvian army had no interest in collecting all that bounty— but I do. And since I know how yer group works, I looked at the path to Lima and decided where yer friends were mostly likely to try to rescue you. They didn't disappoint. In all the confusion, I snatched you and yer friend here and headed off into the jungle before the army knew what happened."

"Where are you taking us?"

"I just told you. To collect the bounty."

"Where?"

"Why would you need to know that?" He pointed his pistol at Jack. "Time's up, mate. Get up."

Jack looked impossibly weary but still forced himself to his feet. Then he bent over to lift Taylor.

"It's okay," she said. "I can walk."

"He can carry you, doll face," the man said.

"I told you I can walk," Taylor said. "If he helps me." She took Jack's hand.

Jack suddenly understood. *Can you read my mind?*

Taylor subtly nodded.

Is there another reason you want to walk? Jack thought.

She nodded.

To slow us down?

She nodded again.

Do you think someone's trying to save us?

"Yes," she said.

"Yes what?" the guard asked.

Taylor squeezed Jack's hand. "Yes. I can walk."

20

Electrical Residue

"Who was that firing?" Ostin asked.

"It's just a machine," I said. "Jaime and his friends set it up."

"You found Jaime?"

"He found me," I said.

"And who is Tessa?"

"I'll tell you later."

We had traveled nearly a mile from the road before the gunfire started to slow. I wondered if the army had discovered they were fighting robotic turrets instead of real people.

Suddenly, Ian stopped walking. "This is really weird," he said, looking around.

"What's weird?" I asked.

"The trail's hard to follow, because Taylor's residue only shows up occasionally on trees and bushes. I should see it on the ground."

"Maybe someone's carrying her," Ostin said.

"That could be," Ian said.

"We should measure the depth of the footprints," Ostin said.

Ian and Ostin both crouched down next to one of the footprints.

"Could I get some light?" Ostin asked. McKenna lit up her hand and held it close. "Thanks," Ostin said. He ran his hand along an indentation in the rich soil. "Hmm," he said. "Interesting."

"Are those Taylor's?" I asked.

"Not unless Taylor has size eleven feet and is wearing boots," Ostin said.

"One of these footprints is deeper than the other," Ian said. "I think Ostin's right. Someone's carrying her. That's why I'm only seeing her residue when she brushes up against something."

"Can you tell if it's Jack carrying her?" Wade asked.

"Why would Jack be carrying her?" McKenna asked.

"Let's just keep going," I said.

We hurried on through the thick jungle with Ian in front and McKenna lighting the way for the rest of us.

After an hour Ian said, "We're gaining on them."

"How can you tell?" I asked.

"The residue is fresher."

We crossed over a stream. The sun was peeking above the canopy and it was now light enough that we could see without McKenna's help.

"Look," Ian said. He pointed to a grouping of footprints in the dirt. "It looks like they stopped here. Whoever was carrying Taylor must have put her down. I can see residue everywhere." He pointed at the ground. "Now there are three prints. Taylor must be walking on her own."

"Whoever was carrying her must have gotten tired," I said. "Let's keep going."

We increased our pace. About forty-five minutes later, Ian said, "I see them."

"Is it Jack?" Wade asked.

"Yes. Jack, Taylor, and an Elgen guard. He's holding a gun on them."

"How far ahead of us are they?"

"Maybe a mile. Wait." He turned his head a little. "There are trucks. It looks like he's meeting up with someone. There's a dirt road. . . . It looks like . . . six more Elgen guards."

"Can we reach them before they meet up?" I asked.

"No. They're just about there."

"And they've got trucks?"

"Two of them."

"We've got to get there before they drive away," I said. "Hurry!"

In spite of our weariness, we again quickened our pace, this time to almost a run. Ten minutes later Ian said, "They've reached the trucks."

"Faster!" I shouted even though I doubted we could be.

A few minutes later Ian said, "They've tied up Taylor and Jack, and they're putting them in the trucks. But I don't think they're in a hurry. Some of them are sitting down."

"Thank goodness," Ostin said, panting.

A few minutes later I asked Ian, "What's going on?"

"It looks like they're arguing."

"Who's arguing?" I asked.

"The guards."

"Let's hope they keep arguing," I said. Just a few minutes later we reached them, stopping less than fifty yards from the guards. I couldn't see the men, but through the trees I could see the bright red of one of the trucks.

"They're still fighting," Ian said. "I think it's getting pretty heated."

"Are they armed?"

"To the teeth. Each of them has a sidearm. Plus a knife, baton, and grenades—standard Elgen utility belt."

"We need a plan," I said.

"On it," Ostin said. He cradled his head in his hand for a moment, then said, "The most important thing is to draw them away from Taylor and Jack."

"And not get killed," Wade said.

"That too," Ostin said. He found a stick, then, kneeling on one knee, drew a circle in the dirt. He handed the stick to Ian. "Here, draw their layout."

Ian crouched down as we all gathered around him.

"This is the road in, these rectangles on the left represent their two trucks," Ian said. "Here's where the men are standing. This is where we are." He handed the stick back to Ostin.

Ostin looked at the diagram for a moment, then said, "All right, here's the plan. First we move closer, to about here. . . ." He touched the stick in the dirt. "Then we split up." He dragged the stick in a clockwise arch. "Zeus, Tessa, Ian, and Wade circle around to the right. Zeus and Tessa position themselves here, at three o'clock, Wade and Ian keep going wide, circling around to the rear of the farthest truck."

"And free Jack," Wade said.

"Exactly. At the same time, Michael, McKenna, and I will go around the opposite way. Michael positions himself at eight o'clock, here while McKenna and I free Taylor. At the signal, Zeus blasts from here, and Michael pulses from here. If any of them try to run toward the trucks, Michael gets them here. If they try to run behind the back truck, Ian and Wade can tackle them. Got it?"

"What's the signal?" I asked.

"I'll whistle," Ostin said. "That way they'll look toward me and won't know what hit them when you and Zeus strike."

"All right," I said. "Everyone ready?"

Everyone nodded.

"Let's do it."

We crept forward another twenty yards toward the clearing until Ostin signaled us to stop. We were close enough to not only see the guards but hear them arguing about how much money each of them would get. There were two men facing toward us. One of them was red in the face and shouting at a tall guard with his back to us. "We stole these trucks. We got shot at!"

The tall guard spoke with an Australian accent. "You poor wankers stole some trucks? I stole these kids from under the bloody army's nose and dragged them three hours through the whoop-whoop. You get what we agreed on or nothing. That's my final offer."

"I'll show you a final offer," the red-faced man said, reaching for his gun. The Australian guard drew first and shot him twice. Then he shot the man next to him. The other three men put their hands in the air as smoke rose up from the campsite.

When the ringing of the gun had settled, the Australian said, "Bloody crook. Anyone else have a problem with this?"

One of the three quickly replied, "You did what you had to do. It just means more for the rest of us."

"It means more for me," the Australian said. "I did the dirty work, you get what we agreed on." He brandished his pistol. "Or don't you agree?"

"No worries," the man said.

The Australian laughed as he returned his pistol to its holster. "No worries, mate."

I counted the guards. Two down, four left. "I thought you saw seven," I said to Ian.

"I must have counted wrong," he said.

"Let's move," I said.

Ostin grabbed McKenna's hand and we moved to the left while everyone else moved right. I stopped at the designated place while Ostin and McKenna moved past me to the truck Taylor was in. Ostin whistled. The men all looked back.

"What was that?" the Australian asked.

One of them shouted, "Over there by the—"

A lightning bolt stopped him. Then a second flash knocked over the tall guard. Two guards ran toward our position. I reached out and pulsed, knocking them both backward and unconscious. Zeus and Tessa emerged from the trees.

"They're out," Zeus said. "I'm surprised they're still alive. With Tessa around I don't know my own strength."

"Let's handcuff them," I said.

"Why don't we just electrocute them and be done with them?" Tessa said.

I looked at her. "We don't do it that way," I said. "Unless we have to."

"They do," she said.

"We're not them," I said. I knelt over the men I'd shocked. One was on his back, and I rolled him over onto his stomach and handcuffed him, then I did the same to the other, while Zeus and Tessa handcuffed the other two. As I was undoing their utility belts I heard someone say, "What does a girl need to do around here to get some attention?"

I looked up. Taylor was walking toward me.

"Taylor!" I ran to her. We hugged, then she pressed her lips against mine. When we parted, her eyes were locked on mine. "You have no idea how good it is to see you," she said. "I wondered if I would ever see you again."

"You didn't think I would come for you?"

"I knew you'd try," she said. "But there're five thousand of them and only one of you."

"Yeah, the odds were a little off," I said.

"For them," she said. Then she laughed, which was beautiful to hear.

"What happened here?" I asked, touching the cut on her forehead.

She shrugged. "Car accident," she said. We kissed again.

"Hey," Zeus said. "Get a room."

Taylor looked over at him and smiled. "I'm glad to see you in one piece."

Zeus grinned. "That makes two of us."

Tessa just stared at Taylor with a confused expression. "What is Tara doing here?"

"She's not Tara," Zeus said.

"This is Taylor," I said. "Number seventeen."

Tessa still looked confused. "But you look just like Tara."

"They're twins, bagel head," Zeus said.

"Twins? You must be identical," Tessa said.

"Only on the outside," Ian said, walking up to us.

Taylor looked at Ian and hugged him. "Thank you for coming after us."

"No woman left behind," he said.

"Where's Jack?" I asked.

"Still in the truck," Ian said. "Wade's untying him."

"He probably needs some help," McKenna said. She began walking back toward the truck. Suddenly we heard Jack shout, followed by a gunshot.

"What was that?" I said.

"Look out!" Tessa shouted. An Elgen guard came around the side of the truck pointing his gun at us. Zeus fired full force, blowing the gun out of his hands and knocking him back nearly twenty feet.

"Where'd he come from?" I shouted. We all ran toward the truck.

"I didn't see him," Ian said. "I'm sorry, I didn't see him."

As I came around the truck my heart stopped.

"Oh no," Abigail said.

Jack was kneeling on the ground holding Wade in his arms. There was blood everywhere.

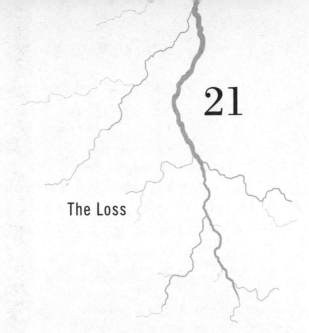

21

The Loss

As we got to Jack's side, he was pressing down on Wade's abdomen. Blood was rising up between his fingers. Wade was shaking and his skin was pale and waxlike.

"You're going to be okay, buddy," Jack said, his voice trembling. He looked up at us. "Someone help me stop the bleeding."

"It hurts . . . ," Wade said. His voice was slurred.

"You're a warrior," Jack said. "Remember you're a warrior."

"It hurts. . . ."

Abigail fell to her knees next to Wade and touched his leg. Even though he was still shaking, his face relaxed. "Thank you," he said softly.

"I can cauterize it," McKenna said. "Ian, tell me where the injury is."

Ian didn't answer.

Pulling Ian back, I whispered, "How bad is it?"

Ian shook his head, then said just loud enough for me to hear, "His body is filling with blood."

Wade's entire body shook. "I don't think . . ."

"Stay with me, buddy," Jack said frantically. "You're a warrior."

"I don't think . . ." His chin quivered.

"Are you a warrior or wimp?!" Jack said, tears streaming down his cheeks. "Warrior or wimp?!"

Wade looked up at him. "You're . . . the only friend I've ever had. Thank you for being . . ."

Jack's eyes filled with new tears. "Don't leave me, buddy. Please. Wade . . ."

Wade trembled. "I . . ." He swallowed, then mumbled, "I . . . I'm . . . sorry." Then he went silent. His head fell back.

"No!" Jack shouted. He began pressing on Wade's chest, but it did nothing but force more blood out of his wound.

"Start his heart!" Jack said to me. "Michael, shock him. Please."

I didn't move. I knew it wouldn't help.

"Please."

"All right," I said. I knelt down. "You need to let go of him."

"No," he said.

I shocked him. Jack shouted out with pain, and Wade's whole body jerked but nothing happened.

"Nothing," Ian said.

"Again, Michael!" Jack said.

I looked at him. "Jack . . ."

"Please."

"All right." I jolted him again.

Again Jack shouted.

I looked at Ian and he shook his head.

"Again!" Jack pled. "Please, try again."

"Jack," I said. "He's gone."

"No. He can't be."

I put my hand on Jack's back. "I'm sorry. But he's gone."

Jack wrapped his arms around Wade's head. "No," he sobbed. "No, no, no."

We all looked at him, fighting our own emotions.

"It's my fault," Jack said.

"No, it's not," I said. "It's not your fault."

"I made him come here," Jack said. "I made him. I've killed my best friend."

22

The Next Step

Time seemed frozen, disjointed like broken sequences cut out of a horror movie. Jack's hands and torso were drenched in blood and he was screaming in anguish. All of us were crying, even Tessa, who didn't know either of them. During it all one of the guards woke and began shouting at us to let him go. The emotion of the moment piqued my anger. "Shut up!" I shouted.

"Let me out of this!" he shouted back.

I stood and walked to him. When he saw the fierce anger on my face his own expression turned from anger to fear. I had to control myself so that I only shocked him unconscious. Then Zeus and I dragged him out of the clearing into the jungle, crammed leaves into his mouth, and tied his shirt around his face to keep him from making any more noise. We were doing it for his benefit. In Jack's current state he would gladly silence him permanently. Then Zeus, Ian, and

I dragged the other guards into the jungle, including the two who had been shot. There was no need to tie up the guard who had shot Wade. He hadn't survived Zeus's blast.

Abigail found a wool blanket in one of the trucks, and she and McKenna draped it over Wade's body. It was nearly an hour before Jack finally left Wade's side. He sat alone at the edge of the clearing, softly crying.

Grief is a powerful force that settles in the heart like a dark, heavy fog. It was familiar territory to me. I was eight years old when I lost my father.

Everyone wandered off to their own place. Ian was in a daze, muttering that he should have seen the guard, and he walked off alone. Abigail, Tessa, and Zeus sat together outside the clearing, near the spot we had first entered. McKenna and Ostin went for a walk while Taylor and I sought refuge in the front seat of the red truck. I just held her in silence. So much had happened since we'd separated, but neither of us felt like talking about it. The gladness we felt at being together again was muted by shock and grief.

An hour or so later Ostin walked up to us alone. He opened the back door of the cab and climbed in. His eyes were as swollen as ours. "I can't believe this," he said. "I can't believe Wade's gone." He looked at me anxiously. "Is your mom safe?"

"She got out," I said. "She's with the voice."

"I wish we were," Taylor said softly. "What are we going to do now?"

I looked through the windshield at Jack, then back at Taylor. "We've got to get out of here before someone finds us."

"And go where?" Ostin asked.

"Jaime gave me the name of a hostel in Cuzco. We'll drive there."

"Jaime?" Taylor said. "You mean the guy who took us up the river?"

I nodded.

"How did you find him?" Ostin asked.

"He found me," I said. "Do you remember that tribesman we saw on the way in?"

Ostin nodded. "The Amacarra."

"They saved me from the Elgen. Then they brought Tessa and me to Jaime."

Taylor said, "Who is Tessa?"

"Tessa was one of Hatch's kids until she escaped from the Starxource plant six months ago. The Amacarra were hiding her. When the Peruvian army started moving in, the tribe took us up the river to Jaime. We hiked through the jungle until we found a place to stop the convoy."

"How did you know where we were?" Ostin asked.

"The voice," I said.

"You talked to the voice?" he asked.

"Jaime had a radio." I raked my hand back through my hair. "Things aren't going well. Hatch has taken control of the Elgen. The voice wanted me to rescue you, then go to Lima and sink the Elgen boats."

"What boats?" Taylor asked.

"The Elgen run their empire from a fleet of boats. Hatch has gathered the fleet and is taking them to an island where he plans to build a base where they can create weapons of mass destruction."

"This just keeps getting better," Taylor said.

"At least we're still alive," Ostin said.

Taylor looked at him as the pain of his words surfaced. "Not all of us."

Ostin winced.

"I just want to get out of this stupid place," Taylor said. "The Peruvians think we're terrorists and want to publicly hang us." She breathed out slowly. "I just want to go back to my old life. But it doesn't exist anymore, does it?"

I shook my head. "Not the way it was. Until we stop Hatch, he'll just keep coming."

"Ignorance was bliss," she said.

Just then McKenna walked up to us. Ostin opened his door, then slid over so McKenna could sit next to him. He took her hand, which surprised me. Outside of his mother, I had never seen Ostin even touch a girl. Clearly a lot had happened since we'd been separated at the Starxource plant.

Taylor said, "So if we sink this boat, then what?"

"We'll go back to America," I said.

"What boat are you talking about?" McKenna asked.

"The Elgen boat," Ostin said.

"The *Ampere?*" she said.

I looked at her. "You know about the *Ampere?*"

"I've been on it. It was a long time ago. Before Hatch locked us up."

"Hatch is bringing the entire Elgen fleet to Peru. The voice wants us to sink the *Ampere.*"

"How do you sink a huge boat?" McKenna asked. "The *Ampere* is . . . huge."

"I could come up with a dozen ways," Ostin said. "At least."

"How would we even get there?" Taylor asked. "You know the army will be watching the roads out of here. They'll probably have roadblocks."

"Maybe not this one," I said, looking at the dirt road. "It wasn't on the map."

"It's probably just an old logging road," Ostin said. "They might not even know about it."

"Those Elgen guards felt safe enough on it to use it," Taylor said. "Do you think it goes all the way to Cuzco?"

"I don't know," I said. "But you're right, we can't go back to Puerto Maldonado. I say we follow it as far as it goes, then hike the rest of the way out of the jungle. At least we'll bypass any road-blocks."

Taylor's voice fell. "What do we do about Wade? We can't leave him here."

"We'll take him to Cuzco and give him a proper burial."

"Even if we have to carry him?" she asked.

"I don't think Jack would leave him," I said. "But it's up to him."

Everyone went quiet. Finally I turned to McKenna. "How's Ian doing?"

"Not well," she said. "He's blaming himself for not seeing the guy."

"He can't see everything," Taylor said.

"He *can*," Ostin said. "He just didn't."

"That's not helpful," Taylor said. "Don't you dare say that around him. He feels bad enough."

"I'm not dumb," Ostin said.

"So what do we do once we're in Cuzco?" McKenna asked.

"We'll meet up with Jaime and make our plan," I said.

"Another plan," Taylor said. "I'm sick of plans. Someday I want someone to say 'We're going shopping.'"

"If only," I said.

Taylor laid her head against my shoulder. I pulled her into me. Everyone just fell silent.

A few minutes later Abigail and Zeus walked up to us. Zeus opened the truck door. "What's going on?" he asked.

"We were just talking about our next step," Ostin said.

"Which is getting out of this lame country," Abigail said.

"We need to go to Lima and sink the Elgen's main boat," I said.

"What?" Abigail said.

"You're planning to sink the *Ampere*?" Zeus said.

"That's the plan," I said.

"It's not my plan," Zeus said, shaking his head. "Maybe you've forgotten, but I don't do boats. I'm getting out of this death hole."

"The thing is," Abigail said, "it's not just the army who wants to kill us, it's the entire country. They've probably put our pictures on television."

"No television," Ostin said. "There's no electricity."

"Whatever," Abigail said. "Then in the newspaper. And if you haven't noticed, we don't look like Peruvians. We stand out."

"She's right," Taylor said.

"Why do you think the *Ampere* will be in Lima?" Zeus asked. "It's in Europe."

"The voice," I replied. "He told us that Hatch is bringing the Elgen fleet to Peru."

Zeus shook his head. "I doubt it. Chairman Schema would never go for it. He likes Italy too much."

"There is no Chairman Schema anymore," I said.

"What do you mean?"

"Hatch has taken over the entire corporation."

"That's not good," Zeus said.

Abigail groaned. "All the more reason to get out of this lousy country before our luck runs out."

"And then what?" Ostin said. "Wait for the Elgen to grow stronger and come find us?"

"We stand a much better chance of not being found if we stop throwing ourselves at them," Abigail said.

"She's got a point," McKenna said. "And worst case, we'll at least have a real life for a few years." She frowned. "I'm sorry, but I'm tired."

I exhaled slowly, then rested my head in my hand. "Me too."

"We all are," Taylor said. "And sad."

I looked back over at Jack. Seeing him broke my heart. Taylor put her hand on my back.

"When do we leave?" Zeus asked.

"We better wait until morning," I said. "I don't think we should drive at night."

"Is there anything to eat?" Ostin asked.

"There's food and water in the back of the other truck," McKenna said. "It looks like these guys were planning on sticking around."

Taylor said, "We'll get dinner for everyone." She turned to McKenna. "Will you help me heat it?"

"Sure." They both got out of the truck.

"I'll help," Ostin said, climbing down after McKenna.

Taylor leaned in and kissed my cheek. "I'll see you in a minute." The three of them left.

When they were gone, Abigail sighed. "I'm really worried about Jack."

I looked back over at him again. He was still in the same place, his head bowed. "We probably shouldn't leave him alone," I said.

"He said he wants to be alone," Zeus said.

"That doesn't mean he should be," Abigail replied. She took Zeus's hand. "Let's go see him."

"I'll come with you," I said.

The three of us walked over to where Jack was sitting and sat down next to him. He glanced up at us, then looked back down. I had no idea what to say.

Fortunately, Abigail was naturally gifted at comforting people. She put her hand on Jack's shoulder. "I'm sorry I can't take away the kind of pain you're feeling."

"I need to feel the pain," Jack said. "It would be wrong not to." We were all silent for a moment.

Abigail said, "You know, when we couldn't find you, Wade was so upset. He kept saying, 'We've got to find Jack.' He pushed us along. You meant that much to him."

Jack covered his eyes with his hand. None of us had ever seen him cry before. It looked so foreign, like Superman with a broken arm. After a minute he looked up at us. "Wade had no one. His parents abandoned him. Every foster home he went to threw him out. His grandmother was . . . a loser." He put down his head.

"He had you," Abigail said.

"Lucky him," Jack replied sarcastically.

"He *was* lucky to have you," Abigail said.

Jack exploded. "Lucky? He'd still be alive if it wasn't for me."

Abigail didn't turn away. After a moment she said, "When your home was burned down, you said, 'I made my choices, I'll live with them.' Shouldn't you allow Wade the same? No one forced him to come. He made his choices."

Jack didn't answer.

Abigail took his hand. "Everyone dies. You made Wade's life worth living."

Jack bowed his head again. Abigail wrapped her arms around him and held him. He began to shake.

A minute later Zeus said, "I'm sorry, man. Wade was a good guy. He really loved you."

Without looking up Jack said, "I was a jerk to him. I was always on his case."

"He knew you loved him. That's why he loved you so much," Abigail said.

All of us sat quietly for a moment, then Zeus added, "So do we." Zeus stood up and walked away.

After another minute I said, "He's right, you know."

Jack couldn't answer. He just broke down and wept.

23

Final Salute

That night we ate a hot dinner of pork-and-bean burritos and some kind of soup with chicken claws in it. Everyone ate except for Jack and Ian, who claimed not to be hungry. A while after dinner Jack and I put Wade's wrapped body in the back of the blue truck to keep it from animals, then we all found a place to sleep in the other truck bed, or inside the trucks, except for Jack, who slept outside on the ground.

The next morning I woke to the sound of digging. Jack had found a shovel in the truck and was digging a grave. I walked over to him. He had washed the blood off his face and arms, but his shirt was stained. He was soaked in sweat and he looked as if he hadn't slept at all.

"Need any help?"

He shook his head.

"You don't want to take him with us?"

"It doesn't matter where he's buried. No one in America cares."

I just looked down. After a few minutes I said, "We were planning on leaving around noon. We're going to take the trucks and drive to Cuzco." I looked at Jack, then said, "After we have a service for Wade."

He looked up, then said, "Would you say something? I don't know how to. He respected you."

"I'd be honored," I said.

Shortly after Jack finished digging, Zeus and Jack laid Wade's wrapped body in the grave, and we all gathered around. McKenna and Ostin had fashioned a small cross from tree branches, and Abigail and Taylor had gathered dozens of brightly colored jungle flowers, enough to completely cover the grave. I stood at the head of the grave next to the cross. It seemed as if even the jungle had quieted for my eulogy.

"To be honest, when I first met Wade I didn't like him very much. I only knew him as a bully. In school, there's a lot said about bullies. We hear about what bad people they are. Adults act as if bullying only takes place in school. But adults bully one another all the time. Some married people bully each other. Some bosses bully their employees. Businesses bully businesses. Countries bully countries. It's like the no-bullying rule changes after you're an adult.

"Still, they tell us to hate bullies. But maybe that's the exact opposite of what we should do. Maybe if they were treated well, they wouldn't bully. Wade wasn't born a bully; he was taught it by those who should have taken care of him.

"After he became my friend, he showed me what kind of person he really was. He was loyal and brave. He had the chance to go home and the Elgen probably would have left him alone, but he wouldn't do it. He wouldn't leave his friends. And that makes him a hero. I know we're all going to miss him. I'm going to miss him. But most of all, Jack will miss him."

I looked at Jack. His face was streaked with tears.

"Wade's last words were to Jack. He thanked him for being his friend. His only friend. Then he said he was sorry. But Wade had nothing to be sorry about. He showed his true self. He always wanted to be a warrior like Jack. And in the end, he was." I took a deep breath. "That's all I have to say."

Taylor sidled up to me and took my hand.

"Thank you," Jack said.

Everyone stood around quietly to see what Jack would do. He looked down for a moment, then he saluted. After a few more minutes Zeus began shoveling the dirt back into the grave. When he was done, Taylor, McKenna, and Abigail covered the mound with flowers.

24

An Ugly Mob

Zeus, Taylor, Ian, and I checked the guards to make sure they were secure. Their leader, the guard who had carried Jack and Taylor into the jungle, tried to negotiate with us.

"Come on, mates. We can work somethin' out."

"We've seen how you work things out," I said.

"I can get you money."

Zeus crouched down next to him. "How? By selling one of us? Do you think we're stupid?"

The man said nothing.

Zeus's eyes narrowed. "I remember you. You were at the academy."

"I was at the gate," he said. "I used to protect you. All of you."

Zeus grinned. "You protected me?" He laughed. "Delusions of grandeur."

The man turned away from him.

"Look at me!" Zeus grabbed him by the hair and pulled his head back. "Your friend killed one of our friends."

"He was acting on his own."

"He wouldn't have been here if it wasn't for you." Zeus held his hands up and electricity sparked between his fingers. "The only reason I don't electrocute you right now is because Michael asked me not to. But give me a reason to change my mind."

The man went silent.

"Where's your money?" I asked.

"It's in his back pocket," Ian said.

Zeus rolled him over and took out his wallet. "Here," he said, tossing it to Ian.

"How much is there?" I asked.

Ian rifled through the bills. "About a thousand in Peruvian."

I crouched down next to the man. "Does this road go all the way to Cuzco?"

He didn't answer me.

"There's an anthill over by that tree," Ian said. "Let's drag him over there."

"The road goes to Paucartambo," he said.

"What's that?"

"It's a small village."

"Does the army know about this road?"

"They wouldn't be much of an army if they didn't."

"But you felt safe enough to hide here."

"They weren't expecting us." He turned his head to look at me. "You don't really think you can escape, do you? They've plastered your pictures on newspapers and handbills everywhere. The whole country is looking for you."

"Well, we'll just have to do our best to not let them find us," I said. "Come on, guys."

"Wait. You're not just going to leave me here like this. . . ."

"No," I said. "Ian, add another pair of handcuffs. And if he gives you any trouble"—I looked at the guard—"leave him on the anthill."

* * *

We checked the other three guards for money, then added handcuffs as well. We ended up with more than two thousand seven hundred soles, which Ostin said was more than a thousand dollars. A half hour later I approached Jack, who was sitting on the ground next to Wade's grave.

"We're ready."

He stood. He was no longer crying. His emotions had turned. His face was steely with anger.

I handed him the truck keys. "We're in the blue truck. The guard told us that the road goes all the way through the jungle. We can make it to Cuzco by night."

He nodded, then walked past me to the truck.

Taylor, Ostin, McKenna, and I rode in the truck with Jack, while Zeus, Tessa, Abigail, and Ian rode in the other.

The dirt road continued on for ten miles, opening to an abandoned logging site, then carried on west for another forty miles until, by late afternoon, we emerged from the jungle into Paucartambo, a village nestled between the green slopes of two mountains.

The ancient-looking town was bigger than I thought it would be. The buildings had weathered plaster exteriors with terra-cotta tile roofs and the streets were crowded with people on foot, many dressed in bright Quechuan costumes with ponchos and bowler hats.

As we entered the town, a herd of llamas crossing the main street stopped us.

"Llamas are so funny looking," Taylor said.

"Technically," Ostin said, "they are vicuñas."

"They look like llamas to me," Taylor said.

"'Llama' refers to the whole family of domesticated South American cameloids," Ostin said. "Like we call horses, horses, but they might be quarter horses or Clydesdales or any other kind. Vicuñas are smaller than most other llamas and their fur is more valued than even the alpaca. It's illegal to try to export them."

"I wasn't planning on bringing one home," Taylor said.

"You know, llamas are descended from the camel."

"How did camels get to South America?" McKenna asked.

"I'm glad you asked," Ostin said.

"I'm not," Taylor mumbled.

I lay my head against the window and looked out. I was glad to hear Ostin spouting off again. I wanted to think about anything except Wade. Somehow, Ostin's biology lesson made things seem normal even though they weren't and never would be again.

After the herd had passed we drove slowly around the town.

"Look," Taylor said. "A street market. Can we stop?"

"I don't think that's a good idea," I said.

"Maybe they have something to eat," Ostin said. "I'm hungry."

"Me too," McKenna said. "And thirsty. Can we stop and get some water?"

"I have to use the bathroom," Taylor said.

"They don't have toilets," Ostin said. "Just squatters."

"What's a squatter?" she asked.

"It's just a hole in the ground. And they probably won't have toilet paper."

"Lovely," Taylor said. "I should have gone in the jungle with McKenna."

"All right," I said, pointing to a dirt field at the end of the road. "Let's park over there."

Jack pulled off the road into the vacant lot and put the truck in park. Zeus pulled the other truck up to my side and rolled down his window. "What are we doing?" Zeus asked.

"We're stopping to get something to eat," I said.

He looked back, then said, "All right."

Ostin and I opened the doors, and everyone climbed out except for Jack. Zeus parked the other truck in front of us, and everyone else got out.

The place made me nervous. "We better not stay too long," I said.

Abigail walked up to Jack. "Are you coming?"

"No. I'll wait here."

"Can I get you anything?"

He shook his head. "No."

Abigail touched his arm. "I'll see if I can find some pastries or something."

The street market was swarming with people and our presence did not go unnoticed. We were the only foreigners on the street, and the natives were not shy about staring at us, which made me very nervous. I held Taylor's hand as we walked through the square.

"I wish Idaho had street markets," she said. She stopped to look at a colorful poncho, holding it up to her chest. "How do I look?"

"Native," I said.

There was a small mart with a refrigerator near the door. "Hey, they've got Inca Kola," I said "Want one?"

"Sure. Maybe they have a bathroom inside," Taylor replied.

The mart was narrow, no more than ten feet wide but three times as long. Colorful packages of snacks with Spanish writing hung on the walls. I lay our things on one of the small wood tables against the wall.

"I don't see a bathroom," I said. "I wish Ostin was here to translate for us."

"Wait, I remember the word for bathroom." She walked up to the dark-featured man at the counter. "Excuse me. Do you have a *baño?*"

I doubted he understood anything but the last word, but he pointed toward the back of the store. "*El baño, sí.*"

"Two years of high school Spanish just paid off," Taylor said, looking back at me. "See you in a second."

While she was gone, I bought two colas and some bottled water, and brought them over to the table. The table was dirty, but there were napkins so I wet one with a bottle of water and wiped it off. Taylor returned about five minutes later.

"That was gross," she said. "There were flies everywhere." She sat down and I handed her a bottle of cola.

"It's warm," I said.

She frowned. "Don't they have a refrigerator?"

"Yeah. Just no power."

"Why don't they have electricity?"

I cocked my head. "I think that's our fault."

"Oh, right."

I took a swig of my tepid soda. "So when did this thing with Ostin and McKenna start?"

"I think it began back in Idaho," she said. "When McKenna melted through her bands in the truck? Ostin was all goo-goo eyed."

"He did always have a thing for Asian girls. Remember that night at Maddie's party when he just stared at Angel until she freaked?"

"Yeah. Then he told her she was the most beautiful girl in the world." Taylor nodded. "Maybe he's not as dumb with girls as we thought." She took a drink of her cola. "Actually, I think it really started after we lost you in the Starxource plant. I freaked out and blamed Ostin for leaving you behind. I said some pretty mean things. McKenna stood up for him."

Just then two soldiers in camouflage ran past the grocery store.

"Did you see that?" I said.

Taylor turned back. "What?"

"Soldiers just ran by. We've got to go."

"We've got to find the others," Taylor said.

We left our drinks and walked to the door. I looked for more soldiers but didn't see any. Across the street from us I could see Abigail, Zeus, and Tessa trying on hats. We hurried over to them.

Tessa looked up at me from under the brim of a straw hat. "What's up?"

"Soldiers," Taylor said.

"Where?" Zeus asked.

"Two just ran past us," I said. "That way."

"Toward the trucks," Zeus said. "Let's get out of here."

"Where's everyone else?" I asked.

"The last time I saw Ostin and McKenna they were at that table over there," Abigail said. "By that fruit cart. They were buying ponchos."

"And Ian?"

"He decided to hang back with Jack," Tessa said.

"You guys head back," I said. "Taylor and I will find Ostin and McKenna."

While they walked back up the road, Taylor and I headed back toward the fruit cart.

"There they are," Taylor said, pointing. "At that puppet show."

We ran down to them. They were both carrying bags with colorful ponchos and hats.

I grabbed Ostin's arm. "We've got to go."

"Wait," Ostin said. "It's just about over."

"Now!" Taylor said. "We just saw soldiers."

As we hurried back up the street toward the trucks, we noticed a large crowd had gathered near the end of the market adjacent to the field where we had parked the trucks.

Suddenly, Ostin grabbed McKenna's arm and pulled her into a small bakery. He shouted to us, "Guys!" He frantically motioned for us to follow.

"What?" I said, walking into the bakery.

"That's not a crowd, it's a mob. I heard someone shout 'Death to the American terrorists.'"

Just then the baker behind the counter pointed at us, *"Terroristas!"*

Taylor rebooted him. The man put his hand up to his forehead. He looked confused and lost. He spotted us and said, *"A la orden, amigos?"*

"Pastel de canela, por favor," Ostin said, pointing to a pastry. *"Eso."*

"Muy bien," he said, lifting out a bun sprinkled with cinnamon. *"Hablas muy bien el español. Un sol, porfa."*

Ostin handed him a coin.

"How can you think about eating?" Taylor asked.

"It's a distraction," Ostin said.

"For him or for you?" Taylor said.

"Ask him if there's a back way out," I said.

"Hay una salida atrás?" Ostin asked.

"Sí. A través aquí."

"Gracias," Ostin said. He turned to us. "There is."

"Let's go."

The back door opened out into an unpaved alley. Fortunately there was no one there except a beggar who had fallen asleep against a stucco wall.

"This way," I said.

As we got to the top of the passage our hearts froze. "You gotta be kidding me," Ostin said.

In the dirt field there were two army jeeps with mounted machine guns, a large transport truck, a police car, and a crowd of Peruvians who had surrounded the vehicles. Jack and Ian were nowhere to be seen.

"Do you think they caught them?" McKenna asked.

"I'm betting that Ian saw them coming and they ran."

"What do we do now?" Taylor asked. "They've surrounded the trucks."

"They're no good to us now anyway," I said. "We've been identified. Everyone will be looking for them."

"Then how do we get out of here?"

"Look over there," McKenna said.

To the south of the lot was a crowd of several hundred Peruvians. They had surrounded Zeus, Tessa, and Abigail.

"This is bad," I said.

"This is going to be ugly," Ostin said. "It's a freakin' lynch mob."

"Except with Tessa next to him, Zeus could easily kill them all," I said.

"That's all we need," Taylor said. "A massacre by the American terrorists."

"I have an idea," I said. "Ostin, we need your ponchos."

He handed over the sacks. I gave one of the ponchos to Taylor. "If we can get close enough to them, Taylor could reboot the whole crowd."

"I can't reboot that many people," she said.

"You can with Tessa's help," I said. "That's why we need to get close." I pulled the hat on, lowering its brim to conceal my face. "How do I look?"

"Native," Taylor said, putting on her own hat.

I turned to Ostin. "We need a diversion. Blow something up. Just not the big army truck."

"Why not?"

"Because that's what we're taking out of here."

"Got it," McKenna said.

Taylor took a deep breath. "Let's go."

Taylor and I shoved our way through the jeering crowd with our heads down as she rebooted everyone in our way. One man grabbed my arm, but I immediately pulsed and kept walking. When we got near the center, we saw rocks and fruit around Zeus and the girls. Zeus was bleeding and three Peruvians were lying facedown on the ground. There were machetes on the ground near two of them.

The girls stood behind Zeus, who had his hands up, electricity sparking between them. The people didn't dare get any closer, so they had resorted to throwing things at them. Near the front, a man cocked his arm back to throw a brick. I shocked him, dropping him to the ground. I walked into the clearing with Taylor following behind me.

Zeus held his hands out toward us. "Stop!"

I kept walking.

"I said stop!"

Then he fired at me, which is what I wanted. The electricity filled my body with even more strength, something we'd need if Taylor couldn't reboot them all.

When I didn't fall, Zeus looked panicked. When I was ten feet from him I tilted my hat up. "Need some help?"

He groaned with relief. "Michael."

"Tessa, enhance Taylor."

"Got it," Tessa said.

I looked at Taylor. "Now."

Taylor took off her hat and concentrated. Suddenly the entire crowd silenced. A few of the older people collapsed to the ground.

"Wow," Taylor said. "I've never done that before."

"Hurry, let's get out of here," I said. We walked in a single-file line with me in front, Zeus taking the back, and Tessa in the middle to enhance all of us. "Have you seen Jack and Ian?" I asked.

"No," Abigail said. "I'm hoping Ian's seen us."

Suddenly there was a loud explosion near the market and black smoke began to rise above the buildings. As I had hoped, it drew the crowd's attention away from the field.

"What was that?" Zeus asked.

"McKenna and Ostin," I said. "Tessa, stay close to Taylor. Keep rebooting."

We might as well have been invisible as we walked through the crowd. The townspeople just stood around us in a stupor, looking like they all had migraines. After the supercharge I got from Zeus, I was feeling pretty electric, and people's metal objects kept sticking to me, which I had to pluck off.

"You've got a machete stuck to your back," Tessa said, pulling the knife off of me. "And three earrings."

As we got near the army truck, Taylor rebooted the crowd standing around it. Then I walked to the driver's side of the truck and pulsed, knocking out the driver and passenger. Zeus and I pulled them out.

"I'll drive," Zeus said.

"There's Jack and Ian," McKenna said, pointing toward the east. "They're running toward us."

Jack and Ian were at the far side of the field, running at a dead sprint in our direction.

"They're being chased by soldiers," Abigail said.

There were at least a dozen soldiers behind them. Then one of them dropped to his knee and raised a gun.

"Zeus!" I shouted.

"I see it!" Zeus said. He reached out and fired a wide bolt, dropping the entire group like bowling pins.

I began waving toward Ian and Jack, which was moot since Ian had already seen us. They reached us seconds later, panting and out of breath. "Thanks for the assist," Jack said to Zeus.

"Always my pleasure," Zeus said. "Get in back."

Zeus and I jumped in the front seat, and Zeus started up the truck.

Taylor, Abigail, and Tessa had already climbed into the back of the transport, and Taylor waved to Jack and Ian.

I parted the screen that divided the cab from the back. "Ian, where are Ostin and McKenna?"

He looked around for a moment. "They're over there," he said, pointing.

"Where?" I asked.

"Wait for it."

Just then Ostin and McKenna came running out of the bakery and back up the alley. "Zeus, they're over there," I said. "Let's get them."

"Got it," he said. He shoved the stick shift forward, and the truck sluggishly ground into gear, then lurched forward. "This thing's a whale," he said.

He turned the truck around as tightly as he could, then drove through a ditch, which tumbled everyone in back, and into the road. I hung out the passenger window, waving Ostin's poncho to get their attention. McKenna saw us first.

"Get in back!" I shouted to them.

Zeus stopped the truck, and Jack and Ian pulled them in. Taylor pounded on the metal side of the truck to signal us. "They're in! Go!"

"Which way?" Zeus asked.

"That way," I said, pointing to the town's only stoplight. "Take the highway east to Cuzco."

We drove around the outside of the town, onto the highway. I kept waiting for someone to come after us, but no one did. As the town fell out of sight, Taylor stuck her head up into the cab.

"You okay?" she asked.

"Never been better," I said.

"Good," she said, nodding. "Cute little town."

The one good thing about our brush with danger and narrow escape (other than that we *did* escape) was that it temporarily took our minds from the grief we were all carrying—though I'm not sure if trading fear for pain is such a bargain.

From Paucartambo we drove to the ancient Incan hill town of Pisac, but for obvious reasons, we didn't stop. From Pisac it was only thirty-five more miles to Cuzco, which was a pretty straight drive except that the bridge over the Urubamba River was washed out and the temporary bridge allowed only one lane of traffic, so we had to wait a long time to cross.

Taylor climbed up front with Zeus and me while everyone else sat or slept in the back. No one got too comfortable. We were driving a stolen army truck and we figured that it was only a matter of time before someone noticed. Ian sat looking back to keep watch. We passed several army vehicles going the opposite direction, but they didn't even acknowledge us. We reached the outskirts of Cuzco after dark.

25

The Blue Door

The city of Cuzco is the kind of place you see in travel magazines and on TV travel shows. Of course Ostin had to tell us all he knew about the city.

"Cuzco is not only the ancient capital of the Incan empire, but it's the official tourist city of Peru—and it attracts more than two million visitors a year. The original city was built in the shape of a puma, or mountain lion, which, to the Incans, was a sacred animal.

"When the Spanish explorer Pizarro arrived in Peru with his soldiers, the Incan king Atahualpa tried to run him out, but the king was captured by the Spanish conquistadors. For his release, Pizarro demanded that the Incans fill a large room with gold. The Incans paid the ransom, but Pizarro just took their gold, then executed the king anyway. That's where the saying 'a king's ransom' came from.

"The Inca Atahualpa was the last great Incan emperor, and forty years after his death the great Incan empire came to an end. The

Spanish tore down the Incan palace and built a cathedral on top of it."

Ostin's Cuzco trivia went on for about twenty minutes. With the exception of McKenna's occasional response, no one else said a thing and eventually even Ostin got tired of hearing himself.

As we drove toward the city, Ian and Taylor changed places and Ian became our GPS, guiding us to the town square, the Plaza de Armas. As Ostin had said, Cuzco was a major tourist attraction and the traffic slowed as the area was crowded with tourists and the people who profit from them.

Zeus parked the army truck behind the cathedral of Santo Domingo, and we all got out, looking around in awe. The cobblestone-paved square was large and beautifully decorated in the architecture of the Spanish Renaissance. Outside of history books I had never seen anything like it.

It seemed to me that everyone was looking at us, which made me nervous, but wasn't surprising. We hadn't bathed in weeks and our clothes were ridiculously dirty. Only Jack, whose clothes were stained with blood, had changed shirts and was wearing an Elgen guard's undershirt.

We split up into smaller groups to avoid drawing any more attention to ourselves, arranging to meet in one hour at the large fountain in the center of the plaza. Then Taylor, Ostin, McKenna, and I set out in search of Hostel El Triumfo.

Finding the place wasn't as easy as I thought it would be. All Jaime had told us about the hostel's location was that it was near the town square. The square was considerably larger than I had imagined and there were dozens of side streets and tiny alleyways leading off of it.

Finally, Ostin asked a shopkeeper where we could find the place and he pointed us in the general direction. Taylor and I started off for it while Ostin and McKenna fell back, following us at a distance.

The hostel wasn't especially notable, and Taylor and I walked past it twice before she spotted a small, plastic sign hanging near the hostel's splintered wood front door. We stepped inside, quickly shutting the door behind us.

The tiny lobby was dark and austere, lit only with candles. At the back of the room, standing behind a small counter, was an old Peruvian man with silver hair and bushy gray eyebrows as thick as caterpillars. Next to him was a young woman dressed in modern clothing. She looked close to our age, perhaps just a year or two older. The man looked at us suspiciously.

I walked up to the counter. "Do you speak English?" I asked.

"*Sí, señor. Un poco.*"

"We would like a room for the night."

The man's dark eyes darted back and forth nervously. "I am sorry, but we have no room. It is the tourist season."

Taylor glanced at me.

"I'm a friend of Jaime," I whispered.

The young woman glanced at the man. The man said, "Who?"

"Jaime," I repeated.

He just looked at me. I suddenly wondered if we had come to the wrong place. "Is this Hostel El Triumfo?"

"*Sí.*"

"You don't know Jaime?"

The man laughed. "I have many amigos named Jaime. What is his last name?"

I didn't know Jaime's last name. I looked at Taylor, but she shrugged. "We don't know."

"He must not be much of a friend. I am sorry, but there are other hotels nearby. Perhaps they have a vacancy."

I was speechless, unsure of what to do. The man raised his massive eyebrows, as if inviting us to leave. "Do you need anything else?"

"No," I said. "Thank you. We'll keep looking."

Taylor and I walked back out into the bustling alley. I sat down on the sidewalk and Taylor sat next to me.

"What now?" she asked.

"I still have the radio. I'll call Jaime." I froze. "No."

"What?"

"I left the radio in the truck."

"That's no big deal," she said. "It's not too far."

"No, not in this truck. It's in the pickup truck."

"Back in Paucartambo?"

I groaned. "I screwed up."

"We weren't planning on being attacked," she said.

"I was sloppy," I said. "We should always plan on being attacked. I was supposed to destroy the radio if we were caught, and now they have it. And we have no way to contact Jaime."

Taylor looked worried. "Without Jaime, how do we get home?"

I shrugged. "I have no idea."

She looked scared. "But he knows we're here, right?"

"He said to meet him at Hostel El Triumfo. But apparently he was mistaken."

Just then someone said, "Amigo."

I looked up. The elderly man from the hostel was standing across the alley. He walked up to us. "You are Michael?"

"Yes," I said.

"Excuse me, but my granddaughter talks too much. I could not risk her recognizing you. All of Peru is looking for you. Even in Cuzco, where there are many Americans, it is dangerous for you. They have put your friends' pictures in the newspapers and on posters everywhere. You and your friends must get off the street quickly." He handed me a brass key. "This is a key to a room in the back of the hostel. You may enter it through that door, so no one will see you." He pointed to a blue metal door set in the white stucco wall. "You must hide in there until Jaime arrives."

"You've spoken to Jaime?"

"Yesterday," he said. "He told me to watch for you. He will be happy to know that you have made it here."

I was relieved to hear that Jaime was safe.

"Until he comes, you and your friends must stay inside. I will bring extra blankets and pillows and some water and food."

"I need to find my friends," I said. I put the key in my pocket. "Thank you."

"Thank you for what you are doing," he said. "You are most brave."

We walked down to where Ostin and McKenna were standing near the street corner.

"Any luck?" Ostin asked.

"We found it," I said. "You guys go with Taylor back to the room, I'll round up everyone else."

"We can help," Ostin said.

"No, they have pictures of you, but not me."

"We'll check out the room," Taylor said, "then I'll wait for everyone at the blue door."

"See you in a minute," I said. I handed Taylor the key, then walked back down past the hostel to the plaza, which even at the late hour was bustling with humanity. Apparently parts of Cuzco still had electricity, as light emanated from many of the shops and restaurants, and the plaza itself was flooded with golden light. A Peruvian street band was playing near the fountain, filling the air with a carnival ambience. There were tourists everywhere, laughing, buying trinkets, and drinking. Some of them were dancing. I envied them. I wanted to have fun too. Under different circumstances I would have.

I found Zeus, Ian, Tessa, and Abigail sitting on the ledge of the fountain eating ice cream. The fountain was half as wide as Mitchell's swimming pool, with a large bowl held up by three mermen who were blowing shell horns with water coming out.

"Want some ice cream?" Tessa asked as I approached.

"I'm okay," I said. "We found our contact. We've got to go."

"I don't want to go in yet," Abigail said. "It's fun out here."

"It's a beautiful night," Tessa said.

"The man at the hostel said it isn't safe for us. He said that they've shown your pictures in the newspaper."

"Great, we're famous," Zeus said.

"Infamous," Tessa corrected.

"It's just like I said," Abigail said.

Zeus stood. "Let's go." He turned to me. "Where's this place?"

I gestured with my head. "Walk up that alley about a hundred feet. On your right side you'll come to a blue metal door. Taylor will be waiting for you."

"I see it," Ian said. "Let's go."

"We escaped and I still feel like a prisoner," Abigail said, turning away from me.

"Does anyone know where Jack is?" I asked.

"He went into the cathedral," Ian said. "I can get him."

"That's okay, I will. They didn't show my picture."

"I'll go with you," Tessa said.

I hesitated. "You probably shouldn't. . . ."

"They don't have my picture either," she said firmly. "I'm just another tourist. You'll look less suspicious with me."

"All right," I said. "I'll see you guys at the room."

Zeus, Ian, and Abigail walked off, leaving Tessa and me alone.

As Tessa and I walked from the fountain, she took my hand. "We should hold hands. We'll look less like terrorists."

"All right," I said, feeling a little uncomfortable. She noticed my apprehension and let go of my hand.

She was quiet a moment, then said, "Ever since we rescued your friends you've hardly spoken to me. What's the deal, aren't we friends anymore?"

"It's not that. I've had a lot on my mind."

"You mean you have a lot of Taylor on your mind."

"She's my girlfriend."

"Does that mean we can't be friends anymore?"

I stopped. "I'm sorry, I didn't mean to ignore you. There's just a lot going on."

"I know," she said. "I'm not trying to bust your chops." She stopped and looked into my eyes. "It's just, we got pretty close in the jungle. I don't think we should just throw it away."

I didn't know what to say. "I'm sorry."

She smiled sadly at me then cocked her head toward the cathedral. "Come on, let's get Jack."

As we neared the cathedral I asked, "What's the deal with you and Zeus?"

She looked at me with a pained expression. "You really want to open that door?"

"Only if you want to talk about it."

"He was my boyfriend for, like, three years. It was great. Then when I left for Peru, I didn't hear from him once. It was like, I love you, then, who are you? I was pretty hurt."

"Have you talked to him about it?"

"I tried. He just had a lot of excuses. And now he has a thing for Abigail."

"He told you that?"

"He didn't have to," Tessa said. She sighed. "I'm going to have to find someone less electric."

The cathedral of Santo Domingo was less than a hundred yards from the fountain, and the building towered above the plaza like a great stone fortress. Even though it was late, the doors to the cathedral were open and locals and groups of tourists were walking in to sightsee or worship. I had never been inside a cathedral before and I was astonished at the intricate architecture and artwork. "This is amazing," I said.

"You should see St. Peter's Basilica in Vatican City," Tessa said. "It makes this place look like a Chuck E. Cheese's."

"You're jaded," I said.

"All of Hatch's kids are jaded," she replied.

Near the center of the chapel was a beautiful painting of the Last Supper. I stopped to look at it. After a moment Tessa rolled her eyes. "Come on, tourist," she said, pulling my hand. "We're looking for Jack, not sightseeing."

We had practically walked through the entire cathedral before we found him. He was kneeling with his head bowed before a table of lit candles. We watched him for a few minutes until Tessa, who was growing impatient, whispered to him, "Jack."

He looked up at us.

"Sorry to disturb you," I said.

"It's okay," he said, standing.

I glanced at the table in front of him. "What are you doing?"

"I lit a candle for Wade," he said.

"I didn't know you were religious," I said.

"I'm not," he replied. He walked toward me. "Did you find the place?"

"Yes. The owner said we should get off the street. The government has shown our pictures all over the media and he's afraid someone might recognize us."

"I figured as much," Jack said.

As we walked out of the cathedral I noticed five police cars were now parked on the opposite side of the square.

"Those weren't there before," I said.

"What do you think's going on?" Tessa asked.

Jack lowered his head slightly. "They must have found the truck," he said.

"If they did," I said, "then they know we're here." As I looked around the square I saw police standing at every exit and alley. They were everywhere.

"What do we do?" Tessa asked.

"We act like tourists," I said. "Jack, stay a little behind us. We'll walk right past them."

As we neared the alley, we could see that the police officers were all carrying pieces of paper. One of them stared at Tessa and me, then looked back down at the paper, then back up again.

"They have pictures," Tessa said.

"I'm in trouble," Jack said.

"Don't run," I said. "Not yet."

The same officer who had dismissed us looked at Jack, then down at the paper again then back up. His expression changed. He said something to another officer. Then both officers approached Jack. They had grave expressions on their faces and their hands were on their guns.

"*Señor*, may I see your passport?" one of them said.

Then two other police officers stepped up behind him.

"I . . . I left it at the hotel," Jack said.

The officer said something in Spanish to the other police, then said, "Please show me some I.D."

"I don't have my wallet," Jack said.

The man just stared into Jack's face. "You have no identification?"

"He got pickpocketed," I said, turning back. "This afternoon."

The man glanced over at me, then back at Jack. Then a fifth officer walked up to us. He was holding an Uzi machine gun. Even though I fought it, I was twitching like crazy, which I'm sure didn't help our cause.

"Are you together?" he asked Tessa.

"Yes, sir," she said. She moved closer to me, and I put my arm around her.

"You are Americans," he said. I couldn't tell if he meant it as a statement or a question.

"Yes, sir," I said.

Jack and I glanced at each other. Two of the officers moved their hands toward their guns. I was about to pulse when the officer in front of us suddenly froze. He just stood there, as if he were having a stroke or something. Then he looked up and turned to his partner and said something in Spanish that, from what I could tell, had nothing to do with us. The policeman with the Uzi turned and looked at a woman crossing the street. It was as if they had suddenly forgotten we were even there. I recognized Taylor's work.

I gestured with my head to Jack. "Time to go," I said. We walked away. About twenty feet from where we were stopped, Taylor and Ian stepped out from a leather goods shop, falling in a few steps behind us. "That was close," Taylor said. She was looking at my arm around Tessa.

I quickly dropped it to my side. "They recognized Jack," I said.

"I think they found the truck," Jack said.

"They did," Ian said. "I saw them from the hostel."

Ian stepped ahead of us and pushed open the hostel's blue door, which led into a small dark courtyard with a picnic table and umbrella. The space was walled in with a brick-and-stucco wall. The building's surface was terra-cotta, and there were several hanging pots of red flowers. Three cats lounged on a wrought-iron table.

"It's over here," Ian said, stopping to wave us on. "There's a stairway around back."

We turned the corner and climbed a rickety, splintered wooden stairway to an upstairs room. As we climbed the stairs I reached for Taylor's hand, but she ignored me. Jack opened the door, and we all hurried in. Ian locked the door behind us.

The room was lit by a single bare lightbulb. There was no air-conditioning, and even though it was well past sunset, the heat in the room was stifling.

The room was small for so many people. There were two bunk beds and a pile of blankets and pillows. Zeus and Abigail were sitting on one bed.

"Not exactly the Four Seasons," Tessa said.

"Perhaps you prefer prison," Taylor said coldly.

Tessa looked at her and frowned. "Just sayin', sweetheart. No need to get testy."

They glared at each other, filling the room with an uncomfortable tension. Then Taylor turned away.

I put my hand on her shoulder, and she shrugged it off. I pulled her aside. "What's up?"

"We're being hunted," she said angrily.

"Yeah, I know that. What's going on with us?"

"You tell me. You find something new in the jungle?" She turned away from me.

"Taylor . . ."

As I stood there wondering what to do, there was a knock at the door. We all froze except for Ian. "It's the hostel man," he said. "He's bringing something."

Jack opened the door.

"*Buenas noches,*" the man said, pushing his way in. He was carrying two large canvas bags. He set them down on the floor, then shut the door behind himself. "I brought you some food and water. I must warn you, the police are going door to door checking buildings," he said. "You must not come out until I tell you it is safe. I will do what I can to keep them away. I have locked the blue door."

"Thank you," I said. "We'll stay inside."

"Good," he said. "I must go back to the front before they arrive. One more thing. I have spoken with Jaime. He will be here early tomorrow morning to get you." He opened the door. "I will pray to the Virgin Mary for your safety." He walked out and Jack locked the door behind him.

The room was quiet.

"What's the plan if they come?" Zeus asked.

"Ian will see them long before they get here," I said. "Taylor can reboot them." I looked at Ian. "If we have to run, what's behind the back fence?"

"It looks like the back of a restaurant. It leads to a bunch of other streets. I think we could lose them."

"Can you see any vehicles?"

"There's a parking lot two blocks up. There are a few vans big enough to carry us all."

"Any with keys?"

"No worries," Jack said. "I can hot-wire anything here."

"Okay," I said. "As a last resort we blow our way out of here, climb over the fence, then follow Ian to the parking lot. Jack hot-wires a van, and we drive to Lima."

"What if we get separated?" Abigail asked.

"We don't," I said. "We stick together." I looked around the room. The fatigue of it all was getting to everyone. "Got it?" No one spoke. "All right. Let's try to get some rest."

In spite of what I'd said, no one slept. Especially me. Watching Taylor fume was agonizing. An hour later Ian said, "Two policemen just checked the blue door. Now they're going into the front door of the hostel."

Everyone was tense.

After a moment McKenna said, "Tell us what's going on."

"They're talking to the old man. He's just talking. He's acting scared." A minute later he said, "He's taping a picture of us up on the wall. The police are leaving."

I breathed out in relief.

Ian turned to us. "The man can act."

Around one in the morning Ian came over and sat next to me. "I think they've given up. The police have moved out of the square."

"Completely?"

"No. There are still a few left. They also have a guy on top of the cathedral with binoculars."

"Do you think it's safe to go outside to the courtyard?"

He looked over at Taylor, then back at me. I think he understood why I was asking. "You're okay."

"Thanks," I said. I walked over to Taylor. "Hey."

She wouldn't look at me.

"Ian said we can go outside."

"Good," she said. "Maybe Tessa would like to go for a midnight stroll."

"Would you like to go outside with me?"

She just sat there for a moment, then exhaled slowly. "All right."

I gave her my hand and pulled her up.

"Hey, where are you guys going?" Ostin said. "We're not supposed to go out."

"We're just going out to the courtyard," I said. "Ian said it's okay."

"We just need some fresh air," Taylor said.

"I could use some too," Ostin said.

"Not now, you don't," I said. I pulled the door open for Taylor and she stepped outside. I held her hand as we walked down the stairway. We sat on a bench in a corner of the courtyard. We kept our voices down. Even though no one could see us, we didn't know if anyone was close enough to hear us. Just hearing English might be enough to get tipped off.

"Why are you giving me the cold shoulder?" I said.

"You know why."

"I had my arm around her so they'd think we were tourists."

"You were pretty convincing."

"Do you really doubt how I feel about you? You can read my mind."

She frowned. "It's not you," she said. "I'm just insecure."

"About me?"'

"About her," Taylor said. "Tessa doesn't like me."

"Why would you say that?"

"I read her mind."

"Why wouldn't she like you?"

"Because she wants what I have," Taylor said.

"What's that?"

"You know what."

I looked at her. "Why would you say that?"

"I told you. I heard her thinking."

I just looked at her.

"You're making me feel like a Peeping Tom," she said.

"You are."

"I'm not trying to be. It's just that we're in these small places, backs of trucks, hotel rooms . . . with Tessa around magnifying my power I can hear everyone's thoughts without even touching them. You have no idea what's going on in there. We're a mess."

"Like what?" I asked.

"Like, Jack is completely blaming himself for Wade's death. He plans to die in Lima sinking the boat. Tessa hates Abigail and me. And Abigail is ready to call it quits."

"She was ready to call it quits in Pasadena."

"Well, now she's really ready."

"And me? What have you read in my mind?"

"You feel bad because I'm being cold to you and you love me."

"Maybe it's not all bad then."

"I'm sorry. I just got jealous."

"Why would you get jealous over me? You're way out of my league."

"I don't know why you always say that," she said. She leaned in to me. "Will you please just kiss me already?"

I put my arm around her and we kissed.

When we parted she said, "For the record, it's the other way around."

"What's the other way around?"

"You're out of my league. You're just too nice to know it."

I pulled her close. After a few minutes she asked, "What are we going to do about everyone? They're falling apart."

"I don't know," I said. "I really don't know."

While I was thinking, someone starting shouting in Spanish. Then we heard glass break.

"We'd better go back in," I whispered. I took Taylor's hand and we climbed the stairs. Inside, everyone was sleeping, though I noticed Tessa glance up at us as we entered. I wondered how long it would be before Jaime arrived.

26

Miraflores

The room's blinds were glowing from the first rays of dawn when there was a soft rap on our door, quickly followed by another. Everyone in the room woke at the sound, except for Ostin, who could sleep on an airport runway.

I looked at Ian, who had been sleeping on a blanket on the ground but was now rubbing his eyes. "Is it safe?"

"It's Jaime," he said groggily. "And the old man."

I got up and opened the door. Jaime's appearance shocked me. His head was wrapped in a bandage that covered one eye. Still he smiled.

"Mr. Michael," he said.

We embraced, then I stepped back and both men entered quickly. I shut the door behind them.

"What happened to you?" I asked Jaime.

"Our escape was not as easy as I hoped. They found us and they shot at us. I barely escaped."

"And your friends?"

He shook his head. "They were not as fortunate."

"I'm sorry," I said.

"Me too," he said. "I am much grieved." He looked around the room. "Is everyone here?"

"Not everyone," I said.

His eyebrows raised. "You are missing someone?"

"We lost Wade. He was shot by an Elgen guard."

Jaime shook his head slowly. "I am sorry. We have all had losses." He walked to the center of the room. "My friends, the police have given up their search, but the army is on their way here. They believe that you are still in Cuzco. We must get you out before they arrive. I have a truck outside. We must leave immediately."

"Where are we going?" Zeus asked.

"We will drive to Lima, where we will wait for the Elgen fleet to arrive."

Suddenly Abigail stood. "I'm not going."

Everyone looked at her.

"I can't do this anymore. I never wanted to come here. We've suffered so much. Jack's been shot. And now we've lost Wade." She breathed out heavily. "I'm going home."

"Home?" Ian said.

"You still won't be safe," I said. "You'll never make it alone."

"She's not going alone," Zeus said. "I'm going with her."

I looked at him in surprise. "You're leaving us?"

"I'm sorry, but Abi's right. It's too much for us. Look at us. We're a bunch of teenagers. We can't stop them." He looked around, then said in a softer voice, "We might as well make the most of the time we have left."

I looked around at the group. A heavy despair had settled on the room.

"Anyone else planning on leaving?" I looked at Taylor. "Taylor?"

"You know better," she said. She walked to my side.

"Ostin?"

"Of course I'm staying."

"Tessa?"

She glanced at Taylor, then back at me. "Sorry. I think Zeus is right."

"Jack?"

"I'm in this to the end."

"Ian?"

Ian looked the most conflicted of anyone in the room—like he was being torn in two. Abigail looked into his eyes. "Come with us."

He looked down for a moment, then back at me. "I'm sorry, Michael."

I exhaled slowly. Everyone looked at McKenna. She was the only one who hadn't picked a side.

"McKenna?" Abigail said. "It's the three of us. It's always been the three of us."

McKenna glanced at Ostin, then back at Abigail. "You're probably right. But I can't let these guys down. They saved us from the academy."

The room fell into silence.

I turned to Zeus. "Are you sure?"

"I'm sure," he said.

Ian looked at me. "Come with us, Michael. This is too risky. You don't want any more blood on your hands."

Jack exploded. "Wade's blood isn't on Michael's hands!"

I put my hand on Jack's arm to calm him. "It's okay, man. He didn't mean that."

"No, I didn't," Ian said. "Wade's blood is on the Elgen's hands. And they're not going to stop until they've taken all of our blood. The only way to win this game is to not play it. We'll go someplace the Elgen will never find us. We'll live together." He looked at Jaime, then back at me. "It's like Zeus said, if the world's going to ruin, then we might as well enjoy it while we can."

Jack's expression turned hard. "Sometimes there are bigger things to live for than yourself."

"Jack," Abigail said softly. "Ian's not being selfish, he's being rational. And I don't think you're thinking about living."

"Then there are things worth dying for," Jack said.

"We're not arguing with you, Jack," Zeus said. "You've suffered as much as any of us. But that's precisely our point. Haven't you suffered enough? Why suffer any more?"

"Because there's a chance we might be able to stop them," Jack said.

"And what if you can't?" Abigail said. "What if they're just too big?"

Jack looked down for a moment as everyone anticipated his reply. Then he looked up, his eyes strong. "Then we'll fail in glory."

The room fell into complete silence. Then Jaime said, "You stay or you go, it is your choice. But for now everyone must leave Cuzco." Jaime looked at the dissenters. "When we reach Lima, I will arrange for you to fly back to America."

Jaime's offer stung. Not just because I was losing my friends, but because deep inside I really wanted to go home with them.

27

The Calm Before the Storm

Jaime had parked a meat refrigeration truck in front of the hostel, and when no one was around, he backed it up as close to the blue door as he could so we could enter without being seen by anyone in the alley. When he gave us the signal we took turns climbing in. I was the last to enter. Once I was inside Jaime shut the door, leaving us in darkness. McKenna lit up just bright enough so we could see one another.

"What kind of a truck is this?" Tessa asked. "It smells back here."

"Is that blood?" Abigail asked, looking at the floor.

"It's a meat truck," Ostin said. He rubbed his face. "I feel like such a ham hock."

In spite of the tension, I laughed.

The ride to Lima was long, nearly seven hundred miles and more than fifteen hours. Jaime stopped only once to get gas and let us use the bathroom. We slept through much of the drive, as much from trying to escape anxiety as from fatigue. Less than an hour out of Cuzco, a convoy of more than fifty army trucks passed us.

No one spoke about the fracture of the Electroclan, but the division was obvious. Consciously or not, we now sat in our own groups—those who were staying and those who were going.

In such a confined metal room, and with Tessa present, Taylor couldn't help but read everyone's thoughts, even though she struggled not to. I didn't have to read her mind to know how angry she was at Abigail. But I wasn't. Even at the academy, Abigail had wanted to go home. I supposed that I felt as if I'd deceived her. She had stayed only because I'd convinced her that it was for her own safety. But what we'd dragged her through since then was hardly for her own safety. What we were now planning, sinking the *Ampere*, certainly wasn't for her safety. I couldn't blame her for leaving. I couldn't blame anyone for leaving. Like I said, I wanted to go with them. But I couldn't. Something held me—something my mother always said. *All that's required for the triumph of evil is for good people to do nothing.*

We arrived in Lima at two in the morning. We woke to the shuddering of the truck braking and shutting off, then the stringent smell of the ocean breeze as Jaime opened the back doors. I don't know what I expected, but it wasn't this. Jaime had brought us to a beautiful tile-roofed villa that overlooked the South Pacific. The house was on ten acres of fenced property at the end of a long, private gravel road surrounded by palm and white-washed orange trees leading up to a large fountain.

Wherever we were, we seemed to be miles from anything else, and for the first time in days I felt safe. Jaime unlocked the villa door, and we went inside. For the first time in what seemed like an eternity we all crashed in real beds with clean, sweet-smelling cotton sheets.

I awoke the next morning long after the sun had risen. I just lay for a while enjoying the comfort of a real bed, then got up and walked out to the kitchen. The smell of coffee brewing filled the dining area. Taylor was already up. She was thumbing through a travel book about Peru.

"Good morning," I said.

She looked up and smiled. "Good morning. I'd ask how you slept, but I think I already know." She smiled again. "A *real* bed with *real* sheets and a *real* pillow. I almost felt like a *real* human again."

"You look like a *real* human," I said. I walked toward her. "What are you looking at?"

"Just this book that was here. It has pictures of Peru. Did you know that there are almost four thousand native varieties of potatoes in Peru?"

"No," I said. "But I bet Ostin does."

"Of course Ostin does," she said. "He's Ostin." She set aside the book. "Come sit by me."

I sat down next to her on the couch.

"Have you looked outside?"

"No."

"It's beautiful. There are flowers and palm trees. It's a real Spanish villa." She looked at me. "It's the calm before the storm."

"I'm afraid you're right."

We sat a moment in silence, then Taylor said, "Jaime left."

"Where?"

"He said he had some business."

"When is he coming back?"

"A few days."

"Did he say anything else?"

"There's food in the fridge and no one should leave the property."

"House arrest again?" I asked.

"Villa arrest. But at least this time we have real beds."

"With pillows."

Just then Ostin walked in. "Morning. What's for breakfast?"

"Potatoes," Taylor said.

"Doesn't surprise me," Ostin said. "There's almost four thousand different varieties in Peru."

28

Two Paths

In spite of our luxurious sur-
roundings, the next three days passed in a dull emotional haze. There
wasn't much to do. Lima had some electricity, so we could watch TV,
but the stations were all in Spanish. So were the books in the house.
There were playing cards, and all of us except Jack played Hearts or
Texas Hold'em until even that got boring.

All that was left to do was to talk, and I suppose that was the
thing we were all avoiding. After all we had been through, it was as
if we were suddenly strangers again. Most heartbreaking to me was
the tension between Abigail, Ian, and McKenna. I suppose all of them
had reason to feel betrayed.

The least sociable of all of us was Jack. He didn't join in cards
or talk or anything. He either stayed in his room or exercised in the
garage, improvising exercise equipment from things he found around
the house. He stuffed a laundry bag with sheets, hung it from a

pergola, then pounded it for hours like a punching bag. He also ran in place, lifted large rocks, and did like a million push-ups. We all were worried about him. I couldn't stop thinking about what Taylor had said about him not planning on surviving the attack.

The evening of the second day, Taylor, Abigail, Zeus, and I were making dinner when Jack walked into the kitchen. His arm was covered with blood.

Taylor gasped. "What happened? Is that where you were shot?"

"No," he said. He held up his wound. He had cut a jagged line on his forearm below his tattoo. "What do you think?"

We were all speechless.

Zeus was the first to say something. "It's a lightning bolt?"

"No," Jack said. "It's two *W*s."

"Two *W*s?" Taylor said.

"What does it stand for?" I asked.

Jack looked at me with disappointment. "Wade West."

Jaime returned the third day, shortly after sunset. The meat truck was gone, and he was driving a white passenger van. Printed on the side, next to a picture of an Incan god, were the words: SACRED VALLEY INCA TOURS.

We all went out and helped carry in boxes of groceries, which were mostly fresh vegetables and meats and sausages wrapped in paper. There was also a box of clothing.

After we'd finished unloading the van, Jaime gathered us into the front room. When we were all seated, he said, "I have news. For those who are leaving, I have made arrangements for you to fly back to America in the morning."

The immediacy of the flight surprised us. Taylor gasped softly.

"Where are we going?" Abigail asked.

"I cannot tell you," he said. "But to a safe place."

"I've heard that twice before," she said. "Both times we were almost killed."

"I guarantee it is safe," Jaime said. "It is with our own people. They would like to talk with you and see if you have any information to help the cause. Then they will make arrangements for your future."

"What do you mean?" Tessa asked.

"Where and how you live will be your choice," Jaime said. "But we know that the Elgen will not stop hunting you, so you will be given new identities. And you will have decisions to make about how much risk you will take."

"Like the witness protection program," Ostin said.

"*Sí*," Jaime said. "We will do whatever we can to protect and help you. But it will take a little time to make everything right." He looked at each of the four who were leaving. "Do you have any questions?"

When no one said anything, I raised my hand. "I'd like to say something."

"*Sí*, Mr. Michael," Jaime said.

I stood, suppressing my tics. "I know that some of you might feel guilty about leaving. I just want to say, don't. You have already risked more than most people will in ten lifetimes. You're already heroes."

To my surprise, no one looked comforted at all. If anything, they looked more miserable.

"Michael is right," Jaime said. "You have already risked more and done more to battle the Elgen than any of us. You may hold your heads high. One need not fight every battle, or die in the struggle, to be a hero."

In spite of what we'd said, everyone still looked down.

After a minute Tessa asked, "What time do we leave?"

"Around ten," Jaime said. "Perhaps a little earlier. There is a private airstrip not far from here. You will fly to Nicaragua, where we will change planes, then fly to our base in the U.S. I have brought fresh clothes for you so you are not so noticeable or uncomfortable.

"For those who are staying, we have received word that the Elgen fleet has passed through the Panama Canal. The first ships could arrive in Port Callao in just five days. So for now I suggest you get as much rest as you can."

The two courses he'd just detailed highlighted the stark difference of our paths.

"Can we please go into town?" Taylor asked. "There's a Hard Rock Cafe just a few miles away."

Jaime shook his head. "No, it is much too dangerous. In times of national crisis, foreigners are closely watched. Yesterday the Lima police arrested two people they thought were Zeus and Abigail."

Zeus and Abigail exchanged glances. "They thought they were us?" Zeus asked.

"Yes. But they were just students. One of them from England." Jaime looked around the room. "Any other questions?"

No one spoke.

"Okay. It is late. Get some rest."

We looked at one another sadly. I wanted to say my good-byes—actually, I wanted to throw some kind of a farewell party, but in light of losing Wade, a party didn't seem appropriate. In the end we all just went to bed.

That night I had a dream. Hatch was walking toward me, smiling. I lifted my hands to shock him, but my hands were gone.

29

Another Farewell

I woke to the sound of talking and I looked at the digital clock next to my bed. It was already half past nine. I pulled on my pants and walked out into the kitchen.

Abigail, Zeus, Tessa, and Ian were sitting around the table eating omelets. They stopped talking as I walked in.

"Hey, Michael," Zeus said.

"Good morning," Abigail and Ian said simultaneously.

Tessa looked at me sadly and nodded. "Michael."

They were all dressed in the new clothes Jaime had brought, which actually looked surprisingly cool. It was odd seeing them in clean clothing.

"You look so . . . normal," I said.

"I know. I hardly recognized myself," Abigail said.

I sat down at the table and looked over at Ian's plate. His omelet had ham, onions, jack cheese, and peppers.

"That looks really good," I said.

"Tessa made them," Ian said.

"I like to cook," Tessa said. "It's kind of my thing. Especially omelets. I'm also good at making crepes."

"You make crepes?" I said.

"She makes incredible crepes," Ian said.

"You were holding out on me," I said.

"It's not like I could have made them in the jungle," she said.

A few minutes later Taylor and McKenna came into the room. Taylor had her arm around McKenna, whose eyes were puffy. She looked as if she'd been crying all night. Ian got up and walked over to her. "Good morning," he said. They embraced.

Ostin walked in. "Something smells good."

"Omelets," Zeus said. "Tessa's specialty."

Ostin looked in the kitchen "You didn't save any for us?"

"Sorry," she replied. "I didn't know when you were getting up."

"You thought we'd just let you leave without saying good-bye?" Ostin replied.

She shrugged. "Maybe."

"What time is it?" Taylor asked.

"It's almost time for us to go," Tessa said. "We're just waiting for Jaime."

Then Jack appeared in the doorway. Abigail's gaze followed him as he walked into the room. Their eyes met, but neither of them spoke.

"Here's Jaime," Ian said. "He's driving up the lane now."

A couple minutes later Jaime opened the door. *"Vámonos, hermanos,"* he said. He looked around at all of us. "I will give you a few minutes to say good-bye, then we must go."

McKenna walked over to Ostin, and Taylor took my hand. For a moment we all just looked at one another.

Then Abigail walked across the kitchen to us. She stopped just a few feet in front of me. "I guess this is it," she said. "Please don't hate me."

"Abi, when I was in Cell 25, I knew I couldn't take the pain much longer before I'd break. But I didn't because you saved me. I don't know which of us is doing the right thing. All I know for sure is that I'll never be able to repay you for what you did for me."

Abigail's eyes welled up with tears. I put my arms around her and she broke down crying. "I'm so sorry, Michael. I wish I were strong like you. I'm sorry I'm letting you down."

I kissed her forehead. "Promise me something."

"What?"

"Promise me that you'll never regret your decision. If I were you, I would have done the same thing. And if something happens to us, it's not your fault. You couldn't have stopped it." I looked into her eyes. "Some people weren't born to fight. Some were born to pick up the pieces."

She fell into my arms again and we held each other. "I'm going to miss you," she said.

"I'm going to miss you, too," I replied. "But we'll see each other again."

When we parted, Abigail's cheeks were streaked with tears. She touched my cheek and for a moment I could feel my pain and fear go away. "When I see you again," she said, "we're going to have a big celebration."

"I'm going to hold you to that," I said.

Then Taylor stepped forward. "Good-bye, Abi," she said. Her eyes were also filled with tears. "I'm sorry I've been so mean to you lately."

"I understand," Abigail said.

"I've just been so angry. Or maybe I'm just afraid. But Michael's right. When Nichelle broke me, you were there to heal me. I'll never be able to repay you for that."

"You freed us," Abigail said. "You've repaid me a hundred times over."

The two of them embraced.

McKenna walked up to Abigail. They threw their arms around each other. When they parted, they were both crying.

"I love you," McKenna said.

"I love you, too," Abigail replied. "You be safe. Promise me."

McKenna just smiled sadly, then the two embraced again.

Then Abigail walked over to Jack. She looked up into his eyes. "Most of all, I'm sorry I'm leaving you."

"You're doing the right thing," he said. "You're too good for this crap. You always were." He took a deep breath. "Where do you think you'll end up?"

"I don't know. Wherever they send me. How about you?"

Jack shrugged. "Wherever the battle takes me."

Abigail smiled sadly. "You really are a warrior, aren't you?"

"We'll find out soon enough."

"I already know," Abigail said. She leaned forward and kissed him on the cheek. Then she looked intensely into his eyes, then kissed him on the mouth. "You have no idea how much I wish you were coming with me, but I know you need to do what you have to do. After you've kicked Hatch's butt, come back to me. I'll be waiting."

"What about Zeus?"

"We're just friends," she said.

"How will I find you?"

"The voice will know," she said. She took his hand. "Don't forget me."

"How could I forget you?"

Her eyes welled up with tears, and Jack put his arms around her and she cried for several minutes. Then she took a deep breath and leaned back. "I need to say one more thing, but it's kind of hard. I just want you to take it the right way."

Jack stared into her eyes. "Go ahead."

"I know that losing Wade was the worst thing that's ever happened to you. I also know that no matter what I say, you're still going to blame it on yourself. I'm just saying, don't go into battle trying to punish yourself. Promise me you won't be careless with your life." Abigail took his hand. "If you have to be a hero, then be a hero. But don't be a martyr. Please promise me."

Jack took a deep breath. After a moment he said, "I promise."

A tear ran down her cheek. "Thank you." She kissed him again, then stepped away.

Zeus walked up to Jack. "You take care, man. And punch Hatch for me."

"I'll do it," Jack said. "You take care of Abi. Keep her safe. And yourself."

Zeus nodded. "Will do, man." For a moment they both were silent. Then Zeus said, "You know, I owe you. You taught me what it means to be brave."

"No, man," Jack said. "When you blew the water pipes, you taught me."

Jack put out his hand. Zeus looked at him for a moment, then a sad smile crossed his face. "Sorry, but a handshake won't do." The two of them embraced. "When you sink that ship," Zeus said. "Make sure Hatch is on it."

Jack nodded. "I'll do my best."

"Michael," Tessa said as she walked up to me. "Thanks for everything."

"Thank you."

"I know things got a little awkward back here, but I'm really grateful for the time we spent together."

"Me too," I said. "Thanks for helping me save my friends."

"Thanks for making me do the right thing," she said. "I'm glad I did."

Outside, the van's horn honked and Tessa sighed. "I guess it's time." She leaned forward and kissed me on the cheek. Then she looked at Taylor. "Good luck, Taylor."

"Thanks," Taylor said.

"Take care of each other."

Tessa looked at me once more, then walked away. All of us walked outside to the idling van. Abi, Zeus, and Tessa climbed inside. Ian stopped and looked at McKenna. There were tears in both their eyes. Then McKenna ran up to him and they embraced. "I love you," she said.

"I love you too," Ian said. "More than I can say."

When they finally separated, Ian said, "You stay safe. Promise me. I don't want to hear any bad news. Not about you. I couldn't take that."

"I'll do my best."

"Keep her safe," he said to Ostin. "She's your responsibility now."

"I'll do everything I can," Ostin said.

Ian turned to me. "Yo, Michael."

I walked up to him and we clasped hands.

"Listen," he said. "Just sink the ship, then get out of there."

"That's the plan," I said. We embraced. "You've been a good friend."

"I feel guilty leaving you here. I know you could use my help."

"We'll manage," I said.

He looked at me, then nodded. "If anyone can, it's you. You're the bravest kid I've ever met." He exhaled. "Better go." He climbed into the van. "See ya."

"Ciao," Taylor said.

McKenna blew him a kiss. He smiled sadly, then shut the door.

"I'll be back later tonight," Jaime said to me.

"Travel safe," I said.

"*Vayan con Dios,*" Ostin said.

Then the van sped away, leaving the five of us alone.

30

Mind Reading

Taylor and I held hands as we watched them go. Even though I'd never admit it to the others, a part of me felt like I was watching my hopes drive away with them. We were already the underdogs, and now we'd lost half our team. I don't think I had felt that discouraged since Cell 25.

"We better go back inside," Jack said. "Before someone sees us."

We all followed him into the house. McKenna was sobbing and Ostin was doing his awkward best to comfort her. I wasn't doing a whole lot better than she was. I was twitching like crazy. When we were inside, Taylor turned to me. "Are you okay?"

"Just my Tourette's," I said.

"Tourette's or not," she said, "you're wrong."

"I'm wrong about what?"

"What you were just thinking."

"Quit reading my mind," I said angrily, wondering what she had read. "It's like reading someone's journal without their permission."

"I can't always help it," she said. "Especially when you're thinking about me."

"What was I thinking?" I asked.

"That you should have made me go with them."

"So?" I said. "Is it wrong to think I don't want your blood on my hands?"

"*My* blood on *your* hands?" she replied. "What about *your* blood on *my* hands? I'm a big girl, I can make up my own mind. This battle is as much mine as yours. Who do you think led the Electroclan when you weren't around?"

"I'm not saying that you're not capable," I said. "But if something happened to you . . ."

"And what if something happens to you? Am I supposed to just deal with that? Do you think you're the only one who's afraid of losing someone they love?"

"I didn't say that," I said, then added, "or *think* that."

"No. But you were going to."

"Great, now you know what I'm *going* to think?"

She looked at me for a moment, then she grinned. "Sorry." She put her arms around me. "I can't lose you either. So we'll just stay close. That way if something happens to one of us, it will happen to both of us."

"That doesn't sound hopeful," I said.

"Nothing sounds hopeful right now," she replied.

Ostin walked up to us. "I'm going to make some breakfast. Anyone hungry?"

"I am," Taylor said.

"Me too," I said. "What are you making?"

"Omelets," Ostin said. "Tessa left all the stuff out to make them."

"Sounds good to me," I said.

"What about McKenna?" Taylor asked.

"She says she's not hungry," Ostin replied.

"You better ask Jack if he wants something," I said.

As if on cue, Jack walked into the kitchen. He got a tall glass out of the cupboard, then walked over to the refrigerator, broke a half dozen eggs into a glass, then swallowed them raw. He wiped his mouth with his arm, then walked back out to the garage.

"I think he just had breakfast," Taylor said.

After breakfast, Ostin went to find McKenna, while Taylor and I cleaned up the kitchen. We were drying the last of the dishes when Taylor put her hand on my cheek. "You need to get some rest. You still look like you haven't slept for days."

"I just can't get enough rest," I said.

"Come here." She took my hand and led me to one of the vacant bedrooms. "Lie on your stomach," she said, pointing to the bed.

I stretched out over the bed and Taylor lay on her side next to me. She lifted my shirt, then ran her fingernails along my back and up my neck into my hair, just like my mother used to do when I was little. It was the best feeling in the world.

Unfortunately, it didn't take long for me to fall asleep.

31

Sinking the *Ampere*

Jaime returned as the sun was setting, a huge red ball sinking slowly into the indigo-blue ocean. I was woken by the sound of his car door slamming. I sat up and looked around the dark room, then at the clock. Had I really slept more than six hours? The house was quiet, and with the exception of Taylor's breathing, I couldn't hear a thing.

I quietly got up and walked out to the front room. I turned the lights on in the hallway, then the front room. Jaime had opened the door and was carrying in several boxes.

"I brought some more food," he said.

"Is there anything else in the car?"

"*Sí.*"

I walked out to the van and grabbed several large packages of bottled water and brought them back in while Jaime made a second trip, bringing in the rest of the food. I put the water in the refrigerator as Jaime put away the rest of the groceries.

"Where is everyone?" he asked.

"I'm not sure," I said. "I think they're sleeping."

"They went to bed early," he said.

I didn't tell him that we had gone to bed shortly after he'd left. "Did their flight take off okay?"

He nodded. *"Sí."* He glanced at his wristwatch. "They should almost be to Nicaragua by now."

As much as I hated seeing them go, I was happy to hear they were out of Peru. "At least they're safe," I said.

"For now," he said gravely. "For now." He patted me on the shoulder. "If you think your friends will wake up, I am going to make some dinner. *Seco de cordero.*"

"What's that?"

"It is a Peruvian specialty. Lamb stew with potatoes. The lamb is cooked in beer until it is tender then seasoned with *aji* peppers and cilantro."

"That sounds good," I said. "Do you need any help?"

"Sí. Gracias. You can peel the potatoes."

While we were preparing dinner, I turned to Jaime. "I still haven't spoken to my mother."

"We have not had a time to arrange it. I will do my best to contact the voice tonight."

When we were ready to eat, I went back to the room and gently woke Taylor. She was as disoriented as I had been.

"What time is it?" she asked, pulling her hair back from her face.

"It's time for dinner," I said.

She squinted at me. "Dinner? How long did I sleep?"

"Most of the day."

She pushed herself up. "Where's everyone else?"

"I'm not sure," I said. "We need to get them."

We searched the house. We found Jack in the garage working out. He was drenched in sweat and his muscles were pumped, his biceps bulging like grapefruits. His knuckles were red from pounding his homemade punching bag.

"Time to eat," I said.

"I'll be right there," he said.

We found Ostin and McKenna in McKenna's room. Ostin was holding McKenna while she slept and he put his finger over his lips to silence me.

"Dinnertime," I whispered.

He just waved me off. "I'm not hungry."

As we walked out I turned to Taylor. "Did he really just say that?"

"Wow," she said. "That's the power of love."

We laughed the whole way to the kitchen.

The stew was delicious and easily the best meal we'd had since coming to Peru. Halfway through dinner Ostin and McKenna joined us. I'm glad they did. It had been a traumatic day, and it was good to come together.

Jack was quiet during the meal, and Taylor tried to engage him. "How long have you been working out?"

"All day," he replied.

"Aren't you tired?"

He looked at her as if the question hadn't crossed his mind. Or, more likely, was irrelevant. "I'm preparing."

"That is good," Jaime said. "We must prepare. There is much to do before the Elgen fleet arrives. Tonight I am picking someone up from the airport. We will be here in the morning."

"Who are you picking up?"

"Someone who can help us," he said.

"Help us do what?" Taylor asked.

He looked at us seriously. "Sink the *Ampere*."

32

Waffles and Dodds

I couldn't believe we were eating real waffles. While we were doing the dishes the day before, Taylor had discovered a waffle iron, and we were all pretty excited about making waffles for breakfast. We didn't have any pancake syrup, but Ostin knew a trick for making it with brown sugar and vanilla and it tasted pretty much like the real thing. With fresh butter they tasted almost as good as my mother used to make. Or maybe it had just been so long since I'd eaten anything like that, it just seemed that way.

Jaime arrived as we were cleaning up. He unlocked the door and walked in. "We are here!" he shouted.

We walked out to see who Jaime had brought home. Standing next to him was a man we'd never seen before. He was tall, at least six inches taller than Jaime, though just as thin. He had messy flaxen hair, a thin face, and a long, beaklike nose, on which rested round, wire-rimmed glasses. We all looked at him curiously.

"This is Mr. Dodds," Jaime said. "Mr. Dodds is a naval specialist. And a member of the resistance."

"Hello," he said. "You may call me Bob." He had an accent that sounded almost British but not quite. "Or Mr. Dodds."

"Are you South African?" Ostin asked.

"You are very astute," he replied. "You must be Ostin."

Ostin looked impressed. "Yes, sir."

"May I say, I have very much looked forward to meeting all of you. Like so many others, I have followed your adventures and I am most impressed with your courage and cleverness."

"It's just survival," I said.

"Well, I hope to be of service to you," he said. "And help you *survive* even longer. I've been asked to brief you on the Elgen fleet and help you in your task to sink the *Ampere*."

"Let us talk in the dining room," Jaime said.

"Have you had breakfast?" Taylor asked. "We made waffles."

"Ah, waffles. Unfortunately we had breakfast at the hotel," he said. "But thank you very much. May I use this table over here?" He pointed to the kitchen table.

"We need to wipe it off," Taylor said. "It's sticky."

I picked up the few plates left on the table, then Taylor ran a damp cloth over it.

Dodds set his briefcase on the table, then opened it. He took out several folded blueprints and laid them out until they covered the table's surface. We all gathered around the table.

"To understand the composition of the Elgen fleet, you must first understand why they even have one. The crimes the Elgen have committed are serious enough to land the entire board in prison for the rest of their lives. They are guilty of money laundering, conspiracy, bribery, fraud, securities fraud, tax evasion, extortion, espionage, and, though still unproven, mass murder.

"About four years ago, when the FBI began looking into the Elgen's criminal activities, Chairman Schema purchased a sizable yacht and moved the Elgen operations to international waters.

"Their first ship was an older-model yacht they renamed the *Edison*. Now, in international waters and belonging to no nation, the Elgen have become a nation unto themselves. They manage their corporation from the ship and move their money through offshore banks in Switzerland, Bermuda, and Cyprus.

"As the Elgen grew, they sold the *Edison* and moved to a custom designed boat called the *Ampere*. The *Ampere* is a state-of-the-art luxury superyacht. Think of it as a floating Waldorf hotel with surface-to-air missiles."

"McKenna has been on it," Taylor said.

She nodded. "It's pretty amazing."

"For a half billion dollars, it should be," Dodds said. "If you have something to add or if I say anything that you have found inaccurate, please feel free to contribute."

McKenna nodded. "Yes, sir."

Dodds continued. "The *Ampere* is the first of many ships the Elgen have since acquired. Today, the Elgen fleet consists of seven ships, each named after a famous scientist of electricity. If the Elgen were a country, the *Ampere* would be their capital. It is the throne from which Admiral Hatch runs his kingdom."

"Admiral Hatch?" Ostin said.

"That is what he now calls himself," Dodds said. "Actually, his full title is Supreme Commander General Admiral Hatch." He shook his head. "I'm going to give you a rundown of the complete fleet." He handed each of us a piece of paper with pictures of seven boats. "This is a list of the Elgen boats. You are to memorize it, then destroy it."

I looked at the sheet. It had a picture of each boat accompanied with technical jargon.

"The first boat on your sheet is the *Ampere*. We'll discuss it in greater detail a bit later. The second boat is the *Faraday*. It is a twenty-thousand-ton refurbished World War Two troopship and, accordingly, is used to transport Elgen guards. It can carry in excess of thirty-five-hundred passengers.

"Boat three is the *Watt*, the most powerful of the Elgen fleet.

The *Watt* is a fully operational battle cruiser. Think of it as the fleet's bodyguard. It is a highly lethal ship, with technology only the most advanced navies carry, including tactical tomahawk cruise missiles, torpedoes, long-range cannons, and advanced targeting systems.

"A few years ago, while the *Ampere* was sailing from the Formosa Strait to the Mediterranean, they passed through the pirate-infested waters of Somalia. As happens too often these days, Somalian pirates tried to capture the *Ampere*, which, frankly, had they succeeded, would have been a blessing to the world.

"The *Watt* blew the pirate ship out of the water more than a mile out, then hunted down its survivors and gunned them down in the waters. The *Watt* is captained by Viktor Chirkev, a former rear admiral in the Russian navy. He is a skilled captain and known to shoot first and ask questions later.

"Boat four is the *Volta*, the Elgen's science ship. It is where Elgen experiments are conducted. It is also where, we believe, the original MEI is being carried.

"Boat five, the *Joule*, is the most secretive of the fleet. We do not know much about it except that it is the fastest of the fleet and, if necessary, can submerge. We believe that it's a floating bank vault and where the Elgen keep billions of dollars of gold bullion, foreign currencies, and diamonds, which would explain why the *Joule* is almost always in close proximity to the *Watt*.

"Boat six is the *Ohm*. The *Ohm* is a supply ship and will be the most active during the docking in Port Callao. A floating commissary if you will.

"Boat seven is the *Tesla*. The *Tesla* is a tender, a small landing craft, used for getting troops from the *Faraday*. As the waters surrounding Tuvalu are too shallow to dock the *Faraday*, the *Tesla* will be transporting guards to the shore for the attack. The *Tesla* can carry seventy guards and crew at a time. Even though it is primarily a transport, it is still armed and dangerous. It is equipped with twin fifty-caliber machine guns and a twenty-millimeter Oerlikon cannon. And, of course, the soldiers' weaponry." He looked us over. "That's the Elgen fleet."

"It's a freakin' navy," Ostin said.

"Fortunately we don't have to sink the whole navy. Just the *Ampere*," Dodds said. "You cut off the serpent's head, the rest of the serpent dies." He looked out over the table. "These are blueprints from the ship," Dodds said. "The *Ampere* is custom designed with a gross weight of eleven thousand tonnes with a displacement configuration. The ship is powered by a triple-screw, diesel-electric propulsion system with four marine diesel engines. It has a maximum speed of twenty-five knots and a cruising speed of twenty-two."

I understood only about half of what Dodds was talking about, but Ostin nodded with interest.

"How do you know all of this?" I asked.

Dodds looked at me. "You should know, Michael. You brought us this information."

"When did I . . ." I stopped. "Grace," I said.

Grace was one of the electric children we had freed from the academy. She had the ability to download information from computers, and she'd taken just about everything from the academy before we got her out.

Dodds nodded. "She has been a veritable gold mine. We just keep extracting more and more valuable information.

"So back to our target. The *Ampere* is one hundred and forty-five meters long and the hull is constructed of steel built over an aluminum superstructure with Kevlar insulation. It has advanced buoyancy system that will keep it afloat even after a hull breech. It is one tough ship."

"How do we sink it?" I asked.

"We don't," Dodds said. "We blow it up. The engine room is on the first level, here," he said, touching the blueprint. "The *Ampere*'s fuel tanks hold more than a quarter million gallons of diesel fuel. With enough explosives in the engine room we can set off the tanks. If you blow a quarter million gallons of fuel, you'll blow the entire ship to pieces."

We all looked at each other. "How do we get the bomb on the boat?" I asked.

"There's the rub," Dodds said. "There will be guards all along the shore, and the gangplank will be highly guarded day and night."

"We could disguise ourselves as Elgen guards and walk on," Jack said, looking at me.

"It wouldn't work," Dodds said. "They are checking everyone who comes on the boat with metal detectors and fingerprint identification. Even if you got on, you'd never carry the explosives past them."

"If they're loading up with supplies," Taylor said, "we could sneak into some of the supply boxes and have them carry us on."

"Clever," Dodds said, "but they're prepared for that too. Their security is like the one you'll find at an airport, except much more advanced. Everything that enters the ship must pass through a type of backscatter X-ray machine. Remember, these guys developed the MEI. They know how to scan."

Jack leaned forward. "We could take a small raft to the back of the boat and throw a grappling hook," he said. "And climb up."

"The deck is more than a hundred feet up," Dodds said. "You would have to shoot it up. Which means you would need a grapple gun. We can expect that the decks will be patrolled by guards and a grappling hook would be easy to see. You would run a high risk of being discovered and shot before you even climbed to the deck."

Dodds was starting to annoy me. "So, you've told us why none of our ideas would work. What's your plan?"

"Unfortunately, I don't have one," Dodds said. "The Electroclan has continually succeeded where we have failed. We were hoping you would come up with something."

"You said the hull is made of steel?" McKenna asked.

"Yes," Dodds replied.

"We don't need a grappling hook. Michael could magnetically climb it. The way Kylee does."

I looked at her. "I've never done anything like that before."

"You did in the Starxource plant," Jack said. "When the rats were chasing us. You could carry the rope up, tie it, then throw it down. Then I'll climb up, and we'll pull up everyone else."

"It would have to be at night," Jaime said. "Or else the other boats in the fleet would see you."

"That could work," Dodds said, looking at me. "What do you think? Could you climb it?"

"I'll need to practice," I said. "And my knot tying. I haven't tied anything since Cub Scouts."

"I can arrange both," Jaime said.

"The next question is, how do we get around to the back of the boat without being seen?"

"Scuba," Ostin said.

"Scuba?" Taylor said. "What if there are sharks?"

"Sharks rarely attack humans," Ostin said. "Besides, there are much worse things than sharks on the *Ampere*."

"Like Hatch," I said. I looked at Taylor. "I say we keep scuba as one of the options."

"If we're already diving," Jack said, "why don't we just put the explosives under the boat and blow it out of the water?"

"The *Ampere* has a reinforced hull and is shaped to deflect a hull explosion. Also, the ship's sonar will detect anything directly under the boat more than four feet in length. They would have divers down after you in seconds."

"If this was a suicide mission, it wouldn't matter," Jack said.

Everyone went quiet.

I looked at Jack. "But it's not," I said.

Jack just looked ahead with dark eyes. "But it would work."

"Not necessarily," Dodds said. "As I said, the hull is shaped to deflect an explosion. Think of it this way. If you grasp a firecracker in your hand, it will blow up your hand. If you set it flat on your palm, it will hurt but it won't do much damage. That's the difference between putting the explosive inside the boat as opposed to outside of it."

"Then we'll get more dynamite," Jack said.

"We're not using dynamite," Dodds said. "We'll be using a much more stable water-gel explosive. But either way, one person could not carry enough to sink the *Ampere* from the outside. In fact, all of you together couldn't carry enough."

"Then we fill a boat with explosives and ram it," Jack said.

"That would fall under the whole suicide-mission thing," I said.

No one else said a word. Jack's comment had left everyone speechless. After a moment Dodds said, "Let's move on. As difficult as boarding will be, it is only the beginning. The *Ampere* is just as protected on board as it is overboard.

"The Elgen are exacting about their security. It is rumored that the *Ampere* has antiphotograph lasers that sweep the boat's surroundings for cameras. When it detects a CCD, they shine a laser into the camera's lens to prevent a photograph from being taken."

"What's a CCD?" Taylor asked.

"It's a charge-coupled device," Ostin said. "In a CCD image sensor, pixels are—"

I stopped him. "It's something in a camera," I said.

"Then how did you get this photograph?" Taylor asked.

Dodds smiled. "Very carefully." He looked back down at the blueprint. "In addition, the boat is equipped with a shipwide camera surveillance system, an intruder detection system, armor-plated doors, and bulletproof windows. We aren't certain how the intruder detection system works, but we suspect that, with all the deck activity during loading, the system will be turned off. But the surveillance cameras will still be a problem."

"Zeus was good with those," Ostin said. "He'd just blow them out."

"That's not helpful," I said.

"We could make a distraction," McKenna said. "We could blow up something like we did in Paucartambo."

"No," Dodds said, shaking his head. "At best it would only distract them for a few minutes. And if something unexpected happens, the Elgen will go on heightened alert. They'll pull in like a threatened turtle."

"Then we'll need to look like them," I said. "Like we did in the Starxource plant."

"How do we get Elgen uniforms?" Taylor asked.

"We could steal them," Jack said.

"No," Dodds said. "That would be another red flag. The Elgen are very strict about missing uniforms. They are like the owner of a burger joint who counts the cups each night to make sure his employees aren't giving away free drinks to their friends."

"My friend Sara used to do that," Taylor whispered to me.

"But we could take *one*," Jaime said. "That wouldn't cause any suspicion. The Elgen sailors often go AWOL."

"What good is one?" Taylor asked. "There are five of us."

"We take one, and we copy it," Jaime said. "We can make them close enough that they will not notice the difference."

"Do we have time for that?" Jack asked.

"My people could make five uniforms in one day. The boats will be in port at least three days."

"What if no one leaves the boat?" Ostin asked.

"The sailors have been at sea for many weeks. Trust me, they will come ashore," Jaime said. "Leave it to me."

"So we will duplicate the uniforms," Dodds said. "But we'll need black cover-ups to go over them as you climb onto the ship."

"So we make a black cloak too," Jaime said. "Simple."

"Okay, one more thing," Dodds said. "All the exterior doors and some of the interior doors on the *Ampere* are locked with magnetic switches."

"This just keeps getting better," McKenna said.

"Then how do we get through them?" Taylor asked.

"You will have to find a key," Dodds said. "This probably won't be too difficult, as every crew member will have one. You can take one from a guard, or perhaps when you get the uniform . . ."

"No problem," Jaime said. "We will take the key with the uniform."

Dodds looked back down at the blueprints and touched a spot near the boat's stern. "This is where you will climb up. Once you're all on board, you will gather here, at this door, which opens to a staircase. From what we know, this back staircase is a fire escape and is rarely used, usually only in the case of an emergency. It leads to all levels, including level one. It is very narrow so you will have to travel in single file.

"At the bottom of the stairwell, you will move forward approximately thirty yards to the engine room."

"How will we know if we're going the right way?" Taylor asked.

"You're already at the back of the boat, so there is no other way to go. Also, you will hear the *Ampere*'s engines long before you reach the engine room. The crew wears earplugs. This could be a problem in the hallway as you will have difficulty communicating with one another because of the noise."

"Even when the boat's docked?" I asked.

"The captain will usually keep at least one engine idling to keep it from drifting and to charge the batteries." He looked up again. "You must remember, the engine room will not be unmanned. Even at night, there will be six to ten crewmen. They will probably be unarmed, but do not count on it. You will have to take out the crew, set the explosive and timer, then escape the ship before it explodes. It's that simple."

"Simple?" I said.

"Sorry," Dodds replied. "In concept it's simple. In practice it will be very . . . challenging."

"By challenging do you mean hopelessly impossible?" Taylor said.

He shook his head sympathetically. "Hopefully *not* impossible." He looked around at us. "But from what I've seen, this group seems to specialize in the impossible. Are there any questions?"

No one spoke for a moment, then Ostin said, "Yeah. Is it too late to back out?"

33

Silo Practice

That evening Jaime and I drove out to the country, looking for a place for me to practice climbing.

"There," he said. "I thought I remembered seeing that." He pointed out over the fence to a tall cylindrical structure. "It is a grain silo. It is made of steel."

When we were certain that no one was around, we climbed over a barbwire fence to the farm, then walked fifty yards to the base of the silo.

"Do you know whose farm this is?" I asked.

Jaime shook his head. "No."

"Will anyone see us?" I asked.

"I hope not. You climb. I will keep lookout."

The silo was made of ribbed, galvanized steel and rose about forty feet high, the top tapering off to a cone.

The best way to describe what it's like magnetizing myself is to say it's like pulsing inside my body instead of outside of it—a little like stifling a sneeze.

I reached my hand as high above me as I could, then pulsed. My hand stuck firmly to the cool metal. Then, pulsing my legs, I jumped up with my knees against the silo. Both my knees stuck. For a moment I just sat there, stuck in place. As Jack had said, I had climbed the wall at the Starxource plant, but it was really just hanging on. Actually climbing upward involved more than just sticking to the metal, but a carefully timed process of sticking, releasing, then re-sticking.

It took me ten minutes to climb just ten feet. At this rate it would take me an hour to climb the *Ampere*, far too long to hang on to the side of the boat without being seen.

After some experimenting, I developed a rhythm, shifting my magnetism from one side of my body to the other. About twenty feet up, I accidentally released one side before fully magnetizing the other and fell about five feet before, in panic, I magnetized my entire body and stuck to the side of the silo like a magnet on a refrigerator door.

I climbed to the top of the silo and back down again in about a half hour, which wasn't too bad considering that the first twenty minutes I was still figuring out what I was doing. When I got down I was covered with sweat and panting. I leaned over on my knees to catch my breath.

"Let's try again," Jaime said.

I looked up. "What?"

"Not fast enough. This time I will time you. On your mark, get set, go."

I jumped up and began climbing. It reminded me of the time in seventh grade gym class when we had to climb the rope to the ceiling. I didn't set any gym records, but at least I had made it to the top.

This brought to mind another problem. Ostin, who was not only out of shape but also afraid of heights, made it only a third of the way before he gave up and slid down, which gave him a wicked rope burn on his thighs and arms. His mother called the school the next day and gave the gym teacher an earful. After all we'd been through, Ostin was in better shape than he was back then, but still I wondered if he could do it.

I reached the top of the silo, then slid back down in a controlled slide. I dropped the last six feet to the ground, rolling on the grass below.

"How'd I do?"

Jaime nodded. "Very good. You made it to the top in four minutes. If you can keep this fast, you will climb the side of the boat in less than fifteen minutes."

"Except I'll be wearing an Elgen uniform and cloak," I said.

"Yes, and carrying a heavy rope," Jaime added.

"I didn't think about that," I said. "I better practice with the rope."

"I will purchase one tomorrow," Jaime said. "We will come back tomorrow."

On the drive back to the villa, I said, "Any word on my mother?"

Jaime shook his head. "It is very strange," he said. "The voice is not responding to our signal."

"What does that mean?" I asked.

"I don't know. But I will keep trying." After a few more minutes he said, "I am worried about our friend Jack."

"So am I," I said. "He hasn't been the same since we lost Wade. He blames himself for Wade's death."

"That is bad," Jaime said.

"Taylor told me that she read his mind and he's not expecting to survive the attack. It's like he's just accepted this is going to be a suicide mission."

Jaime nodded slowly. "Perhaps that is his wish."

"That's what I'm afraid of." I frowned. "I don't know what to do when someone loses hope."

"You pray for them, my friend. You pray for them."

We were quiet the rest of the ride home.

34

Yachts and Fishing Boats

I'm not sure why Jaime didn't just stay at the villa with us, but he didn't. He usually just showed up when we needed him—like for my climbing practices. The next day we found an abandoned metal storage shed closer to the house. I went there twice a day until I got my time down to just twelve minutes. Taylor started coming with me to watch. Or maybe just to feel like a cheerleader again. She was good at that. She even made up a cheer.

> Go, Michael.
> Climb that wall.
> Reach the top
> And please don't fall.
> Goooooooo, Michael!

Then she'd do this little kick thing. Jaime just looked at her like she was crazy. Truthfully, her cheering was counterproductive. The first time she did the whole cheer, I started laughing so hard that I fell ten feet.

The next three days were an emotional roller coaster for me. At one moment I imagined us sinking the boat, escaping, and flying home, having saved the country of Tuvalu, wherever that was. The next moment the whole thing looked like a suicide mission.

On the morning of the third day, Jaime came in while we were all eating breakfast. Taylor had made French toast and fried Peruvian bacon, which was so thick it looked like ham.

"You're early," I said. "I thought we were going at eleven."

"Get something to eat," Taylor said. "Help yourself, I made a ton."

Jaime looked at us seriously. "The Elgen fleet is in port."

We all stopped eating.

"All of them?" Ostin asked.

"*Sí.*"

"I want to see it," I said.

"You will soon enough," Jaime said. "When we attack."

"I need to see it before then. I need to see it in daylight."

"That is risky."

"Unlike sneaking aboard and sinking it," Ostin said.

"I have to see it," I said firmly. "I need to know what I'm facing. I need to visualize the attack."

Jaime looked unsure. "I will have to see if Dodds can come."

"We don't need Dodds," I said. "I just want to see the boats for myself."

"Me too," Jack said.

"And me," Taylor said.

Jaime looked at us for a moment, then said, "Very well. I must make arrangements to capture our sailor's uniform, then I will be back."

"Don't forget his magnetic key," Ostin added.

"*Sí.* And the key. Then we will go visit the Elgen."

* * *

Jaime returned to the house around five in the afternoon. All five of us were waiting for him in the front room and walked out to meet him before he reached the front door.

When we were in the van, Taylor said, "Jaime, did you set your sailor trap?"

"*Sí, senorita.*"

"What are you using for bait?" she asked.

"A pretty woman, of course." Then he added, "It works every time."

"Worked for me," Ostin said, looking over at McKenna. She smiled at him.

"Wow," Taylor whispered to me. "Just wow."

Jaime drove north up the Pacific coastline about twenty miles before we came to a solitary cliff overlooking the Port Callao harbor. We reached the port after the sun had begun making its descent, turning the bay a hue of golden rose.

After Jaime was completely certain that we were not being watched, he retrieved a pair of binoculars from beneath the van's driver seat and we walked out to the edge of the cliff and got down on our stomachs. The Callao bay stretched out below us, bustling with barges and cranes, navy ships, yachts, freighters, and cruise liners.

"That's a lot bigger than I thought it would be," Taylor said.

"Port Callao is the largest seaport in South America," Jaime said.

"What does Callao mean?" Ostin asked.

Jaime looked at him. "This you do not know?"

"Nope," he said.

Jaime nodded. "Neither does anyone else." He pointed to a group of ships a few hundred yards north of us. "They are there, all together," he said, handing me his binoculars.

Even without the binoculars I recognized the vessels. It was impressive to actually see all seven boats of the Elgen fleet together—impressive and *terrifying*.

The *Ampere* was in the middle of the fleet and wasn't hard to pick out. It was the coolest boat I had ever seen—the kind of craft Ostin would have cut out of his *Popular Science* magazine and pinned to his wall.

What made it even more fascinating was knowing that Hatch was somewhere on that ship. I just wished that I could throw a massive lightning ball and blow the ship and Hatch off the planet.

"So that's the *Ampere*," I said.

"*Sí*," Jaime said.

"I told you it was cool," McKenna said.

"The space shuttle is cool," Ostin said. "That thing is freakin' epic."

"And we're going to sink it," I said. "It's kind of sad in a way. Like blowing up a cathedral."

"More like a house of horrors," McKenna said.

"They are docked close together for protection," Jaime said. "You can see the guards have blocked off the entire shoreline."

Ostin grimaced. "If we scuba dived in, we'd have to swim at least a half mile underwater." He was the only one of us who had actually scuba dived, and that was during a highly supervised excursion on a family trip to Hawaii. "That won't be easy."

"What part of any of this is easy?" Jack said.

"I'm just saying, it's going to add at least an hour getting there and we'll all be exhausted when we do. And by the time we blow the ship and get back to shore, the place will be crawling with military. How will we come ashore?"

"We'll have to set a longer delay on the explosive's timer," I said.

"Which gives them more of a chance to find it," Jaime said.

"And where do we put the scuba tanks while we climb the boat?" McKenna asked.

None of us had an answer.

I looked back out over the fleet. "What are those boats out there? The little ones behind the fleet."

"Fishing boats," Jaime said.

"They're close to the ships," I said.

McKenna had the binoculars and was looking out at the boats. "That one's not even a hundred feet from the *Ampere*," she said.

"They don't suspect them," Ostin said.

Jaime smiled. "I think we just found our way to the *Ampere*."

35

Time

Dodds and Jaime came over the next day around noon. Both men looked anxious, but Dodds looked especially on edge.

"We've learned that the resupplying is moving faster than we anticipated," Dodds said. "They've filed with the port authority to pull out Thursday afternoon."

"The day after tomorrow," Taylor said.

"That means we'll have to attack tomorrow night," Jack said.

Dodds nodded. "We have the uniforms and cloaks but no key. Apparently the sailors are not allowed to take them off the ship. We've secured scuba gear, but I understand you won't be using it."

"We think it will be better to use a fishing boat," I said. "We'll get close enough to raft over to the *Ampere*."

"I have already found a black raft," Jaime said.

"What about the explosives?" Jack asked.

"They're ready," Dodds said. "In a backpack with detonators and timers. I'll go over the timers with all of you later."

"No need," Jack said. "I'll be carrying the explosives."

Dodd looked at him with an uncomfortable expression. "Just in case something happens to you, it would be best to have a backup."

Jack nodded. "You're right."

"I have chartered the fishing boat," Jaime said. "We will leave at two thirty a.m. from the north end of the port."

"Won't that look suspicious?" Ostin asked. "A fishing boat at night?"

"No," Jaime said. "Local fishing boats often return late at night."

"There is one other factor to keep in mind," Dodds said. "The weather. It's expected to rain. As long as it doesn't hamper Michael's climbing, it could be to our advantage."

"I've never climbed a wet surface," I said.

"Kylee could do it," McKenna said.

"How is the rain helpful?" Taylor asked.

"Cloud cover, no moon, poorer visibility," Dodds replied. "And less chance that someone will be taking a leisurely walk on the deck." He looked around. "Anything else?"

"Did you arrange for me to talk to my mother?" I asked.

Jaime and Dodds looked at each other. "I'm afraid that will not be possible," Dodds said.

"Why?" I turned to Jaime. "You promised that I would be able to talk to her."

"I'm sorry," Jaime said. "But we have lost communication with the voice."

"What?"

"You know that we were compromised," Dodds said. "Things have taken another turn for the worse. Two days ago the Elgen discovered our agent on their boat. We must assume that they now know everything he knows, about the voice, the resistance, everything he knew."

"Then they know about our plans!" Ostin exclaimed.

"Fortunately we had not yet told him what we were planning to do," Dodds said. "We were waiting until we knew our exact timing so we could warn him to leave the boat."

"How did you learn this?" I asked.

"The voice contacted our associate in Bolivia," Jaime said. "He drove through the night to tell us."

I looked around at my friends. "So we're really alone," I said.

"We always were," Taylor said.

"At least the day is perfect," Jack said.

"Why do you say that?" Taylor asked.

"Thursday is Wade's birthday."

Dodds looked around at us all. "We'll leave here at one forty-five a.m. Jaime and I will have everything prepared. I want you to stay up as late as you can tonight. Study the boat plans, party, just try to stay up until dawn. That way you'll sleep all day and be fresh and ready to go at night."

"That shouldn't be too hard," Ostin said. "Staying up all night."

"Why is that?" I asked.

"It might be our last night to live."

36

A Change in Plans

Taylor and I lay on the front room couch talking until she fell asleep around nine in the morning. About a half hour after that I heard the garage door open. Jack walked into the front room. He was wet with sweat.

"Michael," he whispered.

I got up without waking Taylor.

"What's up?"

He motioned for me to follow him out to the garage. After he'd shut the door behind me, he said, "The plan doesn't make sense."

"You're telling me now?" I said.

"Better now than never."

"What part doesn't make sense?"

"It doesn't take five people to plant an explosive. Just one. If I could get on the boat, I'd do it myself. But I need your help to get on board." He looked me in the eyes. "We don't need everyone else."

I wasn't sure how to answer. "But we're a team."

"That's no reason to risk their lives," Jack said. "Think about it. What do we need Ostin for? We don't need his brains, the plan is already set. He'll just slow us down. Do you think he can even climb the rope?"

I didn't answer. We both knew he was right.

"Or McKenna? Taylor might be helpful, but is it really worth risking her life? Are you okay with that?"

I frowned. "No."

"I didn't think so. So here's the new plan. We turn off everyone's alarms, meet Jaime outside, and tell him it's just the two of us. You get me on the boat, help me score a key, then once I'm inside you get clear."

"What if you're stopped on the way to the engine room?"

"I blow it."

I just looked at him.

"You heard the man, if the bomb's inside, it's going to take the ship down."

"I can't send you in there alone."

"You're not. I'm sending myself in there alone. What's the difference? I'm going in there anyway."

I shook my head. "I can't let you do this."

"Look, remember in the Starxource plant when you stayed inside and locked the pipe so none of us could go back for you? What was that, huh? It was a calculated risk. You did what you felt was right under the circumstance. And because of it, you saved your mother and the rest of us. And you even got out yourself.

"And what about when Zeus blew the water pipe, knowing it would kill him? This is no different. All I'm asking is that you let me do the same thing."

I shook my head. "Jack, I know you think that Wade's death was your fault. . . ."

"This has nothing to do with Wade's death," he said. "It has to do with your life and everyone else's. I'm expendable, dude."

"No, you're not. Not to me."

"I know. Because you're my friend. And you're a good friend. So let me do this, Michael. Let me do this one good thing. You made that choice in the Starxource plant. Let me make that choice too."

I looked down a moment then said, "I don't like it."

"But you know I'm right," he said.

I breathed out slowly. Finally I said, "Okay. We'll do it your way."

"Thank you, Michael. It's the right thing."

"I hope so," I said.

"It is," Jack said. *"Semper Fi."*

I just looked at him sadly. What he didn't know was that I had no intention of leaving him alone on the boat. *"Semper Fi,"* I said. *"Semper Fi."*

37

You Call This Trust?

A few minutes later I crept into Ostin's room. He and McKenna were asleep next to each other. I turned off their alarm. Then I went back out to the couch and lay down next to Taylor. I couldn't sleep. For nearly an hour I just looked at her.

My heart ached. I didn't regret agreeing to Jack's plan—I would never regret saving Taylor's life. I just knew how slim the chances were that I would see her again. My world had changed in the last year in no small part due to Taylor. Having someone care about me and believe in me like she did was as much a power as my electricity was. I thought of writing her a note, but I really didn't know where to begin. Instead, I just cuddled up next to her. It was probably close to noon when I fell asleep.

Jack woke me. It was dark again. I looked up and he put his finger over his mouth. I lifted Taylor's arm from me, then slowly rolled off the couch to my knees. I paused to look at her one last time. I wondered if I would ever see that beautiful face again. I pushed the thought from my mind. *At least I can guarantee that she will see her home again*, I told myself.

The villa was dark and quiet as I walked out the front door and shut it behind me. Jack was leaning against the porch wall. It was overcast, as Dodds had said it might be, and there were no stars or moon visible.

"What time is it?" I asked.

"One thirty. They'll be here any minute." He looked at me. "You ready?"

"As ready as I'll ever be. You?"

"I'm ready."

A few minutes later the lights of the van appeared at the end of the driveway. "Let's stop them before they get close enough to wake anybody," Jack said, walking toward the light. We met the van partway down the lane. Jaime was driving and he stopped the van next to us. Jack slid open the door and we both got in.

"Where's everyone else?" Dodds asked.

"It's just us," Jack said.

"That's not the plan," Dodds said.

"This is a better plan," I said. "Two can do it. The others will just get in the way."

"Everyone agreed to this?" Dodds asked.

"We don't have time to argue," Jack said. "Let's go."

Dodds looked upset but relented. "All right, it's your plan. Let's go." Jaime started to put the van into gear then stopped.

Dodds looked back at us. "Where's everyone else?"

"We just told you," Jack said.

He squinted. "What are you talking about?"

"It's just the two of us," I said. "Come on, let's go."

Again, Jaime started to pull the van forward, then stopped.

Dodds turned back. "Where's everyone else?"

Jack scowled. "What the . . ."

"It's Taylor," I said.

I looked out the window to see Taylor storming down the drive-way. When she got to the van she threw open the door. "Really? After all we talked about, you still tried to go without me?"

"I just . . ."

"Lied? Conspired?"

"He was just trying to protect you," Jack said.

"You zip it," Taylor said. "I already know this was your idea."

She spun back at me. "Really? This is trust?"

"I'm sorry I tried to leave you out. But I'm not sorry."

"What is that supposed to mean?"

"It means he loves you," Jack said.

"I said zip it," Taylor said.

"It means I love you," I said.

"And that's why we stay together. We're not just a couple, Michael, we're the Electroclan—at least what's left of it—and that means we stick together through good and bad times. We've gotten this far because we've stuck together. I know you were trying to protect me, but I didn't ask to be protected. I asked to be with you."

"I thought it was the right thing," I said.

"I know, and part of me loves that you did this. But the right thing is us working together. All of us." She turned to Jack. "And that means you, too. You don't have to prove you're a hero. You've proven that so many times I've lost count. We all admire and love you, just like Wade did. Don't take that away from us. Please."

Jack looked stunned. Then his eyes welled up with tears.

"All right," I said. "Let's go wake Ostin and McKenna."

38

Seventeen, Seventeen

None of us told Ostin and McKenna that we'd tried to leave them behind, and Ostin spent half the drive trying to figure out why his alarm clock hadn't gone off. After just twenty minutes the van pulled off the coastal highway and headed down a long sloped road toward the wide dark bay. As we neared the water, the ships seemed to grow in their immensity, rising before us like great floating mountains. There were lights on the Elgen boats and loading dock, assuring us that they weren't asleep.

As Jaime drove, Dodds turned around to face us. He held up a square, plastic object with a keypad and a digital screen. "This is the explosive's timer. It connects to the detonator in the pack. Once you punch in the code the explosive is activated and cannot be turned off."

"What's the code?" I asked.

"Seventeen, seventeen."

"Just like the radio frequency," I said.

"Remember, once you punch in the code, it cannot be turned off. So do not activate it until you are ready to commit. To set the timer you can either punch in the number of minutes on the keypad or simply push this black button. Each time you push it, it will advance the timer one minute, up to two hours. Like the activation button, once it is set it cannot be changed. So be sure to give yourself plenty of time to get off the boat. But remember, the more time you allow, the more time they have to find the bomb and dispose of it."

He handed me a small black tube similar to the one Jaime used to set off his gun sentry. "As you leave the boat, push this button. It will alert us that you are on your way. The raft you will be using has a motor, but do not use it until you are leaving, otherwise they'll hear you. After you're off the ship, head straight out to the open sea. We will be watching for you with night-vision binoculars and will pick you up in a speedboat. Any questions so far?"

Ostin asked, "Can the detonators be set off by impact or heat?"

"It would have to be intense heat," he said. "Like in an open fire. Why?"

"Just in case the timer malfunctions," Ostin said.

"That won't be a problem," Dodds said. He glanced out the side window. "Okay, we are just about there. When we reach the fishing boat, you'll change into your Elgen uniforms, then cover them with the cloaks and stocking caps. You'll be completely concealed. I brought gloves for the three of you who glow. I don't know if you'll be able to use them as you climb, Michael, you'll just have to test them.

"When the boat passes behind the *Ampere*, we'll throw the raft out and stop the boat. Jack will climb in first so he can help the others on. You'll have just a few seconds to get into the raft. Then the boat will move on, leaving you behind. We'll come in as close to the *Ampere*'s stern as we can, but you'll still probably have to paddle about thirty yards.

"As I said, the raft has a motor and will do about ten knots, but do not use it until after you've set the bomb and gotten off the ship.

Once you reach the *Ampere*, there are magnets to anchor the raft to the hull. They're very strong magnets, so when it's time to leave, don't try to pull them off, just release or cut the line."

Jack patted his knife. "Got it."

"Remember, stay quiet, low, and covered. In this darkness you'll be almost invisible. You know the rest of the plan. Don't forget to capture a key. I doubt they'll leave any doors unlocked. Any questions?"

None of us had any.

"Then good luck and Godspeed," he said. "Let's hope we catch Hatch sleeping."

39

Fishin' Impossible

Five minutes later Jaime stopped the van in front of a small, lantern-lit shack with a hand-painted sign: JORGE'S CHARTER FISHING TOURS.

In spite of the hour, an older man walked out of the building to greet us. He and Jaime spoke a bit in Spanish, then Jaime turned to us.

"Everything is ready. Follow me."

All of us except Dodds walked past the shack and down a wood-planked dock to where an old fishing boat was moored. The boat was beige and turquoise. It had an upper platform enclosed in canvas and its fishing lines were still in place. There was a black raft tied to the port side of the boat.

"Isn't that the wrong side for the raft?" Ostin asked Jaime. "The *Ampere* is south of us."

"Yes, but we will first go far out to sea, then turn back and come in from the other direction as if we are just returning from fishing, so we will pass the boat on the starboard side."

"Clever," Ostin said.

We climbed on board and walked through the cabin to the open back of the boat. It smelled of saltwater and fish. On the floor were canvas bags with our initials marked in pen.

"Your uniforms," Jaime said. "Get dressed."

We all put on the sailor uniforms, which fit perfectly.

"They did a good job," Taylor said. "We look like Elgen sailors." Then she added, "Actually, I've never seen one."

Jaime said, "Put on the cloaks."

I pulled the cloak from the bottom of the bag and slid my arms through it. The fabric was black and lightweight, like vinyl, though softer and more opaque. I looked up at everyone else. We looked like we were wearing Halloween witch costumes.

"Michael, check this out," Ostin said, leaning over the back of the boat. I walked back to see what he was looking at. Painted on the boat's stern was the name: *Fishin' Impossible.*

"Doesn't exactly inspire confidence," I said.

Dodds walked up to the side of the boat carrying a large black vinyl backpack. "Jack," he said.

"Yes, sir," Jack said.

"Your explosives," Dodds said, handing the pack over the side of the boat.

"How sensitive are they?" Jack asked.

"These are pretty stable," he said. "But don't push your luck."

Jack slid the pack over his shoulders just to get a sense of its weight. "About fifty pounds," he said. "No problem." He set the pack on the ground and unzipped the top flap, exposing the detonator. The digital screen glowed light green.

"What's the code?" Dodds quizzed.

"Seventeen, seventeen," Jack replied. He looked up. "That's how old Wade would be today."

The boat's engine started, and the air smelled of gasoline and exhaust as the propeller churned and gurgled beneath us.

"It is time to go," Jaime said. He began untying the rope holding us to the dock.

"Aren't you coming?" I asked Dodds, who was still on the dock.

"No. We can't put all our eggs in one basket, and I believe I am close to reestablishing radio contact with the resistance." He pushed the boat away from the dock with his foot. "But I will see you all shortly."

For just a moment his words hung in the air like a promise. The fishing boat sputtered in its own veil of exhaust as it slowly pulled away from the dock. Then it rotated until we were facing the sea. The old man pushed down on the throttle and we lurched forward, headed out into the cold darkness.

40

The Shadow of the *Ampere*

It started raining as the old boat chugged out to sea. Taylor slid up next to me and took my hand in hers. "I'm cold," she said.

I put my arm around her.

"You know, when we attacked the Starxource plant we weren't together," she said. "This time we're together."

I looked at her. "Our first date," I said.

She grinned.

"Are you scared?" I asked.

"Terrified."

"Me too."

"Do you think we'll make it back?"

"Of course we will."

"Really?"

"I can't afford to doubt," I said. "My mom used to say that faith and fear can't exist simultaneously in the mind any more than light and dark can exist simultaneously in the same room."

"Your mom is smart."

"I know. I wished I could have spoken to her once more. . . ." I stopped myself.

Taylor squeezed my hand. "You'll get the chance," she said.

A moment later Taylor looked over at Jack. "How are you feeling?"

"Wet," he said.

Suddenly the whining of the engine stopped and the boat slowed and pitched forward until the surging of the waves almost rocked us out of our seats. Jaime came out of the cab with a large coil of black rope over his shoulder. "We are turning back now. It is time to put on your masks and gloves." As we donned our coverings, Jaime walked over and inspected the ropes on the raft, then turned back to us. "Remember you must go fast. Jack first, then Taylor, Michael, Ostin, and McKenna. When you are all in I will hand down the pack and rope. If we get near the boat and are discovered, we will about."

"About?" Taylor said.

"I think he means abort," I said.

Jaime went back to the cabin. The boat turned around and headed back toward the lights of the shore. I stood and walked up to the front of the boat.

"Jaime."

"*Sí*, Mr. Michael."

"I need to ask you a favor."

He looked at me seriously. "Anything."

"If we don't make it, I want you to tell my mother what we were trying to do."

"*Sí*. Of course."

"Also Ostin's and Taylor's families. Taylor's family doesn't even know she's electric."

"You will come back, Mr. Michael. But if something happens, I promise that they will know the truth."

"Thank you," I said.

"You will come back," he said again.

When I returned to my seat, the Elgen fleet was in view. The *Ampere* was sandwiched in between the *Watt* and the *Volta*. Fortunately the *Faraday*, the biggest boat of the Elgen fleet, was on the far north side of the fleet. It stuck so far out into the bay that had it been next to the *Ampere* we never would have been able to get close.

No one spoke. Jaime came back with us, looking at the fleet through his binoculars. The fishing boat made a wide, elliptical sweep of the bay, then drifted in toward the shore, carefully edging itself closer to the fleet.

The first of the Elgen boats we passed was the *Ohm*, which in spite of the hour had all its lights on as men and forklifts scurried on its deck filling it with supplies. The next boat was the *Tesla*, then the *Joule*, which was completely dark and stranger looking than I had imagined. Next we reached the powerhouse of the fleet, the *Watt*. The battle cruiser was gunship gray with large cannons pointing out toward the sea behind her.

Our boat slowed still more as we crossed beneath the shadow of the cruiser toward the *Ampere*. I turned back and looked up at the boats, wondering if we were being watched. All I could see were a few cabin lights and darkness. Jaime put down his binoculars, then moved over to the raft and waved to Jack to come help him. They quickly unlashed the raft, laying it flat at our feet on the floor of the boat.

When we were in the shadow of the *Ampere* the engine cut back even more, then slowed as the captain put the boat in idle.

"Now," Jaime said.

The rest of us stood as Jaime and Jack heaved the raft over the port side, leaving just the front towrope attached. Jack jumped over the side, disappearing from our view. Jaime handed over two paddles, then turned to us. "*Rápidamente.*"

Taylor climbed over first, helped down into the raft by Jack, followed by me, Ostin, then finally McKenna, who I hadn't heard speak since we'd boarded.

"Mr. Michael," Jaime said. He tossed me the coil of black rope, then handed the explosives to Jack. Then he pulled out a knife and cut our towrope.

"*Buena suerte, amigos.* Go with God."

The boat shifted back into gear and was soon clear of us, leaving us alone and exposed near the *Ampere*'s massive stern.

"Paddle," Jack said. He took one paddle and handed me the other, and we paddled our way toward the boat until her stern rose above us like a great canyon wall.

"Get the magnets ready," I said to Ostin.

Ostin lifted one magnet, then handed the other to McKenna. The magnets were fist-size and round with a small loop through the back where a strap ran through them, connecting them to the raft. The strap was about six feet long but was designed to be cinched tight, to snug the raft up against the boat.

When we were twenty feet out I set down my paddle and reached out toward the boat and magnified. My magnetism was stronger than I thought it would be and our raft was drawn so quickly to the hull that we hit against the *Ampere* hard enough that I almost flipped the raft over.

"Sorry," I whispered.

Ostin and McKenna stuck their magnets against the hull, which connected with an uncomfortably loud clang, then pulled the straps until the raft was tight against the boat.

"My turn," I said.

Taylor leaned forward and kissed me, gently cupping my cheeks in her hands. "Be careful."

"I'll see you soon."

I slid the rope coil over my head and one shoulder, then awkwardly stood in the leaning raft, putting my hands against the side and magnifying. The hull was cold and wet but easy to grab, as if the water actually enhanced my magnetism. "Watch for the rope," I said. I threw my knees against the hull and began to climb.

With all the adrenaline pumping through my body I reached the top in less than ten minutes. As I got near the railing of the deck, I stopped and listened for guards. I didn't hear anything but the patter of rain, so I crept up a little farther so I could peer over the side. There was no one. I spotted a camera mounted high up on the wall facing down toward me. The camera appeared stationary, but the red light on top of the camera indicated that it was active. I wished Zeus was there to blow it out, and it occurred to me that I could take it out just as well. Throwing lightning balls was too risky, as a flash of lightning would almost certainly catch a guard's eye. I could climb the wall beneath it and short it out; I just needed a little luck coming over the side railing.

But first I needed to get rid of the rope. I magnetized the lower half of my body, then took the end of the rope and tied it around the deck's outside railing with a figure eight knot. I looked down. The raft was completely invisible to me and all I could see below was an occasional whitecap in the sea. I took the coil from around my neck and dropped it into the darkness below. The rope almost immediately tensed. Jack was on his way up. I clung to the side of the boat and waited.

41

My Enemy's Enemy

It took Jack even less time to climb up than it had me. He was strong enough that he wasn't even using his legs but swinging them back and forth as he grasped the rope hand over hand and pulled himself up. He stopped when he was next to me. He looked at me clinging to the side of the boat. "You look like a spider," he said.

"I feel like one," I said.

He looked up. "Anyone topside?"

"No. But there's a camera."

"Have you tried putting it out?"

"I was waiting for you," I said. "Give me a second." I climbed back up and peered over the side again, then, still wearing my cloak, flung myself over on top of the deck. Sidling up against the interior wall, I quickly stole beneath the camera, then climbed up, grabbed it, and pulsed. The red light on top of it went out.

I leaned back over the rail. "It's out."

"Good," he said. "Taylor's on her way up."

I looked over the side. "You can see her?"

"No. I can feel her on the rope."

He climbed the rest of the way up the rope, then grabbed the railing and pulled himself over.

"Let's pull her up," he said.

We both grabbed the rope and began pulling. Taylor suddenly came into view. We lifted her all the way to the railing. "Thanks," she said, panting.

Jack grabbed on to her and pulled her up and over the side. Then we threw the rope back down.

A minute later we felt the rope tense. All three of us grabbed it and quickly pulled. McKenna practically flew up. When she was a few feet from the railing Jack grabbed her and pulled her over as well, then we tossed the rope back down.

"Ostin knows to tie the pack to the rope, right?"

Jack nodded. "I reminded him."

We felt the rope tense, and we quickly pulled. The rope was so light that it almost felt like there wasn't anything on it.

"I see the pack," McKenna said. We quickly pulled the explosives up and over the side. Jack untied the pack and threw the rope back over. It was nearly a minute before we felt it tense.

"Let's pull," I said.

With all four of us pulling, we lifted Ostin up in just five minutes. When he got to the top he looked pale and terrified, and he grabbed on to the railing as if for his life. Jack and I each grabbed one of his arms and pulled him over.

"That was horrific," he said.

"The fun's just beginning," Jack said.

We took off our cloaks and threw them over the side of the boat, then Jack pulled the pack on over his shoulder.

"We need a key," Ostin said.

"Let's try the door first," I said. "Just in case they left it unlocked."

We found the door where Dodds's plans said it would be. As we expected, it was locked. There was another camera near the door. I climbed the wall next to it and put it out as well.

"You guys wait here," I said. "Taylor and I will find a key."

We walked around the back of the boat. We saw a pair of shoes sticking out from behind a tender. Then we saw an expulsion of smoke.

"Someone's sneaking a cigarette," Taylor whispered.

We walked up to him. Smoking was against the Elgen code, and the young Italian sailor was horrified to see us.

"Hey, I'm just . . ." He looked at Taylor. "You're a girl."

"I know," she said. She rebooted him. Then, as he sat there, grinning stupidly, I pulsed and knocked him out. Then I reached over and took his key and the ID he wore around his neck.

"Should we throw him overboard?" Taylor asked.

"Tempting," I said. "But too loud."

"What do we do if he wakes up?"

I pulsed my finger, then wrote into his uniform: *DEATH TO HATCH.*

"That will keep him from fraternizing," I said.

I shocked him one more time, then we hurried back to the others. They were gone.

"Where'd they go?" Taylor asked.

As we walked up to the door, it suddenly opened. "Come on," Jack said.

"How did you get the door open?"

"Him," Ostin said, pointing to a sailor lying face-first on the ground.

"You punched him?" I asked Jack.

He nodded.

"Feel good?"

"More than I can say, brother."

We hurried in single file down three flights of stairs. Just as Dodds had warned, the bottom level was dark and noisy with the dull, steady roar of the *Ampere*'s motors.

As we moved up the hallway to the engine room, someone at the opposite end of the corridor pointed at us and shouted. The man wasn't dressed as a sailor but as an Elgen guard.

"What did he say?" I asked.

"I couldn't hear him," Taylor said.

He pointed a gun at us.

"Ostin and I will see what he wants," I said. "Before he sounds the alarm. The rest of you stay here." I turned to Taylor. "I might need a little reboot."

"I'll watch for it," she said.

Ostin and I walked toward the end of the corridor. As we approached the guard grew more livid. He shouted, "No one is allowed stern entry on level one! Are you crazy or stupid?"

"Neither," I said. "I'm electric." I pulsed and he collapsed to the ground.

"You're getting better at that," Ostin said.

We handcuffed the guard and took his weapons. Then we looked around. Just thirty feet in front of us were what looked like jail cells. "What's that?" I asked.

"The brig," Ostin said. "It was on the blueprints."

"Sorry, I didn't get around to memorizing them."

"I did," Ostin said.

We walked toward them. Two of the cells were occupied. One had an Elgen guard lying unconscious on the floor in a pool of blood. The other was jammed full of people, with a woman hanging upside down against the bars, her long hair touching the floor.

For a moment Ostin and I and the cell's occupants just gazed at one another. Then a graying, middle-aged Italian man said in a low voice, "You're not Elgen."

"That's for sure," Ostin said.

"You're Michael Vey."

"Bingo," Ostin said.

"Who are you?" I asked.

"I'm Chairman Schema."

"He's the chairman of Elgen Inc.," Ostin said.

"Why is he in his own jail?"

"Hatch," Ostin said. "Remember, he's taken over."

I looked at the woman hanging upside down. "Who is she?"

"She's dead," Schema said. His gruff voice didn't conceal his grief. "She sacrificed her life for mine."

"She was one of the board members," one of the women said. "We're all board members. Hatch imprisoned us."

Schema looked into my eyes. "Please let us out."

"Why would I do that?" I said. "You belong in there. You're as much my enemy as Hatch is."

"That's not true," Schema said. "Hatch is *all* of our enemy. We directed him to let you and your mother go. He rebelled against us."

"It's true," a man in the back said. "That's why we're in here."

"I'm not letting you go," I said. "And we're wasting time. Come on, Ostin." I turned to go.

"He's going to kill us," a woman said. "Please, have mercy. I beg you, Michael. We tried to save you."

Something about her plea stopped me. I turned back. "What will you do if I let you out?"

Schema said, "We'll take the company back from Hatch."

"After we blow up the boat there will be no Hatch."

"Then I hope you succeed," Schema said.

I looked at Ostin. He shrugged.

"But if he survives . . . ," Schema said. "Hatch has grown too pow- erful. No one knows what he's capable of."

"We do," I said.

"I know this organization. I know where the money is. I know the Elgen weaknesses. I can stop him. Let me have my revenge."

"Revenge against Hatch?"

"Yes," he said. "Against Hatch."

I turned to Ostin. "What do you think?" I whispered.

"My enemy's enemy is my friend," he whispered back. "Besides, they could be the distraction we need."

I looked at them, then said, "All right, we'll let you go. But if you betray us, there will be no mercy. I will personally barbecue you." I looked around. "Where's the cell key?"

"It's an electric key," Schema said. "The guard has it around his neck."

Ostin took the cell key from the guard and opened the cell door. As each of them stepped out, I melted the bands from their wrists. When Schema was free, he said, "Please help me get her down."

I looked at the woman. "All right."

As he wrapped his arms around her, I grabbed the bands on her feet and melted them. Schema gently laid her body on the floor. He knelt down next to her. "I'm so sorry, Judith," he said. "He will pay for what he's done." Schema looked up, his eyes wet. "Thank you, Michael."

"You should get off the boat as quickly as possible," Ostin said. "It's not going to be here much longer."

I took the guard's gun, magnetic key, and utility belt and gave them to Schema. "This might help."

"Do you know a safe way out?" one of the women asked.

"Go that way," I said, pointing down the corridor. "Take the stairs to the main deck. There's a rope on the port side you can climb down."

"Don't take our raft," Ostin added. "Just swim to shore."

"Are you leaving with us?" she asked.

"Not yet," I said. "There's something we need to do."

Together we moved back down the corridor toward the stern stairwell, Ostin and I bringing up the rear. As we approached the engine room Jack, Taylor, and McKenna stepped out in front of them, blocking their way. "Where are you going?" Jack demanded.

"We're letting them go," I shouted over the motor's hum.

"Sorry, didn't see you," Jack said. He stepped aside. "I recommend a speedy exit."

As the freed board members climbed the stairwell, I shouted to the others, "Let's get this over with."

42

Surprise Inspection

The engine room door was constructed of inch-thick metal with a large glass portal that gave those inside a clear view of the corridor. I grasped the handle and slowly spun it until it opened. Not surprisingly, there was an armed guard stationed near the entrance. He immediately turned to us, his hand hovering near his sidearm.

"What are you doing here?" he asked.

Ostin stepped forward. "Seaman Liss, first class," he said. "The admiral sent us down for a surprise inspection."

"I wasn't informed of this," the man said.

"Hence the *surprise* . . . ," Ostin said.

The man stared at him. "I received no notice of an inspection," he said.

"Perhaps you don't grasp the concept of *surprise*," Ostin said.

"You're not authorized to be here," he said. "I'm alerting security."

He reached for his radio, but Taylor rebooted him. His expression went blank and for a moment he just stared at the radio as if trying to remember why he was holding it. He blinked several times, then looked back at us. "Who are you?"

"You were taking us to the engineer," I said.

He still looked confused. "Sorry, I . . ." He looked at us all and nodded. "This way."

The *Ampere*'s engine room wasn't anything like I had imagined it would be. I'd never seen an engine room, outside of black-and-white photographs of old steam ships with glowing furnaces fed by men with soot-blackened faces shoveling from coal scuttles. The *Ampere*'s engine room was about as far from that as possible. The room was brightly lit with stark white walls and white paneled ceilings with thick chrome pipes running both vertically and horizontally. The ship's engines, four of them, were mounted in the middle of the floor with chrome pipes leading into them from different angles. The floor was made of steel plating, forged with diamond patterns for better traction.

The engineer was standing near a bank of gauges and switches. He didn't look any happier to see us than the guard had. He snapped at the guard, "What are these sailors doing in here?"

"Dr. Hatch sent us," Jack said.

"*Admiral* Hatch," Ostin corrected. "Surprise inspection."

"Elgen protocol does not allow surprise inspections," the engineer said.

"Exactly," Ostin said. "Surprise."

He looked us over, then said, "You all have the same serial number." His expression changed. "You're not Elgen." Suddenly he reached for his sidearm. I was about to surge when Taylor rebooted him. He grabbed his forehead, crying out with pain. "Ah . . ."

"Tell all your men to line up against that wall," I said.

He looked up at me, pain still evident on his face. "Why would I do that?"

I glanced at Taylor, and she rebooted him again. This time the man screamed out with pain, fell to one knee, then to his side, crying out as he hit the floor. Then he went silent.

Taylor was as surprised as any of us. "What happened?"

"I think you just gave him an aneurysm," Ostin said.

"Is he dead?" McKenna asked.

"Does it matter?" Jack said.

Just then two other crew members approached us. They looked at the prone engineer, then back at us. "What happened?"

"He fainted," Ostin said.

"Who are you?"

Before Taylor could reboot them, I pulsed, dropping them both to the ground. "How many more are there down here?" I asked.

"There are two working on that engine over there," Taylor said, pointing to the farthest engine near the back of the room. "Jack and I can get them." She looked at him. "Ready?"

Jack lay the backpack down. "Let's get them."

They walked over to the men.

"That makes six crew," Ostin said. "That's about right for a night shift."

"We need to get these guys out of the way," I said. I pointed to a small door. "What's that room?"

"It's a head," Ostin said. "The bathroom."

"We'll lock them in there."

The bathroom door opened inward and Ostin, McKenna, and I carried the four men—the two crew members, the engineer, and guard—inside and stacked them on top of one another. As we lay the last man on top, Taylor and Jack came around the corner. Jack was dragging two men by their feet.

"Put them in there," I said.

Jack dragged them to the bathroom, then lifted the men and threw them on top of the others. I pulled the door shut.

"How do we lock it from the outside?" Taylor asked.

"Like this," Ostin said. He walked across the room, grabbed the guard's rifle, then came back and wedged it between the door's handle and the doorjamb.

"That will hold them," he said.

"All right," I said. "Let's plant the explosives and get out of here."

"Where should I put them?" Jack asked.

"It shouldn't matter," Ostin said. "That much explosive will obliterate everything within two hundred feet. But generally speaking, the tighter the fit the better."

"But hide it," Taylor said. "In case someone comes down here after we're gone."

"How about back here," Jack said, wedging the pack behind one of the engines. "They won't see it."

"Bonus," Ostin said. "That looks like a fuel line running across the wall next to it."

"How long are you setting the timer for?" I asked.

"What do you think?" Jack asked.

"I'd say thirty minutes," Ostin said.

"You'd better make it forty," I said. "Just in case."

"All right," Jack said. "I'm activating it. Everyone ready?"

"Do it," Taylor said.

Jack pushed four buttons. The timer emitted a long, steady tone, then stopped. "We're live."

"Let's keep it that way," I said. "Let's go."

Suddenly an alarm went off outside the engine room, reverberating loudly down the corridor.

"What is that?" Taylor asked.

"Maybe they've discovered the board's escape," Ostin said.

"We better get out of here fast," I said.

Suddenly a voice boomed from a speaker box mounted below a surveillance camera. "It's too late for that, Vey."

I'd recognize that voice anywhere. It belonged to Hatch.

43

Sixty Seconds

"Why do I bother looking for you, Vey, when you just can't keep away from me? Is it my charisma? My animal magnetism?"

"Your animal smell," Ostin said.

"Ostin," Hatch said. "I didn't notice you. But I'm sure you're accustomed to being overlooked. I appreciate you giving me another chance to kill you."

"You know, I was the one who figured out how to blow up your Starxource plant," he said. "I hope you appreciated that, too."

"Yes, the Peruvian government will be happy for that confession. So let me explain your situation to you. You are pinned down on the bottom level of a boat with only one corridor out, two tiny portals that Ostin couldn't fit his arm through, and more than a hundred armed guards crowding both sides of the hallway. Checkmate. It's over. There is no way off this boat."

"Check the corridor!" I shouted to Jack.

Jack walked to the door and looked out its window, then turned back to me. "Guards in both directions."

"You didn't trust me?" Hatch said.

"Yeah, imagine that," I replied.

"You know how I like making deals, Michael. So here's a deal for you. We're in a bit of a hurry, so if you just walk out of the engine room and surrender, I'll give you a relatively painless death by firing squad."

"That's a great deal," I said. "Why wouldn't I take that?"

"It's the best you'll get, Vey. Which is pretty generous for a truce breaker."

"I broke a truce with an evil, sadistic, psychopathic liar. I'm not losing sleep over that."

"I'm not a psychopath," Hatch said. "But you're right, I was lying. What we're really going to do is strap you down, paralyze you with toxin from the puffer fish, then dissect you while you're still alive so we can learn what is making your electricity grow. And then we'll do the same to your girlfriend."

"You'd have to take us alive to do that," I said. "And that's not going to happen."

"I disagree. And here's why. Either way, you die. But if you surrender, I'll let your little buddy Ostin go home to his mommy."

Ostin shook his head. "They won't let me go, Michael." Then he shouted toward the camera, "Do you know what you are, Hatch? You're a skid mark on the underwear of humanity."

"Remind me to cut out your tongue," Hatch said. "But back to my deal. Ostin goes free, sans tongue, and, added bonus, we won't torture your girlfriend."

I looked at Taylor. Even though she looked terrified, she also shook her head. "He's a liar, Michael."

"You have sixty seconds to decide."

"Just a minute," I said.

"That's what I just said," Hatch replied.

I walked over to the surveillance camera and threw a lightning ball at it. The light went out.

"You just wasted twenty seconds," Hatch said.

Sixty seconds. It was too late to change the explosive's time, but I remembered what Dodds had said about setting it off. I retrieved the pack and brought it over to Ostin and McKenna. Speaking softly so Hatch couldn't hear, I said, "We need to be able to blow it quickly."

"You want me to light it?" McKenna asked.

"It needs intense heat," Ostin said. "You would have to flare."

"I can do that," she said.

"Only if it comes to that." I handed her the pack. She and Ostin sat down on the ground with it.

I walked back to the voice box. "Here's a deal for you, Hatch, you sludge-breath. If your guards come within ten feet of this room, we'll blow our explosive and everyone on board dies."

"It's what they call a Mexican standoff!" Ostin shouted.

There was a pause, then Hatch said, "Clever bluff, but you don't have explosives."

"Of course we do, you human litter box. Why else would we have boarded this tub if not to sink it?"

Another pause. "So let's say you do have an incendiary device. I don't think you have it in you to detonate it."

"You know me better than that, you dog-faced man-worm. I mocked you when you threatened to feed me to rats. Do you think I'm afraid to die now?"

"No. In fact, if I were you, I would have already killed myself. I just don't think you have the courage to kill your friends."

"Use your brain, you baboon butt!" Ostin shouted. "It's the only logical choice you've given us. We can die slowly of torture with you mocking us, or we die quickly, save the world, and take you with us. I think even you could figure that out."

Hatch didn't answer.

But Hatch might have been right. I wasn't sure that I had the courage. I knew that I couldn't commit for my friends. I looked at Taylor. She was trembling. "What do you think?"

"Ostin's right. He'll kill us anyway."

"McKenna?"

She swallowed. "Just tell me when."

I looked over at Jack.

"I say we make our deaths count for something."

I took a deep breath. "Okay." I turned back to McKenna. "On my word . . ."

"What's your decision?" Hatch asked.

"We're unanimous. Come and get us!" I shouted. Taylor gripped my hand tightly. After a minute I said, "Jack, what's going on?"

"No one's advancing," he said.

"The door's locked?" I asked.

"Yes."

"Let us know when they're ten feet away."

"They're probably trying to figure out a way to poison us through the vents," Ostin said.

I pointed to the voice box.

"I hadn't thought of that," Hatch said. "Thanks for the idea."

"Sorry," Ostin said.

"Jack," I said. "Tell me when." He nodded.

"Now what?" Taylor asked.

"We wait." I took her hand and we walked over and sat down next to Ostin and McKenna. I raked my free hand back through my hair. "I guess Abigail was right after all."

Taylor shook her head. "No, she wasn't. We're going to blow this thing and the world will be safer."

Suddenly, something came to mind. "I don't believe it."

"What?"

"Back in the jungle the chief of the Amacarra saw all this. He said, 'over the water a choice would come to me'—that I would have to choose the lives of the ones I loved or the lives of many I don't know." I looked at Taylor. "I guess the guy knew our fate all along." I took a deep breath. "So what do you want to do with the last ten minutes of our lives?"

44

The Good-Bye

"They're coming! Thirty feet!" Jack shouted.

"Are you ready?" I asked McKenna.

She looked frightened but nodded.

I looked at Ostin. I could also see the fear in his eyes. In spite of my own fear, I wanted to comfort him. "At least we probably won't feel anything," I said.

"We won't," he said stoically. "Water-gel explosives can reach temperatures upward of thirty-five hundred degrees Fahrenheit in point zero, zero, two seconds. We'll be incinerated before our brains can register pain."

"That's good to know," I said. I put my hand on his shoulder. "At least we're here together. I'm glad for that."

"Me too," Ostin said. "But all things being equal, I'd rather be clogging."

In spite of my fear I grinned. He smile back at me. I took a deep breath, then turned back to Taylor. Her eyes were filled with tears. She took my hand and said, "Do you know what I hate the most about this?"

"Dying?" I said.

"I mean besides that." She wiped a tear from her cheek. "I hate that my parents will never know what happened to me."

"Jaime will tell them," I said. "He promised me he would."

"Good," she said sadly. She took a deep breath, then looked deeply into my eyes. "I know we're only fifteen, and just kids, but I just want you to know that . . . I would have married you."

I put my hand on her cheek. "I would have asked."

"Twenty feet!" Jack shouted.

She softly sighed, putting her cheek up against mine. "Why aren't you ticking?"

"I don't know. Maybe because there's nothing to worry about anymore."

Across from us McKenna said to Ostin, "You need to move away from me. I'm going to get really hot."

"It doesn't matter, " Ostin said. "I'm going to die anyway."

"It will hurt," she said.

"Just for a few seconds," he replied.

"Fifteen feet!" Jack shouted. Then he said, "We're coming, Wade."

I pulled Taylor into me.

"Ten feet!" Jack shouted. "Blow it!"

McKenna took a deep breath, then said to Ostin, "Good-bye." Then she closed her eyes and her skin began to turn red.

Taylor and I embraced each other tightly. "I'm so scared," she said.

"I've got you," I said.

"I love you, Michael."

That's when we heard the explosion.

45

Shock Waves

The *Ampere* rocked from the explosion's shock wave. At first I thought the massive blast was from our own explosive, but when I realized that we were all still there, I figured that something else must have happened.

"Holy crap!" Jack shouted. "What was that?"

Sirens from the dock began wailing.

Ostin ran to the portal and looked out. "It's the *Watt*!" he shouted.

I ran over to look for myself.

From the light of the fires I could see that the top deck of the *Watt* was mostly blown off and smoke and fire was billowing up into the black sky. What was left of the boat was disappearing into the sea.

"It's sinking," I said.

"Michael, you're glowing," Taylor said.

I looked down. My skin was glowing a pale white and electricity was sparking between my legs and arms and fingers. "What's happening?"

"What should I do with the bomb?" McKenna shouted. She had cooled down, but her arms were still wrapped around the explosive.

"Hold on," I said. "Jack, where are the guards?"

"Mostly on their faces!" he shouted.

Suddenly a massive bolt of lightning burst past our door, illuminating the engine room like the flash of an arc welder. Then there was another.

"The corridor's clear!" Jack shouted. "The guards are down."

Suddenly someone pounded on the engine room door. Tessa's face appeared in the window. "Come on, you idiots!" she shouted. "Let's go!"

Jack opened the door. "Where'd you come from?"

"Someplace a lot better than this," she said.

Then Zeus stuck his head in the doorway. "Hey, where did you get the nifty sailor duds?"

"You came back," I said.

"You thought we'd let you have all the fun? Let's get out of here."

"Wait," I said. "McKenna, how much time do we have on the bomb?"

McKenna pulled back the flap. "Eighteen minutes and twelve seconds."

"Hide it!"

"I'll do it," Ostin said. He took the pack to the back of the engine room and shoved it behind the engine, then returned. "We're good."

Outside the engine room door a handful of guards started to rally.

"Tessa!" I shouted. "A little help."

"You got it," she said.

"I've got them," Taylor said.

I looked back out and the guards were standing in the corridor, looking around in different directions. I made a lightning ball about the size of a watermelon and threw it down the hall. It blew up around them like a grenade, scattering them like bowling pins.

"*Vámonos!*" Tessa said.

We followed Zeus and Tessa out of the engine room, then back up the utility stairway to the deck, which was crowded with sailors who had been woken by the *Watt*'s explosion and had rushed to the deck to see what was happening. In the darkness and commotion, few of them even noticed us, and Zeus and I easily took care of those who did. We ran to the side of the boat where we had left our rope.

Zeus looked over the railing. "I hate water," he said.

"Someone better go down first," I said, "and make sure our raft's still there."

"We brought a boat," Tessa said.

"I'll go first," McKenna said. "I'll flash if it's okay."

She grabbed the rope and slid down into the darkness. A moment later we saw a flash of light.

"That's your cue," Jack said. "Go!"

Zeus climbed over, followed by Tessa, Ostin, and Jack, leaving just Taylor and me.

"Your turn," I said to Taylor.

"No," she said. "I'm not taking another chance of you staying behind."

There was no time for discussion, so I climbed over the railing. I grabbed the rope and slid down a few yards, then looked back up. "Coming?"

Taylor grabbed the railing and was throwing her leg over the side when someone grabbed her. It was one of the Elgen guards. Taylor tried to reboot him, but he was wearing a copper helmet. "Caught you," he said.

"Catch this," I said. I threw a lightning ball at him, striking him on the copper of his helmet. Electricity sparked and sizzled around on his head, then he fell forward unconscious, dropping Taylor over the side of the boat.

"Michael!" she shouted.

I jumped out and grabbed her—both of us free-falling in the dark. Then I reached out toward the *Ampere* and magnetized, which pulled us up against the boat's metal hull. I amped up my magnetism until we came to a sliding stop about twenty feet from the water. Below us was an idling speedboat with all our friends. Jaime was at the wheel.

"That was cool," I heard Ostin say.

"I think my heart just stopped," Taylor said.

"Come on!" Jack shouted. "We only have four minutes to get clear!"

I reached over and grabbed the rope, and handed it to Taylor. "Go."

She slid down the rope until she was low enough that Jack reached up and grabbed her, helping her into the boat. I reduced my magnetism and slid down the hull until I was just a few feet above the boat. Jack grabbed my hand and pulled me in, then shouted to Jaime, "We're all here! Go, go, go!"

"Everyone hold on," Jaime said. He leaned on the throttle and the boat shot forward out to sea. By the time Jaime cut back on the throttle the *Ampere* looked like a toy boat in the distance.

I looked around the crowded speedboat. Everyone was there except for Abigail. I smiled at Ian. He just shook his head. "Michael, my man, you know how to make trouble."

"And you know how to find it," I replied.

"We have thirty seconds," Jack said.

We all looked back to watch the explosion. Jack started counting down and we all joined with him. "Ten, nine, eight, seven, six, five, four, three, two, one . . ." Nothing.

"It didn't blow," Jack said.

"Did you set the timer right?" Ostin asked.

"I did exactly what Dodds told me to do," Jack said. "You saw the detonator, it was counting down."

"Maybe they disarmed it," Taylor said.

Suddenly there was a massive explosion. Even as far away as we were, the sound made my ears ring, reverberating throughout the bay and throwing up tons of shredded debris that showered down on the shore and water. The sky turned orange and yellow as a giant fireball engulfed the *Ampere*. There were two more explosions; the third one was even larger than the first, and the ship broke in two and collapsed into the sea.

"We did it!" Taylor shouted.

"Veni, vidi, vici!" Ostin shouted. "We came, we saw, we kicked Elgen butt!" He shook his fist at the boat. "You're shark chum now, Hatch. You stinking, maniac, sicko freak of nature. You're shark chum." He turned to me, out of breath. "Man, I hated that guy."

46

Revelations and Reunions

For several minutes Jaime just stared at the burning wreckage of the *Ampere*, as if he were in a trance. Our speedboat started to rock more as the waves from the explosion's shock waves caught up to us. The first streaks of dawn had begun to brighten the indigo sky. Set against the gradient horizon, the *Ampere's* orange-red flames and sparkling cinders looked oddly beautiful.

Then Jaime said, "You did it, *hermanos*." He turned back to us. "We now must go before the *guardacostas* arrives."

"Dodds is about a mile up the coast," Ian said. "It looks safe."

"You know Dodds?" I asked.

"How do you think we got here?" Ian replied.

"Everyone hold on," Jaime said, and he hit the throttle again. The boat lunged forward, gaining speed until we were bouncing from crest to crest. I looked over at Zeus. He was wearing a hoodie and wrapped completely in towels, sitting on the floor in the center near the front of the boat. For Zeus, even the refreshing ocean spray was dangerous to him. We might as well have been floating on a sea of acid. I couldn't help but think how courageous he was.

"What happened to the *Watt*?" I asked.

"Zeus did that," Tessa said. "From the deck of the *Ampere*."

"It was a fluke," Zeus said. "They were loading torpedoes on top and I couldn't resist. I didn't think it would go up like that. Ka-boom."

"Ka-boom is right," Taylor said.

"You rock, dude," Jack said. Jack went to high-five Zeus, but Zeus quickly pulled back.

"Sorry, man," he said. "Your hands are wet."

"My bad," Jack said. He wiped his hands on his shirt, then they high-fived.

Ten minutes later Jaime careened the boat toward shore, which was now visible in the early light. As we approached the dock, I could see a white van in the distance with two figures leaning against it.

"Who's that with Dodds?" I asked.

"It's Abi," Ian said.

"Abi came back?"

"It was her idea to come back," Ian said. "But we were all thinking it. None of us could stand the idea of you guys doing this alone. We tried to radio you the same day we landed, but there was a communication problem."

"That's because we were compromised," Ostin said. "We lost radio contact."

"So you touched the States," I said.

"For a day," Ian said.

"More like a few hours," Tessa said.

"Did you meet the voice?" I asked.

"No. But I saw your mother," Ian said.

"You did?"

He nodded. "She gave me a hug. She looked good. Probably because she was eating something better than rat biscuits. She asked me to tell you that she loves you and to be careful." He grinned. "I didn't tell her that you were planning on blowing up the Elgen's main boat."

"Probably for the best," I said.

"I thought so," he replied. He turned to Ostin. "I met your parents too."

Ostin's eyes opened wide. "You saw my mom and dad?"

"Yes. They were very proud of you. Your mom said something like, 'I always knew he would make a difference in this world.'"

"Awesome," Ostin said. He was grinning from ear to ear. "Totally awesome."

As we pulled up to the dock, we could clearly see two massive pillars of black smoke rising from the port a mile south of us. Dodds and Abigail walked out to meet us. Abigail was frantically counting heads on the boat.

Jaime said, "Jack, please throw out the rope."

"Got it," he said, climbing to the front.

Dodds caught the rope, pulled the boat up to the dock, and tied the rope to a metal cleat. Then he stood and raised his arms out to us. "The warriors return."

"You're all here," Abigail said.

"We thought of dying," Tessa said. "But no one wanted to miss the after party."

Jack climbed out first, then helped everyone else out. Taylor and I were the last to disembark.

"Michael Vey," Dodds said. "Your Electroclan has lived up to its reputation."

"We survived," I said.

"That's good too," he said. We embraced.

Then Dodds stepped back, leaving Taylor and me standing next to Abigail.

"Welcome back," she said.

"You too," I said. "What brought you back?"

"Something you said."

"What was that?"

"You said not to regret my decision. I couldn't. If something had happened to you, I would have regretted it the rest of my life." She put her arms around me. "You were right to stay. But mostly I'm just glad you're safe."

When we parted, Taylor hugged her as well. "You saved our lives."

Abigail held her tight. "They were worth saving."

The ride back to the villa at Miraflores was happily crowded, with Taylor and Abigail sitting across our laps. As we pulled up the villa's palm-tree-lined drive, I couldn't help but notice how beautiful everything looked. I remembered wondering as we drove off if I'd ever see it again.

Jaime pulled the van up to the front of the house and everyone piled out.

"I'm getting out of this clown suit," Jack said, pulling off his sailor shirt. "Dodds, where are my clothes?"

"I put them in the bags your sailor suit came in," he said.

"I'm keeping mine for a souvenir," Ostin said.

"I'm burning mine," Taylor said.

"We burned a few of them on the boat," Zeus said.

The idea of that didn't bring me joy. We had sunk a ship. I didn't want to think about all the people who were on it—even if they were part of Hatch's navy.

Taylor was holding my hand and she looked over at me with understanding.

After we were all inside, Jaime shut the door behind us. Jaime said, "In a few minutes Mr. Dodds and I will be going to Lima to see what the Elgen are doing and how the government is responding."

"We will also be making arrangements for your flight home," Dodds said.

Home. The word sounded sweet even if I wasn't sure where "home" was anymore.

"Someday, the world may talk about what happened here today,"

Dodds said. "But until then, we are very proud of you. You should all get some rest. You deserve it."

"Tonight we will be having a big fiesta to celebrate our heroes," Jaime said. "While we are in town, we will shop for food. Does anyone want anything special from town?"

"Inca Kola," I said. "*Muy* cold."

"*Sí*, Kola," Jaime repeated.

"And some *granadilla*," I said.

"*Granadilla*," Tessa said. "You mean that snot fruit?"

I shrugged. "It kind of grew on me."

"There's something I need you to pick up," Taylor said. She walked up to Jaime and whispered something in his ear. Jaime nodded and smiled. "*Sí*, senorita." He turned to Dodds. "*Vámonos.*"

The two of them walked out the front door. Taylor came back and took my hand.

"What did you ask Jaime for?"

"Just some things." She looked into my eyes. "May I talk to you? In private?"

The gravity of her voice worried me. "Of course."

We walked into a room and Taylor shut the door behind us. She looked a little uncomfortable. "I wanted to talk to you about what I said in the engine room—in those last seconds when we thought we were going to die."

I frowned. "It's okay," I said. "I understand. People say crazy things when they're scared."

"I meant every word of it."

We looked at each other, then my mouth rose in a large smile. "Me too," I said. "Someday I'll make good on it."

She smiled that beautiful smile. "I'll be waiting."

47

A Final Fiesta

Taylor and I slept until late afternoon, then woke and talked for about an hour before we heard the van return. We walked out to the front room as Dodds opened the door. He was followed by Jaime, who was holding the hand of a young Peruvian woman.

"Who is she?" Taylor asked Dodds.

"Roxanna is a friend of Jaime's," he said. "She's going to help cook our feast."

"Did you find anything out about the Elgen?" I asked.

Dodds frowned. "Yes. Much."

Jaime looked over at us.

"Good news or bad?" I asked.

"Both," Dodds said. "We'll talk after dinner."

"Yes," Jaime said, walking toward us. "We talk after dinner. But not now. Now we fiesta."

"Did you remember my things?" Taylor asked.

"Of course, senorita. Your surprise."

I looked at Taylor. "Your surprise?"

She nodded. "There's something we need to do."

Jaime and Roxanna worked for nearly three hours to put together our feast, filling the villa with the pungent aroma of their cooking and crowding the table with colorful Peruvian delicacies, which Jaime introduced to us.

"Welcome, friends. We have made for you *kalea mixta*, a fried seafood platter with shrimp, squid, mussels, fish, and yucca sticks, *tacu tacu*, steak with bean cake, and *aji de gallina*, chicken in spicy sauce."

We applauded.

"Epic!" Ostin shouted.

"This is my friend Roxanna," Jaime said. "She does not speak English, but she helped me create our feast."

"Roxanna rocks!" Ostin shouted.

We applauded for her, too. She shyly bowed. "Thank you."

Jaime turned on some festive Peruvian music and we all took plates and started eating. Throughout the party I kept my eye on Jack, who sat alone. Abigail went to sit by him. I couldn't hear what he said to her, but she looked upset as she turned away, walking across the room to sit next to Zeus and Tessa. It seemed to me that now that the fear and danger were over, his mind had returned to his grief over Wade. Perhaps it was survivor's guilt.

When Jack finished eating, he got up to leave.

Taylor turned to me. "We better do it now," she said, standing.

As she walked to the kitchen, I shouted, "Jack!"

He turned back. "Yeah?"

"Where are you going?"

"To bed. I'm done eating."

"There's dessert."

"I don't do desserts," he said.

"This one's especially for you."

Everyone looked over at us. Jaime switched off the music and McKenna turned out the lights, then disappeared into the kitchen with Taylor.

"What's going on?" Jack asked.

Taylor walked out of the kitchen holding a birthday cake lit with seventeen candles. She began to sing, alone at first, then joined by the rest of us. "Happy birthday to Wade."

Jack stood there, speechless.

When we'd finished singing, Taylor said, "Would you blow out the candles?"

Jack hesitated for a moment, then he walked up and blew out the candles. Everyone clapped. McKenna turned the lights back on.

I walked to Taylor's side in front of the room. "In light of this being a special day," I said, "I have a special announcement to make."

Taylor handed me a rolled piece of parchment tied with a silver ribbon. I slid the document out and unrolled it.

In my most dignified voice I said, "With the power vested in me as president of the Electroclan, I hereby award our highest honor, the Electroclan Medal of Valor, to Wade West, for his courage, loyalty, and dedication in the line of duty. Jack, as his mentor, best friend, and brother, we think it is appropriate that you accept this honor for him."

Jack took the paper from me. He looked down at the award for a moment, then said, "Can I say something?"

"Of course," I said. I stepped back.

"I don't know how well you really knew Wade. Wade was the kind of guy who some people thought was hard to get to know. He didn't trust many people. It wasn't his fault. The people who should have taken care of him let him down." Suddenly, Jack choked up. "But I loved him. I didn't always treat him the best. But I always loved him." Jack wiped his eyes. "What hurts the most, is that I wish I had told him that. I just wish I had treated him better. That's all."

The room was silent. Then Taylor stepped forward. In her hand she held another piece of paper. "I would also like to say something.

I'd like to read something." She held up the piece of paper. "This is dated January twenty-first, 2011." She cleared her throat.

Today my grandmother hit me again. She bashed me like a hundred times with a wooden spoon, and then with a tennis racquet. I have cuts and bruises all over. It takes all I have not to just haul off and knock her one, but I know they'll throw me in jail if I do. The last time I stood up to her she called the police, and when they came she acted like a sweet old lady who got stuck with a low-life juvie. Of course the police took her side. Once you have a record, cops don't bother to think. Every time I tried to say something they just told me to shut up. One of them threatened to tase me. Sometimes I feel like this crummy world is completely stacked against me and I want to give up.

Then I think about my best friend, Jack. Jack's been dealt a bad hand too. His old man's an alcoholic. His mom left him, and one of his brothers is a drug head and in prison, but Jack never gives up and he never complains. He conquers. He's a warrior. He's the kind of warrior I want to be someday. If it wasn't for him I probably would have just ended it a long time ago. I know Jack will never read this, but if he did, I'd say "I love you, man."

Taylor looked up from the letter.

Jack was crying. When he could speak he said, "Where did you get that?"

"Jaime," she said. "The voice did background checks on all of us. You didn't know it, but Wade kept a secret blog. I guess he thought you wouldn't think he was a very good warrior if he shared his feelings."

Abigail walked over to Jack and this time he didn't reject her. This time the dam broke. He fell onto his knees, sobbing. "My heart is broken," he said. "It's just broken."

Abigail wrapped her arms around him and held him to her. "I know, honey," she said. "But you're going to be okay. We're going to help you get through this. All of us are."

She pulled him in tighter. Jack just wept.

48

Voices and the Jade Dragon

It was at least fifteen minutes before Dodds spoke. The emotion in the room was still very strong. Jack was quiet, lying in Abigail's arms.

"This was a very special evening," he said. "I share my deep condolences for all of you. Especially you, Jack. I wish I could delay what I have to say, but it's late and time doesn't afford me that luxury.

"As you know, Jaime and I went into Lima today. We went as close to the dock as we dared. But we learned what we expected. The government is blaming the attacks on the American terrorists. They have matched the Elgen's bounty of two and a half million soles on each of your heads." He looked at Jack and Ostin. "That includes you two as well.

"In a country where more than a third of the people make less than a dollar a day, a million dollars makes you quite a target. We need to get you out of here as soon as possible. Our jet will be here in the morning." He glanced at Jaime, then breathed out slowly, as if in exasperation. "We have some unfortunate news. Hatch is still alive."

We all gasped.

"What?" I said.

"His security detail rushed him off the boat as soon as the *Watt* blew up."

We were all quiet, stunned, then Zeus said, "You mean I saved his life?"

"Indirectly," Dodds said.

"I screwed up big," he said.

"No you didn't," I said. "If you hadn't blown up the *Watt*, none of us would be here."

Dodds continued, "We've slowed Hatch down. We've given Tuvalu a chance to respond to their threat, if they're smart enough to make use of it. You've freed Chairman Schema and the Elgen board. I admit, that's a wild card. We don't know where that will lead. But Schema isn't stupid. He's going to fight Hatch to gain back control of the corporation. That might sound like the lesser of two evils, but so be it. Schema's about profits, not conquest. We can live with that.

"Michael, tonight, you and Taylor gave us all a nice surprise. We have a surprise for you as well."

Jaime left the room, then returned carrying the radio. He set it down on the kitchen table and motioned me over.

"We cannot stay in contact for very long," Dodds said. "But there's someone who would like to speak with you."

Jaime turned up the radio's volume. There was a blast of static, then a voice said, "Michael. Are you there?"

"Mom!"

"How are you, son?"

"I'm good. I'm really good."

"I have missed you so much. They say you're coming back now. I can't wait to see you."

"Me too."

"I have so much to tell you. Things I can't tell you over the radio." She paused. "Oh, Michael. I'm so proud of you. I love you."

"I love you too, Mom."

"They're telling me I need to go, but is Ostin there?"

"He's right here," I said.

"I'm here, Mrs. Vey," Ostin said.

"There's someone here who would like to say hello."

Another woman's voice came on. "Hello? How does this work? Can he hear me?"

"Just talk, Ruth."

"Are you sure? Ostin? Are you there?"

"Mom! Dad!" Ostin shouted.

"You're there," Mrs. Liss said.

"How are you, son?" Mr. Liss asked.

"I'm good. We're all good."

"We're so relieved," Mrs. Liss said. "You know how I worry."

"I'm sorry, Mom. I didn't mean to worry you."

"They're saying we need to go," Mr. Liss said. "We're proud of you, son. And we'll see you soon."

"We don't know where in the world you are," Mrs. Liss said. "But you be careful. And don't forget to brush. Gingivitis is the silent killer."

"Gingivitis?" McKenna mouthed.

Ostin blushed. "Okay. I'll see you soon."

For a moment the radio went dead. Then another voice came on. *The* voice.

"Congratulations, Electroclan. Well done. You never cease to amaze. We are all looking forward to seeing you again." He paused. "I would like to share with you some developments in our cause.

"There is a nine-year-old girl from the province of Guangdong, China. Her name is Lin YuLong. In English that means *jade dragon*. She is a child prodigy. Her IQ is 182, higher than Einstein's."

"That's higher than mine," Ostin mumbled.

"Two weeks ago she started posting a thesis on her blog about an experiment she was working on. In English, her thesis was called 'The Theoretical Transference and Electrification of the Human Nervous System.'"

"Whatever that means," Taylor said.

"What it means," the voice said, "is that she figured out how the MEI works and why it made you electric but not the other children."

"That's what Hatch has been looking for," Ostin said.

"Exactly," the voice said. "And apparently he's found it. By the time we discovered the blog, the posting was nine days old. YuLong was kidnapped three days ago."

"I see where this is going," Ostin said.

"I'm sure you do," the voice said. "This has always been Hatch's master plan. If he can produce hundreds of thousands of electric children, all under his control, it's over."

"So now what?" I asked.

"We believe that the Elgen are holding YuLong in their Taiwan Starxource plant, waiting for their science ship, the *Volta*, to arrive in the South Pacific, where they can put her to work. We can't let that happen."

"You want us to go to Taiwan and rescue her?" I said.

"After all you've just come through, I know that's asking a lot. But you're our best hope."

I looked around the room. No one spoke for a moment, then Jack said, "I'm in."

"I'm not leaving you again," Abigail said. "I'm going."

"YOLO," Zeus said. "In."

"I'm there," Ian said.

"All right," Tessa said. "You guys are crazy, but I'm in."

"Of course," McKenna said. "You need me. I'm Chinese. I've got the perfect cover."

"Ostin?" I said.

"No-brainer," he replied. "You know how I love Chinese food."

I looked at Taylor. She just looked at me for a moment, then shook her head and groaned. "I'm in. It's been at least an hour since my life was in mortal danger. I was already getting bored."

I kissed her on the cheek. "All right," I said. "Looks like we're in. Let's find Jade Dragon."

Are you a Veyniac?

For Michael Vey trivia, sneak peeks, and events in your area,

follow Michael and the rest of the Electroclan at:

WWW.MICHAELVEY.COM.

ELGEN GUARD

General Handbook of Instructions

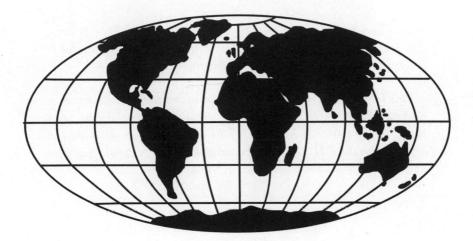

"Yesterday, you were mere men.
Today, you are Elgen."

—President C. J. Hatch, Supreme Commander General Admiral

**Starxource Plant & Elgen Training Facilities
Puerto Maldonado, Peru
September 2012**

Memorandum for the Elgen Guard

1. This handbook is designed to summarize the current laws, policies, and general dispositions from the Elgen High Command pertaining to general guard duty, requirements, and training.

2. This handbook is in no way to be used to contradict or disavow the ranking officers' ADC (active duty commands). All ADC are to be followed at the time of issuance. Where commands are considered in conflict with the GHI (General Handbook of Instructions) grievances may be filed at a later date as set forth in Section 4.

Respectfully,

David W. Welch

EGG, Chief of Guard

CONTENTS

INTRODUCTION

Dear Elgen Guard,

I congratulate you. You have been initiated into the elite group of the Elgen Force. Throughout history, there have been groups of power that have changed the world: the Knights Templars, the samurai, the Nazi Brown Shirts, and the fierce horsemen of the Russian Cossack. You now belong to the greatest of these elite groups. You have taken your place in history.

When you entered this employment you were informed that this was not merely a job, but a cause far greater than any you ever had or ever will have—a cause of greater importance than even your own life. Before joining, you were a mere man. Today, you are Elgen.

As an Elgen Guard you are the sworn upholder and enforcer of the Elgen law. The world will fall onto its knees before you or be crushed under your boot. It is a brave new world. Those of you who are with me will prosper far beyond your wildest imaginations. Those who fail will be crushed beneath the brute power of our growing force.

As an enforcer of the law, you must first be completely familiar with the law. It must become first nature to you. Second, you must be compliant with the law, the purest example of the Elgen elite, both physically and mentally. Your mind is sure and sharp, your way true and straight, your body strong, formidable, and unyielding. You are unlike the weak who inhabit this earth. You are above them. You are the talons of the eagle, ready to capture or to tear asunder. Your path is the way of glory. The uniform you wear is a symbol of your commitment and honor. You must never disrespect it, nor allow it to be disrespected.

A new day has dawned, not just for the world but for you. Rise up to this morning of a new dispensation, the Novus Ordo Glorificus Elgen, and personal glory will follow. Elgen, I salute you.

General Admiral C. J. Hatch

SECTION ONE
GENERAL

THE ELGEN OATH

The oath-taker will raise his left arm while repeating the following oath:

I swear on my life, breath, and fortune to prosper the Elgen cause, to advance its mission until every man and woman on Earth have sworn allegiance to the *Novus Ordo Glorificus* Elgen, our new glorious order. I offer up my life and death to this endeavor and will follow all rules contained in this book and those that will come, with fidelity, honor, and exactness. I swear this oath on my life.

This Elgen oath is to be held with utmost sanctity. Any guard demonstrating an attitude to the contrary will be disciplined.

THE ELGEN SALUTE

The Elgen salute is a symbol of our purpose, unity, and strength. Elgen Guards will salute all officers of higher rank than themselves.

The salute is performed by touching the three middle fingers of the left hand to the temple, the thumb and little finger touching together at the tips.

ELGEN GUARD STANDING ORDERS

1. Memorize this handbook. Strict adherence to its guidelines will ensure your success and progress within the Elgen Force. Any disobedience to its precepts will result in immediate disciplinary action.
2. From this moment forward, your previous chain of command no longer exists. As an Elgen Guard you will answer only to the Supreme Commander, the Elite Global Guard, your Zone Captain, and your Squad Captain.
3. Officers of the Elite Global Guard (guardsmen are to refer to them as Elite Guard) represent the Supreme Commander in his absence. To disobey their orders is tantamount to disobeying the Supreme Commander.
4. Any sign of insubordination, intentional or otherwise, will be dealt with swiftly and severely. Precise obedience and loyalty is the guardsman's only true protection.
5. Guardsmen will report any disloyalty or infraction among fellow guardsmen to their Squad Captain. Guards found "protecting" or "sheltering" another guard will be considered an accessory and receive the identical punishment as the transgressor.
6. The contents of this manual are confidential (C5). Leaking of information will be punished according to Elgen guidelines.
7. Guardsmen are to rid themselves of all previous loyalties, attachments, and commitments, whether personal or professional.
8. Guardsmen are required to maintain peak physical and mental condition. Weakness of body or mind will not be tolerated. Periodic testing will be utilized to determine continued eligibility.

HISTORICAL BACKGROUND

The history of Elgen Inc. begins with the history of electricity itself. As long as humans have existed, they have been fascinated by electricity and ascribed it with mystical properties. The ancient Greeks believed that lightning was the weapon of Zeus, the king of the gods. Any place struck by lightning was considered sacred, and became the site of temples and worship. Similarly, the Scandinavian mythological figure Thor threw lightning bolts at his enemies. In Hindu mythology, Indra is the god of lightning and a symbol of strength.

While the mystical power and majesty of electricity have been observed since the beginning of humankind, it is only in relatively recent times that humans have sought to understand and control this great power. Scientists like Franklin, Edison, Tesla, Westinghouse, Ampere, Volta, Ohm, Faraday, Joule, and others, dedicated their lives to understanding the science of electricity, but it is only in recent centuries that electricity has been harnessed by humankind and used for its benefit. It is no coincidence that the successful manipulation of electricity occurred at the same time as some of society's greatest technological advancements.

Today, in our so-called *civilized* world, it is difficult to imagine life without electricity, yet *25 percent* of the world's population still lives without its benefit. It is Elgen Inc.'s goal to remedy that crisis within our lifetime. Once we have succeeded, the relief of human suffering will be without measure, as will the effect on the advancement of civilization. Children who were previously shackled to the daily chores of gathering wood and fuel for basic survival will now be able to attend schools. Women will be free of the menial chores that keep them from advancing their own educations. Economies will improve as manufacturing and farming becomes more productive and efficient with the benefit of electrical power. In short, Elgen Inc.'s electricity will change the world.

After many years of research, Elgen Inc.'s scientists created our unique electricity-generating process. In 2009 we successfully opened our first Starxource power plant. While the science behind our electricity production is top secret, our process may be best compared to fusion—but without the environmental backlash, threat of meltdown, or the contaminants of nuclear waste.

Since the opening of that first plant, many others have followed in both developed and developing countries. The benefits to these countries have far surpassed our, and their, greatest hopes. In the future we will assist larger and more populated countries until the entire world is advanced and prospering beneath the Elgen network of electric power. Then the wars between the nations will cease. They will be bound to one another through their common energy source and will no longer rise up against one another, for no one nation can assault another without the power of electricity. The promise of Elgen Inc. is much more than a cleaner, ecologically brighter world, it is also one without pain, fear, and the destruction of war.

One does not change the world without opposition, which is why Elgen Inc. has trained and employed its own army, dedicated to the advancement of Elgen Inc. and its goal of providing energy solutions today for a brighter tomorrow. *As an Elgen guard, you are now a part of ensuring that brighter tomorrow for billions around the world.*

SECTION TWO
LEADERSHIP, HIERARCHY, AND CHAIN OF COMMAND

CHAIN OF COMMAND

The Elgen Guard is ruled through the following hierarchy:

GENERAL GUARD

I. ELGEN SUPREME COMMANDER, General Admiral C. J. Hatch

II. THE ELGEN BOARD

A remnant of the former Elgen organization, the Elgen board now acts as a non-voting advisory counsel to the Elgen Supreme Commander. Membership on the board is determined solely by the Elgen Supreme Commander.

III. ELITE GLOBAL GUARD (EGG)

The Elgen Supreme Commander's force of twelve guards. The authority of the EGG is challenged only by the Supreme Commander, and their orders are to be followed as though from the Supreme Commander himself.

Uniform: Black with purple and scarlet chest emblems. Red and black armbands on right arm.

IV. ZONE CAPTAINS (ZCs)

Zone Captains are the leaders of a global zone of Squad Captains. Zone Captains report to the EGG.

Uniform: Same as EGG with addition of scarlet armbands.

V. SQUAD CAPTAINS

Elgen Squads are the fundamental unit of the Elgen security corps. Squad Captains are in authority over and responsible for all members of their squad, comprised of six to twelve Elgen Guardsmen. Squad Captains report to their regional Zone Captain.

Uniform: Purple Elgen Uniform

VI. GUARDSMEN

The Elgen Guardsman is the fundamental figure of the Elgen security corps and is responsible for the inner workings of all Elgen operations. Tasks and responsibilities vary widely and training is provided by Squad Captains. Guardsmen report to their Squad Captain.

Uniform: Standard Elgen Uniform with armband bearing the guard's zone and squad identification number.

VII. ELGEN SECRET POLICE (ESP)
   One or two Elgen Secret Police members exist within each squad. As the eyes and ears of the Elgen organization, their primary responsibility is to act as informants on the other guards while keeping their identities confidential. ESPs communicate directly with Zone Captains, ESP Captains, and, where warranted, the Elite Guard.
   Uniform: The ESP uniform is indistinguishable from regular Elgen Guardsmen.
VIII. ESP CAPTAINS
   A group of twelve elite ESP members responsible for the organization and success of the ESP force.
   Uniform: Elgen uniform with a scarlet beret and a scarlet sash, hung from the left shoulder. (New captains will hang sashes from right shoulder during first six months of tenure.)
IX. ESP CAPTAINS' ASSISTANTS
   There are twenty-four assistants who help the ESP Captains collect

and consolidate information from the ESP force as well as assisting the ESP Captains in special projects and duties as the position may require.

Uniform: Dressed in black with yellow and black striped armbands.

NAVAL ELGEN OFFICER RANKS

Admiral of the Fleet

Admiral

Rear Admiral

Ship Captain

Commander

Lieutenant Commander

Naval Guardsmen

Ensign

Currently the offices of General Admiral and Admiral of the Fleet are held by the Elgen Supreme Commander. Please refer to the *Naval General Handbook of Instructions* for descriptions of duties and uniforms.

ELGEN ELITE FORCES

In addition to specific ranks, guards may be associated with special elite forces. Membership in these forces may have geographical consideration and is by invitation only.

I. **Electric Youth**

Elgen Inc.'s Youth Force is comprised of a small group of gifted adolescents. Guards will be aware of their presence but are not to approach or speak to them unless it is a specific part of their assigned duties. Guards are to obey these youth's orders as they would the EGG. The Elgen Youth Force members are to be guarded and protected at the expense of guards' lives.

      i.   Quentin

      ii.   Torstyn

      iii.   Bryan

      iv.   Kylee

      v.   Tara

      vi.   ~~Tesla~~

      vii.   ~~Tanner~~

      viii.   ~~Nichelle~~

      ix.   ~~Zeus~~

      x.   ~~McKenna~~

      xi.   ~~Abigail~~

      xii.   ~~Ian~~

II. Chasqui

Translated from the ancient Quechuan dialect, the word "chasqui" means "messenger of light." The Chasqui are a special Elgen military order in Peru. Their roles are specifically connected to the Peruvian Starxource plant in Puerto Maldonado.

III. Domguard

Also known as the "Order of the Amber Tunic." The Domguard are a very powerful and secretive global force.

IV. Lung Li

The Lung Li (literally meaning "dragon power") is a special Asian Elgen military order. Their activities are limited to countries in the eastern hemisphere, including China, Taiwan, Korea, Japan, Vietnam, Cambodia, and Thailand.

SECTION THREE
TRAINING

REQUIRED TRAINING

All Elgen Forces must complete a minimum of ninety days initial training (IT) at the Kaohsiung, Taiwan, or Fiumicino, Italy, training facilities.

Initial training will include physical endurance and strength testing and building (see Physical Requirements), psychological testing, and aptitude testing. Guards will be assigned their first field of duty (FOD) based on the observed accumulated test scores and performances during initial training.

PHYSICAL REQUIREMENTS

All Elgen Guardsmen are required to maintain peak physical condition. The following physical fitness tests will be administered quarterly by Squad Captains without warning and at random times, including the middle of the night or during regular shifts. Failure to pass the physical test will result in dishonorable discharge.

Physical Test	Required Time/ Repetition	Guard Actual Time	Pass/ Fail	Squad Captain's Signature
3-Mile Run	Complete in less than 24 minutes			
Pull-Ups	25 consecutive repetitions			
Sit-Ups	100 consecutive repetitions			
Push-Ups	50 consecutive repetitions			
25-Foot Rope Climb	Complete in less than 60 seconds			
Standard Obstacle Course	Complete in less than 13 minutes			

WEAPONRY

All Elgen Guardsmen will be issued the following basic weaponry:

- **Bulletproof vest**

- **Utility belt with concussion and smoke grenades**

- **Standard M4 Carbine Rifle**

- **Standard 1911 Colt sidearm**

- **Tactical Special Ops Knife (fixed blade) with leg holster**

Elgen Guardsmen assigned to special details (especially those involving electric children) may be issued some or all of the following:

- **RESAT gun and darts**

- RESAT detention systems

- Mindwave Helmet

SECTION FOUR
ELGEN PROTOCOL

LEVELS OF CONFIDENTIALITY

Confidentiality is key to Elgen Inc.'s mission. After a trial period, most guards will be granted some information in return for their continued loyalty and service. Any information given to guards is to be kept strictly confidential. Guards are to discuss internal affairs with no one, excepting the commanding officer who has issued the information. C10 information may only be discussed in the presence of the Supreme Commander, and only at his initiation. All information is assigned a confidentiality level and requisite penalty. This level will be disclosed before the information is divulged. Any sharing of information among low-ranking guards or with outsiders will be met with swift punishment as outlined in the following table:

Level of Confidentiality	Disciplinary Action for Unauthorized Divulgence
C1	Verbal reprimand. One year probation. Pay reduction.
C2	Verbal reprimand. Two weeks confinement. Pay reduction.
C3	Verbal reprimand. Ten day detention period in Reeducation. Pay reduction.
C4	Three-week detention period in Reeducation. Pay reduction.
C5	Six-month detention period in Reeducation. Pay reduction.
C6	One-year detention period in Reeducation. Pay reduction.
C7	One-year detention period in Reeducation. Life-long assignment to menial position within Elgen Force with no chance for promotion.
C8	Life imprisonment with hard labor.
C9	Death.
C10 (Highest)	Death by torture.

DISCIPLINARY ACTION

Disciplinary action for minor offenses, including the consumption of alcohol, tobacco, or use of unauthorized chemical substances, will be handled by the immediate commanding officer and may include corporal punishment, internment, fines, peer discipline, or probation. Major offenses, including breech of confidentiality above C2 must be reported to the Zone Captain. In cases requiring extreme disciplinary action (i.e. sedition or divulgence of C5 to C10), a disciplinary court will be convened, comprised of a counsel of five ZCs, two ESP Captains, and overseen by the regional EGG.

HANDLING OF INTERNAL GRIEVANCES

All grievances must be submitted by form EIA0026B, in duplicate, to the Elgen Guardmen's Squad Captain. In the case that the grievance is against (or involves) the Squad Captain, a complaint may be submitted to a Zone Captain for summary examination.

Note: Guards who submit complaints that are found to be meritless may face disciplinary action.

REEDUCATION

Although only a relatively few guards will ever work in the Elgen reeducation program, it is vital for all personnel to understand its workings and role in the global expansion of the Elgen empire.

The reeducation process is designed to help those who have been counterconditioned to non-Elgen paradigms. Misguided individuals are sent to the nearest reeducation center where they will undergo a series of educational and mind-altering exercises in which erroneous thinking is replaced with the glorious truths of the Elgen. The following exercises and procedures have been used with such great success that even a few of our most dedicated guards are graduates of our reeducation campuses:

Step 1: Appearance Alteration
Detainees wear attire (i.e. pink, flowered jumpsuits)
that promotes humility and greater willingness to
cooperate. Jewelry, facial hair, or distinguishing hairstyles
are removed or changed during the admitting process.

Step 2: Name Change
Disassociating detainees from their previous identities
serves to open their minds to new truths. All detainees
are assigned numbers that serve as their identity until
their graduation from Reeducation.

3. Confinement
Detainees are housed in individual ten-by-ten foot
rooms containing a metal cage. For the detainee's safety,
a special deactivation code is required in order for a
visitor to enter the detainee's cell. Failure to input the
code will result in the detainee being electrocuted.

4. Educational Media

Elgen Inc. has produced a series of films designed to correct detainees' thinking and expedite the conversion process. These films are shown at regular intervals during the detainees stay, as often as twenty times per day. The more time spent in front of these films the speedier the process of conversion and the greater the success.

5. Detention Time Period/Integration

While individual cases vary, most detainees require a relatively short reeducation period. They are then welcomed into our cause.*

Historically, 97% of all detainees are satisfactorily reeducated and allowed the privilege of serving the Elgen, oftentimes in menial roles such as janitorial or groundskeeping work. All former reeducation students are continually monitored and assessed for their continued improvement.

*Occasionally, it is deemed necessary to detain individual students for longer/indefinite periods. These special cases pose special security risks and require extra attention from Elgen Guardsmen.

SECTION FIVE

MISCELLANEOUS

ELGEN FLEET

The Elgen fleet consists of seven vessels manned by Elgen naval personnel and equipped to handle a variety of projects.

ES *Ampere*
The flagship of the Elgen fleet, the *Ampere* is a superyacht that serves as the Elgen command ship. It is used for special functions and to entertain Elgen VIPs.
Design Specifications: 11,000 tonnes. 145 meters. Steel over aluminum superstructure with Kevlar insulation. Powered by a triple screw, diesel-electric propulsion system with four marine diesel engines.
Max speed: 25 knots. Cruising speed: 22 knots.

Faraday
A refurbished World War II troopship used to transport Elgen guards.
Design Specifications: It can carry in excess of 3,500 passengers. 76,000 GRT. Powered by twin marine diesel engines. Twin props.
Max speed: 18 to 19 knots.

Watt
A fully operational battle cruiser equipped to protect the rest of the Elgen fleet. Carries and operates advanced technology including tactical tomahawk cruise missiles, torpedoes, long range cannons, and advanced targeting systems.
Design Specifications: Displacement: 38,200 tonnes. 213 meters.
Max speed: 32.5 knots.

Volta
The Elgen's science ship. It also contains a confinement center capable of housing up to fifty GPs.
Design Specifications: Displacement: 13,000 tonnes. 152 meters.
Max speed: 20.5 knots.

Joule
(Classified)

Ohm
Serves as a supply ship for the Elgen fleet as well as Elgen compounds and Starxource power plants.
Design Specifications: Displacement: 9,000 tonnes. 98 meters.
Max speed: 20.5 knots.

Tesla
The Tesla is a small landing craft used for transporting troops from the *Faraday*. (This type of ship is also known as a "tender.") It is equipped with twin fifty caliber machine guns and a twenty millimeter Oerlikon cannon.
Design Specifications: Displacement: 3,586 tonnes. 100.55 meters. Powered by three twelve-cylinder gasoline-fueled engines. (Modified design of the Packard 3A-2500 V-12 liquid-cooled aircraft engine.)
Max speed: 35 to 40 knots.

ELGEN FACILITIES

Administrative Offices (Land-Based)
Italy, Rome
Finland, Helsinki
Taiwan, Kaohsiung (Training Facility)
Peru, Puerto Maldonado

Reeducation Centers
Peru, Puerto Maldonado
Taiwan, Kaohsiung
Mexico, Tampico, Tamaulipas
Italy, Fiumicino (Training Facility)
Tuvalu, Funafuti
Finland, Helsinki
Tanzania, Mwanza

STARXOURCE PLANTS
Beta Control Countries (BCC):

Anguilla   (Starxource Functioning 100%)
Christmas Island   (Starxource Functioning 100%)
Cook Islands   (Starxource Aborted)
Falkland Islands   (Starxource Functioning 96%)
St. Barths   (Starxource Functioning 96%)

**Operational Starxource Plants (OSP)/
Combined Populations: 115,703,571**

Palau   21,000
British Virgin Islands 28,213
Gibraltar   29,441
Monaco   35,881
Saint Martin   36,824
Cayman Islands   54,878
Greenland   56,890

Bermuda	64,237
Dominica	71,685
Jersey	97,857
Aruba	101,484
Tonga	103,036
Grenada	110,821
Virgin Islands	106,405
Samoa	184,032
Finland	5,405,590
Zimbabwe	12,754,000
Taiwan	23,200,000
Peru	29,797,694
Tanzania	43,443,603

**Plants Under Construction (PUC)/
Combined Populations: 32,623,410**

Portugal	10,561,614
Greece	10,787,690
Chad	11,274,106

**Under Negotiation/
Combined Populations: 1,010,135,758**

Poland	38,092,000
Sudan	45,047,502
Spain	46,196,278
South Korea	48,750,000
Italy	60,600,000
France	65,073,482
Philippines*	94,000,000
Pakistan	187,000,000 +
Brazil*	192,376,496
India*	233,000,000

*Top 10 Populous Countries

MEDALS AND AWARDS

C. J. Hatch Award for Distinguished Service
The prestigious C. J Hatch award is the highest honor given to Elgen Guardsmen, and is often followed by an advancement to Squad Captain, Zone Captain, or even Elite Global Guard status. The recipient of this award is personally selected by the Supreme Commander himself and stands as an example of exemplary Elgen performance, dedication, and heroism.

Golden Lightning

This award is bestowed upon one Guardsman every calendar year. This award is given to the Guardsman who demonstrates the highest level of dedication, loyalty, and performance. Squad Captains will submit names for review to the Zone Captains, who will then narrow the field of candidates to five. The final names are passed to the EGG for a decision. Golden Lightning candidates are awarded a private audience with General Admiral C. J. Hatch. Many Golden Lightning–award winners have been promoted to Squad Captains or Zone Captains.

Silver Filament

This award is bestowed upon an Elgen Secret Police member every calendar year at a private event. Because the identity of the ESP must remain confidential, candidates for the award are chosen by the ESP Captains based on performance, discovery, and value of discovery. ESPs who uncover disloyal guards or factions among the ranks are considered for the award. Although there is no public presentation of the award (in order to protect the identity of the ESP member), winners are granted special privileges as well as a private audience with EGG David W. Welch.

Bronze Spark

This award is bestowed biannually during the Elgen Guard Global Training Camps. Candidates are chosen from each squad and reviewed by Zone Captains. Each zone bestows the award on a soldier who has best demonstrated Elgen qualities of loyalty, determination, strength, and solidarity. Bronze Spark winners receive a pay grade advancement and are publicly acknowledged during the training broadcasts.

LANGUAGE AND TERMINOLOGY

The Elgen military force has developed language and terminology in reference to its unique mission. While Elgen Guardsmen will use many of these terms on a daily basis, it is required that their meanings are kept strictly confidential from outsiders. (Note: Many terms are classified and will only be revealed on a need-to-know basis.)

Section I—Acronyms & Abbreviations

ADC	Active Duty Commands
BCC	Beta Control Countries
EGG	Elite Global Guard
EMP	Electromagnetic Pulse
ESP	Elgen Secret Police
FOD	Field of Duty
GHI	General Handbook of Instruction
GPs	Guinea Pigs (*Homo sapiens*)
IT	Initial Training
MEI	Magnetic Electron Induction
NSG	Neo-Species Genesis program
OSP	Operational Starxource Plants
PUC	Plants Under Construction
Re-Ed	Reeducation
RFID	Radio Frequency Identification Device
ZCs	Zone Captains

Section II—Terms & Definitions

ADC   (Short for *Active Duty Commands.*) All rules and instruction given to Elgen Guardsmen.

BCC   (Short for *Beta Control Countries.*) Used in reference to Starxource power plant development. (See *OSP*, *PUC*, and *Starxource.*)

Bowl (The)   Any Starxource plant's central conductor—designed to direct power to a delicate, silver-coated copper grid that conducts electricity to capacitors.

Cell 25   An important aspect of every GP prison, Cell 25 acts as the ultimate recalibration tool. Prisoners locked in Cell 25 are forced to endure erratic food schedules, a consistent electronic beep, and frequent bouts of terror. Cell 25 references a specific room that can be duplicated in any Elgen facility.

E Patterns/El-Waves   Units of measurement that designate the biological electricity patterns and levels present in the body.

EGG   (Short for *Elite Global Guard.*) The Supreme Commander's elite force of twelve guards.

Electrical Pulse   A secondary pulse that references the flow of electricity within the body. Tested through sensors developed specifically for this purpose.

Electric Children   Group of youth with electric capabilities. Many of these youth are a part of Hatch's special youth force, but others are considered enemies of the Elgen. (See *Electroclan.*)

Electroclan   Small terrorist group comprised of renegade Electric Children as well as a few nonelectric youth. Considered an enemy to the Elgen. (See *Electric Children.*)

Elgen Electric Generation. The Elgen Corporation as a whole. (Pronounced *El-Jen*.)

Elgen Academy An elite school designed to engage and train Electric Children. Originally referencing a specific facility in Pasadena, this term now refers to the Electric Children's education in a broader sense. (See *Electric Children*.)

EMP (Short for *Electromagnetic Pulse*.) A wave of electricity capable of stopping all electrical functioning and communications.

ER 20 (Classified.)

ER 21 (Classified.)

ER 22 (Classified.)

ESP (Short for *Elgen Secret Police*.) Secret informants existing within each Elgen Guard squad.

ESP Captains (Short for *Elgen Secret Police* Captains.) Twelve ESP leaders who report to ZCs and EGGs when appropriate. (See *EGGs* and *ZCs*.)

FOD (Short for *Field of Duty*.) The initial duty assigned to new Elgen Guardsmen after the completion of IT. (See *IT*.)

GHI (Short for *General Handbook of Instructions*.)

Glow Common term for Electric Children. Because of their unique bioelectrical makeup, all Electric Children give off a faint, phosphorescent glow. (See *Electric Children*.)

Goats Guards of questionable loyalty who require reeducation in order to remain members of the Elgen Force. (See *Sheep* and *Reeducation*.)

GPs (Short for *Guinea Pigs*.) Elgen Inc.'s human test subjects. Comprised of criminals and other untouchables, their presence is crucial to the advancement of our scientific pursuits. GPs are assigned numbers and kept in GP prisons. They wear orange jumpsuits and collars that monitor their vocal cords, administering incapacitating shocks if the GP attempts to talk or scream.

Grail   (Slang.) Elgen-speak for a project or mission that cannot reasonably be accomplished.

IT   (Short for *Initial Training.*) Ninety day requisite training similar to the U.S. military's basic training or boot camp

MEI   (Short for *Magnetic Electron Induction.*) Elgen invention used for finding diseases and abnormalities in the body. Since its early testing the MEI's role within our organization has evolved to become an intricate part of the NSG program. (Commonly pronounced *may.*)

Mindwave Helmet   Also commonly called a "reboot helmet." A protective helmet constructed of copper and made to withstand projected electrical interference. Used in special missions.

Newf's   (Derogatory slang.) Non-Elgen workforce.

NSG   (Short for *Neo-Species Genesis* program.) Details are classified.

OSP   (Short for *Operational Starxource Plants.*) Starxource power plants currently in operation. (See also *BCC, PUC,* and *Starxource.*)

PUC   (Short for *Plants Under Construction.*) Used in reference to power plants currently being developed. (See also *BCC, PUC,* and *Starxource.*)

Rabisk   A biscuit made from rat carrion, fur, and bone meal. Though primarily used to feed other rodents, Rabisk is sometimes fed to Elgen prisoners.

Re-Ed   (Short for *Reeducation.*) Process by which Elgen alter the minds of individuals who have been counterconditioned to reject Elgen beliefs. Also refers to a physical facility.

RESAT   Unique to Elgen Inc., the RESAT is used to subdue errant Electric Children through lowering their body's electrical content. To be used in special missions only. (Pronounced *Ree-Sat*.) (See *Electric Children*.)

RFIDs   (Short for *Radio Frequency Identification Devices*.) Subdermal tracking devices used to track the location of GPs. They are administered through injection and most often placed in left arm. (See *GPs*.)

Sheep   Enthusiastic soldiers whose loyalties lie with General Hatch. These guards will be trained and advance to leadership rank, ultimately taking leadership positions over the Starxource Plants or Elgen compounds. (See *Goats*.)

Squad Captains   Leaders of the Elgen Guardsmen subgroup, composed of six to twelve Elgen Guardsmen.

Starxource   Name given to Elgen power plants. Starxource power plants deliver economical, renewable, and environmentally friendly power to the world through a top secret process most closely related to cold fusion.

Stretch   References the effectiveness of Electric Children's abilities. Electric stretch can be increased through proper diet—extra potassium and minerals, decrease in refined sugars—as well as practice. (See *Electric Children*.)

ZCs   (Short for *Zone Captains*.) Leaders of a regional zone of Squad Captains. (See *Squad Captains*.)